Praise for the Hanley & Rivka Mysteries

"[Pirrone] has painted a complex and intriguing portrait of her native Chicago, with a mix of crime, religion, and cultural division in a time of despair."
*Publishers Weekly*

This "deeply nuanced mystery is bolstered by fine writing and historical detail."
*Kirkus* (starred review)

"A meticulously penned historical mystery [that] weaves complex characters into an intriguing plot...a gripping mystery that troubles the very notions of innocence and guilt. [It] is an eminently consumable and intelligent read...Pirrone recreates a roiling time period in Chicago with skill, paying homage to the cultures of those at its margins."
*Foreword Reviews*

A "complex tale of hidden identities and motives"
*Publishers Weekly*

"Readers with a love for, or burgeoning interest in, Chicago will find *For You Were Strangers* as satisfying as a richly coursed meal of the era."
*Foreword Reviews*

Also by D. M. Pirrone

*No Less in Blood*

The Hanley & Rivka Mysteries

*Shall We Not Revenge*

*For You Were Strangers*

# PROMISES
## *to the* DEAD

# D. M. Pirrone

 ALLIUM PRESS OF CHICAGO

Allium Press of Chicago
Forest Park, IL
www.alliumpress.com

This is a work of fiction. Descriptions and portrayals of real people, events, organizations, or establishments are intended to provide background for the story and are used fictitiously. Other characters and situations are drawn from the author's imagination and are not intended to be real.

Book/cover design and maps by E. C. Victorson

Front cover image: Adapted from *Night Scene at a Junction*.
Currier & Ives, c1885.
Courtesy of the Library of Congress, Prints and Photograph Division
Title page image: Detail from *Rymning*. Cecilia Baath-Holmberg, 1896.
Courtesy of Schomburg Center for Research in Black Culture,
The New York Public Library

Library of Congress Cataloging-in-Publication Data

Names: Pirrone, D. M., author.
Title: Promises to the dead / D.M. Pirrone.
Description: Forest Park, IL : Allium Press of Chicago, [2020] | Series: A
    Hanley & Rivka mystery ; 3
Identifiers: LCCN 2020018041 (print) | LCCN 2020018042 (ebook) |
ISBN 9780999698259 (trade paperback) | ISBN 9780999698266 (epub)
Subjects: GSAFD: Historical fiction. | Mystery fiction.
Classification: LCC PS3616.I76 P76 2020 (print) | LCC PS3616.I76 (ebook)
    | DDC 813/.6--dc23
LC record available at https://lccn.loc.gov/2020018041
LC ebook record available at https://lccn.loc.gov/2020018042

*To all the voiceless people from America's bitter past.*
*May your lives be remembered and honored,*
*and your voices finally heard.*

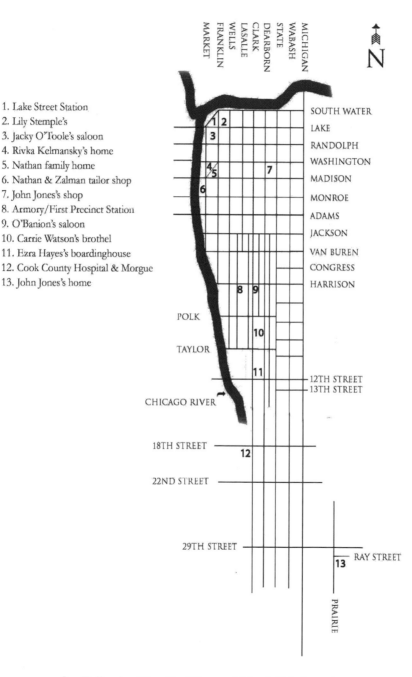

1. Lake Street Station
2. Lily Stemple's
3. Jacky O'Toole's saloon
4. Rivka Kelmansky's home
5. Nathan family home
6. Nathan & Zalman tailor shop
7. John Jones's shop
8. Armory/First Precinct Station
9. O'Banion's saloon
10. Carrie Watson's brothel
11. Ezra Hayes's boardinghouse
12. Cook County Hospital & Morgue
13. John Jones's home

See Following Map For West and North Side Locations

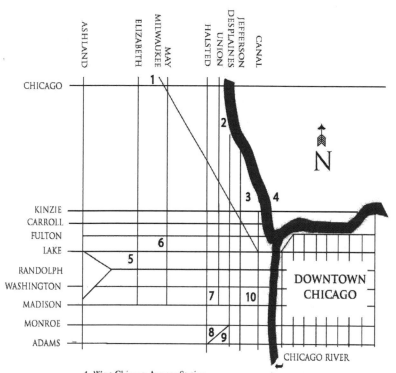

ASHLAND  ELIZABETH  MILWAUKEE  MAY  HALSTED  UNION  DESPLAINES  JEFFERSON  CANAL

CHICAGO — 1

2

N

3  4

KINZIE
CARROLL
FULTON
LAKE — 6

5

RANDOLPH
WASHINGTON

7  10

DOWNTOWN
CHICAGO

MADISON

MONROE

ADAMS — 8 9

CHICAGO RIVER

1. West Chicago Avenue Station
2. Liam Mahoney's boardinghouse
3. Illinois, St. Louis and Grand Southern rail yard
4. Cleary's Saloon
5. Coughlin family home
6. O'Shea family home
7. Second Precinct Station (Union Street)
8. Ida Kirschner's boardinghouse (Hanley family home)
9. St. Patrick's Catholic Church
10. Chicago and Alton Railway depot

West and North Side Locations

# Promises to the Dead

# PROLOGUE

*July 9, 1872*

Wet heat, the thick air of summer midday by the Mississippi clinging to him like a damp blanket. Beaten ground beneath his bruised body where he lay shackled around that damned iron pole. Taller than a man, the pole was sunk deep into the packed dirt. No chance of pulling it over or freeing himself any other way. Nothing for it but to lie there, breathing the stink of river mud and the swamp nearby and his own sweat and blood, until they decided he'd suffered enough. *At least they won't kill me,* Ezra thought. *Not while they figure I'm still good for another year's work or more.*

Dizzy, head pounding, he lost track of time. After a while, someone dragged a limp body over and dropped it in the dirt by another iron stake a few feet from where he lay. Pale face and neck above a tan homespun shirt and dark trousers. Even bloody and battered, there was no mistaking the white skin. A young man, from his face and the scant mustache on his upper lip. Still breathing but with frequent catches of pain. Dazed eyes blue as a spring sky gazed at Ezra without seeming to see him. A pink strawberry mark stood out by one ear. The camp overseer bent and shackled him like Ezra was, wrists to ankles around the iron, then kicked him in the ribs and walked away. Who was this man—this boy—and what was he doing here, beaten and a prisoner?

The answers came slowly as the afternoon wore on, and Ezra did his best to ignore his aching head and ribs and the nagging itch of drying blood on his face. The white boy recovered his wits enough to talk, of all the fool things. Ezra resisted at first, but then gave in. It beat listening to the whine of mosquitoes and tasting his own sour spit, and he couldn't help a flicker of curiosity. They exchanged names, and what they'd done to earn their punishment. On hearing that Ezra had tried to escape, the boy smiled. "You'll do it again," he said, making a question of it.

Why not answer true? This boy—a Yankee from the Freedmen's Bureau, a dead man for sure—would hardly betray him. "Till I make it or they kill me."

"When you do make it…" The boy closed his eyes and grimaced as if some new pain had stabbed through him. "My family's in Chicago. They won't know what's happened to me. Can you go there and tell them?" He shifted one hand, wrist straining against the shackle, until his fingertips rested on Ezra's shoulder. "I've a room in New Orleans. On Dauphine Street. There's money there you can use. And…" His fingertips pressed into Ezra's flesh. "I was here before. I hid in the trees by the cane fields and in the bayou. I saw things…I wrote it all down. Made sketches. A record." He swallowed and licked blood off his lip. "I told the bureau. They can't do anything. They're all but gone now. But my family…my father…I wrote him I'd send everything. He can get the word out. People need to know."

Ezra's disbelieving laugh jarred his sore ribs. "What's that got to do with me? Who the hell cares about a bunch of damned darkies, anyhow?"

"Someone has to." The boy locked eyes with him. "I'm a dead man. I know it. Bring my father the papers. Tell my parents what happened. What I died for. Tell my mother to pray for me. Please."

# ONE

*August 1870*

All your accounts should be in order." Ezra closed the ledger he'd been working with and replaced it on the shelf behind him. Through the open door of the tiny back office, he could see the rest of Daniel Lucien's store, where Lucien sold herbs, simples, and tinctures. A refuge of sorts for the past month, this little apothecary's shop, with better pay and easier work than unloading cargo off the New Orleans riverfront. He preferred earning his keep with his mind rather than muscle and felt a certain satisfaction in doing so by his own choice. It wasn't enough, though. *Never enough. Not until I find her.*

"That's twenty dollars I owe you, then." A smile spread across Lucien's narrow face. Tall, thin, and sharp featured, light as hazel wood, the apothecary reminded Ezra of a heron. Lucien went to a small safe in a corner of the office, unlocked it, extracted a few bills, and handed them over. "You're sure you won't stay on? I'd be happy to pay you full time. Lord knows I could use the help. I'm better with medicines than numbers."

"I'll think on it." Ezra pocketed the money, with a faint sense of shame at near lying to the man. Truth was, he felt restless and rootless, had ever since the Rebellion ended. *Five years,* he thought, not for the first time. *Five years free again, and I still don't have a belonging place. I should leave, start over somewhere a black man can breathe.* Not the first time he'd had that thought, either. What held him here was a fool's hope of finding what slavery had cost him...or at least a part of it. His heartbeat quickened as he eyed the street outside. Too late to start today. He'd not get where he meant to go before sundown, and to be out after dark in the back country nowadays was killing foolish for a black man. *First thing tomorrow.*

Lucien's affable grin gave way to a somber expression. Ezra had come to know it well over the past several days, ever since the evening he'd drunk too freely of his employer's home brew and confessed his fragile hope. Seeing that look on Lucien's face again now, he felt warmed by and resentful of it at the same time. "You're still going, aren't you?" Lucien said.

"Wouldn't you, in my place?"

Seconds passed. Then Lucien sighed. "At least let's lessen the risk, if that's possible." He stepped past Ezra to the cramped desk and dug a rolled-up paper out of a drawer. A map, Ezra saw when Lucien spread it across the desk's surface and weighted it with river-smoothed stones. "Show me where the settlement is. We'll figure a safe route as best we can."

Ezra moved to join him and stared down at the map, which showed Orleans Parish. The tiny settlement Ezra sought was southwest of New Orleans, a ten-mile journey on foot. Some longer, if he stayed off the road. He knew the stories...everyone hereabouts did. How a black man walking the roads or fresh off the train might find himself jailed, or worse, by any passing white with a mind to cause him trouble. The lucky ones were harassed and beaten, then let go. The rest? Killed or set to hard labor, the rumors said. They never came back, so no one knew for sure.

He and Lucien spent the next half hour plotting his journey, based on Lucien's best guess of where potential danger lay. At the end of it, Ezra shook Lucien's hand, noting by reflex the contrast between his own dark skin and Lucien's paler brown. Not light enough to save this man trouble if some white chose to make it for him, but here among the *gens de couleur libres* there was a certain safety in numbers. He should stay, take Lucien up on the offer of permanent employment. Maybe after, if he found who he sought.

Lucien let go of Ezra's hand and clapped him on the shoulder. "I'll pass the word, let folks know you're a good man to hire."

"Thanks. I appreciate it." Ezra walked out of the apothecary shop and into the hot, dusty, busy street, feeling more hopeful than he had since the last time he could remember.

❧

Michael O'Shea stood by the rail of the *Queen of Cairo*, dashing off a short letter he would post as soon as they docked.

> *Dearest Mother,*
>
> *I am sending a brief note to let you know I am now in New Orleans. I'm told I'll find use for my energies there, aiding the freedpeople whose hard-won liberty remains too much in doubt. I need to do more for them than draw pictures and collect stories. I know you understand, even if Father doesn't yet. This wanderer's life I've been leading has taught me a great deal, settled ghosts from the war in ways I didn't expect. That may be all I can ask—that, and the chance to be of service to those who need it most…*

The letter finished, he remained, sketchbook in hand, charcoal pencil flying over the paper in a vain attempt to capture the spectacle before him as the riverboat neared its destination. The riverfront was all noise and motion, sailboats and steamboats crisscrossing the water, the latter belching smoke at the cloudless sky. Along the docks' expanse, mule carts and hurrying men moved amid towers of cargo—barrels of rum, sacks of rice, hogsheads of molasses and sugar, bales of cotton—bawling orders and shifting loads. Chaos, impossible to set down on the page. Michael should have felt discouraged, but the sheer energy of it all made him laugh out loud as he lowered his sketchbook in amused defeat. Largely spared destruction in the late Rebellion and back on its feet in the five years since, New Orleans was a marvel.

A gruff voice sounded in his ear. "Share the joke?"

Michael turned toward the first mate of the *Queen of Cairo*, suddenly and sharply aware of how much he would miss the old sailor. Brady was somewhere past fifty, of an age with Michael's father. A pang at the thought of the elder O'Shea tugged at Michael's heart. *I wish he understood how the war changed things, why I had to leave home after. Come back South, go where I could, bear witness with the skill of my hands. Little as that is against what's needed.*

His thoughts must have shown in his face. Somber now, Brady held out a fat envelope toward him. "Godspeed, lad. Come see us when we're next in port."

"I'll try." Michael took the envelope and peered inside. Startled, he looked up. "What's this? I worked for passage, not pay."

"Captain thought a few greenbacks'd be useful. The rest of us put in our bit." Brady scratched the edge of his beard. The riverboat bumped and scraped as it glided into its slip. Around them, sailors shouted and tossed ropes, while others jumped from the deck to the weathered boards of the slip and began tying up. "It's a good thing you're doing, helping those people. God knows they can use all the help they can get." A clap on the shoulder, accompanied by a gentle shake. "You watch yourself, hear? Plenty of folks'll be ready to fight another Yankee as soon as whistle at you. I'd not see you come to harm."

"I'll be all right." Michael wasn't sure of that but, for Brady's sake, he made himself sound it. "Take care. And tell the captain and crew thanks for me."

He felt the first mate's gaze on him as he disembarked and threaded his way through the waterfront bedlam, heading toward the nearest street. Was the field office he'd been told of still in the same place? There was every chance it might not be, what with all the political wrangling in Washington over the Freedmen's Bureau. President Grant's election two years prior had done little to stop that. Still, there must be some use to which Michael could put himself here. Something more concrete for the freedpeople than collecting their stories and sketching their lives… when they let him. "Baronne Street," he murmured as he strode along. "Baronne and *what*?"

A few helpful passersby gave directions, and eventually he found his way. Ten minutes' brisk walk down Baronne Street brought him to the place he sought. A sign by the front door, nearly hidden in the recessed archway, read *Bureau of Refugees, Freedmen, and Abandoned Lands.* He stood there a moment, contemplating the sign. Small, unassuming, almost as if not meant to be seen except by those, like him, already looking for it. The building itself was narrow and old, its stone walls worn and pitted in spots. He hesitated on the doorstep. Was he doing the right thing, joining up here? What dangers might he face, Northerner that he was, in this unfamiliar place so far from home?

*I fought in the war. I survived. Too many didn't. I owe them. All of them, Negro and white.*

He drew a deep breath and gripped the knob, then opened the door and went in.

# TWO

## July 14–15, 1872

Sunday Mass was the last place Frank Hanley wanted to be, but it mattered to his mother and sister, so he came. He decided to forego Holy Communion, not feeling sufficiently in a state of grace. The long, hot summer was dragging on, the city of Chicago still reviving in the wake of last October's Great Fire, yet Hanley felt as stuck in the doldrums as if it were the dead of winter.

The thought of winter made him drift into memories as Father Gerald droned from the pulpit. He was thinking of Rivka again, though he knew better. Walking with her not six months ago through the little Jewish neighborhood where she lived on Market Street near Washington, talking to her people on that first day after her father's murder. Snowflakes settling on her dark kerchief and shawl, brushing her cheeks, and clinging to her lashes. Two months ago, at the May *ceilidh* dance, she'd been odd woman out in her kerchief and brown calico amid the others' bright dresses and bared heads, but still the only girl in the dance hall his eye lingered on. He'd walked her home after, holding her hand in the soft spring night. That kiss before she left him, a brush of her lips on his, as light and unexpected as the touch of falling snow.

He stood for the closing hymn and sang along with the rest of the congregation, though his heart wasn't in it. As the music ended, Mam snuck him a sideways glance, which he pretended not to see. Then it was out of the pew and down the long nave of St. Patrick's, the obligatory stop to compliment Father Gerald on another fine homily, and at last they were out on the boardwalk ready to head home. Where Hanley didn't want to be, either. He wanted to be at Lake Street Station, hard at work. No, he wanted to be at Market Street. With Rivka.

Mam laid a hand on his arm and raised her voice above the clatter of passing wagons. "It's for the best, Frankie." She wore a look he'd come to loathe since May, a combination of pity and certainty. "She's not right for you."

"Not Catholic, you mean." His tone was too harsh, he knew it as soon as he saw his sister, Kate, flinch beside him. The air smelled of horse manure, and a train whistle shrieked from the distant lakeshore as he shook Mam off and stepped away. Kate would change the subject, trying to head off another argument, and just now it was more than he could stomach. "I'm going for a walk. Don't wait dinner for me." He turned and strode down Adams Street, losing himself among passersby, heading east instead of west toward home.

His steps took him where he knew they would, past Canal and over the South Branch of the Chicago River until he reached the corner of Adams and Market. Not giving himself time to think about it, he turned north, then halted at Market and Madison. Sunday was an ordinary day here. People were going about their business, visiting the tailor shop or the butcher's or wherever else their errands took them. He envied them such simple, everyday purposes.

Another hundred yards down Market Street and he'd be at Rivka's front door. He started that way, got most of the distance before permitting the thought, *And then what?* But he already knew. Aaron, Rivka's brother, blocking the door. Telling him Rivka was busy or not at home, not to him. Himself thinking of shoving past Aaron, calling Rivka's name, not leaving until he saw her. But that would only make more trouble for her than she was already in. Why had he invited her to the ceilidh? Why had she come? What had possessed either of them to think she could cross into his world for even one night without repercussions?

He stood on the street, within sight of the Kelmansky house, while people flowed around him as if he were a rock in a stream. The front door remained closed. Finally, feeling foolish and angry at himself, he turned south and walked away.

❧

Monday morning, he was back at work writing up his latest case, a fatal shooting in the Hairtrigger Block near Wells Street. Two liquored-up gamblers fighting over a woman, or the rigged card game the shooter had just lost, or both. Half a dozen witnesses, though four refused to talk to the police on principle and the other two were blind drunk. Hardly worth the trouble for Lake Street's twelve-man detective squad. He hadn't bothered taking Rolf Schmidt with him for the canvass—there wasn't much for the patrolman to do that was different from his usual job walking the beat. The young German officer was sharp eyed and a fast learner. He'd be more than qualified to step into the next detective's job that came open. Or maybe the City Council would increase the department's budget and they could expand the detective squad. Hanley gave a sour laugh. *And maybe dead politicians will lie their way through the Pearly Gates.*

"Your turn, Hanley." The deep voice, with its hint of challenge, belonged to Jack Chamberlain. Hanley looked up. Built like a bear and rumpled as an unmade bed, the senior detective loomed near the door to the station lobby, a paper sack in one hand and a partly eaten cruller in the other. He jerked his shaggy head toward the doorway, through which the desk sergeant was coming with a woman in his wake. "One of your own Micks, from the sound of her. That should make it easy."

He ignored Chamberlain's slur and stood to greet the woman as she reached his desk. She looked to be Mam's age, around fifty or so—well dressed, though not expensively, save for the fine straw hat she wore. Her eyes were red rimmed, her fingers twisted in a lace-edged handkerchief.

"He said you can help me," she murmured, her gaze locked on Hanley's face. He noted the brogue, put it together with the respectable clothes and the handkerchief, and pegged her as a few rungs up the ladder from "Paddy" Irish. One of his own, indeed. If she'd started out in a slum like Conley's Patch where he'd grown up, she looked long gone from it.

"It's my husband," she went on, pulling the handkerchief taut on the last word. "Mr. Lawrence O'Shea. He's gone missing."

# THREE

*July 15, 1872*

Missing?" Hanley pulled a chair over from an empty desk and gestured for Mrs. O'Shea to sit. "Tell me about it," he said gently. "And if I could have your full name?"

"It's Mrs. O'Shea...Grace O'Shea." She sounded dazed as she perched on the chair's edge. "My Lawrence never came home Saturday night. I didn't know what to do, who to tell at first. I spoke to Father about it. He told me to come here."

"Your father?"

"Father Gerald. We go to Saint Pat's, Lawrence and I." She clenched her hands and stared down at her lap, fighting for composure.

He couldn't recall seeing her at Saint Pat's of a Sunday, but the congregation was large enough that he didn't know everyone in it. Saint Patrick's was the heart of Irish life in Chicago, all the more so since the church had survived the Fire. "So Father Gerald sent you to the police?"

Beyond them, Chamberlain gave a snuffling laugh, then crammed the last bite of cruller into his mouth. Mrs. O'Shea's gaze flicked toward him as he ambled to his desk, sat, and pulled a logbook out of a drawer. She bit her lip and looked back at Hanley. "I came Sunday, after Mass, to tell about Lawrence. Only..." Another glance at Chamberlain, her cheeks flushing pink. "*He* said there was no need yet, that Lawrence was likely just...that he'd turn up. And now it's Monday, and he's still gone." She blinked at Hanley, her blue eyes wide and guileless as a child's. "Can you help me?"

"Best get right on the case, *Detective*," Chamberlain said, brushing crumbs from his shirtfront. "No time to waste, is there?"

Hanley's anger flared at the thought that Chamberlain had ignored this woman's plight. "We'll do our utmost." He stood and was gratified to see Mrs. O'Shea ease her grip on her handkerchief as she stood, too. He reached out and cupped her elbow, turning her away from Chamberlain and back toward the lobby doorway. "Let me take your statement somewhere more comfortable, ma'am. The squad room's no place for a lady."

☙

Lily Stemple's eatery, a dining room and enlarged kitchen tacked onto a small frame house half a block from the station, was sparsely tenanted this late in the morning. The local patrolmen had long since breakfasted and were out walking their beats, while the rest of Lily's clientele—workingmen and the occasional clerk looking for a good meal cheap—had likewise started their day. Lily's oldest daughter, Jenny, was clearing tables, while Lily herself wiped down the jerry-built counter at one end of the room where meal orders were taken. "Could we get a pot of tea, please, Lily," Hanley called to her as he guided Mrs. O'Shea to a table. The little money in his trouser pocket ought to just cover the expense if he sacrificed his horsecar fare. The day promised to stay fine, so he'd have a pleasant walk home at the end of his shift if it didn't get too hot.

"Coming right up." Lily gave him a warm smile. Just past forty, she had the well-padded, comfortable look of a favorite armchair. And a soft spot for Hanley, ever since he'd rescued her youngest boy from a pack of street toughs on his patrolman's beat a few years back. "Kettle, Jenny," she called as her daughter headed toward the door to the kitchen, carrying a tray laden with dirty plates.

Hanley thanked Lily and pulled out a chair for Mrs. O'Shea, then sat opposite her. "So your husband went missing on Saturday?"

"Yes." She settled into her seat, spine straight, hands folded in her lap. A lady's pose, held just a little too carefully. "I didn't worry at first, when

13

he didn't come home for supper. He said he'd be working late, and then I thought maybe he'd gone for a drink with the men. He did that sometimes of a Saturday night. Only, when I woke up Sunday morning and he still wasn't home...and he wasn't at Saint Pat's either..." She blinked hard and drew a breath. "He'd have met me at Mass if he was all right. He *never* misses Sunday Mass."

Something to ask Father Gerald about. "Where does he work?"

"At the Illinois, St. Louis and Grand Southern Railway." A note of pride colored her voice. "He's a clerk. He works with papers and numbers, checking shipments and such. 'Twas Mr. Coughlin gave him the chance, and he made the most of it."

"Mr. Coughlin?"

She nodded. "He's the railway's senior man in Chicago. He runs things at the rail yard. A fine fellow, Lawrence always said—" She broke off, swallowed hard as the last word sank in. "Says."

Hanley felt a pang of sympathy. With extra gentleness, he continued. "You said Lawrence sometimes went drinking with the men. Do you know their names, or where they usually went?"

"A place near the yard...Clancy's, or Cleary's, something like that." She stared down at her lap. "I don't remember anyone's name. He'd say them in passing, you know? They weren't close friends. Just...the workingmen. And he didn't go out with them often. The odd Saturday here and there, that's all." She glanced up, her eyes brimming. "So when that man, that other detective, when he said my husband was 'sleeping it off' somewhere..."

*Holy Christ. That English bastard.* Hanley fought down renewed anger, lest it upset Mrs. O'Shea further. Her husband missing since Saturday night, not a habitual drinker, no word to his wife that he'd stayed with a friend, not turning up as expected the next day...it didn't look good, and Mrs. O'Shea had to know it. *And Chamberlain damned well should've.*

Lily's appearance with the pot of tea, two plain china cups, and a small bowl of brown sugar came as a welcome distraction. "If you take milk, I can fetch it from the icebox," Lily said. Hanley declined, as did Mrs. O'Shea with a slight shake of her head.

Lily moved off, and Hanley sugared his tea. "So your husband didn't drink often. That's good to know. Was there trouble at work? Anyone who had a quarrel with him?"

Her answer was barely above a whisper. "You believe me, then. That... that something's happened to Lawrence."

Briefly, he touched her hand. "I'm sorry to say, yes. *Was* there trouble at the rail yard?"

"Not a quarrel with anyone. Something else." She fished in her string purse, pulled out a carte de visite and a folded sheet of paper, and laid them on the table. "That's my Lawrence," she said, pointing to the photograph. "The letter's from our son, Michael." The faint smile that crossed her face gave it a sudden beauty. "Our youngest. Twenty-six this past June. He draws the most wonderful pictures, he sends them to me sometimes, you've no notion—" She shook her head abruptly, her lips pressed together. "Never mind that." She unfolded the letter and tapped a paragraph partway down the page. "Here. He said there were stories...about slaves, if you can believe it. After the war and all, such terrible things going on. It upset Lawrence. I could tell, even though he told me not to bother myself over it."

"And where is your son?"

"New Orleans...with the Freedmen's Bureau. Michael served in the war, you know. Enlisted in '63, claimed he was twenty-one instead of seventeen. Had no notion what to do with himself when he came home, except that he wanted to draw. He's always wanted to draw." A shadow passed over her face. "The war changed him. He tried to talk about it, but we couldn't really understand. So he left Chicago again. In '69, that was. I've not laid eyes on my son since."

A double tragedy, if Lawrence O'Shea was dead instead of merely missing. Hanley read the letter, picking out relevant phrases. *Troubling rumors...freedmen snatched along the roads...put to labor...Sweetbay Sugar Company... plantations along the river, near the bayous...captives languish in bondage anew.* That last sent a chill through him. He'd glimpsed a little of slavery's horrors as a Union soldier, and that was more than enough. "I can see why this letter bothered your husband. But I don't see how it means trouble at the rail yard."

"He knew the name…the sugar company. They ship on the Illinois, St. Louis and Grand Southern. He told Mr. Coughlin about it. Mr. Coughlin was shocked. Promised he'd look into things, Lawrence said."

Hanley wondered what *look into things* meant. The shipping contract, presumably. Keep the railway clear of anything unsavory, whether the stories were true or not. Assuming the railway owners cared, as O'Shea himself clearly did. "And your husband believed him."

She drew herself up, as if startled by the question. "He'd no reason not to. Mr. Coughlin's always been as good as his word to us."

"I don't doubt you, Mrs. O'Shea. It's the kind of question policemen have to ask." He smiled to put her at ease and, after a moment, she relaxed enough to sip her tea. He watched her, wondering whether to bring up other questions that inevitably sprang to mind when a man went missing. *Does he gamble? Does he have a sweetheart or a doxy somewhere?* She hadn't even hinted at any such thing, but married men often kept secrets from their wives, and she seemed the trusting type.

As he sipped his own tea, deciding what to say next, she spoke again. "He told me not to wait supper for him. On Saturday, I mean. And he was worried again. He'd been better after talking to Mr. Coughlin, but then…" Her grip tightened on her teacup. "When he kissed me goodbye…he held me so tightly. Like he was afraid to let me go, like… like he knew it might be for the last time."

Disquiet stirred in Hanley. A distraught woman's fancy, yet she was so certain. "Could've been anything. A bad night's sleep, some personal regret he wasn't comfortable confessing."

A rueful smile crossed her face. "Lawrence and I were married thirty-two years ago, Detective Hanley. After all that time, a wife knows her husband inside and out."

Rebuked, if gently, he sat back. "I'll do what I can, Mrs. O'Shea. One way or another, we'll find out what happened."

# FOUR

I know the way to Onkl Jacob's shop, Aaron." With a touch more force than necessary, Rivka tightened the carrying strap around her copies of McGuffey's Third and Fourth Readers. "I am perfectly capable of walking there on my own."

She might as well not have spoken. Arm's length from her in the small front parlor, cool disapproval clear on his face, her brother nodded toward the books. "If you're ready, we should go."

Rivka drew breath for an angry retort, then pressed her lips shut. What could she say that Aaron would hear? *It was only a dance. It was only one night. I only wanted...*

Heat rose in her cheeks as she picked up the books and stepped out the front door into the too-bright afternoon sunshine. She had wanted exactly what she got. She had wanted Hanley to take her hand, hold her, look at her like she was the most important person in his world just then. She had wanted to be with him in that world, instead of in her own where he didn't belong. Just for a few hours. Stolen time for a daydream, with no one to know of it but her. And him.

How foolish she'd been to think that could happen. How foolish she was still.

Distant bells chimed the three-quarter hour as she and Aaron walked without speaking down Market Street. They passed two women out doing the day's shopping. One gave Rivka a nod. The other averted her gaze. Aaron pretended not to notice, but his strides lengthened, and he was soon ahead of Rivka. It hurt, watching him and knowing the reason. *Because his wife is a* goyische *mulatto, and some of our own can't accept that.*

The day's heat made the air heavy, the baked-wood smell of the boardwalk mingling with the pungent odor of horse manure from passing traffic. Sweat ran down Rivka's back, and her scalp itched beneath her kerchief. She gritted her teeth and did her best to ignore the discomfort. The walk to the tailor shop wasn't long, and at least in the back room she and her students would be out of the sun. Five girls now, down from ten, as Aaron's supposed disgrace touched Rivka, too. Well, she would devote herself all the more to those who were left.

Light glinting off the shop's front window made her squint as they drew nearer. No sign of Moishe Zalman, Onkl Jacob's assistant, who polished the glass every day. He must be inside, working on a suit or a shirt. As if he'd read her mind, Aaron laid a hand on her sleeve. "Be polite to Moishe. All right?"

She sidestepped out of reach. "I am always polite to Moishe." Apart from Onkl Jacob and Tanta Hannah, Moishe was one of the few people who didn't go out of his way to avoid them. Rivka knew she should be grateful, but the reason for it made her anxious. Especially now.

"You barely speak to him when you arrive."

"He's working. I have work to do as well." A sliver of guilt broke through her irritation. She did avoid speaking to Moishe beyond the most perfunctory greeting, fearful that anything more would prompt him to tell her things she didn't want to hear. *I have spoken to Reb Nathan about us*, for example. Or—now that Aaron had fully recovered from the beating he'd suffered a few months earlier—*I will speak to your brother*. With Papa dead since January, it was Aaron and Jacob's place to decide Rivka's future. That was how things were. Why did it make her want to fight, or run somewhere far away? Her breath came fast, and she steeled herself as she walked around to the rear entrance. The girls still permitted to come would be arriving soon.

Aaron normally left her at the door to her classroom, a onetime storage room for extra cloth that Onkl Jacob had emptied and allowed her to use. Today, he came in with her. Surprised, and fearful of what this might mean, she snapped at him. "I don't have Detective Hanley hidden in a corner. You don't need to check."

"Rivka." He kept his voice low, so as not to carry into the shop, but there was no mistaking his scolding tone. "This is exactly why I'm doing what I'm doing. Because you have not acted with good sense, I can't trust you to behave yourself as you should, and Detective Hanley is—"

"He saved my life. And yours."

"He endangered you! If you hadn't tried to help him—" Abruptly, Aaron turned away from her. "It doesn't matter. What matters is your future, and it doesn't lie with an Irish policeman."

She closed her eyes and counted silently to five. "It was one night," she said when she could trust her voice. "Two hours. A dance."

"A kiss," he said, his voice as hard as his look.

She flushed. "Yes. One. For a moment, just one moment of..." What could she call it...madness? No...but she couldn't name it yet, even to herself. "Whatever you may think—"

"It doesn't matter what I think. It *does* matter that no one else thinks it."

*Especially Moishe*, he might have said, but mercifully didn't. The question, *Do you?* rose to her lips, but before she could say it, he brushed past her toward the curtained doorway into the shop. "Where are you going?" she asked instead, as if her words could forestall him.

He glanced toward her, his expression softening. "It's high time to settle things. You know it, Rivkaleh."

The endearment only made her angrier. "So you are taking Papa's place now, deciding my life for me? You haven't even been home half a year, you have no right—"

"I have every right. And every responsibility." He spoke gently as he moved closer to her. "I haven't been much of a brother to you for a long time. I'm sorry for that. I know how alone you've been, how much you've had to depend on yourself since Papa died. Too much. But there's no need anymore. I promise."

"But I don't *want*—"

He brushed her cheek with a fingertip as if shushing a small child, pushed back the curtain, and stepped through the opening.

She stared after him as he walked over to Moishe, who was cutting fabric at a slanted table. Moishe glanced up and set down his shears. Within seconds, Jacob came over and joined the conversation.

She yanked the curtain shut, then turned away and pressed her hands flat against the long table where her students sat. The surface felt hard and unyielding. She stared a moment at her fingers, splayed like pale fans against the dark wood. Unbidden, a memory came of her hands clasped in Hanley's as he whirled her through the Irish reel, both of them laughing, so close to each other she could feel his warmth. She hadn't seen him since the ceilidh dance. Because Aaron kept him away, or because he'd lost interest? Maybe he had. Without seeing him, reading his feelings in his face, she couldn't know.

*Enough.* She fumbled at the book strap and began laying out the readers. The girls would arrive any second. *Think of today's lesson. Then home for chores and supper. And after that…*

She blew out a breath, feeling weighed down in the hot back room. She had no answer for *after that.* Maybe she never would.

# FIVE

## *August 1870*

*hould've known.* The thought in Ezra's mind was so bitter, he could taste it at the back of his tongue. *I should've known it wouldn't be her. That kind of luck, I don't have. Not since mine first turned bad, all those years ago when the slavers—*

He shook his head sharply, the motion breaking the memory's painful hold. He was in pain enough here and now. The woman he'd come to see—not who he'd sought after all—stood a few feet away from him, a girl child of nine or so clinging to her skirt. Both of them stared at him, their faces brown-gold like ripe wheat, the girl with somber curiosity, the woman with pity. She'd been through a fruitless search of her own, she'd told him, after the first shock of his disappointment wore off. *My man's name was Silas,* she'd said, over fresh milk and the plate of fried salt pork she'd gently urged him to eat. *I spent three years looking. Asked at the Freedmen's Bureau, first chance I had. Friend of mine, she found her man and one son that way. But my Silas, he was gone. For good, most like. Where he was sold to, the sugarcane plantations…they chewed people up like gristle, spat 'em out dead often as not.*

Ezra's woman might well be dead, too. Or dead to him, long gone to someone else. They'd loved each other once, but then he was sold away. After the war ended, he'd moved from place to place, tracing rumors of a woman who matched her description, but never managing to find her. Thinking on it hurt so much, he feared he might sick up what little he'd eaten right there. He took a shaky breath, fought to master himself. The woman touched his shoulder and he flinched. She drew back her hand as if scalded, her face pinched with embarrassment.

"You sure you won't stay?" she said after a moment, low and gentle. "Can't be more than a few hours till sundown. You're safer here. Get some sleep, go back in the morning."

He shook his head. Even first light felt like too long to wait. He'd come here with such hope, and now all he wanted was out, so badly it heated him like a fever. "I'll be all right. I don't think it's gone three yet. Sunset's past six. That's time enough."

She looked as if she might argue more, but something in his face must have told her it was futile, for she nodded without further word. Instead, she bent and whispered to her daughter, who glanced down and fished in the pocket of her worn calico dress. The girl drew out a pawpaw, then slowly left her mother's side and came near enough to offer Ezra the fruit.

He took it and thanked her, forcing the words out over a hard knot in his throat. At least this woman and her child had each other. Ezra was alone. Again.

❧

A steady walking pace took him six or so miles toward New Orleans before fatigue forced a halt by the bank of a creek. He didn't recognize it and wiped sweat from his face as he tried to work out exactly where he was. He was so tired, and it was harder than he'd thought to keep to Lucien's safe route when his brain felt fuzzy as Spanish moss. How had he gone off, what landmarks had he missed? Not that there were many out here. He couldn't stop thinking of outrages against black men by whites whose paths they were unlucky enough to cross. The Freedmen's Bureau was next to useless, except as a place to report such incidents and hope word would reach what federal authorities were left. Though the Union troops remaining in Louisiana were spread too thin to counter white violence much, and he'd heard they were all on their way out soon. *So what happens to us then?*

With effort, Ezra shook off his grim thoughts and knelt by the creek. He dared not linger, but his dry throat made the cool water too enticing to pass up. He'd eaten the pawpaw a while ago and wished vainly for another. He scooped handfuls of water into his mouth, splashed his face and neck, resisting the temptation to dive in. He carried too much anguish still to baptize himself clean of it. He shook out his damp hair, got to his feet, and set off once more. The buzz of insects and the calling of birds blended with the rhythm of his stride, lulling him as he walked. He crested a small rise, looked around for habitation, saw only a copse of trees. Unfamiliar, like the creek, but promising shade and shelter from anyone whose notice meant danger.

He hurried toward the little woodland, breathed easier as its cool green embraced him. Kept going until the click of a rifle and a man's harsh voice pierced his ears. "Stop right there, boy!"

Ezra froze. A white man stood near, pointing a shotgun at his chest. Terror narrowed his vision to the dark hole of the gun barrel, the sneer on the white man's face above his untrimmed beard. Then more details filtered in—a second man walking up beside the first, a tin star pinned to his homespun shirt. The star glinted in the late afternoon light that filtered through the trees.

The rifleman held his gun rock steady. "You're trespassing on my land, darky. Lucky for you, I'm feeling kindly today." He nodded toward the second man, who favored Ezra with a cold blue stare. "All yours, Sheriff."

☙

The jail they threw him in was a single cell with slits between the bricks in the outside wall. The stifling air brimmed with stale sweat, piss, and fear. They'd taken Ezra's traveling bundle. Thank God he'd left his pay from Lucien back in his rented room, or they'd have gotten that, too. He had little sense of time passing, except by the light through the slits. Despite the heat, he shivered as he paced the tiny cell. If they meant to kill him, why hadn't they done it already? *I stayed off the road,* he thought desperately, as if arguing with God or whatever cursed fate ruled him. *I steered wide of any farmhouse I saw.* Yet here he was, snatched up like the poor bastards in the stories. *Is this torture? Do they want me extra terrified before they string me up?*

More time passed. He tired of pacing and sat on the floor, leaning against the rough brick wall. Watched what light there was fade into darkness. Slept eventually, overcome by sheer exhaustion. Next thing he knew, it was morning, the cell door creaking open. Ezra slowly rose to his feet as the sheriff stepped in. Whatever awaited him, he would meet it standing proud.

"You're lucky again, boy." The sheriff moved aside to let a second white man into the cell. Not the rifleman from earlier. This man was taller and thinner, in a fine suit and hat. He wrinkled his nose, at the stench or the sight of Ezra, or both. "Mr. Elihu Hammond says he'll pay your debt. Tell him thank you."

Dry mouthed, Ezra swallowed. "What debt?"

The sheriff's expression hardened. "For trespassing on Cottingham's bottomland yesterday. Forty dollars. Thank Mr. Hammond, I said. And make sure you call him 'sir.'"

The words came hard to Ezra's lips. *No choice.* "Thank you. Sir." Sourness on his tongue made him want to spit, but he knew better. "Am I free to go?"

He wasn't, of course. He'd known that when he asked. Elihu Hammond smiled—a wolf's grin, predatory and cold. "You are. With me. Two years' labor you owe for the money I'm out." He tapped his breast pocket. "It's all in the contract. You'll make your mark on it when we get to the plantation."

A chill like the ague hollowed his gut. "Plantation?"

Hammond nodded. "You look strong enough to cut sugarcane. Work the boiling house, too." His eyes narrowed. "You're older than I like. How old *are* you, boy? Never mind. You'll do. Don't shirk, or you'll regret it."

*Run*, said a wild voice in his head. *Knock them down, get* out, *get free*. The pistol on the sheriff's belt told him that was suicide. Unless he'd be better off dead. No. They'd love that—a Negro shot trying to escape. He wouldn't give these men that satisfaction, cost him what it may.

Moving slowly, he followed Hammond out of the cell. Whatever hell he was headed for, he vowed to survive it.

# SIX

*July 15, 1872*

The noise of the rail yard hit Hanley from more than a block away, as he turned from Wells to go west on Kinzie toward the bridge. The yard lay on the far side of the Chicago River, in a triangle four blocks long of crisscrossing railroad tracks and beaten dirt bounded by Kinzie, Jefferson, and the river's North Branch. Clanging metal, chuffing steam, thundering booms, and the high, thin whine of wheels on tracks grew louder as Hanley approached. He reached the edge of the yard, then stood for a few minutes marveling as the iron and wood behemoths lumbered through the smoke-hazed, wide open space.

Some trains had stopped, and they dwarfed the men who swarmed around them—brakemen and engineers, laborers unloading boxcars and flatbeds, here and there a uniformed employee with a ledger apparently inspecting each load. Men shouted, cattle bawled, freight cars boomed as they bumped each other, crates and lumber swung through the air on giant pulleys as they were offloaded and lowered to the ground. Beyond the train cars and to the west, mule carts and wagons took on cargoes of their own—stacks of shingles and boards, bales of cotton, sacks of wheat and corn, barrels and crates of Lord knew what, all for sale to eager customers somewhere.

Not for the first time, Hanley felt a fierce pride in being a Chicago man. Born in Ireland he might have been, but he barely recalled the place.

Chicago was home. Every cargo in America came through this city—lumber, grain, cotton, pig iron, cattle and hogs, ready-made clothes, furniture, and hardware. Chicago truly was the trade crossroads of the United States, the indispensable place that would make the country rich. *Or at least a piece of it,* he thought as cynicism took hold. *The money-grubbers who own the railroads and lumberyards and stockyards and want to own everything else.*

He glanced around and spotted the yard office, a sturdy one-story brick building with a sign hanging out front, just off a raised boardwalk that led past a cargo area crammed with tracks and freight cars and hurrying workmen. Not far beyond the small building, the Chicago River glittered in the sunlight. Hanley strode toward the office, ducking between two mule carts being loaded and detouring around a third. As he passed the team of men hoisting tied shingles onto the third cart, one of them stepped back, bumping straight into him.

"Christ's sake, look where you're—" The man broke off, frowning at Hanley. "Not seen you before. You new? Go see the yard foreman. He's over unloading boxcars at the moment."

Hanley sized the man up as he dug his badge out of his trouser pocket. Tall and craggy faced, the fellow had a south of Ireland brogue thick as potato cakes. Hanley's own scant Irish lilt deepened in response. "Detective Frank Hanley, Chicago Police. I'm looking for Mr. Patrick Coughlin."

The man's eyebrows rose. "Are you, now? He's not here. Away on business."

"When will he be back?"

The man shoved a stack of shingles further into the cart. "Wednesday, I heard. Don't know for sure. Yard boss don't tell us his comings and goings."

So much for talking to O'Shea's employer, but he needn't waste the trip. "Anybody else in the office today I could talk with?"

"A clerk, maybe. There's two, O'Shea and Jamieson. O'Shea's senior." The man frowned. "I've not seen O'Shea yet today, now I think on it. Strange, that is."

"It's O'Shea I'm here about. He's gone missing." Hanley tucked his badge away. "When was the last time you saw him? Any of you?"

"He was here Saturday." The new speaker looked barely out of his teens, brown hair flopping over one eye, his expression like a friendly dog's. "Said he'd come drinking with us after work."

"Did he go with you? Where? When's 'after work'?"

The third member of the loading team scowled at his mates. Square built and brawny, he had copper-penny hair, pale blue eyes, and a nose crooked from at least one ill-healed break. "No time for talking. We've a cart to load, case you'd forgot."

"I only need another minute." Hanley kept his tone affable, a bare whiff of authority behind it. The mule cart driver had turned to watch them, avid as a spectator at the races. Clearly, he wasn't in any hurry. "I take it the three of you know Lawrence O'Shea?"

"A bit. Enough to bend the elbow with now and then." The first man dusted his hand on his pants and held it out. "Gerry Sullivan. Sully. The youngster's Conn Rourke, and Mr. Sweetness there"—he gestured toward the redhead—"is Liam Mahoney. Something happen to O'Shea?"

"That's what I'm finding out. When did you last see him on Saturday? And was it here, or wherever you went afterwards?"

"We went to Cleary's. Our usual." Sully pulled a wrinkled bandana from a trouser pocket and mopped sweat off his face. "O'Shea was still here when we left the yard. Whistle blows at dusk, that's near half past seven these days. He said he'd papers to finish with, he'd catch us up in a bit. An hour, probably less." Sully frowned and scratched his neck. "I don't remember seeing him at Cleary's. Then again, I had more'n a drop or two pretty quick." He gave a sheepish grin. "*Uisce beatha* to start, beer after. You know how it is. O'Shea could've come later and I'd not recall."

Rourke and Mahoney told similar stories, the latter as grudgingly as a miser. Lawrence O'Shea was in the yard office when they left, said he'd catch up with them shortly. They'd all had drinks and a meal, then played some cards in hopes of adding to the week's pay they'd just received. Rourke lost money, Liam and Sully won a couple of dollars apiece. No one remembered whether Lawrence O'Shea ever turned up.

"Maybe he went in the river," Rourke suggested, wide-eyed. "If he did come to Cleary's and had a bit...or even just leaving the yard, if it was dark by then. He might've slipped, fallen in."

A simple, and plausible, explanation. Hanley thanked the men and let them go about their business. He spent another hour at the yard, talking to the cargo foreman and other laborers whose attention he snagged, but learned little more than he already had—O'Shea was friendly but kept to himself, a devoted family man, went drinking with "the boyos" only on occasion. A passing rail cop, patrolling near the yard office Saturday night, confirmed its windows were dark by "near a quarter to nine." Hanley ventured briefly into the office to talk with the junior clerk but took pity on the harassed-looking young man clearly up to his ears in paper and ledgers. He settled for confirming O'Shea's presence in the office when everyone else left on Saturday evening. More questions could wait until tomorrow.

Before leaving the yard, he detoured by the river and spent a few moments watching ripples cross its gray-brown surface. The stench was enough to choke him, and he breathed shallowly through his mouth. Just upstream, clouds of flies hovered over a floating island of rotting swill and cattle waste from nearby breweries. Closer at hand, the bloated corpse of a dead cat drifted through a patch of something slick and oily that Hanley couldn't identify. For Mrs. O'Shea's sake, he hoped her missing husband wasn't down there, buried amid Chicago's stinking refuse in a watery grave.

# SEVEN

## June 1872

D*ear Father,*
*I hope this letter finds you well. I fear you will not be after you read it, but I am much troubled in mind, and must unburden myself on paper at least.*
*Disturbing rumors reach us here, of freedmen snatched along the roads and byways and never heard from again. It's said they are put to labor, most often cutting sugarcane, without pay and harshly treated.*
*Sweetbay Sugar Company is named more than once, though its owners disclaim all knowledge, and they are powerful men hereabouts. The freedpeople speak in whispers of sugar plantations along the river, near the bayous, where captives languish in bondage anew…*

"Tell me your name," Michael said gently to the woman in the patched calico dress who sat across the makeshift table from him in the Freedmen's Bureau field office.

"Bessamy," she whispered, holding the tin mug of strong tea he'd given her as if it anchored her in place. She'd barely sipped but had spent so long staring into the liquid Michael wondered if she was reading auguries there. "Bessamy Moses. 'Twas Harris, before the Jubilee." The ghost of a smile passed over her face. "Henry chose our name. Moses, for the Promised Land…" She sucked in a breath, gripping the mug tighter. Looked up, her brown eyes glistening. "I didn't know where else to go…who could help. Don't know if the bureau can. But if there's any chance…"

In fits and starts, he drew the story from her. How her husband, Henry Moses of Beulah Town, had gone by train to visit his ailing aunt some miles away and never came back. "Not that Sunday like he said, nor any day after. No word, neither. He'd have sent, if he meant to stay longer. His cousin Samson could write, would've if Henry asked. And then, one day when I went to the depot to see if…" She bit her lip. "Henry wasn't there. But Fanny was. Fanny Williams. Healer woman in Beulah, goes around where she's needed, curing the toothache and ague and such. She saw me, told me come with her. Someone I needed to see, she said."

Again, Bessamy faltered. Michael waited, then murmured, "Not your husband, I take it."

"No." She gulped tea and set the mug on the table. "A stranger. Dragged himself to Fanny Williams's door, bad hurt like a beaten dog. They beat him so hard, not an inch of him wasn't bruised. Arm broke, ribs broke. Dried blood on him, Lord knows from what."

"Who beat this man? Where, when?"

"The pattyrollers." She shuddered. "That's what he told Fanny. They chased him into the bayou, after he ran off from the sugar plantation where they'd made him a slave again. And he…" She shook her head, her hands curling into fists.

Michael leaned toward her. "He what, Mrs. Moses?"

"He saw Henry there. Being whipped." Tears welled up, spilled over. "I told him, no. That can't be. But he said it was. Henry Moses from Beulah Town. They'd tell their names, talk if they could, cutting cane or in the boiling house. Pattyrollers caught 'em, there'd be trouble, but…" Her shoulders sagged. "He died, this man. Three days after I spoke to him."

Michael sat back, a sickness in his gut. He'd heard rumors of slave labor—they all had, one time or another—but this story had more to it than others. Enough to find the place, maybe. Rescue poor Henry Moses and the rest, if luck and the few federal troops still hereabouts allowed. "Do you know where the plantation is, Mrs. Moses, or what it's called? Did the man tell you anything before he passed?"

She raised one hand and wiped her damp cheeks. "Sweetbay Sugar, downriver from New Orleans, a mile past the lightning tree on the way to Poydras. You got paper? I never learned my letters, but I know the river and the bayou, and I can draw a map."

⁂

Seated at a rickety desk in his cramped office, Captain Julius Lowell let out a long-suffering sigh. "I'm sorry, O'Shea. I can't authorize such an expedition. The men I still have are stretched thin enough, responding to outrages all across this military district. Need I remind you that Louisiana alone covers over fifty thousand square miles?"

Michael's fists clenched at his sides. "But we know freedmen are enslaved at this plantation, sir. And—"

The captain held up a hand. "Save your breath, son. We both know what I want to do. I'm telling you, I *can't*. Not without more than a couple of women's word for a claim by a dead man. God knows I feel for poor Mrs. Moses, but—"

"If I can get more details, confirmation, will you send men? Will you at least consider it?"

Lowell laid down Bessamy's map and pinched the bridge of his nose, as if staving off a headache. "If and when you learn more, come back to me. We'll see then."

⁂

"You're crazy, you know." In the tavern next door on Baronne Street, Lieutenant Jack Wilkie tossed back his whiskey and signaled the barman for another. "Going downriver to the sugar plantation, to *ask* if they're using slave labor? They'll just tell you lies or run you off. *If* you're lucky. Sweetbay Sugar's company toughs will gladly break your Yankee head for you, or worse. And, even if they don't, there's no guarantee Captain

Lowell will send troops to storm the place. What can he spare you for your goose chase, one soldier at most? It's not worth the risk." He picked up the new full glass the barman set next to him. "Henry Moses is a lost cause, Michael. After damned near two years here, you must know that. Give the poor woman some money for a train ticket, somewhere she can start her life over, and get on with building schools and seeing to it the teachers get supplies and pay for as long as we've still got. Don't go looking for trouble. We can't do anything about the damned slave plantations, anyway."

Michael looked up sharply from his beer. "What do you mean, 'as long as we've still got,' and there's nothing we can do?"

"You haven't heard? The story is, Congress wants to close us down at the end of this month. Our assistant superintendent's spent the past two weeks with a face grim as yellow fever every time I've seen him. Something's in the wind. And it isn't good."

"If I paid attention to every rumor, I'd never do a damned thing. You really think they're shutting us down? Truly?"

Wilkie sipped his liquor. "I wish I could tell you no. And even if that weren't so, Sweetbay Sugar's big hereabouts. They make a lot of money and grease a lot of palms. The bureau couldn't compete with that before, and we sure as hell can't now." He met Michael's gaze, his expression haggard. "Mark my words, we won't be here much longer. Best accomplish what we can that'll be of use after we're gone, not go hunting game you can't bag. You'll get beaten like that luckless fellow who died, maybe even get killed outright. If not on this little expedition of yours, then later in a dark street or alley somewhere. And for what?"

Michael couldn't muster a reply. Wilkie finished his whiskey and bade Michael goodnight, with a look on his face as if he regretted saying too much. Only as the lieutenant's lean figure vanished through the doorway into the gathering night did an answer finally come—spoken softly to himself, but a promise, nonetheless. To Bessamy and Henry Moses, and countless others he'd never know. "Because as long as we're still here, someone has to try."

# EIGHT

*July 11, 1872*

Ezra ran through the darkness, the baying of dogs still too loud behind him. The rough ground beneath his bare feet dipped and rose, making him stumble, slowing him down. He couldn't slow down. They'd catch him. Catch him and do what they wanted with him, then leave his body in the bayou for the gators to eat. After what he'd lived through at the plantation, and what he'd seen there, he had no intention of ever going back. He would make it to safety or die trying.

He forced his legs to pump harder. A stitch burned in his side, and sweat stung the day-old stripes across his back. Harsh, sobbing breaths drew hot, damp air deep into his lungs. It smelled of swamp rot, decaying wood, and the sharp burnt tang of a storm coming. He gagged on the odors and thought of the dogs. How far could the pattyrollers follow him through the watery channels of the bayou? He'd heard tell running through water washed off human scent, but the hounds chasing him were still on his trail. How far would they follow?

*Far enough.*

His foot thudded on a tree root. He slipped, flailed, managed by a miracle to stay upright and moving forward. Harsh shouts from behind mingled with the dogs' deep-throated belling. "Won't git far...turn west and flank 'im...fuckin' darky's a dead darky." Laughter, loud and cruel. *Faster,* he thought, his heart climbing into his throat. *The cypress.*

*Find it.* He flicked his gaze from side to side as he ran, straining to see in the faint starshine that filtered through the canopy of trees, vines, and Spanish moss.

Dark trunks, dark water, dark everywhere. The ground turned spongy, sucking at his toes. He angled away from it toward firmer earth. A smothering curtain closed around him, as if the darkness had turned solid. He bit his tongue to keep back a yell, tasted blood, fought through the curtain into clear air. A fragment of Spanish moss clung to his lip. He wiped it away with a shudder.

Ahead, he could just make out the rest of the cypress grove he'd blundered into, narrow trunks and moss-draped branches stretching upward from bulging, cone-shaped feet. A landscape as alien to him as the moon, adding to the terror he'd gulped back like wormwood ever since being brought to this benighted place. Was it the right grove? Picking his way around its edge, over gnarled roots and deadfall, he strained to see. Cypress crowns hid the Drinking Gourd, the stars he'd meant to follow. The memory of singing that song, his own deep rolling voice shaping the words, pulled a panicky laugh from him on a puff of labored breath. He imagined the dense web of growth high above, closing in on him like his pursuers. The dogs' barking and men's voices were louder now, behind and to the west. He'd lingered too long.

They'd do for him like they'd done for the Yankee boy. Make him bleed and beg before they strung him up. The boy's face flashed through his mind, thin white cheeks mottling red, blue eyes bulging over the rope knotted around his skinny neck. *Freedmen's Bureau*, the lynching boss had said, and spat on the ground as the dying youth jerked and twitched above them. *Now he knows what free men are.*

A howl rang through the dark, followed by a shout of triumph. Ezra turned east and ran again, weaving through the cypress grove until he felt water splash around his feet and knew he'd reached a shallow channel. He changed course to follow it, running alongside—the splashing would give him away. He had no sense of where he was now, whether the marked cypress tree he sought was ahead of him or behind or anywhere he could reach in this goddamned swamp. His legs shook and his side burned, and he was going to die of a burst heart before the bastards got hold of him again, and maybe that was the best he could hope for, better than being torn apart by the hounds or strung up or dragged back to the plantation and whipped to death so all the others would see and learn their lesson—

A flash of white at eye level, shaped like a jagged cross. The shock of relief almost brought him to his knees, but he forced himself up the sloping bank toward the mark that hung in the darkness like a disembodied thing. His searching fingers found the cypress trunk, the rough bark around the fresh blazon in it. He took a precious few seconds and bent to scoop mud, straightened, and slapped it over the cross-shaped mark. *Just a little farther, turn right past the tree, keep going…*

Footsteps ahead. Not his own. No dog. Before fresh fear could prompt his tired body into action, someone spoke. A low murmur, pitched not to carry. "This way. There's food and a place to hide."

He knew the cadence, though the man's voice was unfamiliar. That, plus the tree mark and no telltale glimmer of pale skin as the speaker drew closer, told him he could trust. He stumbled forward, was caught by strong callused hands, held upright by well-muscled arms. "Easy," the stranger murmured in Ezra's ear. "Y'all are safe now."

# NINE

*July 16, 1872*

Cleary's was a ramshackle but clean saloon on Kingsbury a little over a block north of Kinzie, described by Sully as a place "where the beer and whiskey aren't watered, and a workingman can get drunk at a fair price." A chalk slate menu at one end of the bar offered ham sandwiches, cold chicken, and buttered bread, the latter two slices for three cents. Drinkers were sparse at this early hour—an elderly man at a corner table with a plate of bread and a glass of beer, and a pair of rivermen chowing down on a breakfast of chicken legs. Hanley ordered a ham sandwich and a beer. When the barman set them in front of him, Hanley took a swig before getting down to business. "You make a good brew," he said.

The barman grinned. He looked nearer forty than thirty, round faced, with black hair and eyes courtesy of long-dead shipwreck survivors from the Spanish Armada. "My da's recipe. Eamonn Cleary that was, God rest him these ten years. You a Galway man?" He tapped an ear. "I can always hear it, me. My folk're from Galway. Good to meet a countryman, if I'm right."

"You are." Hanley couldn't help grinning back. "Though I left there young. You've a gift." He held out a hand. "Frank Hanley. Francis, for the saint."

The barman shook it. "Gabriel Cleary. My mam was mad for angels."

Hanley picked up his sandwich. "I'm here for more than a drink and a bite, if you don't mind talking a bit. Police business. A man's gone missing. Would you know a Lawrence O'Shea, clerk at the Illinois, St. Louis and Grand Southern rail yard?"

Gabriel frowned in thought. "Not by name, though I get plenty from the yard in here most nights of the week. He your missing fellow?"

Hanley nodded. "Since Saturday." He ate a bite of sandwich, then set it on the plate and fished the carte de visite Mrs. O'Shea had given him out of his shirt pocket. "This is O'Shea. I'm told he planned to join some friends after he finished work. Was he here Saturday evening?"

Gabriel eyed the photograph, lips pursed. "I don't think so. He's not a regular customer, drops in once every few weeks or so. Nice fellow, generally stands his mates to a round before he leaves. I've never seen him drink more than two. Never stays late, or plays cards or dice. 'Got to get home to the wife,' that's what he tells the other boyos. The look in his eyes when he says it, I'd say she's a lucky woman."

"What about some other men from the yard?" He described Sully, Connor Rourke, and Liam Mahoney. "Were they here?"

"They were. Came in about half past seven, give or take." Gabriel leaned forward, arms braced on the bar. "The redhaired fellow— Mahoney, is it?—likes his whiskey more than's good for him. I've known him start a ruckus once or twice when the cards don't run his way. Never an outright brawl, mind you, but he's quick tempered when he's losing. The big fellow, Sully, usually calms him down before anyone throws more than words."

"Did Mahoney play cards that night?"

"Yeah. Sat down with a couple guys, big boyos. Not Irish. Norwegians, I think. Couldn't tell you their names, but I knew their faces. Regulars."

"And the other two...Sully and Rourke?"

"They watched the card game awhile, played a hand or two. Sully making sure his pal took it easy, maybe. Then him and the youngster bowed out and got to drinking together. None of 'em made any trouble."

"What time did they leave?"

Gabriel shrugged. "Ten, bit after." Another customer came in then, with a wave to the rivermen already there as he strode up to the bar and ordered a beer. Gabriel moved off to draw it, leaving Hanley alone with his meal. He finished the sandwich, reflecting on what he'd learned, which wasn't much more than he already knew. Lawrence O'Shea had worked late, just as his wife and the workmen had said. He'd meant to join his mates at Cleary's but never arrived. From Gabriel's description, he didn't sound like a gambler, or a heavy drinker likely to fall in the river and come to grief. Then again, it didn't always take drink to make a man lose his footing or drown.

Hanley swallowed the last of his beer. With Saturday evening accounted for till ten o'clock, it didn't seem likely that Mahoney and his companions had done O'Shea harm, assuming any of them wanted to. *Stop thinking like he's dead. He might be alive and in a holding cell or hospital somewhere.* Hanley doubted it, but he could be wrong. Worth checking police station lockups, though the notion of O'Shea as a drunken Paddy sleeping it off rankled. He should check the morgue, but he shrank from that. *For Mrs. O'Shea*, he told himself, comforting half-truth that it was.

The West Chicago Avenue station wasn't too far away. He might as well start there.

 හ

Two hours later, Hanley stood in front of Lake Street Station, footsore and frustrated. Lawrence O'Shea hadn't turned up at any hospital near the rail yard, or been assaulted or hauled in for drunk-and-disorderly at the West Chicago Avenue station. Hanley'd gone west to the station on Union Street Station as well, in case the missing man was attacked or picked up closer to his home, but no one there knew anything of him, either. Proprietors of the ten-cent gambling hells near Cleary's and the rail yard didn't recognize O'Shea, nor did any beat cop at Hanley's own stationhouse. He stood by the front steps, letting the river breeze dry his sweat-damp shirt. Sympathy for O'Shea's wife stirred in him. Poor woman, hoping so hard for good news while surely bracing for the worst. He didn't relish delivering it when the time came.

Thoughts of Mrs. O'Shea reminded him of the letter she'd showed him from her son. Matthew? No, Michael. Michael O'Shea had written his father about rumors of slave labor near New Orleans. What had she said of him? Something about the Freedmen's Bureau…he worked for them down there, if Hanley recalled right. So had someone else Hanley knew—Seamus Reilly, a fellow soldier from Hanley's company in the Irish Brigade. Seamus was back in Chicago now, trying to settle into a normal life. Worth finding out if he'd heard the same stories during his time in Louisiana and if there was truth to them.

Aaron Kelmansky had worked for the Freedmen's Bureau as well, though not in Louisiana as far as Hanley knew. He might shed some light on the matter, if only about how the bureau functioned and what it did. If there was any point in Hanley asking him about anything. If Aaron was even home at this time of day. Getting on for noon, it must be. Maybe he *wasn't* home. If so, then…

*Fool. You don't even know if she'll be there.* He ignored the mocking voice in his head that told him he was kidding himself, this trip had nothing to do with his case, as he fluffed his shirt in a vain attempt to dry it and smoothed his hair. Then he turned and strode toward Market Street.

Even though he'd hoped for it, he still felt caught by surprise when Rivka answered the door. For a moment he could only stand there and savor the sight of her in her brown workday dress and kerchief. He remembered the shine of her dark hair beneath it, from the ceilidh dance when the kerchief slid down, letting loose some strands that brushed her cheek.

She said his name, so softly it was scarcely a breath, which recalled him to himself. "Miss Kelmansky. Rivka." Heat rose in his face as he collected his wits. "I, um…I wondered if you can tell me where your brother's working today. I've a case, and the Freedmen's Bureau came up, and I remember he was with them after the late Rebellion, before he came back here…" Impossible to govern his tongue when all he wanted to do was look at her. Better yet, go inside and be with her, hold her close—

"*Ver iz*, Rivkaleh?" The familiar male voice from inside the house dispelled Hanley's daydream. Aaron came into view, his expression turning cool when he saw Hanley on the stoop. He nudged Rivka aside.

"What are you doing here? You have no business speaking to my sister—"

"My business is with you. May I come in so we can talk?" It wasn't a request, though Hanley kept his tone casual for Rivka's sake.

"There is nothing to talk about." Aaron moved as if to shut the door.

"The Freedmen's Bureau," Hanley said. "It came up in a case. A woman's husband went missing a few days ago. She's frantic. You worked for the bureau. You may know something that'll help me find this man...or find out what happened to him."

He watched an internal debate play out on Aaron's face. Refuse to help and demand Hanley leave? Step outside and talk with him in full view of the neighbors? Let Hanley in, where Rivka was? Aaron pursed his lips, then stepped back. "A few minutes. Then you go."

☙

Predictably, Aaron banished Rivka to the kitchen. "There is dinner to make and your English class to prepare for," he said as he gestured for Hanley to precede him into the tiny front parlor. "See to it. I will join you shortly."

Rivka bit her tongue. Snapping back at her brother's high-handedness would make her look like a shrew, and she had no desire to give Hanley *that* memory to carry away with him. The look in his eyes when he saw her...she hugged it close like a blanket against the cold that would come when he left again. How could she have feared he'd lost interest, even for a second?

She went to the stove, lifted a lid, stirred the banked coals beneath. Tea. No. There wasn't time to boil water. *Water. Yes. It's a hot day.* And poor Hanley, his hair was matted with sweat and wilder than usual, as if he'd already walked some way in the unrelenting sun. She fetched two glasses, dipped up water from the rain barrel to fill them. Set them down, opened the icebox, hunted amid the sawdust that slowed the ice's melting for pieces large enough not to dissolve when rinsed. There were three. She cleaned sawdust off them, dropped two in Hanley's glass and one in Aaron's, then wiped her wet palms on her skirts, picked the glasses up, and headed toward the parlor.

The door was closed. She nudged it open with a foot and went in. Aaron looked startled, then disapproving. "Water," she said, handing him a glass. She turned to Hanley, unable to keep a smile off her face. "I thought you would like some. There's ice in it." Of course there was, he could *see* that, she sounded like a babbling idiot. But he didn't care, he was smiling back at her, thanking her as if she'd brought him rubies.

"Rivka. Dinner is waiting."

Aaron's tone brooked no defiance, but she felt impervious to it. "Can I get you anything else? A bit of bread, a piece of fruit?"

"Nothing else," Aaron said. "Go tend to dinner."

With effort she swallowed a snappish reply, left the parlor, and retreated toward the kitchen, dragging her feet. Hanley's voice carried through the parlor doorway—he was asking what Aaron knew of the Freedmen's Bureau. "The missing man's son, Michael O'Shea, worked for them in New Orleans. He wrote to his father, Lawrence, about—"

"I cannot help you." A clipped dismissal, clearly meant to make Hanley give up and go away. "I left the Freedmen's Bureau three years ago. I know nothing of it since, aside from accounts in the newspapers. According to those, the bureau is being disbanded and hardly exists anymore."

"You must know something. Anything may help. What the bureau's been doing, how it works—"

This time, Aaron's reply held a shade of regret. "The bureau is enormously large, you understand. While I was there, it encompassed ten states and five districts, each of those divided further. I worked for them in Virginia, the First Military District. Louisiana was in the Fifth, more than a thousand miles away. Anything that happened in New Orleans, I can shed no light on. I'm sorry."

A brief silence fell, broken by Hanley's murmured thanks. A chair creaked as someone stood. Then footsteps. Swiftly, she turned around.

Hanley stepped out of the parlor, holding his water glass. He looked down the hall and saw her, came toward her. Was that regret she read on his face, that he couldn't prolong their time together, such as it was? She walked forward to meet him. Aaron hovered a step behind Hanley, his face stiff with disapproval. Rivka ignored her brother's presence as best she could. When Hanley handed her the empty glass, their fingers brushed, and her breath caught. "Thank you again for the water," he said, as if he meant more.

How much feeling could she put into a few words? "It was no trouble. I hope you find the man you're looking for."

"I hope so, too. Alive and well." A last glance, longer than it should be, and then he was through the front door and gone.

# TEN

*July 14–15, 1872*

Three days of relative safety, three blessed days, yet too often Ezra still heard the baying of hounds. Real or fancied, he wasn't always sure. The little bayou cabin on its foot-high stilts was clean and dry, his Underground Railroad rescuers kind enough not to press him about the horrors he'd endured. They'd fed him, cared for his hurts, bought him a train ticket for where he'd told them he wanted to go. The word surprised him even as it came out of his mouth. "Chicago." It seemed he meant to keep his promise to the white boy whose lynching he'd witnessed, after all.

He ate the last morsel of bread set out for his breakfast, then pulled on a pair of shoes, stood, and took up the small bundle that held spare clothing, a shaving kit, the ticket, and some food. One last glance around the empty cabin, a furtive touch on the handle of the knife sheathed at his belt. The man he knew only as Cal—"Safer that way," Cal said—had left it for him along with the other things. Ezra had expected a word of caution as well, considering the risks his rescuers were taking to get him out of Louisiana, but Cal had kept silent. *No sense saying what we both already know when it won't change what needs doing.*

He left the cabin and moved silently through the bayou, picking his way northwest across the boggy ground. Patches of sucking mud forced small detours, and once he froze in the shadow of a cypress as the belling of a hound reached his ears. Or was it a heron's cry, or some other creature entirely? The sound faded, and he wiped cold sweat off his forehead. The sooner he reached New Orleans, the sooner he could leave it.

Dauphine Street first. Then Lucien's place, a final haven until it came time to board the train.

&

He found the white boy's rented room easily enough, in a two-story building of weathered gray stone with a green-painted front door. The olive-skinned Creole woman who ran the boardinghouse let him in right away when he gave her the boy's name.

"Something's happened," she said, her voice taut, as Ezra crossed the threshold into the dim front hallway. "Is he dead?"

"Afraid so, ma'am."

She closed her eyes, then opened them and gestured toward the stairs. "Second floor, room on the left. Whatever you came for, get it and go." No questions, for which Ezra felt grateful.

He thanked her and went up. The room on the left was sparsely furnished, as if its former occupant had spent little time there. A bed with a blue-and-green quilt, a washstand with pitcher and basin, a straight-backed chair and a rickety table by a narrow window that faced the street. The table held a china mug, a spoon, a book that might be a Bible. A small cedar chest at the bed's foot stood open, clothes peeking out. Ezra went to it, knelt, pushed aside shirts and trousers and undergarments until he felt a bulging envelope beneath. *Evidence*, the white boy had said.

Ezra pulled the papers out of the envelope without so much as a glance at them. Nothing more in it, no money. Where else could the money be? He stuffed the papers back in, then stood and glanced around the room. *The Bible*. He strode to the table, flipped through the leather-bound volume, and found a few folded bills inside the back cover.

He scooped up the money, then stood with it in his hand instead of leaving as he ought. It was dangerous to be here, to be anywhere except on the train going north. That was it, he realized. Going north meant safety, a chance at a new life…alone, away from the woman he loved.

*You don't know that. She could be anywhere. Up North, even.* But he couldn't make himself believe it. Every rumor he'd heard of her, every story he'd chased, put her in the South still. Danger or no, how could he leave it, and his last hope of her, behind?

*Five years searching and you've found nothing.* The thought pounded in his head. *She could be married, she could be dead. You won't ever know. Live with it.*

He clenched his fist around the white boy's money. The paper bills crackled in his hand. The sound made him think of flames, burning his hope to ashes.

&#8494;&#8485;

The New Orleans depot was crowded, noisy, full of steam and smoke and unfamiliar faces. Mostly white ones, brown faces of varying shades sprinkled among them like wood chips in a fast-running stream. Ezra's gut clenched whenever a white man looked his way. Stranger, or pattyroller? Hunting him, or not? To calm himself, he conjured up Cal's voice, from the bayou cabin early that morning. *Keep calm. Look like you belong where you are. With fresh clothes and no lash marks showing, people will believe what they see*—a libre couleur *going about his business. That's you now, Ezra.*

A free colored man. Ezra drew a deep breath, settled his tight shoulders. He'd been free once, long before the war. Even slavery couldn't steal his own past from him. Sure as hell Sweetbay Sugar couldn't. He steered through the flood of people, seeking a porter to ask about departures. Within minutes he found one, a man as dark as he was in a navy-blue uniform and flat cap. "Where do I board the next train for Chicago?"

"Platform No. 4." The porter pointed. "Down there, near the end. You'll see the number. Second-class cars are the fifth one and back."

Ezra thanked him, wishing he had a coin or two to slip the man. All he had were greenbacks, and those too few. He threaded his way through still more people, every inch of him alert for the shout of recognition, the grabbing hand, the blow to knock him senseless and render him no trouble. *The pattyrollers are in the bayou, not here. I'm safe... as much as any Negro can be.*

He found the platform, eyed his ticket, made his way along the waiting cars in search of the right place to board. What had the porter said, the fifth car back? The fourth? It was all a muddle in Ezra's head, exhausted as he was from his journey into New Orleans. The young man's envelope full of drawings and writings, hidden in Ezra's bundle, seemed to weigh it down. He wished he hadn't taken them, didn't want to deal with them. But he'd given his word, and he wasn't the kind to easily break it.

He'd lost count of the cars. A shout nearby made him start, but it was only one white man greeting another near the first car behind the huge, whuffing engine. Ezra saw an open door ahead, mounted the steps to it and boarded the train. As he turned and walked into the car itself, shocked faces—all of them white—stared at him. A whisper ran through the car, and a ruddy-faced ticket taker built like a side of beef came up to him with a glare. "Next car, *boy*," the ticket man said. "This one's for decent people. Not your kind."

Ezra felt his arm muscles twitch, his free hand ball into a fist. He wanted to smash the man's sneering face, make him choke back that *boy* and all that followed it. He also wanted to get to Chicago alive and in one piece. Impossible to do both.

*Keep calm.* He willed his hand to open, his head to bow a fraction because this bastard would expect it. "Sorry." Before the ticket man could demand a *sir* from him, he ducked back through the entry door and off the train. He hurried down the platform past two more cars, just for good measure, and boarded again. The right car this time, the skins of those in it a reassuring collection of browns. He found an empty seat, settled in by the window, leaned back, and closed his eyes.

A hand on his shoulder jolted him awake, ready to fight, until the dark face above the uniform registered, and he gave his ticket to be torn. The ticket taker moved on, and Ezra sagged back against the windowpane. Twenty hours or more to Chicago. Plenty of time to sleep. He craved sleep like a drunkard craves liquor.

He tucked his bundle with its spare shirt and trousers, small store of provisions, and the white boy's papers securely in the crook of his arm, then closed his eyes again and let exhaustion overwhelm him.

❧

Curls of steam drifted across the platform as Ezra left the train and hurried through the crowded Chicago depot. Stiff as he was from hours of sitting, it felt good to move. He thrust a hand into his pocket and felt the smooth fold of the bills nestled there. Enough for a couple of days at a cheap boardinghouse, even at prices likely to be high. As he strode past the engines and through the milling crowd, the words of the Our Father formed in his head. *Forgive us our trespasses….* He'd be forgiven for taking the money as well as the papers he'd been told to. And surely the white boy's soul would be forgiven whatever he was guilty of. Not so those who killed him, or there was no justice in Heaven.

He turned his thoughts to practical matters—food, shelter, a place to lose himself a time while he earned his keep. "John and Mary Jones," he murmured, stepping around a porter with a laden baggage cart who was following a well-dressed white woman with two fretful children in tow. "119 Dearborn." He could have written down the names and address, but it was safer just to remember. The pattyrollers, or the man who employed them, might send somebody after him even this far. Kill him for defying them, if nothing else. Or because he'd seen them lynch that white boy, or both. He'd gotten safely out of New Orleans, but how could he be sure they hadn't spotted him in the crowd at the train station there? Jubilee or no, the slave catchers hadn't changed in anything but name. They did what they wanted. And they never gave up.

The thought made him cold, even with the summer heat folding around him like a blanket as he finally reached the street. The air stank of mud and horses. For a moment, he felt dizzied by the passing traffic and the rattle of wheels echoing off brick and stone walls. Delivery wagons, brewers' drays, hackney cabs, and people by the dozens, no one so much as glancing at him as they went about their business. Chicago was a maze, a wonder. A place of freedom, or a trap. Too soon to tell.

*John and Mary Jones, Dearborn Street.* A respected couple in Chicago's colored neighborhood, and beyond it, from what he'd been told. Cal had said their business and home remained sanctuaries, still a vital part of the Underground Railroad that nowadays helped freed blacks move up from the South to the safer North. Ezra dug out a map, purchased from a vendor on the train, and traced a finger along it until he found Dearborn. Then he turned east and started walking.

# ELEVEN

*July 17, 1872*

A burglary case took up most of Wednesday morning after Hanley's arrival at Lake Street, so it was closing in on noon by the time he returned to the rail yard in search of Lawrence O'Shea's boss.

"Aye, Mr. Coughlin's here," said Jamieson, the lone clerk in the office. His thick brogue rolled off his tongue like fog off the lake. Straw-colored hair that stuck up in the back made him look even younger than he likely was. Behind him, a closed door in the partition wall bore gold lettering across opaque glass that read *Patrick M. Coughlin, Shipping Agent.* "I remember you from Monday. Detective…sorry, what's the name again?"

"Hanley."

"Right." Jamieson's eyes widened. "D'you know yet what happened to Mr. O'Shea? I hope he's not come to harm."

"I hope so, too." Hanley gave it extra warmth, to put the young man at ease. "If you've a minute, can you tell me what Mr. O'Shea does, what sort of paperwork he handles—"

The closed door opened. The man framed in the gap had an air of restless energy even standing still on the threshold. His broad shoulders and barrel chest strained his suit coat and made him look more like a laborer than a businessman. Bright blue eyes framed by a shock of brown hair and a neatly trimmed mustache favored Hanley with curiosity. "Can I help you, sir? What's your business here?"

He spoke with a brogue as well, much slighter than Jamieson's but stronger than Hanley's own. Hanley held up his badge and identified himself. "I'm here about a missing employee of yours. Lawrence O'Shea."

Coughlin frowned. "O'Shea, yes. I'm most concerned. You've not found him, then?"

"Not yet." Hanley chose his next words with care. "I'm told he spoke to you about a business matter recently, connected with a shipping client in New Orleans. He had concerns—"

"Yes. Yes, he did." The frown gave way to a wry smile. "Can I stand you to a meal while we talk further? Or would that be bribing an officer of the law?"

〇〇

They went to the Carroll Street Tavern, a choice that surprised Hanley. The well-off boss of a thriving rail yard hardly belonged amid the typical noon crowd of low-paid shop clerks, omnibus drivers, dock workers, and bricklayers in rolled-up shirtsleeves, laughing and joking as they wolfed down fried fish and sandwiches and beer. Coughlin should be more at home in a chop house with expensive steaks and white linen tablecloths. Then again, maybe he'd worked his way up and preferred to stay true to his roots, in his choice of eateries at least.

"I'm afraid I can't tell you much that's any use," Coughlin said after the waiter set down their plates of fried perch and a loaf of crusty bread. "The men said O'Shea's been missing since Saturday evening? If anything happened to him after work—if he was set upon by footpads or toughs anywhere near the yard—"

"We're looking into that angle, of course. At the moment, I'm interested in that 'business matter' he told you about. The rumors of slave labor. Did you know of them when the client company—Sweetbay Sugar's the name—signed on? How does the railway get clients, by the way? Is that your job?"

Coughlin forked up a chunk of fish. "I don't recall hearing such tales about any of our shipping clients in New Orleans, until O'Shea

51

brought these to my notice. Though the Illinois, St. Louis and Grand Southern hasn't the means or obligation to dictate how anyone else does business…and even if we did, that would be our concern, not the police department's. Poor Lawrence must have met with mischance somehow. Shouldn't you be focusing on that?"

Hanley dug into his own perch. "Lawrence's wife says the stories troubled him quite a bit."

Coughlin ate the bite of fish and cut another. "They did. He couldn't abide slavery. Before the war, he was halfway to being an abolitionist, from some of the things he'd say around the yard. I think he wished he was young enough to fight in it. God knows he was proud of his son when the boy enlisted. Did you serve, Detective?"

"Chicago Irish Brigade." The fish was excellent, cooked to a turn and served with early carrots and young onions. "Yourself?"

Coughlin shook his head. "War's a younger man's game. I was past forty when they fired on Fort Sumter. I did my bit for the Union by keeping the trains running and supplies flowing." He raised his beer glass and sipped. "You're sure you won't have some? The brew here's excellent."

"Not on duty, thanks." A shrewd operator, Coughlin was, deftly turning the subject from Lawrence O'Shea. "So what did Lawrence say when he came to you?"

"With his son's tales?" Coughlin reached for the bread loaf and tore off a sizeable piece. "He expected the lad to settle down, you know. After the war. Then the boy went off to work for the Freedmen's Bureau, if you can believe it." He said *Freedmen's Bureau* as if speaking of Barbary pirates. "Waste of time, helping *those* people. Might as well expect children to make their own way in the world as darkies to do it. But that's neither here nor there. Anyway, Lawrence asked about Sweetbay Sugar…wanting to know if stories about slaves had reached my ears. He thought I should tell the owners and stockholders at the Grand Southern. I told him the same as I've told you…not a word was breathed to me when I landed the contract. Though they'd hardly admit it to a Yankee Irishman if they *were* using slave labor, now would they?"

"So you didn't look into it, like you told O'Shea you would?"

Annoyance flashed across Coughlin's face, swiftly suppressed. "Of course I did. The railway's reputation means a lot to me." He gave Hanley a confiding smile. "Hugh Denham—he's a major shareholder, I've known him for years—he spoke up for me when the shipping agent's position here in Chicago came open. It's thanks to him I got the job. I owe him, and the Grand Southern, for putting their trust in me." He broke his bread into two smaller pieces. "Hugh was an abolitionist before the war, still votes solid Republican. He'd never condone slave labor or have any truck with a client tainted by it. When Lawrence told me about Sweetbay, I wrote the company's owner. We'd met briefly, months ago, to settle the details of the shipping contract, and he seemed an honorable sort. But you never really know, do you?"

Privately, Hanley agreed. If Sweetbay Sugar was re-enslaving freedmen, they'd hardly say so. Either way, it wasn't Coughlin's or the railway's responsibility. Still, it stood out that O'Shea had gone missing not long after receiving his son's letter. Hanley didn't like things that stood out. "And?"

Coughlin bit into the bread, chewed and swallowed. "Haven't heard back yet. But there's no proof, and I'm sure there won't be—nothing for the railway to be bothered with." Another practiced, friendly smile. "We're in the railroad business to make money. While no one wants to be connected with anything scandalous, a few rumors from darkies down South hardly amount to that. Proof, now, that'd be different. But I can't imagine there is any. And I'm sure you understand the importance of making money, Detective. Getting ahead. As an Irishman…and a plain workingman to boot. Like I was once."

*Not a gent after all. A working-class boy who's done well for himself.* Hanley tore his own hunk of bread from the loaf. Coughlin was sparing no effort to win him over. So he'd be satisfied and go away? That kind of charm would be an asset to a man moving up in the world. "When did O'Shea come to you about the slave labor?"

Coughlin looked thoughtful as he speared an onion. "Around the middle of June, it was. Three, maybe four weeks ago? Three, I think. A Saturday, I do recall that."

Hanley buttered his bread and took a bite. Lawrence O'Shea had vanished on July 13th. Too long between his inquiry about Sweetbay Sugar and his disappearance? Maybe his vanishing act stemmed from something else, after all. "How well did you know O'Shea? His wife says you gave him his clerking job here."

"That I did." Coughlin ate the onion and washed it down with beer. "A steady fellow, he was, and quick minded enough to do more than haul cargo all day. I saw myself in him, to be honest. So I gave him a leg up, and he's more than repaid my confidence in him since."

"What does he do, exactly?"

"He keeps track of cargo shipments, makes sure the numbers are what's contracted for. What comes in from where, what goes back out. We don't let trains run empty. The Illinois, St. Louis and Grand Southern has one of the most efficient operations in Chicago. I like to think I've contributed to that. Earned my keep, so to speak." Coughlin said this as if expecting Hanley to share his obvious pride in his achievement.

"Does O'Shea gamble much? Or have a mistress, would you know?"

"A mistress? Lord, no. It's always and only been his wife he loves. You can see it in his face every time he speaks of her. I suppose that's the kind of thing you policemen have to ask. Suspicious minds and all that. If I dealt with criminals all day, I'd think that way, too. But no, Detective. He's not run off with some doxy, unless I've badly misjudged him."

"And gambling?"

"I wouldn't know. I'm not much for it myself."

Hanley ate more fish, then sipped water. "So what about Saturday?"

Coughlin blinked. "What about it?"

"O'Shea worked late, I'm told. And he was worried about something. Did you talk to him that day?"

"I'm sure I did. About what, I couldn't tell you. Nothing significant I can recall." He leaned toward Hanley across the table, his expression earnest. "Keep me apprised, won't you? Lawrence O'Shea is a valued employee. If anything's happened to him, the railway—and myself personally—want to see justice done."

# TWELVE

Hanley had run out of excuses to avoid his next stop, so he gave in to the inevitable and hopped a southbound horsecar that took him most of the way. It was just past two when he finally reached the morgue, recently relocated to a new building at the rear of the County Hospital lot. He'd kept clear of the place since May and the end of the Champion murder investigation. God only knew what reception he'd get. Still, if Lawrence O'Shea was dead—which seemed likely—the morgue was the logical place to start.

He walked through the doors and found himself in a large front room, partly given over to the superintendent's office. The remaining space was empty except for a large glass case that housed a motley collection of clothing, presumably taken from the dead. He passed through and kept going toward the examining room beyond, gagging as the smell reached him. After better than two months' avoidance, he'd lost some of his tolerance for the chemical sting of carbolic mingled with the sickly sweetness of dead bodies.

In the examining room, he found Will Rushton stitching up the chest of a portly, middle-aged corpse. Will's olive skin looked darker than usual in contrast to the dead man's pallor. *Stop it*, Hanley told himself, embarrassed he'd paid it any mind. Will was the same person he'd always been, mulatto or not. Only Hanley's knowledge had changed.

He cleared his throat. Will glanced up. At the sight of Hanley, his expression turned flat. "Something I can help you with, Detective? I'm afraid I can't spare you much time."

So that was the way of it. Hanley had hoped for better but hadn't really expected it. It pained him to recall that just a few months earlier, he'd trusted Will so little that he'd accused him of murder. He moved further into the room and nodded toward the examining table. A second, sheet-draped body lay on the slab adjacent. The third table was unoccupied. "Just looking for a corpse that might've turned up recently. Go ahead and finish. I'll wait."

Will held his gaze a moment, then returned to his work. Hanley noted his precision with the needle and sutures. No wasted motion, total focus on his task. A seasoned battle surgeon during the late Rebellion couldn't have done better.

"You learn that in the war?" he asked, just for something to say.

"I learned it at medical school. The battlefields were a practicum." Will pulled the suturing thread taut, picked up an odd-shaped pair of scissors, and cut the thread close to the dead flesh. He took his time washing his surgical tools and his hands in preparation for the next corpse. No remarks about the one he'd just finished with, no inquiries about which dead body Hanley was interested in, no joking about work or comments about the newly built morgue. As the seconds ticked by, Hanley felt the slow burn of anger. He wrestled it down, not ready to acknowledge the guilt that fueled it. He hadn't come here to have things out with Will Rushton, but to help a frightened woman who would probably soon find herself a grieving widow.

Will dried his hands, folded the small towel with meticulous care, and set it on the sink's edge. Finally, he glanced at Hanley. "You're looking into a murder?"

"Missing person. Lawrence O'Shea. Railroad clerk, worked late on Saturday and never came home. Someone suggested he might've fallen into the river, though I've nothing definite to say so."

A spark of interest showed beneath Will's cool exterior. "I may have something for you." He turned to the second examining table, where the sheeted corpse lay. "This one came in around ten o'clock. Some bargemen fished him out of the river just north of Carroll Street in the wee hours this morning."

With the same gentle respect he gave to all the dead, Will folded the sheet back. "Is this your man? You have a description?"

Hanley flinched. The puffy, mottled face was still recognizable as Lawrence O'Shea's. "A photograph. His wife…his widow gave it to me. Looks like it's him. How long was he in the water?"

"Given the condition and color of his skin, I'd say at least three days but not more than four. I can't be more precise, not with him waterlogged. Not much bloating yet, thank God."

Hanley did some quick figuring in his head. "O'Shea was last seen around seven thirty Saturday evening…so he probably went in sometime Saturday night, but no later than the early hours of Sunday."

"Sounds about right." Delicately, Will reached out and turned the head rightward, revealing a caved-in rough oval as large as his two fists at the back of the skull. "Good God," he murmured, then retrieved his surgical kit.

"What in hell's name made that injury?" Hanley asked. "It's too big for a cosh, wrong shape for a mallet or a wrench or a crowb—"

"Leave the professional judgment to me, please. If you still trust it."

"Christ, Will." The retort escaped before he could stop it, but Hanley's brief regret vanished in a heartbeat. They might as well have this out after all. "If I wasn't willing to trust your judgment, I wouldn't be here. Grant me that at least."

Will folded his arms. "You didn't grant me anything in Ben Champion's murder. You couldn't make up your mind if I was lying or incompetent. And for *no good reason.*" He laid out the last three words like hammer blows.

"Your adoptive father was a suspect at the time. So were you."

"Horse leavings. That's not why. You can lie to yourself if you want, but don't lie to me. I can spot it quicker than you can spot a criminal."

*Because you've spent half your life lying to everyone about being white.* Hanley just managed to keep the words back. If he said them, Will would never forgive him. He couldn't afford a permanent breach, considering they both worked for the police department. As to their friendship…he shook his head, angry with his own inability to sort it out. Angry with Will, too, for making it harder. "I've told no one about you, except your sister Ada," he said instead. "And I won't. Doesn't that count for something?"

Uncertainty replaced Will's glare. Then he looked away. Moving with taut control, he took a long, thin instrument from the surgical kit and delicately moved a torn flap of scalp aside, then probed a section of cracked bone. "The pieces are still connected, and there's beveling on the edges. That means fresh bone, not dry." A queasy pang rolled through Hanley as Will probed some more. "Depressed fracture, posterior right cranium. Whoever hit him was plenty strong, or the weapon was damned heavy. Or both." He moved a sliver of skull aside, and his eyes narrowed. "Something here besides bone fragments. Hand me the tweezers, will you?"

Fumbling in the kit at first, Hanley found them and handed them over. Bile rose in his throat as Will poked at O'Shea's shriveled brain, but he choked it down. After another minute, Will held the tweezers up, a flake of something dark caught between them. "See that? There's more than one. Black flecks in the brain matter. Whatever the murder weapon is, it left those behind."

Hanley forced himself to look more closely. "Dirt? Mold from three days in the river?"

"Or metal. Iron, from the color. And corroded some, to flake off like that. So deep in the tissue it was still there, even after seventy-two hours or more in the water."

"Did the head injury kill him before he went in, or did he drown?"

"Fresh bone and beveling says the head injury, but give me a few more minutes and I'll tell you for sure." Carefully, Will set the tweezers down and pulled the sheet further back, exposing the corpse to the waist. "If he went in while dying, as opposed to dead, there'll be water in his lungs." He took up a scalpel, sliced through O'Shea's chest, and folded back the skin and muscle, exposing the sternum and ribs. Next, from a corner cabinet, he fetched an odd-looking implement, a rectangular frame with a cleaver-like handle sticking out. Only when he set it against a rib bone did Hanley realize the base of the frame was a hacksaw blade.

The grating noise it made set his teeth on edge. Bone dust spattered Will's hands and the dark mass of what Hanley assumed were lungs beneath. Eventually, Will set the saw down and moved the cut rib aside.

He poked one lung with a finger, then eased his hand beneath the rib cage and pressed gently downward. "No water. He was dead when he went in."

"Any notion where?"

Will shifted the rib bone and muscle flaps back into place. "The North Branch flows south, toward the junction of all three stems at Wolf Point. The current is pretty sluggish, and we haven't had any big rainstorms lately, so a body could meander. If I had to guess, I'd say Erie or so."

"You're sure?"

"As I can be." Will said it with professional crispness, the brief camaraderie of moments ago vanished like a blown-out flame. "Lucky you, Detective. You've got a murder on your hands."

# THIRTEEN

*July 18, 1872*

W e'll start you out with inventory." John Jones led Ezra down a wide, sturdy staircase to the basement floor of the building he owned, where his sizeable tailoring and clothes-cleaning establishment was housed. He reminded Ezra of a preacher—kindly and dignified, with a presence that commanded respect. "We just got a shipment that needs recording. You've a neat hand, and I'm happy to pass that job on to younger eyes than mine." Jones gave him an easy grin. "Then we'll test your head for figures, see if you can help with the account books as well. I'm still straightening out the mess since the Fire. We've only been open in these premises for the past few weeks. You kept accounts before the Jubilee, you said?"

Ezra nodded. "In Louisiana. Near enough to New Orleans that I was let to hire myself out to local merchants. When the master didn't need me." The word *master* came out with bite. Sympathy glimmered in Jones's eyes, and Ezra took a calming breath. His days of living as someone else's property—whether named as such or not—were done with, had been since he escaped through the bayou. He didn't know yet whether he'd stay in Chicago or only stop here long enough to earn money for a grubstake somewhere else. Somewhere a black man could go for a fresh and fair start, if there was any such place in the so-called land of the free.

The basement was high ceilinged and spacious, well lit by sunshine pouring in through windows that rose partway above the street. An interior wall divided it in two, with a wide double door partway down, from behind which came splashing sounds and the smell of strong soap. A washhouse, Ezra guessed. He followed Jones past a group of men and women seated at separate tables, stitching garments—shirts and suit jackets, a few ladies' skirts—toward a doorway at the rear. They passed through it into a storeroom, where Jones took a logbook and pencil from a side table. "The fabrics are labeled," he said. "Cottons, cambrics, wools, and flannels. Write down the quantities of each and check them against the manifest."

He reached into the pocket of his suit coat and brought out a thin sheaf of folded papers, while Ezra gazed around at the towering shelves laden with bolts of cloth, most in shades from white to cream, tan to brown, and gray to black. Among them, a few brighter hues glimmered—deep blue, pale green, a warm rose that made him think of sunrise. More fabric rolls in somber shades were stacked near a door in the back wall that likely led to a street or alley.

Jones handed him the papers, then nodded across the storeroom toward a tall cabinet with rows of tiny labeled drawers. "Buttons, thread, trimmings, needles, thimbles and such are all in there. I inventoried those last week, so you needn't bother with them. Just the fabric shipment. When you're finished, let me know. I'll be in my office." He clapped Ezra on the shoulder and left.

Ezra eyed the stacked bolts by the rear door. He opened the logbook and read over a few pages, getting the sense of it, then turned to the nearest blank sheet, tucked the pencil behind his ear, and squatted by the fabric pile. The labels were neatly written on white cardboard tags that dangled from the bottom of each bolt. Carefully, he noted them in columns by number and fabric type, then compared them to the manifest Jones had given him. Everything matched. He stood and stretched, working stiffness out of his knees from crouching for the past while, then left the storeroom.

Jones's office was somewhere on this floor, he assumed, which was devoted to the cleaning and tailoring establishment. The first floor of the building was let to a bank, Jones had told him, the upper three stories to offices of various types—lawyers, a grain dealer, a real estate agent, even a photographer. The pride of ownership in Jones's voice as he spoke of his tenants gave Ezra an odd feeling, something between aspiration and envy. Jones had never been a slave. Born free like Ezra, he'd been lucky enough to stay that way for all of his fifty-plus years. Still, if Ezra could do half as well as this man had, he'd count himself more blessed than many.

As he glanced around the large open space, his gaze swept across the people at the sewing tables. Five men worked in one group, four women in another. The women were talking, their soft voices a pleasant undertone through the room. One voice rose briefly. "...homesteaders, as soon as we can afford to. Won't be much longer now."

"But the land's free," another woman said. "I heard you pick your place and stay on it for five years, and then it's yours. Isn't that so?"

The first speaker shifted in her seat enough for Ezra to see her face clearly. Shocked stillness took hold of him as he absorbed the details—fine bones, golden skin, and gray-green eyes, their color unforgettable even if he could have forgotten everything else about her. His heart thudded against his ribs, and his skin flushed hot from head to foot. He drew breath to say her name, then choked it back. She would know him if he spoke. Did he want her to, here, in front of strangers? What would she do, what would she say? Indecision mixed with longing held him silent and motionless, his whole body tight as a clenched fist.

"Takes money to make a go of farming." She reached for a pair of scissors and snipped a thread from the seam she'd been fixing. "Seed, tools, food to keep you through the months before there's anything to harvest and sell. I'm hoping we'll earn enough this summer so we can go west soon and file a claim before winter sets in."

A third woman shook her head. "I hear winter's terrible out West. Bad enough here, where there's folks around to help you. Out there, with nobody for miles..."

"We'll manage. We have to." The first woman stood and shook out the mended garment, then noticed Ezra standing there like the thoughtless fool he was. "Can I…" She trailed off, a furrow between her brows. Recognition struck—he saw it in her widened eyes, the slight parting of her lips. *Did they still taste the same?* he wondered. A thought he'd no business having, not here and not now. Surely not after so many years between them, in which God only knew what had happened. That she was here at all was…what? Fate's joke? An act of Providence? Both?

He cleared his throat, taking hold of his feelings as best he could. Despite his efforts, his voice shook as her name left his mouth like a prayer. "Ada," he said. "It's been…quite a time."

℘

At one, Mr. Jones came out of his office and announced a dinner break. Two of the men left, discussing which nearby tavern served the best soup, while the rest of the workers fetched tins and baskets from a table in a corner of the workroom. Ezra hung back, shy of mingling with them. Shy of getting close to Ada with other people around. He still couldn't fathom her being here, couldn't quite accept that she was real. He made a trip to the outhouse instead. By the time he came back, his dinner was the only one unclaimed.

The other workers had settled in groups, eating and talking with the familiarity of long acquaintance. Ada sat listening, peeling a hard-boiled egg, as an older woman sang the praises of her newest grandson. Ezra walked past them, past the three remaining men who were pitching coins at fruit pits in friendly competition, and sat on the floor to eat. As he unwrapped his sandwich, one of the coin pitchers invited him to join them. "Too rich for my blood," he said, with a joking smile he didn't feel, and a nod toward the pennies and nickels scattered across the floor. The other man shrugged and returned to the game. Ezra resumed eating and tried not to think of anything but his food.

He was halfway through his sandwich when he heard a soft footfall behind him. He guessed who it was before she spoke. "Ezra," Ada said softly. "How…how are you keeping? Are you well?"

He turned and saw that her cheeks were flushed, likely at the absurdity of her own words as much as any feeling for him. *How are you* and *are you well*—thirteen years, a war, and an unsettled peace after he'd last set eyes on her. Last held her close, breathing the scent of her hair, storing up the memory of her before they came to take him. Not that any of it was her fault. Not even the way he'd left Virginia and Angel Oak Grove, back before the Rebellion. Fetching up in Louisiana, Deep South sugarcane country, convinced he would die there. Time was, he'd thought nothing worse could happen to him.

Buying time to school the turbulence in him, he took a bite of his sandwich, chewed and swallowed. "Well enough to live this long," he said finally. "You?"

She rested her back against the wall, hands twisted in her skirt. There was wonder in her eyes, and regret, and a touch of anxiety. *And love, still?* "I didn't think I'd see you again. After you were…"

"Sold," he finished for her, sharp and bitter. "But all that's done with, thank God."

"Yes." She kept gazing at him as if he were a haunt, a restless spirit of the beloved dead come back to finish something left undone. "How…how are you nowadays? What are you doing in Chicago?"

He wished fiercely they were someplace private where he could wrap her in his arms, lose himself in her, erase every second of their lost years. *Hiding,* he thought of saying. But there was no sense bringing her into his current situation. "Worse than some, better than others. Glad to be here instead of where I was." That much was true. He cleared his throat. "How about you?"

The flush in her cheeks deepened and she glanced down. "Doing all right. Earning money to go west."

"I heard." Too much was held in those few words he'd overheard her say. *I'm hoping* we'll *earn enough. We.* Acid curdled in his gut. Defying it, he ate another bite of sandwich. Cured bacon on fresh crusty bread, both in short supply in the old slave quarters on the plantation where he'd spent most of the past miserable two years. The rich, salty taste in his mouth made him bless the Lord and his boardinghouse landlady. "It's a hard life, homesteading, they say."

"No harder than we're used to." She gave him a small smile, then tucked a wisp of loose hair behind her ear. He recalled the gesture as one she made when she felt anxious but didn't want to show it.

He looked away from her, crumpling the empty sandwich paper in his hand. "Did you ever find any of your family?"

"I found my brother Will," she said. He waited for more, but she didn't go on.

"Well. That's something." He chose not to ask who else she'd found, or come to be with…who *we'll* and *we're* referred to. He wanted her to leave, yet he also wanted to keep talking with her. She was the only one he'd ever told how it felt to be born and grow up free, then be taken and made chattel. The only one he'd let see him weep over the life and family he'd lost. That meant something, even now.

"Are you…are you staying on here?" she asked.

He wasn't sure of his answer until the words came. "For a while. Don't know how long. I'm at Mrs. Kelvin's boardinghouse on Twelfth Street. Paid by the week."

She nodded, her expression solemn. As if he'd answered a question she hadn't asked, and she wasn't sure she liked it.

# FOURTEEN

Hanley spent the first hour of Thursday morning writing up preliminary notes on the Lawrence O'Shea murder case. Setting it down on paper helped distance him from it, though not enough to keep from thinking of Lawrence's widow. She'd managed not to break down when he brought her the news yesterday, but her empty stare and white-knuckled handclasp told him what it cost her to keep her anguish inside. Pity for her made him grip his pen tighter, concentrate harder on each word as he wrote. Grace O'Shea might have been his own mother, staving off collapse when his father died. Hanley'd been too young to remember much, but the frightening blankness of Mam's unspoken pain stayed with him still.

He shook off the old hurt and glanced up, in time to spot his old friend Seamus Reilly entering the stationhouse lobby. Hanley had sent him a note asking him to drop by. He closed the logbook and tucked it in a drawer, then stood and headed out of the squad room. "Seamus. Thanks for coming. How've you been keeping?"

Behind Seamus's jaunty grin, Hanley read exhaustion. "Tolerable. Yourself?"

"Same." He suppressed the impulse to ask how his friend was sleeping these days, knowing Seamus would hate it. Like many fellow Irish Brigade veterans, Seamus could be touchy about other people's concern. "Let's walk by the river. At least there'll be a breeze, even if it smells."

"All right." They left the station together, and Hanley turned their steps toward South Water Street. There was plenty of open space amid the docks and warehouses along that stretch of river, so he and Seamus could hear themselves talk over the noises of the busy waterfront and the rail yard not far away.

"I've questions about New Orleans, for a case I'm working," Hanley said as they turned onto South Water. "When you were with the Freedmen's Bureau there, did you run across a Michael O'Shea? Young fellow, mid-twenties, came from Chicago. Likes to draw, so I'm told."

"O'Shea…" Seamus gnawed his lip, then nodded. "I remember him. Didn't know him well, but we crossed paths not too long before I quit the bureau and came home. He always had a sketchbook by him, everywhere he went. Why?"

Hanley filled him in about Lawrence O'Shea's murder and Michael's allegations of slave labor at Sweetbay Sugar Company. "Did you hear the same stories? Were they ever proven?"

A puff of breeze ruffled Seamus's scraggy hair and beard, bringing the stink of fish and mud and rancid distillery swill along with the cries of wheeling gulls. "We heard things, sure. In whispers, everywhere the Negroes gathered. Saloons, eateries, the general store. In New Orleans, in little towns outside it. But when we'd ask questions, looking for names or places—anything we could act on—folk'd clam up. Even when the ones asking were colored troops working for the bureau, instead of white ones. People were scared, plain and simple. They figured the bureau couldn't take on the big boyos, the ones that still had money and pull even after the war. 'Specially after '68, when Congress and bloody Andrew Johnson shut us down on pretty much everything that wasn't to do with schools and teachers. Hard enough before then to stand up for the freedmen when local whites caused 'em trouble. I can't blame 'em for not talking. Why should they risk what little they had…for nothing?"

"What kind of trouble did the bureau deal with?"

"Labor contracts, mostly." Seamus glanced sideways at him, bitter amusement on his face. "Once the war ended, all those plantation owners…cotton, sugarcane, rice…still needed workers to till the fields and plant and harvest the crops. Only now they had to pay them, in wages or food or both. Some took their medicine and paid up, though you'd have thought it half killed 'em. Others refused. When Negroes came to us after being cheated, or run off, or beaten and threatened with murder for seeking what was due them, we'd send field agents back with them, usually with a few soldiers as well to make the point. Mostly, it worked. Sometimes there'd be a standoff, until cooler heads prevailed and the guns went down. And there were always outrages against the freedpeople. Beatings, rapes, even killings. It never stopped."

Hanley felt sick. He forced his mind back to his own murder case. "Was Sweetbay Sugar one of the 'big boyos' around New Orleans?"

Seamus sighed, his gaze on a gull circling in the cloudless sky. "They were, still are. The bureau sent agents to the company office a couple of times. Early last month, not long before I came home, a few of us even took a trip downriver to the Sweetbay plantation where the cane's grown. I was one. O'Shea was another. We never got a chance to talk to a single Negro, what few we got close to. The overseers didn't exactly give us the run of the place. We lodged a formal complaint with the city government afterward, but nothing happened. Sweetbay Sugar greased palms when they had to, broke heads when they wanted. What they told us when we went there, you could stuff up my nose and I'd have room to breathe."

He sounded like Patrick Coughlin all over again, no proof of slave labor and none likely forthcoming. More disturbed about it than Coughlin was, though. Coughlin had been...*philosophical* was the kind word. *Lackadaisical* struck closer to the mark. "There's a lot of money in sugarcane, I take it?"

Seamus watched the gull as it banked, dove, and snatched a fish from a riverboat's churned-up wake. "Enough to buy damned near anything...politicians, coppers, silence. Sugar and molasses, they're part of what's keeping Louisiana afloat these days. Chicago gets a fair portion of what's produced. The rates the railroads charge to ship it would make your eyes pop, but the cane growers can afford it." He gave Hanley a mirthless smile. "Isn't that something to think on...you might be helping slavery come back every time you sweeten your coffee. Even if they don't call it slavery anymore."

They fell silent briefly, looking out over the water. Thoughts swirled in Hanley's head, of boxcars loaded with hogsheads of sugar speeding north toward Chicago, courtesy of the Illinois, St. Louis and Grand Southern. He might never look at sugar or molasses the same way again. "So you're saying we *can't* know if the stories are true."

Seamus's shrug belied his grim look. "That's the way of it, worse luck. I couldn't prove it before I came home and I can't now, any more than anyone else. So, if you're thinking slave labor at Sweetbay has to do with your murder case, I have to tell you, I don't see how."

☙

After parting from Seamus, Hanley turned his steps toward the rail yard for another talk with the junior office clerk. On his last visit there, Coughlin had interrupted things before young Jamieson could say much and sidestepped the question of whether something was bothering O'Shea the day he died. Maybe Jamieson could shed light on the matter.

He crossed the Wells Street Bridge and headed north toward Kinzie. The river breeze felt refreshing in spite of the sun beating down. The smell had long since ceased to bother him, and the rhythm of his steps blended pleasantly with boatmen's shouts, crying gulls, and the rattle of surrounding street traffic. Too soon, he reached the yard, crowded with trains and wagons and hurrying men. A whistle shrieked, sharp and high over the normal commotion. Hanley glanced toward the sound. Far down a clear stretch of track, some distance west of the yard, an oncoming train was approaching.

The engine looked toy sized at first but rapidly grew larger as it neared. Hanley could see men on it now, running atop the boxcars it pulled. The nearest man reached the far end of a car, knelt, and spun a smallish wheel jutting out from the top. He straightened and backed up a few paces, then sprinted toward the following car. Heart in his throat, Hanley watched him hurtle the gap between them. The runner landed hard on his feet and dashed toward the next wheel. Brakemen, Hanley realized, slowing the train car by car. He'd seen advertisements for them in the papers. A job for a daredevil gambler, willing to bet his life he wouldn't fall and get crushed between the freights. *How many lose that bet in a given month, or a year?*

The incoming train was whuffing to a halt, workers gathering close to start unloading as quickly as they could. Hanley turned away from the spectacle and headed toward the yard office, keeping an eye on his surroundings. He dodged a mule cart, pulled up short by inches a few seconds later before a second one hit him. The driver swore, at either Hanley or the mule, slapped the beast's rump, and kept going.

Hanley reached the office and went inside. A harassed looking Jamieson glanced up from his work. "Mr. Coughlin's not here now, Detective, if you're—"

"Actually, I've come to talk to you." Hanley made his tone friendly, confiding. "You look like you could use a break, if you don't mind my saying so."

"I could, that." The youngster ran a hand through his hair in a failed attempt to smooth the cowlick. "I'm still getting used to doing the whole job on my own, all the things Mr. O'Shea kept track of. Pay's higher as senior clerk, though. Me mam and sisters are happy about that."

Hanley leaned against the counter. "You were here this past Saturday, July thirteenth, weren't you?" Jamieson nodded. "Did you talk with Mr. O'Shea? Do you remember anything he said, how he seemed… his usual self, or anxious, upset?"

"We didn't talk much. A quiet fella, O'Shea was." Sadness crossed Jamieson's face. "He always had a good word when he came in and when he left. Took care with his work, too, especially the numbers he gave Mr. Coughlin for the monthly account books. Cargo in and back out, what each company owed and paid. He was that proud of it. Sometimes he'd say a bit about his son or daughters, or his grandchildren. Or ask about me mam and sisters. Maire, the oldest, she's getting married in September. We talked about family a time or two, how they can drive you mad. Well, I talked. He listened, mostly."

"And last Saturday? Was anything worrying him?"

"Hard to tell. Like I said, he was a quiet fella. He was here eating a sandwich, working on the ledgers, when I left around seven. Didn't seem too bothered."

"Did anyone else talk to him, more than a hello? Mr. Coughlin, say?"

Jamieson's expression brightened. "Mr. Coughlin's a fine man. Gives me a nod when he sees me, asks after me mam and sisters and all. I don't remember him speaking to Mr. O'Shea…not more than the usual good morning and how's the wife. But O'Shea said something later about 'meeting with the boss.'"

Coughlin hadn't mentioned that. "Did he say why?"

The youngster looked regretful. "Sorry, not a word. Just that they'd be having one."

"When did O'Shea bring it up…morning, afternoon?"

"Afternoon, late. Just before quitting time, it was."

&

Back outside the yard office, Hanley stopped a moment to watch a group of laborers unload cotton bales from a boxcar. Four men swung each huge bale out, two men to a side, then hefted it onto the flat base of the a scale. A fifth man reached toward the long iron bar at the scale's top. Noting his red hair and stocky build, Hanley recognized Liam Mahoney. On the far side of the scale, a uniformed conductor stood with a sheaf of papers, pen at the ready.

Mahoney's hand closed over a dangling chain with a large weight on the end. He moved the weight across the bar until the giant cotton bale hovered a foot or so off the ground, then made an adjustment and eyed the bale. He called out something to the conductor, though Hanley couldn't hear what over the noise of the yard. Some number of pounds or feet, he guessed, as the conductor scrawled on the paper.

The unloaders grabbed the bale and swung it onto a nearby pile, clearing the scale for the next one. The scale's iron bar looked longer than Hanley was tall, with a spiked curve at one end like an eagle's talon, and the cotton bales towered over the workers hefting them. As

Hanley edged closer for a better look, Mahoney let go of the chain with its moveable weight. Something about the weight nagged at Hanley as it swung gently in the air. He clenched both hands and brought his fists together, conjuring the cracked-egg hollow in O'Shea's skull. *Size and shape are right. And those black flecks embedded in his brain—iron, Will said. That weight looks like a solid chunk of it.*

A thrill passed through him, like a dip in cold water. He headed toward Mahoney and the others just as Mahoney glanced up. A wary expression crossed the man's face. He beckoned to a passing worker, then strode off as the fellow came over and took his place. Hanley started after, but Mahoney moved too fast and soon vanished amid the snaking lines of freight cars. Not worth pursuing him, surly cop-dodger that he was. Hanley approached the other men, careful to keep clear of the cotton bales. One of the workers was Sully, and Hanley hailed him. "D'you have a minute?"

Sully tilted his head. "A minute, yeah. No more, with cargo waiting."

Hanley nodded toward the cotton scale, the iron weight on its chain. The chain was shorter than his forearm, though not by much. "Does that weight come off, or is it fixed in place?"

"'Course it comes off. How else would we move it up and down?" Sully's face showed puzzlement that Hanley would ask such a thing. Then he turned somber. "We heard about O'Shea. I'm sorry he's dead. Was it some bullyboy got him? They're in the streets near the yard sometimes of a Saturday night, knowing payday means money in a man's pocket."

Word had gotten around quickly since yesterday afternoon. Hanley wasn't surprised. "We're looking into it. I don't suppose you know any more than you've already told me?"

"No. Though I guess O'Shea didn't make it to Cleary's." Sully cleared his throat and spat sideways into the dirt. "Whoever killed him, hanging's too good for the bastard."

Hanley agreed, then nodded toward the dangling scale weight. "Can I borrow that? I'd like to show it to the police surgeon."

Sully bit his lip. "I don't think…I mean, that's railway property."

"It could help solve O'Shea's murder."

"I don't know…I'm not the man to ask. Maybe Mr. Coughlin—"

"What's the trouble here?"

Hanley turned. The new speaker wore a blue uniform, emblazoned with a stitched gold copper's star. Around it, matching thread traced the words *Illinois, St. Louis & Grand Southern Railway*. A rail cop. He'd have to tread carefully. "Detective Frank Hanley, Chicago Police," he said, fishing his badge from his pocket. "I'm looking into Lawrence O'Shea's murder."

"Officer Thomas Walker." The rail cop's wary expression eased a trifle. "Shame the man's dead. But it didn't happen here, I'm sure, so it's nothing to do with us."

"That's to be seen. He worked here, after all." Hanley nodded toward the cotton scale. "The injury that killed O'Shea—"

"Didn't happen here." Walker kept it polite, but Hanley heard the underlying chill in his voice. "And these men have work. Best get to it, boys."

A train whistle split the air as Sully and the others moved back to the boxcar they'd been emptying. Four tracks beyond, toward the western edge of the yard, an engine belching steam and smoke pulled slowly southward past its motionless brethren. Walker nodded in the direction of Kinzie Street. "I'm sure you've work to do as well, Detective Hanley. Don't let me keep you from it."

Hanley held the rail cop's gaze for a couple of seconds, but he knew when he was beaten. "Of course," he said. *Safeguard the railway at all costs, whether there's need or not.* He knew the behavior. He'd seen it before. He nodded to Walker, then turned and walked away. He felt the rail cop's eyes on him all the way to Kinzie Street, but deliberately didn't look back.

# FIFTEEN

Fraylin." The voice belonged to Moishe Zalman.

Rivka had known he would come eventually, had braced herself for it throughout her English classes for the past few days. She glanced up from collecting the readers her students had left behind. Moishe stood in the schoolroom doorway, hands in his pockets, eagerness and anxiety written on his face. She nodded toward him, not trusting herself to speak.

"A good day today, Fraylin," he said. "Many customers. And I have finished a fine suit for Reb Klein. My own work, every bit. Reb Klein was most pleased. Reb Nathan as well."

Why was he talking about suits? For lack of anything else? Given what he, Onkl Jacob, and Aaron had surely discussed in the shop on Monday, that couldn't be the case. "That's good," she said and reached for the last reader.

Moishe hurried over, grabbed it, and gave it to her. "Reb Nathan says I can make more suits. Take over some customers, even. You should know this, Fraylin." He drew in a breath. "Rivka."

She stared at him as his meaning, and his use of her name, sank in. If Moishe made whole suits instead of piece work, he earned more of their price. He was telling her he could provide for her as a husband should. "Reb Zalman—"

"Please." He laid a hand near hers atop the stack of readers. "Call me Moishe?"

She looked down. A quarter inch of brown leather binding separated the curves of their palms. "I…I, ah…"

"Forgive me. You are modest. As you should be, when we have not yet reached an understanding."

"Understanding?" *Hashem*, could she not get anything sensible out of her mouth—only stammers and echoes, like a parrot? "Have you not already reached one with Onkl Jacob and Aaron?" The bitter note in her voice shamed her, but only for a moment. Moishe didn't deserve it, he was only doing what everyone thought he should. *That* was what rankled—that her life should be decided by what everyone thought. Especially what Aaron thought.

He gave her a solemn look. "I have spoken to Reb Nathan and your brother, yes. Now I am speaking to you."

"What for? If they, and you, have decided things, what say do I have?"

He eyed the table between them, then met her gaze again. "It matters that you should be happy, Rivka. You will not be happy if you are not at least asked what you think."

Despite herself, she was touched. She hadn't expected that Moishe would seek her opinion. "And if I tell you? Then what?"

"Do you know your answer already? Have I no chance to persuade you?"

*Yes. No. I don't know.* "I don't know what I think yet." Hanley's face rose in her mind, him smiling down at her as they danced to the wild, skirling pipes and fiddle at the ceilidh. That same tender look two days ago, as he sat in her front parlor and thanked her for a simple glass of water as if it were all he'd ever wanted. She closed her eyes, willing the memory away.

Moishe slid the readers from her grasp and tucked them in the crook of his arm. "I will see you home, Fraylin. Let that be a beginning."

༄

She was quiet at supper that night, more so than usual. Aaron made a few attempts to draw her out, asking how her students were doing and talking of his own experiences teaching Negro children at the school in Virginia where he'd first met Nat and Ada after the war's end. His affectionate gaze went to his wife as he spoke of this, and she met it with a brief, strained smile. That was unlike her. Usually, the warmth between Ada and Aaron shone like sunlight, even in passing moments. Rivka put it down to fatigue—Ada was working hard these days, earning money so she and Aaron could go west. Rivka concentrated on eating. The meal was nearly finished, so she could soon be alone with her thoughts while she tidied up.

Finally, pushing a potato around on his plate, Aaron brought up the subject she'd been dreading. "Has Moishe spoken to you?"

"Yes."

"And you said…?"

She licked her dry lips. "Nothing, one way or the other."

He set his fork down and stared at her. Though his features resembled Papa's, in that moment he reminded her more of Mameh—the disappointment, the disapproval. "Moishe has waited long enough, Rivka. Jacob tells me—"

"Jacob tells you entirely too much." She stabbed a carrot and brought it to her mouth. If she was eating, he couldn't make her talk.

Confusion crossed his face. "What is that supposed to mean?"

"It means you don't know me, Aaron. You don't know anything."

"I know enough to know what you should do."

Her fork clattered against her plate, the piece of carrot untasted. "I am not one of your students to be lessoned. What I should do, *I* will decide."

"The way you have been? Absolutely not. You will marry Moishe. Nothing else needs to be said."

His certainty brought her to her feet. "You think *you* can decide my life after ten years gone? Who I will marry, *if* I will marry…you have no right, it's not your place—"

Swiftly, Aaron stood too. "It *is* my place. With Papa gone, I—"

"With Papa gone." She threw the words at him like stones. "That's what this is about—everything that's happened since Papa was killed. Hanley and I coming to know each other, my feelings for him, and his for me. You're afraid I'll make the same choice you did—marry a *goy*, bring disgrace on our heads. Well, it's too late for that, Aaron. You've disgraced us already, and I'm suffering as much as you are for it."

Across the table from her, Ada drew a sharp breath. Abruptly, Rivka felt ashamed. She hadn't meant to say all that—not in front of Aaron's wife and stepson—but she was right, Aaron was wrong, and she had to make him see it.

"That's different," Aaron said through gritted teeth.

"Why? Because you're a man? Because of the war? Because you fell in love? None of our people talk to us, Aaron. Only Jacob and Hannah... and Moishe, who does it because he thinks he'll get me as a prize. All because you married a Christian and a—" Just in time, she bit back the word *mulatto*. She couldn't keep going, not with Ada staring at her in shocked reproach and Nat hunched as if his stomach hurt.

"I didn't know you felt that way about me and Aaron. I'm sorry I was wrong." Ada's quiet voice held an edge that cut like a knife. She stood, the scrape of her chair and the rustle of her skirt seeming loud in the sudden silence. "It's been a long day. I'm tired. Excuse me." She carried her plate and silverware to the sink, then left the room. Nat, wide eyed, mumbled his own request to be excused and followed.

Rivka sipped water to ease her dry throat. Righteous anger toward her brother, mixed with guilt at her runaway tongue, was a hard, hot ball in her stomach. Aaron stood rigid, staring down the hall where Ada and Nat had gone. The silence in the kitchen felt brittle enough to break.

"How dare you." Aaron bit off each word. "Selfish, spoiled, ignorant—how dare you speak of Ada like that? How dare you judge my family, or me?"

Her anger flared anew, burning away regret. "I'm following your example. With one difference—*I* only judge. *You* judge and condemn."

He stepped toward her, fists clenched, and for a terrifying, unreal moment she thought he might strike her. "Think what you want. But you'll do as you're told." He stalked past her out of the kitchen, after his wife and stepson.

Rivka steadied herself against the table. The lingering odors of supper threatened to choke her. She swallowed the sick feeling and cleared the remaining plates while the argument replayed in her mind. *You will marry Moishe. It's too late, Aaron, you've disgraced us already.*

She set the plates in the sink, then leaned against it, resting her head in her hands. After a moment, she straightened slowly, fetched the dishpan, and filled it from the rain barrel by the back door. A scattering of stars glinted overhead in a clear patch between clouds. She stood awhile, gazing at the faraway lights, then turned and went back inside.

# SIXTEEN

*July 19, 1872*

The odor from the deadhouse left a bitter taste at the back of Hanley's tongue. The morgue examining room was empty except for a corpse, small and slender beneath its sheet. The sight made him flinch. He was no stranger to violence, but children always got to him. There was no right in such deaths, no decency. Useless though it was, he murmured an Our Father from habit on his way to Will's cramped back office, where he found the police surgeon writing in a logbook.

"Got something to show you," he said when Will glanced up. Ignoring the man's guarded look, he held out his sketchbook, open to a drawing he'd made from memory the night before. "It's a cotton scale. Long skinny thing, seven feet at least, with an iron weight as big as my two fists, on a chain that moves up and down. They use them at the Illinois, St. Louis and Grand Southern rail yard, where Lawrence O'Shea worked. The weight comes off, and the chain is a good foot long. Any chance this thing is what crushed the back of O'Shea's skull?"

Curiosity glimmered in Will's eyes. He took the sketchbook and studied the drawing. "Could be. The shape looks right, and the size surely is. What's that number on it, sixteen? Sixteen pounds swung at you would have one hell of an impact. It'd crush a man's skull for certain." He caught Hanley's gaze. "I don't suppose you can bring me one? I could fit it to the head wound, see if it matches up."

"O'Shea's body is still here, then?"

Will nodded. "I'm releasing it later today. The funeral's tomorrow, I'm told."

Hanley suppressed the fresh sorrow he felt for O'Shea's widow. "I can't get a scale weight here, unless I steal it. Company property. I did get a close look at it, though. It's made of iron. Black, like those flakes you found in O'Shea's brain. It even looked corroded in a couple of spots, like you said it'd have to be to leave traces behind."

Sympathy flitted across Will's face. "At least the poor devil went quick. Probably dead at one blow." He set the sketch down and eyed the logbook he'd been writing in. "I was just making additional notes on O'Shea. Found a few more interesting details. Care to see?"

*Of course* was on the tip of Hanley's tongue. Then Will's too-casual tone registered, and he recognized the blazing obviousness of the question as an olive branch he'd be a fool to miss. "Lead the way," he said.

He followed Will to the deadhouse and over to the shelf that held O'Shea's body. Will pulled the covering sheet back. "Those discolorations on the shoulder and neck are bruises, post mortem. The neck bruising looks almost like a ligature mark—I'm guessing his shirt got caught on something in the river that pulled the collar tight. There's a scrape along his right arm that never bled. So it happened after death, too."

"There's plenty of junk in the Chicago River he could've bumped against or got stuck on. Or a bridge piling might have caught him." It felt good to hash things over with Will, like they had before the Champion case came between them. "Did he have a wallet on him?"

Will nodded. "Still attached to his belt. There wasn't much in it, though. Just a pair of soaked greenbacks."

Hanley frowned. "He was murdered on a payday and never got to the saloon to spend his earnings. He should've had more on him. But I can't see a thief leaving any money behind." He ran a hand through his hair. "Anything else?"

Will pulled a glass jar down from a nearby shelf and extracted an organ from it. "I opened up his stomach and found that he'd eaten just before he died…not more than two hours before, by the look of things. Might have been bread and ham, something like that. Should help you pin down when he died, if you know when he last ate."

Hanley gagged at the sight of the partially digested food. The junior clerk, Jamieson, had mentioned O'Shea was eating a sandwich in the office at the end of the workday on the Saturday he went missing. Two hours would definitely put his time of death no later than nine o'clock or so that night. Was he still at the rail yard then, or had he left? If the latter, where might he have gone, other than to Cleary's Saloon like he'd planned?

Will leaned against the shelf and folded his arms. Hanley envied his ability to be so easy here, so apparently untroubled by the restless shades of the dead. "If O'Shea got stuck on debris or a bridge, that changes things," Will said. "You remember I told you he probably went in around Erie Street? Given how long he was in the river, he must've gone in further downstream."

"How much further?"

"More like Illinois Street or even Kinzie, I'd say."

Hanley let out a breath. That meant O'Shea could have died—or been dumped—in the rail yard. "You're sure?"

Will's wary look came back. "I can't be precise. But if you're willing to trust my expertise—"

"Oh, for—" With effort, Hanley reined in his irritation. "I am," he said, with an uncomfortable sense of guilt. "I always was. I just…forgot for a while." He knew *I'm sorry* should come next and wondered why he couldn't say it. Was he really that stiff necked, as his mother often claimed? Or was he still treating Will as if being mulatto made him lesser in Hanley's eyes?

Will regarded him in silence, a look on his face as if Hanley'd disappointed him. "Well. Now you know everything I do. For what that's worth to you."

☙

81

The conversation in the morgue replayed in Hanley's head all the way back to Lake Street. Will had offered him an opening, and they'd edged closer to bridging the gap between them...until Hanley couldn't manage a forthright acknowledgment of fault, and his failure pushed Will away again. How pig stubborn was he? He pushed through the stationhouse doors, relieved at the need to report to Sergeant Moore. At least he could spend the next little while focused on something besides his own shortcomings.

He was heading for the stairs when Jack Chamberlain wandered out of the squad room, stained coffee mug in hand. The sight of Hanley brought a sneer to Chamberlain's face. "Where's Rosie O'Grady, little old lady? Haven't seen her since Monday. Her nothing case too tough for you?"

The senior detective stood within arm's reach and, for a moment, Hanley imagined the sweet satisfaction of knocking the man's teeth into his spine. Instead, he drew a slow breath. "Her name is O'Shea. And her husband is dead. Murdered. Which you'd know if you'd lifted a damn finger when she first came on Sunday to report him missing. You should try actually helping people who come to us, Jack. Earn your keep for...what is it, another month before you quit?"

Chamberlain snorted. "If you think you're taking over my job, Paddy—"

"At least I'd *do* your job." Hanley set a foot on the bottom step. "Ask any man on the squad. It'll be a relief to stop carrying your dead weight." He started up, conscious of Chamberlain staring daggers at him as he went, but not caring a damn.

Moore stood by an open window in his office, though there wasn't much breeze to catch. "Sweat bath in here," he said, mopping his neck with a handkerchief as he turned to face Hanley. "Not much better out there, from the look of you. What've you got on your murder case?"

"The weapon, maybe." Hanley handed his sketchbook over, explaining about the cotton scale and its weight at the rail yard. "Will Rushton says the poor fellow likely went into the river around there. Based on the medical evidence, the most plausible time frame would be sometime between seven thirty and nine o'clock, nine thirty at the outside."

"Anyone at the rail yard he had trouble with?"

"Not apparently…though there *was* trouble. I'm still working out how it could be worth killing over." Swiftly, Hanley related what Mrs. O'Shea and Seamus Reilly had told him about Michael O'Shea's letter and the rumors of slave labor. "I'm not sure how much credence to give those stories, and I doubt Sweetbay Sugar would breathe a word. Coughlin said as much when I asked, and he's right. Still, O'Shea most likely being killed at the rail yard, plus that scale weight, points toward something to do with his workplace instead of a random street crime. Not one of his fellow workmen I've talked to knows of, or admits to, any grudge against him, but it only takes one liar. Or one of them jumped for his pay and hit him too hard. Will Rushton found two greenbacks in his wallet, when there should've been a week's salary."

"What about gambling debts? Or an angry husband whose wife O'Shea seduced?"

Hanley shook his head. "Gabe Cleary says he never played cards or dice at the saloon, and they didn't know him at any gambling hells nearby. As to a mistress, so far everyone who knew O'Shea says he loved his wife to distraction." Pity made his throat catch, but he shook it off. "Maybe everyone's wrong. Or there's a reason I haven't uncovered yet."

Moore nodded. "Keep me informed."

જ

Back on Kinzie Street by the rail yard, Hanley considered the place as a crime scene. O'Shea might have gone in anywhere along the stretch of river that bordered the yard on the east. Of course, it was always possible he'd gone in on the *other* side of the river. But Hanley didn't think that was likely, given the man's connection to the rail yard.

Hanley moved into the yard proper, keeping shy of tracks and freight cars and catching no one's eye. He wasn't here to ask questions.

O'Shea had been finishing paperwork in the yard office. Hanley called up a memory of the interior on his way toward the building, visualizing details as best he could. Had the blow that cracked O'Shea's skull been a closed wound, or open? He thought of Will, narrow metal instrument in hand, pushing a torn flap of scalp aside. A lacerated scalp bled profusely. *There'd be spatter. Hard to clean up. If he was struck inside the office, I'd have noticed something.*

Lured out, then. Or the killer lay in wait for him to leave. Hanley halted just shy of his destination, gnawing his lip. Almost a week since the murder, rainstorms between, and gangs of railmen crisscrossing the ground nearby like busy ants storing food for winter. No chance of any footprints distinct enough to identify. He'd come here on a fool's errand, most likely. But the riverbank lay so close—maybe ten feet away, a short distance to drag a man, and plenty of water to wash fresh blood from hands and arms, even clothing if necessary. So he kept going. Sometimes it paid to be stubborn. You never knew what you might find.

The outside wall of the office looked clean of week-old bloodstains, though nothing much would show on red brick. Discouragement overcame him. *Sometimes being stubborn gets you nowhere.* The square front windows on either side of the door were dingy and dust spotted. The left-hand window looked dirtier than its mate and sported a crack in the lower right corner. Old or new? He brushed a fingertip across the spot. Something on the glass, rough and dried and dark. Blood, mud, impossible to tell.

He fished for the handkerchief Mam always insisted he carry. The cotton square was clean and more than big enough. Prying the cracked glass loose took several seconds, but the laborers within eyeshot were intent on their work, and no one asked what he was doing. Finally, the little corner piece popped out. He wrapped it in the handkerchief and stuffed it in his pocket.

He turned the corner of the building and found behind it a long, empty freight shed with a low, overhanging roof. The ground under the eaves was largely undisturbed and dry, prompting him to look more closely for evidence of a struggle.

His perseverance paid off. He found scuffled boot marks in the dirt, then spied what looked like a dent in the wall above them where something had splintered the wood. He brushed his fingers over the spot, getting a rough sense of its size and shape. Maybe where the scale weight landed after hitting O'Shea's head? The shadows made it too dark to see if there were blood stains, but he searched further and finally found drag marks headed toward the riverbank. A swift glance around showed him that the yard office itself largely hid this area from prying eyes.

He got out his sketchbook, moved out from beneath the eaves into the late afternoon sunlight, and quickly sketched what was almost certainly the scene of O'Shea's murder.

# SEVENTEEN

*July 21, 1872*

The pan of cornbread was still warm in his hands as Ezra approached the yellow clapboard house with the wide porch. A fine place for black folks to be living in, finer than Ezra had known even as a child in Baltimore—but, no question, John Jones had earned it. From humble beginnings, Jones now counted Chicago's elite among the customers at his tailoring shop and had amassed the wealth to join them. Ezra's father, a free Negro and skilled carpenter, had done well enough in Baltimore to afford rent on a small home and workshop, and to feed, clothe, and school three children before his death, but quarters were cramped and money tight, and often Ezra had resented it. If only his family hadn't needed him to work the river docks, where his brawn stood out, making him a target for—

He shut down that thought and mounted the porch steps, shifted the bread pan to one hand, and knocked on the door. Light footsteps sounded on the other side, and then the door opened. Mary Jones stood in the gap, graceful in her gray silk Sunday dress, black hair with hints of silver framing her strong-boned face. Her dark eyes lit up as she caught sight of him.

"Ezra! Come in and make yourself at home." Her gaze fell on the pan he held, wrapped in a blue-striped dishcloth. "But you didn't have to bring anything, except yourself."

"I wanted to." He handed her the pan as he stepped inside. "Just cornbread. Least I could do, considering what I owe you both that I can't ever pay back."

She shook her head. "No talk of that. It's God's work, getting you and others to freedom." A shadow crossed her face. "We thought we were finished with it after the war, but some things don't change, even when folks die for it. More's the pity."

"You think things ever *will* change?" His reply held more bitterness than he'd meant.

For answer, she laid a hand on his arm. "Mr. Jones is in the parlor. Go on and join him, why don't you."

He nodded, then turned and walked into the front room.

Jones sat in a cushioned chair, a book in his hand and a full tumbler on a small round table beside him. He looked up at Ezra's entrance and set the book down. "I thought I heard you in the hall. Mary tells me we'll be ready to eat in ten minutes or so. You've time to join me in a drink, if you like."

"Thank you." Following the older man's nod, Ezra perched on one end of the sofa. He still felt out of place here—in the dubious refuge of this unfamiliar northern city, in this well-appointed parlor with its polished furniture and thick carpet and tall shelves full of books. So far from the Sweetbay Sugar plantation, and from his few years of hardscrabble freedom before that. How much did he dare trust that his fortunes had changed?

He watched Jones at the sideboard, pouring a shot of whiskey. Six feet tall and broad as a prizefighter, in a fine suit of his own tailoring that set off the middling brown of his skin, Jones looked like the substantial man of business he was. A living reminder of what was possible, a refutation of everything from which Ezra had fled.

Jones handed him the whiskey. "Your health," he said as he retrieved his own glass and raised it. They sipped in silence. "How are you settling in at Mrs. Kelvin's?"

"All right, thanks." The liquor burned pleasantly in Ezra's throat and loosened something inside him he hadn't realized was clenched so tight. He gave Jones a tentative smile. "I can't remember the last time I ate so well."

"Mrs. Kelvin's a treasure. We've sent people to her before. She'll be glad to have you for as long as you want to stay."

Was there an unspoken question in that? If so, Ezra wasn't ready to answer it. Instead, he nodded toward the bookshelves. "My mother would've sold her right arm for those. She and my father taught us to read, said it would let us make something of ourselves." He eyed his whiskey glass. "Back then, I thought she was right. Now?" He shrugged. "Doesn't seem there's much of any way a black man's allowed to make something of himself. Jubilee notwithstanding."

"Depends on where you are," Jones said. "Chicago's done all right by Mary and me. We just have to keep working until that's true everyplace."

"If a war couldn't do it, I don't know what will."

Jones tilted his head. "Did you finish the Frederick Douglass I lent you?"

"Nearly." His second day in Chicago, still under the Joneses' roof while they worked out details of his lodging, he'd found Douglass's *My Bondage and My Freedom* and begun reading. Mary, seeing him absorbed in it, had mentioned it to her husband. By suppertime, Ezra had the book and a promise of employment at Jones's establishment as well. "I wonder what he'd do about what I ran from outside New Orleans. What anyone *can* do about it, with things going like they are."

Jones's expression turned somber. "A few years ago, I'd have been more hopeful. Now…" He trailed off and sipped his drink. The quiet suddenly felt heavy. "Still," he said after a while, "we can't lose faith. Things may get better."

Ezra had saddened his benefactor, and he didn't want to do that. He was here for a pleasant Sunday dinner, after all. "I read in the *Tribune* about your campaign for commissioner," he said.

Jones brightened. "The *Trib*'s all right. No endorsement yet, but they're favorable enough so far. The *Times*, now…" He shook his head, lips pursed. "Wilbur Storey prints a rag, if you ask me. Something ought to be done. Mary thinks I'll win again, in spite of them, but we're taking nothing for granted."

Ezra sipped again, marveling at the contrast between where he was and where he'd come from. Down South, black men held public office at great risk—those who hadn't yet been beaten bloody, strung up, or shot dead by white mobs. Here in Chicago, John Jones could be elected county commissioner and likely re-elected with relative ease. His wealth surely had a good deal to do with it. An odd pang, not quite envy, ran through Ezra. What might *he* be by now, if those damned slavers hadn't snatched him off the Baltimore docks at nineteen?

He shook off the old anger, but his face must have given him away. "You could stay here," Jones said gently. "There's opportunity, if a man's willing to work for it. Even for a black man."

"I don't know." Ezra turned the whiskey in his hands. "I don't know what I want to do. I don't know what's safe, or right, or—" An unexpected jolt of fear made him tighten his grip on the glass.

Jones's brow furrowed. Ezra looked away but felt the older man's gaze on him.

"You *are* safe now," Jones said after a while. "It's not like before, when any white man who wanted might lay claim to you off the street."

"I know." Ezra still couldn't look up, couldn't ease his hold on the smooth curve of the whiskey tumbler. *Pale face, bulging eyes, dark slash of rope around the throat. Body swinging from the cypress branch while the other white men spat and laughed.*

Jones spoke again. "Any one of those pattyrollers from the bayou fool enough to come all the way here and try something, he'd have one hell of a fight on his hands."

Ezra knew that, too. More seconds ticked by.

"You don't have to tell me," Jones said finally. "But if you want to…"

Ezra looked up at that, saw concern in Jones's face. Suddenly, powerfully, he was reminded of his father. Jones wasn't quite old enough—the man didn't look beyond his mid-fifties—but Ezra felt the connection all the same. They'd been good to him, the Joneses. Shown him every kindness since he turned up on their doorstep, travel weary and starting at shadows. Saved his life, helped him get a roof over his head and money coming in so he could keep himself and plan for the future. And he was tired of carrying alone the burden of what he'd witnessed.

He drew a deep breath. *Hot sun hammering down. Mosquito whine in his ears, blood on his lip. A voice, young and pain soaked. Making him promise, promise to go to Chicago and tell…*

He knocked back the last of the liquor and wiped his mouth. "On the plantation," he said slowly. "By the old quarters, in the back, where no one could see…there was a boy. A white boy…"

# EIGHTEEN

*July 22, 1872*

Penny, Frankie," Mam said, seated across from him at the kitchen table.

"Hmm?" He glanced up. His mother was watching him over a slice of toast spread thick with raspberry jam from last autumn's harvest in Ida's backyard. The Great Fire hadn't reached this far west. "Sorry. Just thinking about the widow in my murder case. I need to talk to her again, and I'm not looking forward to it." He sipped his coffee, savoring its bitter edge. Their landlady, Ida Kirschner, brewed it strong enough to stand a spoon in, just the pick-me-up he needed.

"The one buried her husband Saturday? Poor thing." Mam nibbled her toast. "Can it wait?"

"Maybe." Lawrence O'Shea hadn't been much for cards or dice, but that didn't rule out other types of gambling. Horse and dog races, for example. Or there could be things in the dead man's personal life his widow hadn't known about or wanted to mention. "I'll have to ask some difficult questions. A little delay won't hurt." He swallowed the last gulp of coffee and stood, then went to his mother and kissed her cheek. "Don't know if I'll be back for supper."

"Ida'll keep a plate warm," she said with a smile, then turned serious again. "About the widow, when you do talk to her? Women like her and me, we're stronger than we look."

❦

He left the boardinghouse and hurried down the front steps in the bright sunshine. Another hot day, judging by how warm the air was already. He should go straight to Mrs. O'Shea's, get the difficult questions over with, and try to confirm the junior clerk's story of O'Shea's planned "meeting with the boss" on O'Shea's last day alive. Instead, he stayed on Madison until he crossed the river, then headed north on Market toward Lake Street Station. He told himself he meant to check for messages before starting work, but deep down he knew better. Christ, what an idiot he was. *You won't see her. She'll be inside, cooking breakfast or sewing, or something else women do. Or she'll be out at the butcher's or greengrocer's.* His feet refused to listen to his head. *Five houses, four, three, two.* Rivka's house was visible now, including its small back porch and a slice of rear yard. If she came out…if he could catch a glimpse of her, just for a moment.

The back door opened, and his heart leapt. A second later, it plunged into his stomach. Golden-brown skin, no kerchief over the smooth black hair. Not Rivka. Ada Kelmansky, Aaron's mulatto wife.

Ada walked down the steps, dinner pail in hand, and rounded the house. At the sight of him, she halted. Surprise crossed her face, swiftly replaced by guarded civility. "Good morning, Detective Hanley," she said, approaching the boardwalk where he stood.

"Ma'am." The damn fool in him wanted to ask, *How is Rivka? Is she well? Has she mentioned me since last Tuesday?* He swallowed the words, shamed by his own longing and tense as a cat in the rain, more than ready to be on his way.

"It's no good, you know," Ada said quietly. In her eyes, he saw compassion. "Aaron's set on how things'll go for her, and he's a stubborn man."

Maybe it was her expression that did it. He answered from his heart. "So am I."

❦

Grace O'Shea answered when Hanley knocked at the door of the two-story clapboard house on North May Street a short while later. The widow was dressed for the day, but she'd made a mess of pinning her hair, in contrast to its stark neatness at her husband's funeral two days before. She looked drawn, as if she hadn't slept much since. She focused on him with a vague, puzzled frown. "Detective Hanley...I wasn't expecting you."

"I need to talk about Lawrence," Hanley said gently. "If you're up to it."

She blinked, then nodded. "I suppose I am. Come in."

He followed her into a small front parlor, so painfully clean the sunshine gleamed off every dusted surface. She settled on the sofa by the window. For the first time he noticed a sheet of paper in her hand. Old love letter? Sympathy washed through him as he sat on the sofa's other end.

Before he could decide how to begin, she spoke. "I'm sorry I wasn't...I meant to thank you for coming to Saint Pat's on Saturday, but I couldn't face up to..."

"It's all right." He couldn't ask about her husband and other women, not while she sat there with Lawrence's letter across her lap. Coughlin had quashed any notion of a mistress, though he'd evaded the question of how well he knew O'Shea. Mrs. O'Shea had called the yard boss a fine man who'd always been as good as his word...*to us,* she'd said. Hanley hadn't noted it then, but the intimacy implied by that phrasing struck him now. He wondered how deep it ran, and with whom.

He chose to start with an easier subject. "You told me your husband was worried about something the day he died. Did he mention a meeting planned with Mr. Coughlin that day?"

She blinked, as if collecting her thoughts. "Not that I remember. He didn't always tell me things like that, though. Work things."

"And he didn't say what was bothering him? Not even a hint?"

Her answer was barely above a whisper. "No. I should've asked. I wish I had."

He wanted to take her hand, comfort her like he would've with Mam, but such a gesture from him would be unbearably intrusive. "How close was Lawrence to Mr. Coughlin? Were they friends?"

Mrs. O'Shea drew a breath and nodded. "Since they were boys back in Ballymaloe, in County Kerry. They met at the village school. Patrick helped Lawrence learn to read. Lawrence looked up to him. Like an older brother, or…" A pink flush rose in her cheeks. "You didn't grow up in Ireland, did you, Detective? It's not much in the way you talk, the music of it. Were you born there?"

"I was. The Great Hunger hit when I was four." He barely remembered the land of his birth, but speaking of why they'd left never came easy.

"Then I don't know if you'll understand." She stroked one edge of the paper she held. "Patrick wasn't plain folk like us. He came from the lodge, up by the manor house. That…means certain things. Even here. Patrick's family…they weren't the landlords, they only collected the rents, but still…they were Protestants, and our betters. My Lawrence made something of himself here that he couldn't have back home, but it was thanks to Patrick he did it. So much of what we have comes down to Patrick taking care of us."

"And that's why your husband trusted him so much?"

"Patrick's a good man, a kind man. He's always done right by us." She looked back down at the paper, then turned it over. Not a letter, a pencil sketch of a Negro woman holding an infant. It reminded Hanley of the Madonna and Child at Saint Pat's.

He gestured toward the drawing. "Your son's?"

"Yes. Michael loves those people he went to help. He writes me about how hard they work, how they share what they have with anyone, poor as they are. They aren't at all what we've been taught to think of them. They're just like us, only wanting a home and hearth to call their own." She said it as if the idea was surprising, but not unwelcome. One fingertip traced the Negro woman's cheek. "Lawrence was so proud of our boy. They quarreled after the war, when Michael went wandering instead of settling down, but I know Lawrence felt sorry for it. I wish—" She swallowed hard and closed her eyes. When she opened them, moisture glistened. "Was there anything else you needed to ask me?"

"Only this." If a love triangle gone wrong lay behind Lawrence's death, his widow wasn't knowingly a part of it—he'd stake his badge on that. "Did your husband owe anyone money? At the racetrack, say, or—"

"No." She straightened, sounding irked at the notion. "He never went places like that. He saved what he could for our daughters and Michael, took pride in every penny he earned. He told Patrick once it was cheating fate, to win on the horses or dogs by fool's luck. He never would go to the track, even when Patrick asked him."

Hanley sat back. Coughlin had claimed not to gamble, disclaimed knowledge of whether O'Shea did. "Did Patrick ask him often?"

"He used to, years ago. He gave it up once he realized he'd never get a 'yes.'"

She looked paler now than when he'd first arrived, fatigue clearly taking its toll. Hanley thanked her for her time and stood. "If you think of anything else to tell me, Mrs. O'Shea—anything at all—send word to Lake Street Station. I'll come see you as soon as I can."

He left her sitting there, hands clasped over her son's drawing, head and shoulders bowed with the weight of her loss.

# NINETEEN

By the start of his second week in Chicago, Ezra's days had settled into a pattern. Work, meals at his boardinghouse or a cheap tavern, nights spent reading by lamplight in his room until the need for sleep overcame him. He read his Bible, or a newspaper, or the book John Jones had lent him, sometimes aloud simply for the sound of a human voice. Whenever he moved through Chicago's streets, especially the downtown area where Jones's tailoring business was, he kept aware of people around him, never wholly at ease until he reached his workplace or the solitary refuge of his room at the end of the day.

The horrors printed in the papers didn't help. Riots, burnings, murders by Ku Klux night riders and vigilantes, with the federal armed forces overwhelmed or indifferent to the outrages. What he read made him think of going out West, like Ada planned to do—she and the man she was with now. Even though he'd expected it, it still cut deep that she'd married someone else. She'd told him so on his second workday, as gently as she could manage. Not that he blamed her. How could he? She hadn't known what plantation he was sold to all those years ago, or if he'd survived the brutality of sugarcane country. He hoped she was happy, though she'd looked under strain the past couple of days. More than once he'd caught her watching him, then hastily glancing away when their eyes met. Nagging worry got the best of his caution, and he went up to her at the dinner break on Monday. "You doing all right? Everything okay at home?"

"Everything's fine." Her thin smile, meant to reassure, did nothing of the kind. She grabbed her dinner pail and walked over to sit with the other women. The oldest, a ripe tomato in hand, was regaling the rest with another story about her grandson. Ada settled among them, smoothed her skirt, and took out a sandwich, but didn't eat it. She just sat there, apparently absorbed in the old woman's tale.

Ezra turned away. *None of my business.* Ada wasn't his woman anymore. He told himself it was just as well, considering his situation, though the hollow in his heart gave the lie to that. He left the workroom, intent on spending the next half hour safely anonymous in a tavern with only a drink for company.

෧෨

To his surprise, he found Ada waiting by the front door of his boardinghouse on Tuesday morning. She looked like she hadn't slept well and clutched her small string purse in both hands. "Ezra," she said.

"What are you doing here?" He moved toward her, took her hands. Slender and delicate as ever, they felt cool despite the heat already in the air. Worry clawed at his throat. "You all right? You need help? Tell me."

"I'm fine. I'm not here on my own account." She drew a deep breath. "It's just…we'll be leaving soon…and I wanted to tell you—" She broke off and glanced down at their joined hands. "I've thought on this awhile. I've prayed on it. It's hard to know how to say it right."

What could she be talking about? They'd barely spoken since his first two days at Jones's place. He tightened his grip. "Just say it. Please."

The anxiety in her face gave way to a softer look as she met his eyes again. She took another slow breath, as if steadying herself. "You have a son. Our son. His name is Nathaniel. He'll be thirteen come August."

For a moment he couldn't take it in. He felt dizzy, like he'd drunk deep of corn liquor and only her handclasp was keeping him upright. "Thirteen. Nathaniel. Our son."

"Yes." She paused, watching him, a tentative smile on her lips. "He goes by Nat. He's near as tall as me. He works hard in school. He wants to be a lawyer. He'll grow to be a good man, like his father."

Her words washed over him, clear as water, yet he couldn't make sense of them. *Thirteen.* Thirteen years ago, he'd been sold away. From

Angel Oak Grove, from Ada, from what little sense of home-place he'd scraped together with her as they'd eased each other's loneliness. He groped for a reply. "Why didn't you tell me?"

"I didn't know until after you were gone." She slipped her hands from his grasp, opened the string purse, and fished in it. He watched every motion she made like a drowning man reaching for driftwood—anything to anchor him in the here and now. *A son. I have a son.* He still felt like he might fall down and braced himself with a hand against the boardinghouse wall.

She brought out a folded paper and held it toward him. "I wrote this when Nat was born. I'd no place to send it. But I had to tell you about him, even if only in my heart."

He took the paper in numb fingers. It felt dry and worn, the folds making deep creases in the written lines they crossed. He opened it and read slowly, absorbing the words, a sentence sticking out here and there. *He's strong, with a good cry. I wish you were here and could hold him in your arms.... All I can do is pray that somehow, some way, you'll know of him—that come the Jubilee, if it ever does, God will make a second miracle and show you your child.*

His eyes were wet as he refolded the letter. "Keep it," she said when he tried to give it back. "It's yours."

"And Nat?" He marveled at his son's name on his tongue, the sound of it in his ears, as he tucked the precious letter away in a pocket. *Nat. Nathaniel. My boy.* "Is he here in Chicago with you? Does he know about me? When can I see him?"

She glanced down at the grass. "He knows about you. He knows you had to leave us before he was born. I never said *sold*. I didn't have to." She looked up at him. "I talked to Aaron. Nat loves him like a father. But he has a right to know his real one. Aaron agreed." A heartbeat's pause, as if gathering her strength. "Come back with me after work Saturday afternoon. Aaron is...busy then. Nat'll be home, waiting."

# TWENTY

Hanley spent the morning showing O'Shea's picture at inexpensive brothels and a few panel houses, just to be thorough. No one recognized him, and the offer of coin didn't loosen any tongues, which confirmed Hanley's impression that the whores and madams were telling the truth. He even ventured out to Brighton Trotting Park on the city's far south side, but no one there recognized O'Shea, either.

Hanley had no real reason to think Coughlin had killed O'Shea. But the man's lie about gambling—his own habits and having no knowledge of O'Shea's—nagged at him. Mrs. O'Shea had said Coughlin invited her husband to go to the racetrack with him, apparently on multiple occasions. So why did Coughlin claim not to gamble at all...unless he had something to hide? Hanley drew a quick sketch of Coughlin from memory but, when he showed it at the trotting park, it produced only scratched heads and muttered *maybe-can't-be-certains*, even though he kept it casual and didn't mention murder.

A roast beef sandwich and a beer, consumed at the first acceptable tavern he ran across back in the city, and then Hanley was off to the morgue on his second errand of the day. Unfortunately, he had no luck there, either.

"Well, the color along that crack is right for dried blood. Unfortunately, that's all I can say for sure." Will Rushton stepped back from his desk and gestured toward his prized microscope. He looked overstretched, probably from working too hard. "See for yourself."

Will's office felt close, the warm air tainted with carbolic. Hanley mopped sweat off his neck as he bent over the eyepiece. The lens showed the piece of window glass from the rail yard office as a bright-edged triangle speckled with dusty rain spots, one side marred by a brownish-red stain.

He straightened and turned to Will. "What would *make* you sure?"

"Nothing." Will held up a hand to forestall Hanley's protest. "I know…you know what dried blood looks like. So do I. But this"—he tapped the microscope—"won't confirm it. I can tell fresh, liquid blood from the shape of the cells. A dried stain on glass? There's no examination I can make that'll prove a thing."

"Damn." Hanley ran a hand through his hair, then rolled his shoulders to relieve a cramp. "Never mind. I'll find another way. I'm certain poor O'Shea was clubbed down outside the yard office or very nearby, then dragged to the riverbank and shoved over. Maybe I'll get lucky, and some passerby saw something."

"No notion who hit him yet?"

"Not unless there's more you can tell me. How tall the killer was, if he's right- or left-handed?"

"Sorry." Will meant it, Hanley could tell. "Not a midget or a giant, and plenty strong. If I had to guess, I'd say left-handed. But it's not—"

"Conclusive." Hanley sighed. The office was too small for pacing, worse luck. He slouched against Will's desk, hands in his pockets. Anyone could've taken the weight off the scale…though, as Will had said, it would take a lot of strength to swing sixteen pounds at a man's head. He thought of Sully and the other men tossing cotton bales around, Mahoney moving the scale weight up and down. Mahoney had ducked off when he saw Hanley taking an interest. Was it only distaste for talking to cops? He frowned, remembering Gabe Cleary's words about the man. *Likes his whiskey more than's good for him. I've known him start a ruckus once or twice when the cards don't run his way.*

Hanley let out a breath. It was a long way from being a poor loser at cards to killing a man for extra money at the faro table. And Mahoney had been at Cleary's all evening. Hanley was reaching, and he knew it. Desperate for a decent lead, if only for the widow's sake.

⁂

From the angle of the light, it was near four o'clock when Hanley left the morgue. Thunder muttered in the distance, but the gray-blue tower of clouds on the horizon looked far enough off that he should make it home before the storm broke if he took the horsecar. Lucky enough to catch one right after reaching the stop, he boarded and rode north up State Street. His stomach growled, reminding him it had been a time since dinner. Home a little early for a decent meal and a long think in the quiet of his room—that was what he needed. *Soon*, he promised himself.

He got off at Madison and headed west, preferring a walk to another long, jolting ride. The street grew more crowded as he neared the river bridge, with the Chicago and Alton depot on the far side. He jogged over the bridge and threaded through the stream of people toward the next street corner. Carts and drays vied for space with hackney cabs and horsecars, filling the air with creaking wheels, hoofbeats, and shouts from exasperated drivers. Hanley edged to the curb, keeping an eye out for a gap.

A hoarse whisper—"Mind your business!"—then a hard shove in his back. He fell, sprawling, in the street. A woman screamed. He jerked his head up. An omnibus bore down on him, the driver swearing, hauling on the reins. He staggered upright. Not fast enough. The horse reared. A flailing hoof struck his head. White-hot pain exploded through him. Then darkness.

# TWENTY-ONE

Something wet splashed his face. Wet and cold. *Water…the lake? Christ, the chill of it deep in his bones, Mam and Kate shivering next to him while the fire roared hot at their backs.*

"…coming around," someone said. Slowly, more sensations filtered through. Damp shirt. Fire in his head. Hard ground beneath him. Hoofbeats, rattling wheels. Not the lake. The street.

Hanley opened his eyes. Blurred faces peered down at him… three, no, four. He blinked, tried to focus. The morgue. Will. He'd gone there about the glass shard…then left and started for home… got near the train depot, and then…

"Give him some drink." The speaker was an older man, graying beard, spectacles. "Who's got brandy? Whiskey?"

"Lemme through." A hint of Galway brogue, as familiar to Hanley as the streets of Conley's Patch. Its owner moved into sight. Craggy faced, sandy hair over darker brows and bushy mustache, piercing eyes. Near Hanley's age, in his thirties. *Seen him before?* Uniform and flat cap. Not a copper's. Horsecar or omnibus driver. The fleeting sense of familiarity faded. Dizziness roiled Hanley as the newcomer knelt on the boardwalk, a silver flask in hand. "Here. Good for what ails you. Take a swig. Not too much at once, mind."

Hanley fought to sit up. He made it as far as a propped elbow, head throbbing like a drum. He swore, squinted through the pain, pinpointed the flask and grabbed it. The owner's rough hand steadied his. "That's it."

Hanley gritted his teeth and raised the flask to his lips. The liquor burned like fire. His head hurt too much for more than dim surprise at the taste—whiskey, and not the cheap stuff. He swallowed, wiped his mouth, and handed the flask back. "Thanks. I owe you, Mr. ...?"

"McDonald." The driver tucked the flask inside his uniform coat. "Mike McDonald. Need a hand up?"

❧

He rode home in McDonald's omnibus, grateful not to have to walk. McDonald had declined the fare—"It's only a few blocks. Least I can do. And you're a Galway man, I can tell." The fellow kept up a patter the whole trip, though most of it bypassed Hanley. He floated on the river of words, throwing in conversational noises now and again, while he puzzled over the burning question of who had shoved him into traffic. Accidentally or on purpose? That rough whisper, so close. *Mind your business.* Meant for him? Who'd said it? Why? The effort to think it through made his headache worse. The crowd had been thick—new arrivals fresh off the train, friends and kinfolk come to meet them, plus the usual bustle of Chicago's streets. He couldn't pick out a face or form among them, try as he might.

The jolting of the omnibus—a ten-seater, smaller and more comfortable than a horsecar, likely serving one of the fancier hotels— sent darts of pain through his skull. The same omnibus that damned near hit him? No wonder McDonald was being so kind.

Relief washed through him when they pulled to the curb in front of Ida's boardinghouse. McDonald rose from his seat, eyed Hanley, and pulled out his flask again. "Have another swig. Looks like you need it to get you in the door."

Hanley took the flask. Tipping back his head to drink didn't hurt quite as much this time. "Jameson's. You've good taste."

McDonald chuckled. "For important things." He retrieved the flask and squirreled it away again.

"Did you see me get pushed into the street?" Hanley asked.

"Pushed? God, that's terrible. I thought you'd lost your footing, or maybe..." McDonald shrugged. "Maybe you'd had a bit? No offense."

"None taken. So you didn't see anyone shove me?"

"In that crowd? Be damned hard to pick 'em out."

Hanley felt unreasonably disappointed. He watched McDonald step off the omnibus and head toward the patient horse between its shafts. He took a few seconds to muster his strength, then followed. McDonald was speaking softly to the horse as he fed it a carrot. "Thanks for the lift," Hanley said. "If you recall anything, will you tell me? The name's Hanley. Frank Hanley. I'm a detective at Lake Street Station. You can ask for me or leave a note there."

"Detective, is it?" McDonald's light tone suddenly held an edge beneath. "You didn't say so before."

Hanley blinked, bewildered by the change. "You didn't ask."

McDonald patted his horse, then turned back to his vehicle, passing Hanley without a look or word. With one foot on the omnibus step, he tossed over his shoulder, "That'll be a half dollar you owe me, next time you ride my 'bus."

*What the hell?* Anger spiked in Hanley's chest. He forced it down, dug in his pocket, and came up with a ten-cent piece. "Here. I'll settle the rest later." He held the dime out toward McDonald. The man made no move to take it.

"Suit yourself." Hanley dropped the coin onto the street and walked away.

# TWENTY-TWO

## *July 24–25, 1872*

A cup of Mam's strong-brewed willow bark tea dulled Hanley's headache enough for him to manage a halfway decent sleep. He spent Wednesday resting, under protest, at his mother's insistence. "A kick from a horse is nothing to shrug at," his sister said. She, their mother, and Ida had all nagged him to see a doctor as well. But he felt well enough when he woke Thursday morning and begrudged the expense as well as the time. It was only a glancing blow. A direct hit would've cracked his skull, like poor Lawrence O'Shea.

He got up and dressed, wincing whenever an incautious move caused a fresh spike of pain. A glance in his shaving mirror showed a purpling bruise the size of a child's fist peeking out from his hairline. He scowled. Who wanted him injured or dead? With a sharp sigh, he turned away from the mirror. Useless to speculate. Finding a witness to the attack on him was next to impossible—if it *was* an attack and not just an unlucky accidental shove, the muttered "Mind your business" meant for someone else nearby. Apart from the omnibus driver, McDonald, Hanley couldn't put a name to anyone who'd been there.

The junior clerk's story about O'Shea's "meeting with the boss" stuck in Hanley's mind. If O'Shea *had* arranged a private talk with Coughlin on July 13th, he hadn't told his wife, protective of her as he clearly was. Yet she'd been so insistent that something new was worrying him on his last day alive. More about the slave labor stories? Something to do with shipments or payments? Jamieson had said O'Shea handled those records and gave Coughlin numbers for the monthly account books. Had O'Shea found some discrepancy of sufficient concern that he couldn't help bringing his worry home?

*Might as well ask the boss.* Feeling renewed by the thrill of the hunt, Hanley strode out of his room and hurried down the stairs.

☙

Luck was with him when he reached the rail yard. Coughlin sat at his desk in his private office, an open ledger in front of him. The yard boss greeted Hanley affably enough, though his eyes widened as he glimpsed the bruise on Hanley's forehead. "Good lord, Detective. What happened to you?"

"Traffic accident. Nothing a day of rest didn't fix." Hanley eyed the ledger. "Going over accounts? O'Shea's death must make that harder."

Coughlin's smile faltered. "I'm sorry...I don't follow."

"Breaking in the new clerk. You told me O'Shea kept track of cargo shipments, making sure all the numbers were correct. Things brought in and shipped out. Must be complicated for an operation the size of your railway."

"Not my railway," Coughlin said with a chuckle. "I have my own bosses to answer to. Shareholders as well."

"Yes. You mentioned them before."

"What is this about, Detective? If you've questions for me, ask them. There's no one here more interested than I am in helping you find out who killed Lawrence O'Shea."

"I appreciate that. Did you arrange to meet with him the day he died? To go over the account books, for example? I understand he kept track of payments as well as shipments. You didn't mention that when we spoke before."

Something flickered in Coughlin's eyes, there and gone in a heartbeat. "I didn't think of it. But there wasn't any meeting arranged. No need. Going over the accounts was part of the job."

"I'm told he mentioned a meeting with you. He spoke of it shortly before closing time on July thirteenth. There might have been a different reason than the accounts, I suppose—"

"There was no meeting." Coughlin looked irritated now. "I left the rail yard at five o'clock for a musical evening at Hugh Denham's. Closing time is dusk, half past seven this time of year. Is there anything else? Because, if not, I've work to get on with. I hold a highly responsible position, in case that's not yet clear to you."

Hanley nodded toward the open ledger. "Mind if I have a look?"

"I'm afraid I can't allow that." Coughlin covered the pages with a spread hand, as if to keep Hanley from leaning in for a peek. "Our accounts are proprietary. I'd need to consult the company lawyer."

"And he is?"

"Really, Detective." Coughlin let out a sigh that said *Give me patience* as clearly as if he'd spoken it. "Lawrence's death has nothing to do with the railway. He was set upon—"

"By someone here at the yard. Who cracked his skull like an eggshell and dumped him in the river." Hanley watched Coughlin blanch at the blunt words, but the man said nothing. "Not the usual place for assault by a street thief. Unless you're suggesting the railway has lax security, and some ne'er-do-well just wandered in."

Coughlin's expression hardened. "If you're making some sort of allegation, against the railway or me—"

"I'm not." *Yet.* "I'm doing my job. Looking into things. Finding evidence, not jumping to conclusions. That's how justice gets done... for Lawrence O'Shea or anyone."

Coughlin gave a wintry smile. "I stand corrected."

Hanley pulled his sketchbook and a pencil from his shirt pocket. "So you left the yard for a musical evening at...what's the name, Hugh Denham's? The gentleman who gave you your highly responsible position, I believe you told me. Where does he live?"

"Sheldon Street, near Union Park." Coughlin gave a number, and Hanley wrote it down. "Hugh's sister is amazingly accomplished, and there was a professional violinist as well." The yard boss leaned forward, elbows on his desk. "Really, though, isn't it likely poor Lawrence was set upon by some bullyboy after his pay? The rail yard's near four blocks long. Officer Walker and his men do their best, but they can't be everywhere." For a moment, genuine sadness glimmered in Coughlin's eyes. "Lawrence would've fought back if someone jumped him. Fifty on his last birthday, but he was a brave man. He'd not have submitted tamely to an attack by footpads."

"When did you leave Hugh Denham's on Saturday?"

A flicker of renewed annoyance. "I got there at seven. Went home to change first. The musical program ended at half past nine. Satisfied?"

"One more thing," Hanley said. "Who's the railway's lawyer, and where might I find him?"

✑

He'd intended a quick stop by Lake Street Station to report to Sergeant Moore but halted in surprise as he came through the doors and saw Grace O'Shea standing in the lobby. "Here he is now, ma'am," the desk sergeant said, but she was already heading toward him, looking pale as new milk and tense enough to fly apart.

"Mrs. O'Shea." Her appearance alarmed him. "Are you all right? What's happened?"

"I found another letter. From Michael." She stopped a foot from Hanley, fumbled in the string purse she carried, and drew out a folded paper. "Read it. It's awful, it's..."

He pressed her fingers gently as he took the letter, hoping the brief touch might calm her. A glance at the page showed a hasty scrawl, addressed to Lawrence O'Shea. He read it swiftly, a chill rising inside him as the words sank in. *Dear Father, I hardly know how to write this. The stories of slave labor are true. I saw it with my own eyes...Freedmen chained together in the Sweetbay cane fields...overseers lashed a man bloody, then marched him into the bayou...I cannot unsee what they did to him, waking or sleeping...*

Sickened, Hanley skimmed the second paragraph. *The bureau can do nothing. Its power is ended, its offices closing...made a record, drawing and*

108

*writing down everything I saw...another trip, to document more horrors...sending you everything once I have enough. Bring it to the newspapers—the* Tribune, *the* Times, *everywhere. There will be an outcry. There must. Otherwise, what in God's name did so many die for?*

He looked up at Mrs. O'Shea. "When did you get this? Why didn't you tell me before?" His tone was harsher than he meant, and guilt swept through him when she flinched.

"I only found it this morning." She swallowed hard, fighting for composure. "I was going through Lawrence's things...he never said a word, tucked it away in his book of devotions, like he didn't want me to know..."

"Shielding you," Hanley said, more gently, ashamed he'd added to her distress. "Do you know when this letter came?"

"It was postmarked July eighth. It must've got here a few days later... July eleventh or twelfth. I remember...Lawrence was upset again that day. Weighed down, like after Michael first wrote him about the slaves." Her voice cracked as she went on. "Friday and Saturday, the last days of his life."

"Did he show this to anyone, or talk about it? To Mr. Coughlin?"

"I don't know." She clutched the string purse, her knuckles white. "But I've not heard from Michael since, even when I sent word about his father's death. A week ago, it was, but he's not replied or come home. He has money for the train, I don't understand it. I can't believe he wouldn't be here by now..."

Hanley held up the damning letter. "You've gotten nothing that might be the evidence he says here he'd send?"

Tears spilled over as she shook her head. "No. Nothing at all."

# TWENTY-THREE

## *July 25, 1872*

J
ohn Jones's tailoring shop was larger than Will had expected, taking up the entire half basement of the handsome brick building the county commissioner owned on Dearborn Street. Will lingered outside it, wondering which door Ada would use when she came out for dinner. If she came out. She probably brought her own midday meal, rather than spend precious coins she and Aaron and Nat needed for homesteading out West. A pang of envy cut through him, sharp as a blade. *To go somewhere else, start over, be who you want instead of who you have to be...*

He shrank from the thought of going inside to find her. Something in him still wasn't ready to face other people seeing him with Ada and noting his resemblance to her, risk them knowing him for mulatto instead of white. Though no one was likely to recognize him here, unless they were patients at the Fifteenth Street clinic where he volunteered or were kin to some poor soul who'd turned up on a morgue slab. Coppers from Lake Street or Central, the closest stations to this stretch of Dearborn, had plenty more to pay attention to than a respectably dressed man and woman going about their business. He bit his lip and stared at his shoes, marked with the dust of the summer-dry streets. What a coward he was, even now.

*Well, then, I'm a coward.* He lifted his chin, as if defying himself, and snickered at his own absurdity as he walked around the building, looking for a side or rear exit. The front door would mostly be used by customers, as well as patrons of the bank on the building's first floor and the offices above. Uncle Josiah, his adoptive father since Will was thirteen, often said there was no finer tailoring shop than John Jones's. Ada felt lucky to have gotten a job here, had told him as much the last time he dropped by the Kelmansky house after work. *The one place I feel safe being with my own sister. Aaron and Rivka don't care what color I am. And they'd never tell anyone who does.*

He rounded the back of the building and halted. Ada was there, leaning against the brick wall, face turned skyward and eyes shut in the noon sunshine. He watched her a moment, his heart a knot in his chest. His sister, restored to him by a miracle after the war, yet he couldn't simply go to her. Instead, here he stood like a halfwit, waiting for her to see him and speak first, give him his cue.

Impatient with his own dithering, he called her name as he walked toward her. When she opened her eyes and looked at him, he plastered a smile on his face. "Have you eaten yet? I thought we might go somewhere. You pick the place."

☙

They settled on a small eatery that offered lake perch with fixings for twenty-five cents a plate. "Mr. Jones comes here sometimes," Ada said as they walked through the door. "He says the fish is always fresh, and the fixings can't be beat."

The eatery boasted eight tables, whites at two of them and Negroes at three more, and brimmed with the scents of frying fish, onions, and potatoes. Once seated with their food, Will found himself at a loss for words. Ridiculous to be so tongue-tied when he'd sought out Ada's company. He smiled at her over his plate, cut a piece of fish, and raised it to his lips. "How are things? Nat doing well?"

Disquiet glimmered in her eyes, swift as lightning and gone. Then she was smiling gently, her usual expression with him, and he wondered if he'd seen anything else at all. "Yes. Same as when you asked a couple of weeks ago." She ate a potato chunk, washed it down with coffee. "You didn't come here to talk about Nat. You've never come to find me at work before, only to the house. Something on your mind?"

"You know me too well." It bewildered him how that could be, considering they'd spent more years apart than together since she was sold away when they were children. Him ten when that calamity struck, her just fourteen…and by the time he found her again, twenty years on and mere weeks after the war's end, he'd long since run away with their family to Chicago and grown up and become a white man. The hard choice he'd made before the war, and kept to after, lay between them still, like a wall he couldn't climb, or a river he'd no notion how to navigate.

He ate the bite of perch and cut a second one, sidestepping his own confusion with another harmless question. "So, when do you leave Chicago? Do you know where you're going yet?"

"Nebraska, we're thinking." Her smile showed strain and, for the first time, it struck him how tired she looked. "We have almost enough saved up. Aaron has a last thing to settle, and another payday or two will help, but we'd like to go before August is out."

The "last thing to settle" was Rivka, Will guessed. As far as he knew, Aaron's sister didn't plan to head west with them. From what little he'd picked up on his infrequent visits, Aaron had a husband for her in mind…and Ada wasn't saying so outright because of Will's friendship with Hanley, who wasn't likely to take well whatever *settling* occurred. *Does she think I'll talk out of turn to him? I wouldn't know how. Not anymore.*

Ada's next words—"How's your work? Everything going all right?"— brought Hanley's last visit to the morgue sharply to mind. They'd both reached for their old easy partnership, actually got hold of it for a minute or two. But Will couldn't sustain it, only its appearance. That he understood why made it no simpler to deal with. He couldn't *un*-know what Hanley knew of him, couldn't stop second-guessing every word and look they exchanged. Nor could Hanley, or so it seemed to Will. Though it wasn't just Hanley. It was the whole damned police department, the morgue orderlies, the coroner. He couldn't stop thinking, *What if they know, too? What will they say, how will they act around me, if they ever guess?* He knew, and feared, at least part of the answer to that. No way at all, because he'd lose his job faster than he could open his mouth to protest. How much more would go with it of the life he'd built for himself he couldn't be sure and didn't want to find out.

He watched his sister calmly eating her meal. No, not calmly. More as if forking up food and engaging in conversation were sapping what strength she had. Suddenly alarmed, he leaned forward and touched her wrist. "Are you all right? You don't look well."

"Don't doctor me, little brother." The affection in her eyes robbed the remark of its sting, though the warmth came with a warning not to pry further. He recognized that look, had surely worn one like it too often on his own face. "I just need sleep. Working too hard."

"There'll be more of that once you're homesteaders. Work, I mean, not sleep." He sipped coffee, then grinned at her. "Maybe I should come with you. An extra hand around the place, and I'm sure they could use a doctor out in the wilds of Nebraska. That's one way to escape."

She tilted her head. "Escape what?"

Now they'd come to it. The reason he'd needed to see her today, so much that he'd broken from his usual safe pattern and gone to find her, then walked with her in public to dinner someplace, even though someone he knew might see them together. Of everyone he knew in Chicago, only Ada might understand. "The morgue. The police department. The need to be white every hour of the day I'm there." He shrugged. "It used to be…well, not easy, but…tolerable. Nowadays…" Another shrug. "Less so. A lot less."

She laid her knife and fork across her plate. "Maybe you should come west. Start fresh. It's worth thinking about."

He speared a potato and slowly ate it, while her words settled in him like windblown seeds come to rest in new-turned soil. "So it is. And I will."

# TWENTY-FOUR

After seeing the widow home and making sure she was all right, Hanley stood outside the O'Shea house on North May Street and considered his next move. *The slave labor stories are true.* That notion shocked him, though on reflection it shouldn't have. Not with the violence reported in the papers, Ku Kluxers and white mobs wreaking havoc where they could. Not given Aaron and Ada Kelmansky's experience last spring with night riders in Alton, Illinois.

He headed down the street, toward Randolph and the nearest horsecar stop. A car drew in a few minutes later. He boarded and settled on a rear bench. Watching the city go by, he couldn't stop thinking of Michael O'Shea—the second letter, the drawings and written testimony that hadn't turned up, and Michael's…how many days' silence was it? Too many for a son who wrote his mother regularly and knew his father'd been killed.

The car neared Halsted. On impulse, Hanley got off and headed south down the boardwalk. His friend and fellow veteran, Seamus Reilly, had taken a room near here. With luck, Hanley might catch him at home.

He arrived as Seamus was walking out the front door of his boardinghouse. Hanley greeted him, then said, "I need a favor," as they fell into step together. "Can you find out if Michael O'Shea is still in New Orleans?"

"If the office there is still open. I doubt it is, though, so probably not. Why?"

"You know those stories about slave labor you heard when you were down there?" Hanley drew a deep breath. "They *are* true. Michael found out. He was sending his father—my murder victim—evidence to prove it."

ભ

Back on the horsecar, Hanley rode further east, thoughts chasing through his mind like rabbits. Who'd want to bury any hint of slave labor connected with Sweetbay Sugar Company? Who would Lawrence O'Shea have told about his son's discovery and purported evidence? Patrick Coughlin was the obvious answer. But Coughlin had been elsewhere, he'd claimed, when O'Shea met his death. And who knew if O'Shea had ever breathed a word of what Michael found, to Coughlin or anyone?

*If it would even matter a damn.* Hanley fidgeted in his seat, uncomfortable from more than the hard wooden bench and a dull headache starting where McDonald's damned horse had kicked him. The country was tiring of outrages and "the Negro question," as some of the papers put it. He didn't read them often these days, not wanting to deal with ugly realities he felt powerless to change. He got enough of that as a cop. If Sweetbay Sugar's use of slave labor came to light, would people care? More to the point, would any of Coughlin's bosses at the Illinois, St. Louis and Grand Southern care?

What had Coughlin said about his patron among the railway shareholders, Hugh Denham? A former abolitionist who'd have no truck with slavery, or any client tainted by it. Coughlin owed Denham the "responsible position" he was so proud of, and whatever wealth he'd earned through it. If hard evidence emerged that Sweetbay Sugar—a shipping client Coughlin had personally cultivated—enslaved its workers, would Denham believe Coughlin hadn't known? If not, the truth might well cost the rail yard boss his livelihood and everything that went with it. Or was Hanley wrong, and the fat profits from shipping hogsheads of sugar and molasses by the hundreds outweighed all else?

The car pulled in at Canal Street and took on more passengers. Hanley wished vainly for a breeze. The thought of fat profits circled in his head. *As senior shipping agent in Chicago for the Illinois, St. Louis and Grand Southern, Coughlin's well placed to pad his salary by skimming off the top. Sweetbay Sugar's an obvious source. But why risk it? Gambling. He lied about that, said he wasn't much for it. To hide debts? Who does he owe, and how much?*

A puff of wind brought the smell of the river. Hanley wiped sweat from his neck. *How would Coughlin manage a scheme like that? Fiddle with cargo numbers, shipping rates? Lawrence O'Shea kept track of both. But so far nothing says he uncovered any wrongdoing…or that there is anything to uncover.*

The car rattled over the bridge. As they neared Randolph and Market, Hanley stood and made for the exit, swaying with the car's motion. He'd disembark less than two blocks from Rivka's house. A sudden desire to see her left him dizzy with its force, but he reined it in. She'd be at the tailor shop by now, teaching her English class. And what business did he have even thinking about dumping this tangled mess in her lap, just because he needed to talk it out?

*Tell Moore the latest. Make some sense of things. Then we'll see.*

ᘓᘔ

"Something for you, Detective," the desk sergeant called when Hanley walked in. "Came about ten minutes ago." He held out a folded slip of paper.

Hanley went over and took it. In bold, slanting script, the note read, *I spoke to our attorney after you left and received permission to show you some accounts. Feel free to return today, if that is convenient. If not, send a reply and I will make other arrangements.* The name scrawled at the bottom was Patrick Coughlin's.

Reporting to Moore would have to wait. Hanley pocketed the note, thanked the sergeant, and hurried back out of the stationhouse.

As before, Coughlin was at his desk when Hanley arrived at the yard office. This time, a closed ledger lay on the blotter in front of him. "This is for June," Coughlin said. "You can look through it here. If you've questions about it, I can answer some of them."

Hanley raised an eyebrow. "Some?"

"Enough so you can understand what you're looking at." He made no move to hand the ledger over.

*Wants me to ask him for it.* The pettiness of it amused more than annoyed Hanley. He held out a hand and counted silently to five before Coughlin gave him the book. "Thank you," he said, and started flipping through it. The entries were clear enough—company names, type and amount of goods or commodities shipped, money paid in, dates of receipt. The Illinois, St. Louis and Grand Southern shipped a wide variety of things from a vast number of clients—Georgia pine lumber, pig iron, raw cotton and finished cloth, rice, sugar, molasses, tobacco. Fresh fruits and vegetables, too, plus furniture and ready-made clothing. Hanley perused the pages, looking for Sweetbay Sugar. The company was there, listed most weeks as shipping several hogsheads of sugar and molasses. Weekly totals paid ranged from $38 to $50.

Hanley did some quick figuring in his head. On Sweetbay Sugar alone, the railway was making close to $200 a month. That worked out to near twice what Hanley earned in a year. He glanced at Coughlin. "Who determines what the railway gets paid to ship goods?"

"It depends on what's being shipped. Generally, rates are for pounds per mile. Twenty cents, thirty, sixty...over a dollar, sometimes."

"What do you charge for sugar and molasses?"

"Mid-range. Forty cents per pound. Some shippers charge higher, but I wanted the best deal for the Grand Southern. The lower rate's more than made up for in volume of goods."

"Must be a lot of pounds in those hogsheads." Hanley frowned as he examined more pages. Nothing looked altered, no figures changed. The names and numbers were all in Coughlin's hand. "Do you normally write up the accounts? I thought O'Shea's job was making sure of the numbers."

"Lawrence and I worked together on the ledgers." Smooth as butter on a corncob, not a second's hesitation. "I took the figures from the final cargo manifests he gave me. They're accurate." A shadow crossed his face. "Lawrence was good at his job. We'll miss him."

Hanley closed the ledger and handed it back. "I'd like to see another. Any month will do."

Coughlin shook his head. "One month's account book, that's what I've permission for. If that's not good enough for the Chicago police—"

"Where do you deposit the money your clients pay you?"

Coughlin frowned at the question but answered readily enough. "City Savings Bank. Go ahead and check, if you must. You'll find everything in order."

❧

The sight of his badge and the mention of Coughlin's agreement netted Hanley a look at the railway's bank account for June. Deposits from Sweetbay Sugar matched what he recalled from the ledger at the yard. Large weekly withdrawals were labelled *Payroll*, smaller and less regular ones, *Expenses*. Hanley pointed out one of the latter to the bank clerk hovering at his elbow. "Who do these go to?"

"Mr. Coughlin." The clerk's glasses slid down his nose, and he pushed them back up. "He travels a lot, drumming up new business for the company. They reimburse him for meals, hotel rooms, that kind of thing."

That made sense, worse luck. "Does he have a personal account here?"

The clerk frowned. "Yes. Why?"

Hanley gave him a reassuring smile. "Just being thorough. I'm sure it's all right." It probably was, and he couldn't push things without a warrant. Which he'd no reason to get, apart from unproven suspicion about debts and annoyance that Coughlin had thwarted him. If the man was skimming profits to pay off gambling princes, he was hiding it well. Maybe he wasn't skimming. Maybe it *had* slipped his mind that O'Shea recorded payments as well as cargo, and his defensiveness about the account books was simply meant to protect his employers from a bumptious, bumbling copper.

There was one more thing to check before diving into the gambling hells. Hanley thanked the clerk and left, then turned his steps toward the Denham residence on Sheldon Street.

# TWENTY-FIVE

*July 26, 1872*

Early on Friday, Hanley knocked on Sergeant Moore's office door. Sleep had come hard the previous night, as the impossibilities of the O'Shea case whirled through his brain. No evidence of street thievery or other criminal encounter gone wrong, no whisper of a killing grudge by any of O'Shea's workmates. A trusted supervisor who'd lied about gambling and was linked to slave labor by a company the railway did business with, but who might not know that hard evidence of it existed to threaten his position, and couldn't have killed O'Shea regardless, as he was elsewhere at the time. A surly fellow laborer at the rail yard, who avoided Hanley like yellow fever and seemed the type to have jumped O'Shea for his missing payday cash, but was playing cards and drinking at Cleary's Saloon when the murder occurred. There had to be something Hanley was missing. By the time he'd given up on sleep and boiled himself some coffee at six o'clock that morning, he thought he'd found it.

"That's some bruise you're sporting. What happened?" Moore asked, when Hanley came through the door.

"Near miss with an omnibus a couple of days ago, by the Chicago and Alton depot. I got shoved into the street. It could've been accidental... the crowd was pretty thick."

"You don't sound like you think so."

"I'm not sure. Right before it happened, I heard someone mutter,

'Mind your business!' I don't know if whoever said that meant me or somebody else. Anyway, that's not what I wanted to talk to you about."

He paced in front of his sergeant's desk, working out how best to start. The more he thought about the ledger Coughlin had shown him the day before, and the yard boss's failure to mention that O'Shea tracked payments as well as cargo, the more it bothered him. "I've no suspects, because the only two that looked good were both elsewhere when poor O'Shea was killed. Yet the murder more than likely happened at the rail yard, outside the office or close by, and according to Will Rushton a sixteen-pound scale weight was almost certainly the weapon. Not the kind of thing a bullyboy or street thief carries around. Apparently, none of O'Shea's fellow workers had a grudge against him, let alone one worth caving in his skull over. Everyone says he was well liked. No one's so much as hinted that he was anything but a hardworking, honest soul."

"And?" Moore tilted his head. "You didn't come here just to tell me you're dead in the water. What do you need?"

"A search warrant." At Moore's raised eyebrows, Hanley explained about the account ledger, the junior clerk's story of O'Shea's "meeting with the boss," Coughlin's convenient omission about O'Shea's work, and his own suspicion that the yard boss was up to something. "Coughlin swore there was no meeting the day O'Shea died, but the widow says her husband was worried over something significant...and new, when he left for work. The clerk's story backs that up. Not two days beforehand, O'Shea got word from his son that Sweetbay Sugar *does* use slave labor, and the boy had proof. What if O'Shea went back over the account books, looking at Sweetbay Sugar, and stumbled over some kind of payment fiddle? It's damned convenient that yesterday morning Coughlin was adamant the accounts were off limits and he couldn't let me have even a quick look without the company lawyer's permission. But, a couple of hours later, he was singing a different tune. Except he wasn't, really, because I could only see the June ledger, which he handpicked. I don't trust that. Maybe O'Shea didn't, either. A look at a few more ledgers could show if there was funny business going on."

"Are you thinking Coughlin killed O'Shea?"

Hanley sighed. "Not personally. He spent that Saturday night at a home near Union Park. Hugh Denham, a major shareholder at the Illinois, St. Louis and Grand Southern, hosted a musical evening. Coughlin got there at seven, stayed the whole time, left after ten. I spoke with Denham late yesterday. He confirmed Coughlin attended the musicale, swears he never left. Not even at intermission. Apparently, the man spent it paying court to Denham's sister, who was pleasantly flustered at his attentions."

"You don't care for Coughlin, do you?"

"I don't much, no." Until Moore asked, Hanley hadn't fully recognized his distaste for the rail yard boss as anything more than a copper's instinctive suspicion of people who acted helpful while dancing around questions. "He spent a lot of effort trying to charm me the first time we talked. Made a point of telling me how much Denham and the other railway higher-ups trusted him, how much he valued that. Even yesterday, with the bloom well off the bluff-good-fellow rose, he still put on the act once or twice. And now paying court to Denham's sister… the man's desperate to be liked. Or he's conning people whenever he thinks he'll get something out of it."

"Which makes him an opportunist, but no worse. And why steal from his employer, if that's what he's doing?"

"Gambling debts. He claimed he wasn't much for gambling when I asked if O'Shea had the habit. The widow says otherwise, and I know whose word I trust more." Hanley ran a hand through his hair. "If Coughlin owes serious money, there's his motive for skimming the railway's books. Sweetbay Sugar may be one of many clients whose shipping fees he's pocketing. He'd do anything to protect his racket. And he could easily hire a bullyboy to commit the actual killing. They're ten a penny at the gambling hells."

Moore shook his head. "It's all conjecture. Can you put him at any gambling houses? What about the railway's bank account? I assume you checked it."

"I did. Everything looked in order…based on that one ledger. That's why I need a warrant for more."

"Which you won't get, based on suspicion alone." Moore stroked his mustache, a habit of his when thinking. "If you can get more information, something solid…"

*The lawyer.* "I might be able to do that."

&

Harrington, Brooks and Lackland was one flight up in the office block off Dearborn and Lake. Hanley walked in and saw a white-haired man, in a suit that'd cost two weeks of a cop's pay, chatting with a thirtyish fellow at a reception desk nearly the size of a dining table. Behind the two men, a partial wall gave onto a short hallway with three doors along it. One for each lawyer, Hanley guessed. He fished out his badge and held it up. "Detective Frank Hanley, Chicago Police. I'm looking for Thomas Brooks."

The secretary answered first, with practiced politeness. "Do you have an appointment? Otherwise, I'm afraid—"

"It's all right." The older man eyed Hanley as if sizing him up. "I'm Thomas Brooks. What's your business here, Detective?"

"I've a case involving one of your clients…the Illinois, St. Louis and Grand Southern Railway. A question about the accounts." He nodded toward the little hallway. "It's probably best we discuss this in private."

Footsteps sounded in the corridor outside. Then the outer door opened, and Coughlin strode in, a rolled-up sheaf of papers in hand. "I've brought the contract I'd like to go ov—" He halted abruptly, scowling at the sight of Hanley. "What are *you* doing here?"

"Talking to your lawyer." Hanley turned to Brooks. "Mr. Coughlin informs me he needs permission from you to show me the rail yard's account ledgers. You gave it for one of them yesterday. I'd like to see more."

"I…" A slight frown, hardly more than an eyebrow twitch, passed over the lawyer's face. His gaze flicked from Hanley to Coughlin and back again. "May I ask why?"

"Murder. The victim, Lawrence O'Shea, handled—"

"That's enough, Detective," Coughlin broke in. "You've no right to come here and sully the railway's reputation with accusations of—"

"I'm not making accusations. If I see more accounts, I might not need to."

"I told you, that's proprietary information." Coughlin glanced at Brooks. "Isn't that so, Thomas?"

"It is." The lawyer's tone was carefully neutral, but Hanley read alarm in his eyes. "I'm afraid I must defer to my client. Unless you can prove sufficient need that a search warrant is granted. In that case—"

"There *is* no need." Coughlin folded his arms, bristling like an attack dog. "The Illinois, St. Louis and Grand Southern had nothing to do with the unfortunate death of Lawrence O'Shea. He was valued and will be greatly missed. And if you use what happened to him as an excuse to harass the railway, or me, I'll file a complaint with the Police Department. Do we understand one another?"

The bluff-good-fellow act was gone for good. Which only made Hanley more determined to keep digging. "We do," he said, holding Coughlin's gaze until the yard boss looked down. To Brooks, he said, "Pleasure to meet you. Good day."

☙

"I'm sorry, Frank." Sergeant Moore shook his head. "It's still not proof, or anything close. There has to be more before you bring it to a judge."

"For well-off business owners and other rich folk, you mean." Frustration edged Hanley's voice, even though there was no point getting angry at his boss. He and Moore both knew the realities of pull in Chicago. Fighting it was as futile as griping about the weather. "Damn it, the man's lying to me. About his gambling, about that June ledger...I'd swear he never asked the lawyer permission to show me anything. Brooks had no idea what I was talking about. I could see it in his face."

"If you can get the lawyer to confirm it..."

"Right. Land his own client in trouble. That's about as likely as a blizzard in June."

"Then find another way. Put Coughlin at a gambling hell or two, then go from there. Unless it *was* a random attack, and Rushton's wrong about the weapon. A common footpad could've snuck into the rail yard to rob O'Shea, then bashed him over the head with a cosh or something else. A chunk of pig iron, say. Those yards are big places. The rail police can't be everywhere."

The notion left Hanley cold. "If that's the case, we'll never find the culprit. I hope to hell it isn't, for the widow's sake."

❧

He should go home, he knew. Leave the case behind, relax over supper with Mam and Kate and Ida, play a fiddle tune or two afterward to clear his aching head. Fatigue gnawed at him, and his bruised temple was throbbing like a fresh horse kick. But the encounter at the lawyer's office wouldn't leave his mind as he crossed the river at Lake Street. Brooks's startled, wary response to Hanley's mention of the ledger, then talking of a warrant, then Coughlin interrupting with bluster and threats. Had the lawyer brought up a warrant as a hint, unable to be clearer, since his client was right there?

He passed Canal Street and kept going, ignoring the inner voice that told him to turn south toward Monroe like he usually did. *Go home. Rest. Come at it fresh tomorrow.* Why was he so stuck on Patrick Coughlin, anyway? That question brought him up short, and he halted in the middle of the boardwalk. *Because that damned ledger, and Sweetbay Sugar's slave plantation that might have cost Coughlin everything, or led O'Shea to uncover thievery that'd do the same, are the only leads I have? Because I don't like Coughlin? Because Mrs. O'Shea reminds me of Mam, and I can't let her down?*

He let out a sharp breath, prompting a startled glance from a passing woman with a laden grocery basket on her arm. Moore was right…check more gambling hells, put Coughlin at some, use that as leverage. The rail yard could wait. Which was where he was heading, he admitted to himself…to sneak into the yard office and look at the ledgers. A mad idea. He'd risk his badge if he were caught. Especially with Captain Mike

Hickey on the prowl to do him hurt. The First Precinct's commander couldn't forgive Hanley for besting him in their fight by the river last May, or for uncovering Hickey's role in the attempted Confederate takeover of Chicago back during the war. *Don't hand him ammunition. Fat lot of good you'll be to O'Shea's widow if you're off the force.*

Reluctantly bowing to common sense, he turned and started homeward.

# TWENTY-SIX

*July 27, 1872*

They left work at early closing, Ezra dry mouthed as if he'd eaten dust. So focused was he on tamping down his excitement—*my son, I'm going to see my son!*—that he felt only mild surprise when Ada led them to Madison and then turned west instead of where he'd expected, a block east to State Street where they could catch a horsecar. As far as he'd learned in his time here, the city's Negro area lay mainly southward, starting around Jackson and stretching down to Sixteenth, though some Negroes lived elsewhere in Chicago. Clearly, Ada and her man did.

"We've a little ways to walk," Ada murmured as he kept pace beside her. "Almost to the river. It's not far."

He nodded, not trusting himself to speak. He'd have given a week's pay for a glass of water, a month's to be at their destination and in the same room with his boy. Maybe then the persistent sense of unreality would leave him.

A horsecar rattled past as they continued down the street. The smell of road apples carried on the warm breeze, but Ezra didn't mind it. He was going to see his son. *Nathaniel. Nat.* He said the name softly, testing how it felt. Ada briefly clasped his hand. He squeezed back. They went on in silence. All around them, buildings loomed large and solid, three- and four-story cliffs of brick and stone. Carts and drays and omnibuses clogged the streets, and Ezra saw people everywhere, hurrying about their business. Did Ada and her family live in some hotel? Surely not. He doubted they could afford it, even if such a place would have housed Negroes. Here and there amid the stone and brick buildings he spotted smaller wooden structures—a wheelwright's, a cobbler's shop, a few homes. He took them all in, soaking up details as he tried to guess which house might be the one where his boy lived. The one with new shingles on the roof, or yellow flowers by the door, or some other they hadn't passed yet.

At Market Street, by the river, Ada turned north. Passersby had grown sparser in the last block or so. Plenty of wagons still, but not near so many folk on foot. All that he saw were white. Some gave them wide-eyed glances, others looked hastily away. Ada seemed oblivious to it. Unease tightened his stomach. He didn't care for strangers, especially white strangers, so close.

A soft touch on his arm claimed his attention. "Just up there," Ada said, gesturing. He hurried after her through a short stretch of clapboard houses and storefronts amid the stone giants of banks and hotels and other commercial establishments. The damp scent of the river hung in the air. The street was quiet, the few stores they passed apparently closed. Even a butcher's and a greengrocer's, which seemed odd on a Saturday.

Ada led them to a house in the middle of the block. He stepped up beside her, nerves taut as telegraph wire. She pulled a key from her string purse and unlocked the front door. He drew in a slow, deep breath, like a swimmer about to dive under.

She led him into a tiny front parlor. Bookshelves, a sofa, pale curtains fluttering. Near them, by the window, a boy. Tall, slender, skin golden brown like Ada's. Face like hers, too, though not her light eyes. Dark eyes, black as Ezra's own.

Nat had his hands in his pockets. His gaze met Ezra's—clear, open, a question in it Ezra couldn't trust himself to read. Ezra swallowed hard, fought to speak through the surge of feelings that closed his throat. Love, longing, fear. He was barely aware of Ada moving toward Nat with a rustle of calico.

She laid a hand on the boy's shoulder. "This is Ezra Hayes," she said, her quiet voice somehow sounding loud as Gabriel's trumpet. "Say hello to your father."

$\diamond$

Rivka stayed close to Tanta Hannah as they left the *shul*. The men would follow shortly, everyone going home for a brief midday meal before the afternoon service. She snuck a swift glance around for Moishe, in case he'd come out in hopes of catching her, but didn't see him.

She shrank from the notion of going home. Ada would be there by now. Since the blazing argument at supper ten nights ago, Ada had spoken to Rivka only when necessary, with a clear-eyed coolness that made Rivka's face burn. Nat mimicked his mother when he acknowledged Rivka at all. It hurt. Five months ago, she hadn't known either of them existed, yet now the thought of the pain she'd caused them knotted her stomach.

She jumped at a touch on her elbow. Aaron steered her toward the Nathans' house next door. "We're going to Jacob and Hannah's. Moishe will be there as well."

"What? Why?" Aaron had said nothing of it when they left for shul this morning, nor had Tanta Hannah mentioned it. Then the answer came to her. The next step in the courtship dance, under everyone's watchful eyes. She wasn't ready, felt trapped at the thought. "Aren't Nat and Ada expecting us?"

His expression reminded her of a shuttered window. "Not today."

Hannah and her daughters had drawn ahead. A glance behind showed Onkl Jacob and the rest of the men coming out of the shul, Jacob speaking earnestly to Moishe. The others kept a little away from them, as the Nathan girls were keeping away from Rivka. No more than arm's length, but enough to make a point. Aaron's grip tightened on her elbow, as if he expected her to break free and run home. Sudden shame made her flush. Maybe this wasn't only about her and Moishe. Maybe Aaron was trying to spare Ada and Nat the discomfort of her presence. A spark of anger flared. It was *his* fault. If he hadn't brought up Moishe, hadn't dictated to her as if she were a child—

*He deserved what I said. They didn't.* As quickly as it had come, her anger fled. "The other night…when I said…I didn't mean to—"

He let out a weary sigh. "It doesn't matter, Rivkaleh. We'll be leaving before long. The important thing is to get you settled before we go."

જી

Ada had left them alone to get acquainted. Ezra stood mute, drinking in the sight of his son while questions churned inside him. *Are you well? Happy? What do you do every day? What do you think about? Did you ever think of me before now?* Piling up like a fast creek blocked by a beaver dam. Something would break through, and it would be the wrong thing, and he would ruin this first precious meeting with this boy who was his blood, a gift from the God he'd almost stopped believing in.

Nat drew a breath, let it out, picked up a palm-sized chunk of wood from a small table nearby and turned it over in his slim fingers. Next to the wood were a pocketknife and three figurines. A fish, a frog, a rabbit, none bigger than Ezra's two thumbs put together. Ezra moved forward, reached out and stroked the rabbit's ears. The rough curve brought back a memory clear as day of his own hands, child-small, working with a two-inch blade at a peeled pine stick destined to become a snake. "You whittle?" he said. "I did, when I was a boy."

Nat's somber expression brightened. "I started when I was seven and Mama bought me my first pocketknife."

Ezra nodded toward the unfinished piece of wood. "What you working with?"

"Pine. It's easy to get 'round here. Lumberyards always got scraps."

"Pine's good for carving. Soft." The tension in Ezra's chest was easing, words coming more freely now. He picked up the rabbit. Precise scratches made with the knife tip hinted at eyes and a nose.

Nat had given the tiny animal a whimsical expression, as if it were surprised to have emerged from scrap lumber. "This is good. Better than I made at your age. What's that one going to be?"

"Bird. A cardinal, if I can do it right. Papa Aaron taught me—" The brightness in Nat's face fled. He bit his lip and stared at his feet.

"It's all right." Meaningless words, Ezra unsure if they were lie or truth, but they seemed to ease the boy. *Nat loves him like a father,* Ada had said. "You can say his name. He been good to you?"

"Yes." Nat looked troubled as he said it.

It hit Ezra then like a gut punch—the weight of thirteen years stolen from them both. His boy had another father now. Another life, without Ezra in it. And he was leaving. Going west. This day, this hour, might be all the two of them ever had together.

He clenched a fist around the rabbit. *I shouldn't have come,* he thought, and only realized he'd spoken it when Nat flinched. More words, desperate words, came tumbling out. "I'm sorry, God, I didn't mean that...I wanted to come, I *had* to come, since the first minute I knew you existed in this world I wanted to see you, be with you..."

Nat came up beside him, laid a hand on his sleeve. "Pa," he said. As if that word alone held magic enough to change things.

A shiver ran through Ezra. He turned and swept his son into his arms.

# TWENTY-SEVEN

The long horsecar ride to Twenty-Ninth Street passed in a blur for Ezra. His mind was full of his son—how he'd looked, what he'd said, the warmth and strength of his sturdy frame in Ezra's arms. He wished Nat was beside him now on the hard, polished bench, the two of them talking or sharing silence as the city streets rolled past.

He still held the little wooden rabbit, hadn't let go of it since leaving the house on Market Street. He brushed his fingers across its nose. Nat had given it to him before he left, the look on the boy's face saying what words couldn't. Sadness rose, threatening to choke him. This couldn't be all he had of his son—this one afternoon, this one work of Nat's hands.

He got off the horsecar and started walking east until he reached Prairie Avenue, then jogged one short block south to Ray Street. He turned there and continued on until he reached a familiar two-story clapboard house, butter yellow with black shutters and a graceful sweep of porch. He stopped in front of it and blinked, unsure for a moment what he was doing here. But he'd nowhere else to go, no one else to talk to who might begin to understand. He climbed the porch steps and knocked on the front door.

John Jones opened it. The older man's inquiring look gave way to recognition, then concern. "Ezra? You look done in. Is everything all right?" He stepped back, ushering Ezra inside. "Come in. Mary's got coffee on the boil."

☙

The coffee eased his tight throat, though he couldn't bring himself to eat any of the biscuits Mary Jones offered. "I don't know what to do," he said, finally relaxing a bit in his seat at the kitchen table. "He's my son. I can't just let him go from me in a couple of weeks, knowing I'll likely never see him again." His voice turned bitter. "But I can't do anything else with things as they are. There's a damned target on my back that white men put there. Long as that's so, what can I offer my son except trouble?"

"You want him with you, then," Jones said. "To stay."

Hearing him say it, Ezra realized it was true. "Yes. He's thirteen next month, near a man grown. Not so young he needs his mama." Part of him flinched at that, thinking of Ada—she loved her boy, it would hurt her to lose him—but he quashed the feeling. *You had him for thirteen years,* he thought, as if Ada were there to hear.

"You ask him about it?"

"No. Didn't know I wanted to until I got here."

Mary spoke up. "His mother'll have a thing to say."

"I *know* that." He heard the sharpness in his tone and curbed it. "But I'm his father. Don't I have a right in him? Doesn't he have a right in me?"

"Maybe so, but you don't know what he thinks," Jones said. "Ada's married, if I remember. What about her husband, the stepfather? How does Nat feel about him?"

"I don't...I haven't—"

"Have you ever cared for a child?" Kind but firm, Mary sounded like his mother as he remembered her from decades ago. "Thirteen's a far cry from twenty-one. Those aren't easy years without a woman's touch to smooth things. And how will you keep him, along with yourself? Feed him, clothe him, see to it he keeps up his schooling?"

Ezra's fists clenched on the table. "You make it sound impossible."

"No." She poured him more coffee. "Just hard. Hard enough to think on awhile."

Jones took a biscuit and buttered it. "Talk to the boy." He glanced at his wife. "Mary and I will help you if we can, however you work things out."

Gratitude swept through him and relief so strong that for a moment he wanted to cry. Nothing had been settled, they hadn't even agreed he was right. But, for the first time in years, he felt like he wasn't alone. "Thank you," he managed to say.

Silence fell while he sipped coffee and Jones slowly ate the biscuit. Finally, Jones dusted crumbs from his hands. "Did you ever go see those white folks? Tell them about their boy?"

Ezra shot him a look. There was no judgment in his face, or in Mary's, only gentle concern. He drew a breath and stared into his coffee cup. "I'm thinking on it."

♥

He did, in his little rented room later that night. Since coming to Chicago, he'd done his best to shut out the memory of that day at the plantation and the white boy's death. Now it wouldn't go away. He sighed, lay back on his bed, the soft mattress beneath his back and Nat's wooden rabbit in his hand. He gazed at it, thinking of fathers and sons, and promises to the dead.

He sat up, tucked the rabbit in his trouser pocket, and went downstairs to the parlor in search of letter paper. Mrs. Kelvin had a supply and gave him several sheets. Back in his room, he turned the oil lamp a little higher, then sat on his bed with the paper on his knee and began to write.

# TWENTY-EIGHT

*July 28, 1872*

Early Sunday morning, well before Mass, Hanley left the boardinghouse for Mrs. O'Shea's to see if there'd been any word from her son. He couldn't be certain Lawrence's wife would make it to Saint Pat's, or that he'd find her in the crowd if she did. He hoped Michael O'Shea had turned up since she came to Lake Street with that damning second letter. The young man's silence for two full weeks since his father's death, even more than the lack of his promised evidence, suggested catastrophe waiting in the wings.

A thunderstorm in the wee hours had tamped down the heat, so he opted to walk to North May. He passed brick two- and three-flats that gave way to small clapboard houses with painted shutters and neat squares of grass in front. Here and there kitchen gardens grew in side yards—curling lettuce, bunched green onions, cucumber and squash vines loaded with summer bounty. Rather than dwell on Michael O'Shea's fate, he turned his thoughts toward more productive channels. After another day of rest foisted on him by his mother, he'd spent Saturday finally getting somewhere with regard to Patrick Coughlin. He'd been able to prove the man was indeed a gambler, and a liar to boot.

☙

"Tell me what he's done, and I'll tell you if he's been here," was the tart comment offered by Carrie Watson, whose bordello on Clark Street catered to rich patrons. Just the sort of place to appeal to Coughlin, who clearly reveled in being a wealthy and prominent businessman despite his professed kinship with the workers he employed. Hanley had started there, knowing plenty of card games went on in the parlors at 441 South Clark. "He rough up a girl?" Carrie asked. "Settle a debt with his fists, or a knife? Better yet, a pistol duel. That's the type I like. Romantic."

Used to Carrie's bite, Hanley ignored the sarcasm in her reply. "Is Coughlin the dueling kind? From what I've seen, he'd rather not dirty his hands. You know different?"

"All I know is, he doesn't fight here. I don't allow it. Though I can't see him bloodying anyone's nose even when he gets mad enough. Might soil his fine French cuffs."

"But he does gamble? Faro, poker, and so on?"

She pursed her lips. "I provide entertainment for respectable customers. Not my business what else they get up to under my roof." She fixed him with a sharp look, waited for him to nod, and continued. "But, yes, he's played a card game or three. He also brags about winning streaks at Brighton Park and the dog tracks. And he doesn't like to lose. Gets red faced, stalks around like an angry bear. Especially lately. I don't know why, so don't ask."

That *lately* piqued Hanley's interest. "Who might?"

"You go see O'Banion, down on Custom House Place. Your man Coughlin was complaining about O'Banion's Saloon one night a few months back. Somebody cheated him at faro or something. If anyone knows what's up, O'Banion likely does."

Carrie was being remarkably free with her information. Not her usual style. "And you're telling me all this because…?"

She folded her arms. "Because I don't like complainers. Or the kind of fellow who sweet-talks every girl in the room, makes her think it's True Love, when she can't afford to be such a silly little fool. And then she finds out he lied to her anyway. That man's cost me two perfectly good girls in the past six months, charming them just because other gents took an interest. Like a child who wants another one's toy. He's done something wrong you can put him away for, saves me the trouble of tossing him out next time he shows his face."

✲✲

It had taken some persuading, plus a few greenbacks from Lake Street's petty cash, but O'Banion had delivered the goods. The question was what Hanley could, or should, make of what the saloon owner told him.

"You didn't hear this from me," O'Banion had said, over a glass of rotgut whiskey Hanley'd paid too much for. "Word is, your fellow owes Johnny Dowling a packet. I make it my business to know who owes who. Johnny and me, we go back a ways. He's got a big place now, out west by Halsted and Madison. Runs all kinds of games there." O'Banion nodded at the rough sketch of Coughlin that Hanley'd laid on the table between them. "This fella's showed up here a couple-three times. Slumming, I figured. Johnny told me a few weeks ago to watch out for him. He doesn't pay up when he loses, not unless he has to. If you know what I mean."

Hanley did. "And Dowling's after him?"

"What do *you* think?"

Hanley'd talked to the bullyboys, too, the ones hanging around O'Banion's and elsewhere. Not one admitted to knowing Coughlin beyond, "Seen him around, yeah," and "Sure, he plays cards. Wins some, loses some," not even through the usual dodge of "a friend of a friend who knows a fella." Familiar as he was with the loafers, thugs, and confidence men who frequented gambling dives, Hanley could generally spot them lying. He didn't think they were. Which left him with…what, exactly? Coughlin in serious financial trouble, as well as lying about gambling and probably about that June ledger. None of which proved he'd hired out O'Shea's murder, or that he had reason to. *But damn it, it has to be him. There* isn't *anyone else. Except a random thief I'll never find without an eyewitness I haven't got.*

❧

He reached May Street and turned onto it. Here, the kitchen gardens were tucked out of sight around the back and the houses had lace curtains in their front windows. The area was largely Irish, but as different from rough-edged Conley's Patch where Hanley grew up as an ocean was from a mud puddle. A place like this was a notch up from a laborer's life, or a fresh-off-the-boat poor Mick's. From the careful respectability of North May Street, a man might aspire to a profession, or to work in business…or hope his children could.

The O'Shea house was in the middle of the next block. Hanley reached it and knocked on the front door. To his surprise, Patrick Coughlin opened it. The man's grim face turned grimmer at the sight of Hanley. "Detective," Coughlin said. "If it's Grace you've come to speak to, I'm afraid she's not at home today. To anyone." He cleared his throat. "We've only just learned…her son's been killed."

# TWENTY-NINE

K illed? Michael O'Shea?" Though part of him had feared exactly this, the reality of it stunned Hanley. "What happened?"

Coughlin's jaw tightened. "If we can believe what the darky said—"

"Darky? What darky?"

Coughlin glanced backward over his shoulder, then met Hanley's gaze again. "This is a house of mourning. Whatever you came for can wait, surely...and what happened to poor Michael is none of your business."

Hanley made a split-second decision not to mention Michael's second letter, at least not yet. Let Coughlin trip himself up with it, if he knew. "You're right. I understand Mrs. O'Shea isn't in a fit state to talk with me. But I've a matter to raise with you, and here you are. Let's not stay at the door and disturb her further, shall we?"

Coughlin stared at him a moment longer, then gave a chilly nod. "All right." He stepped across the threshold and pulled the door shut behind him.

Hanley moved a little way down the front walk. Coughlin followed. "Tell me about the darky," Hanley said.

"Why?"

"Because I asked." He softened his tone. "And because it'll make things easier on Mrs. O'Shea when I speak with her again. I'm thinking that matters to you, seeing as you're here. Why are you here, by the way? Sunday morning's an unusual hour for visiting."

"I came to take Grace to Mass." Coughlin sighed, and the hostility in him eased a little. "The darky turned up right when we were getting ready to leave for Saint Pat's. Knocked at the back door and asked for Lawrence. I said Lawrence was dead and told the darky to clear off, but Grace heard him and came over, and…" He sighed. "Poor thing. First her husband, now her only son. It's more than any woman should bear."

"So he asked for Lawrence and said Michael was dead? How did he know? Did he say what happened?"

Coughlin shrugged, moving further down the walkway. "He didn't give much detail. Just said he spoke to Michael not long before the boy died and that Michael asked him to bring word to his parents." For a moment, the yard boss looked bleak. "It happened outside New Orleans, he said. Someplace Michael 'shouldn't ought to have been' was how he put it. Considering Michael worked for the Freedmen's Bureau, I'm guessing it was bad. Bad enough the darky didn't want to burden a woman with it. Especially Michael's mother."

"But she believed him? Did you?"

"First chance I get, I'll send a telegram to New Orleans, see if I can confirm the story. But he described Michael perfectly, right down to the strawberry mark by his left ear. And he didn't ask for money. Flat refused it, in fact, when I offered. He—" Coughlin searched for words. "I could see in his face he felt for Grace. I know some say they're like children, the Negroes, they don't feel things as deeply as we do, but this fellow did. You couldn't *dis*believe him."

He seemed easy enough discussing the incident. Maybe he *didn't* know about Michael O'Shea's promised evidence of slave labor. "What did this man look like? Did he give a name, an address?"

"Something Biblical, the name. One of the prophets. I've no notion how to find him again, even if Grace wanted to. As to looks…" Coughlin paused. "Big fellow. Muscles like a ditchdigger. Dark, like mahogany wood. More than thirty but shy of fifty, I'd guess. Honestly, most of them look the same to me. I was concerned for Grace, not paying much mind to anything else."

The man's tone held extra warmth when he spoke of O'Shea's widow. Maybe skimming the till, or burying the slave labor story, weren't his only motives for murder. "How close are you to the O'Sheas, Mr. Coughlin?"

"I'm not sure what you mean. Lawrence worked for me, of course—"

"You called Lawrence's widow 'Grace' just now, and you're squiring her to Sunday Mass. I know you're a friend of the family, but—"

Coughlin's face darkened. "What are you suggesting?"

He'd unsettled the man. Good. "Never mind. Just a passing thought." Deliberately, Hanley switched tactics. "So tell me why you lied to me."

Bewilderment crossed Coughlin's face. "Lied to you? About what?"

"Gambling. You're 'not much' for it, you said. Except you owe people money. Unpleasant people. People who hurt folk that don't pay up. I can see where you might be tempted to do anything to get out of that kind of trouble."

"I have no idea what you're talking about."

"Carrie Watson does. So does Johnny Dowling, and who knows what other gambling princes. A few too many big losses at faro and five-card stud, especially lately. Plus more on the horses and dogs. I'm sure you earn a decent salary, but those kinds of debts can drown a man before he knows how deep he's in."

Coughlin laughed, a mirthless bark. "So what are you accusing me of? No, don't tell me. The account books, isn't it? You think I'm stealing from the Grand Southern...the people who put their trust in me, helped make me who I am. That's a load of rubbish. How dare you suggest I'm a thief—and you a fellow Irishman. Have you no decency at all?"

Pitch-perfect indignation. Hanley felt tempted to applaud. "Not where murder's concerned. Let me see your ledgers and I'll believe you. And this time you don't choose which."

"You've a damned suspicious mind."

"I'm a cop. Comes with the job."

"If you're accusing me, say it plain and haul me off. But I've not stolen a penny. And you know damned well I didn't kill Lawrence O'Shea—over that, or anything else." The man glanced toward the house. "It's time I got back to Grace...Mrs. O'Shea, *if* you don't mind."

He wasn't breaking through Coughlin's bluster. Time to give him an out, see if he took it. "What about Liam Mahoney?"

Coughlin's stone-faced glare gave way to a startled look. "What about him?"

"He likes a good card game. He doesn't like to lose. The two of you have those things in common. Did he owe anyone money?" The fellow's alibi for O'Shea's murder was as good as Coughlin's own, as far as Hanley knew—but O'Shea's wallet had held only two dollars instead of a week's pay, and Mahoney was strong enough to swing that scale weight as if it were made of feathers.

Coughlin blinked and wet his lips. "I wouldn't know. Mahoney pulls his weight at the rail yard and likely drinks more than is good for him. So do most of the men. Not my business how they spend their time, as long as they show up for work sober."

"So you've never seen Mahoney at a gambling hell, or played cards with him at Cleary's, say?"

"I don't gamble at saloons. I'll admit, I bet on the horses and dogs sometimes. And yes, I play faro now and again…with other men of means, where I know the games are honest. Not the sort of places Mahoney can afford, if you get my drift."

Another lie. O'Banion knew Coughlin by sight. Why didn't he take the chance to cast blame on Mahoney, shift it off himself? He couldn't know Mahoney was in the clear. And mention of the fellow had definitely spooked him. "What happened to your being a plain workingman once? You called yourself that when we first spoke, at that eatery on Carroll Street. Not so much where your pocketbook's concerned?"

"I'm sentimental, Detective. I'm Irishman enough for that. But I'm not stupid, and I won't be cheated." Coughlin folded his arms. "I'd like to get back where I'm needed. Are we finished?"

One last question, though Hanley didn't expect an honest answer. "Did you ever hear back from the owner of the Sweetbay Sugar plantation? You said you wrote him about those rumors of slave labor Michael O'Shea dug up."

Coughlin went still, the tension in him sharpening like the air before a storm. "I told you before, there won't *be* any proof, and they'll hardly confess," he said, his voice hard as a steel rail. "Michael is dead and those stories with him. Let the dead damn well rest in peace."

# THIRTY

*July 29, 1872*

Monday morning found Hanley on Rolf Schmidt's beat, joining the big German patrolman's daily rounds. "Mahoney?" Schmidt said, slouched against a lamppost as he eyed the sketch Hanley showed him. "*Ja*, I know him. Likes to drink at Cleary's on Kingsbury and Jacky O'Toole's on Franklin. I book him at O'Toole's a few times for fighting." He snorted and shook his head. "Some Irishman, him. Fella can't handle his whiskey. What kind of trouble he's in now?"

"Don't know yet," Hanley said. "What were the fights over, d'you remember?"

"Cards. Twice, he swears the other guy cheats. Third time, other guy says Mahoney cheats. Not the same guy. All different." He frowned. "Fourth time, he jumps a fella in the street. Fella owed him money, I guess, the way Mahoney's yelling, 'Pay up.' Other guy didn't want to talk, ran away like a rabbit soon as he could."

"How long ago was that fourth arrest?"

"Three months. May, early. I wrote it up."

Hanley clapped Schmidt on the shoulder. "Thanks."

He heard similar stories at other stations in the Second Precinct. Mahoney was a brawler and a hard drinker, used to dealing with the world fists first, brain second. "Your man's a hothead, for sure," said a patrolman at the West Chicago Avenue station whose beat included streets near the rail yard. "I arrested him a while back...middle of

March, I think…when he beat up a fellow at the dog track. Turned out he picked the man's pocket, and the dumb sap went after him to settle things. Mahoney was with a friend at the time. The friend paid his bail and persuaded the victim not to swear out a complaint. Said Mahoney had a widowed mother to support and if he got a name as a troublemaker, he'd lose his job." The patrolman shrugged. "Fellow was a soft touch. Mahoney got lucky."

"Who was the victim? And the friend…d'you recall his name?"

"The friend was Irish, that's all I remember. The other gent, who got his pocket picked, talked like an American. No arrest, so no names." Another shrug. "Sorry about that."

Hanley blew out a breath. "All right, then. What did Mahoney's friend look like?"

બ

An hour later, Hanley stood fidgeting and fuming amid the small crowd waiting to cross the Chicago River at Lake Street. The bridge was open, the fourth of five schooners passing through the gap, bound for the lumber yards and grain elevators that lined the South Branch. Hanley stared at the masts of the last two vessels, willing the damned things to move faster.

His conversation with Sergeant Moore not a quarter hour earlier buzzed in his brain, infuriating as a cloud of gnats. After all he'd found out about Coughlin, it still wasn't enough for a warrant. *You're asking the Illinois, St. Louis and Grand Southern to share proprietary business information with the police department in hopes of incriminating a fine, upstanding citizen in a heinous crime we know he personally didn't commit,* Moore had said. *That's how a judge will see it.* And, *You don't know it was Coughlin who talked Mahoney out of trouble at the dog track, let alone why he would've. No names, and the description of Mahoney's "friend" could apply to most middle-aged Irishmen in Chicago. Besides, aren't Mahoney's whereabouts at the time of O'Shea's murder accounted for?* All of which was true and sat like sour milk in Hanley's gut. One rule for ordinary folk, another for the rich and important. The railroads had major pull, even smallish ones like the outfit Coughlin worked for. That, as much as his no doubt respectable salary, protected him from the law. Though not from the gambling princes. *Which is why all this happened in the first place, if I'm right.*

The final schooner sailed through the gap. With a mechanical howl, the swing bridge began to close. Hanley craned his neck, using his six-foot-plus height to see over the people in front of him. When the ends of the bridge met the boardwalk again with a rattling clang, he hurried forward with the rest of the throng. Five more minutes took him to the edge of the rail yard, where he halted. What was he doing? He'd no new information with which to pry the truth out of Coughlin—about his relationship with Mahoney, about thieving from the railway, or about the evidence of slave labor at Sweetbay Sugar. He had nothing to pry any truth out of Mahoney, either. Just a cop story about the dog track incident, which proved nothing about who murdered Lawrence O'Shea.

He stood on the street corner, gnawing his lip. What had Gabe Cleary said about Mahoney the night O'Shea died? The surly railman had played cards with his mates...and with two Norwegians, regular customers. They'd likely be at Cleary's tonight. If Mahoney *hadn't* been at the saloon all evening, if he'd left the place between, say, eight and nine thirty, for long enough to club O'Shea down behind the rail yard office and dump him in the river, and then returned to Cleary's, the Norwegians would probably know.

Still unsettled, he turned and walked south a little way along the river. Gulls' cries reached him on the breeze, along with boatmen's shouts and the usual stink from the filthy, debris-choked water, made worse by the summer heat. The foul atmosphere matched his mood. Coughlin knew he was after the railway account ledgers and must have guessed he was spinning his wheels. What other ways might the man dream up to safeguard himself? What if he went to Hugh Denham, his patron shareholder in the Illinois, St. Louis and Grand Southern, and asked Denham to intervene? The railway itself wasn't implicated in O'Shea's death, so its bosses hadn't brought pressure to bear. If they did...

He shook his head. No use borrowing trouble. Still, he couldn't shake his misgivings. What if the Norwegian card players confirmed Mahoney *was* at Cleary's Saloon all night from seven thirty to ten? Even if they said otherwise, what proof did he have that Coughlin hired Mahoney instead of some random bullyboy to kill O'Shea? Or Mahoney might have clubbed O'Shea down on his own to steal the clerk's missing pay.

The chuffing and clanging of arriving and departing trains, accompanied by the shriek of a whistle, reached him from the nearby rail yard. He could go back there. Find Mahoney's drinking partners on July 13th, Sully and Rourke, see if they recalled Mahoney ducking out during the evening. But Sully'd already said he was drunk enough, soon enough, not to remember if O'Shea ever showed. And besides, Mahoney was one of them. Ten to one they'd close ranks against a copper on principle if they thought Hanley meant the surly Irishman serious trouble.

He looked toward the yard, an idea forming in his mind. Risky, probably too much so. But it might be the only way to get what he needed.

*For Mrs. O'Shea*, he told himself as he finally turned and walked away.

# THIRTY-ONE

Rivka's steps lagged as she headed downstairs for breakfast Monday morning. The smell of coffee reached her, along with the sound of voices. Aaron, Ada, and Nat, all bustling around getting ready—Nat for school, Ada for work, Aaron for another day of seeking odd jobs. *I could go back up. Sit in my room for five minutes, or ten, until they've all left.* She drew a steadying breath and continued downward.

"—home for supper." Aaron's words echoed from the rear of the house, followed by the *chunk* of the back door closing. One gone, not to be faced until evening. She reached the kitchen and saw Nat gulping dregs from a coffee mug. He set it down, turned to grab his schoolbooks from the table, and caught sight of her. A wary look crossed his face. He snatched the books by their strap, murmured, "'Bye, Mama," and ducked out in Aaron's wake.

Ada gave her a cool glance as Rivka moved further into the room. "Coffee's still hot," she said as she untied her apron. "Four eggs this morning. We left you one." She hung the apron on its wall peg, snagged a dinner pail from the counter, and turned toward the door.

"Ada—" Rivka raised a hand, then checked the gesture. "That night at supper, when I—"

"Never mind. It's done with." The crispness in Ada's voice gave the lie to her words. "I can't be late for work." She yanked the door open, stepped out, and shut it behind her. Rivka heard her footsteps, light and brisk, going down the back stairs.

There was no point following. A wave of frustration washed over Rivka and she clenched her fists. Aaron and his family would leave Chicago soon. Two weeks, he'd said, definitely before August was out.

She *had* to set things right, mend what her harsh words several days ago had broken. She couldn't let them go with matters as they were.

A cup of coffee restored her spirits somewhat, as did the egg she boiled and made herself eat. She washed the breakfast dishes and headed toward the front room for her sewing basket. Mending would take up the rest of the morning until it was time for dinner and her English class.

As she neared the parlor door, the flap of the letter box caught her attention. The morning post had arrived. There wasn't much, she saw when she retrieved it. An advertising circular for women's shoes; the *Chicago Daily Journal*, a subscription of Papa's she couldn't bring herself to cancel; and a letter. For Nat, she noted, surprised at both the letter and the name. *Nat Whittier*—not Kelmansky—was scrawled on the white envelope in a clear, bold hand. The return address read *E. Hayes, 148 Twelfth Street.*

She eyed it with curiosity. Letters rarely came here since her father's death. One for Nat was even more unusual. Who had sent it? A schoolmate? It must be. She frowned at the envelope, troubled by the surname. Aaron had adopted Nat, she knew. Maybe he hadn't wanted his classmates to think he was Jewish.

She carried the mail into the parlor and laid it on the side table, then settled in her favorite chair with her sewing basket at her feet. A shirt of Nat's needed mending. She pulled it from the basket and got to work.

❧

She managed to teach her afternoon class while avoiding attention from Moishe and Onkl Jacob, though her relief at this was short lived. A stop at the butcher's on the way home, to buy a chicken for supper, reminded her yet again how precarious her situation was. When her friend Sisel Klein came forward eagerly to help her, Sisel's husband ordered his wife away. Lazar Klein stopped short of telling Rivka her custom was no longer welcome, but tended to her order with brusque distaste, as if she carried a disease to which he didn't wish Sisel exposed. She caught Sisel's eye before leaving but took no comfort in the regret she saw there. It wasn't fair that Rivka should be judged by what Aaron had done. Was it fair to judge Aaron and Ada, come to that? Goyische and mulatto or not, Ada was a good person, and they loved each other. And poor Nat, a child caught up in adults' decisions. *We offered them shelter, yet now we treat them like this. How can this be what Hashem wants of us?*

Foolish thoughts. Dangerous ones. She forced them from her mind and hurried homeward, walking through her own door with a sense of gratitude. However difficult the rest of the day might be once the others returned, at least she had some refuge here.

Nat came home from school as she was digging young carrots in the garden. She greeted him with a tentative smile. He stood watching her, swinging his books from their strap. Then he gave a brief nod and started up the back steps.

"Nat," she called as he reached the door. He turned to look at her.

What to say next? She seized on the first thing she could think of. "A letter came for you. It's on the table in the parlor."

He looked startled, then murmured, "Thanks," and went inside.

Well, it was something. She blew out a breath, pulled another carrot from the clinging dirt, and tossed it on the pile.

At supper that evening, Aaron complimented her on the chicken stew, a sign the breach between them was on the mend. Nat was unusually quiet, no stories about who pitched the best ball game at recess or flicked slate chalk at which girl. He pushed his food around on his plate until Ada asked with a worried look, "Something wrong, honey?"

"Just tired is all." He shoveled a forkful of carrot and onion into his mouth and chewed with gusto, then sawed at a gravy-soaked chicken leg. Ada watched him, frowning, but said no more.

Afterward, as Ada washed and Rivka dried the dishes, the silence pressed down. Gradually, it dawned on Rivka that the shadows in Ada's face were more than lingering anger or awkwardness in her presence. Ada looked preoccupied, even anxious. About Nat? About going west? About being here, where hardly anyone looked her in the eye when she ventured out of the house? After her own experience at the butcher shop, Rivka felt the injustice of that more keenly. Finally, she asked, "Is everything all right?"

Brief surprise glimmered in Ada's face. "Fine." She dunked forks into the dishpan and scrubbed them, paying meticulous attention to each. The silence thickened.

"I'm sorry for what I said. I was angry at Aaron, but that's no excuse." Rivka took the forks from Ada and dried them, thinking of Lazar Klein—his scornful voice, his refusal to even glance in her direction as he wrapped her parcel and took her money. "We like to think we're good people, kind people. But so many aren't kind to you and Nat. I'm sorry for that, too."

Ada said nothing. When Rivka looked up from her task, she saw a softness in Ada's eyes. Forgiveness? Maybe the beginning of it.

"None of us has it easy these days." Ada nodded toward the stewpot on the stove. "Hand me that, will you? We'll set it to soak awhile."

☙

Hanley went home from the stationhouse for a light meal, then ventured out again. The air felt soft, the day's heat slowly easing as twilight gathered. A distant church bell tolled the three-quarter hour. Hanley headed east on Madison, then turned north onto Jefferson Street. Ten more minutes' walk brought him to the rail yard. At near eight o'clock, there was still light enough yet to see. He'd timed his arrival as precisely as he could, enough after the workday ended for the men to have gone, but before full darkness fell. Lantern light in the office window would draw attention, the last thing he needed on this mad venture.

*It'll only take a few minutes. Then I'll go on to Cleary's, find those two Norwegians, see what they tell me about where Mahoney really was on the night O'Shea was murdered.* He lingered on the far side of Jefferson and Kinzie, watching the yard. A minute crawled by, then another. In the ebbing light, a figure in the uniform and flat cap of a rail cop ambled past and vanished amid the motionless freights in the cargo area. Hanley waited some more, counting to thirty in his head, but no one else appeared in the portion of the yard he could see.

He let out a breath he hadn't known he was holding. The crisscrossing tracks at street grade just ahead of him were empty. *Now or never.* He hurried across the tracks and Kinzie Street into the yard, then halted to get his bearings. The cargo area where he'd watched the men unload cotton bales lay to his right, boxcars and flatbeds crowding it like slumbering giants. The yard office stood past it, deeper in and slightly to the north by the riverbank.

He crept through the cargo area, keeping close to the freights. A bull's-eye lantern flashed up ahead, and he flattened himself against a boxcar as the railroad bull walked past, whistling a haunting and familiar tune. After a moment, Hanley recognized it as "The Parting Glass." The rail cop vanished from sight, and Hanley breathed easier. The office lay a few yards ahead. Pray God it wasn't locked—or, if it was, he'd manage to make good use of the hook pick he'd brought along. He slid a hand into his trouser pocket and touched the slender length of metal. Years ago, long before the war and joining the police, when he'd been a petty criminal thieving off the docks, he'd watched Crowfoot Abe and other cracksmen at work a time or three. Paid good attention, too. He *should* remember how to do it...

One last check for motion, a lantern flash, the sound of a whistle or a footfall nearby. Nothing. Hanley took a cautious step away from the boxcar. The light was nearly gone. Would he be able to see the damned door lock clearly enough to pick it? Maybe he'd get lucky and wouldn't have to. Another step forward, glance right, glance left. Still nothing. He drew in a breath, ready to run across the open ground into the shadow of the building.

"Hey! You!" The shout came from behind and to his left, amid the hulking freight cars. A man's figure coalesced in the spill of light from the bull's-eye lantern he held up, and Hanley recognized Officer Walker.

He resisted the instinct to run, stood his ground as Walker came closer. Surprise, then suspicion, crossed the rail cop's face. "Detective," Walker said, as if what he meant was *sonofabitch.* "Yard's closed for the night. You mind telling me what the hell you're doing here?"

150

❦

Late that night, voices woke Rivka from fitful sleep. Ada and Aaron, sharp with worry.

"—don't know what to *do*," Ada said.

"I don't know, either. How can I advise you about a man I've never met?"

"You didn't *want* to meet him."

"And *you* didn't want me to." Silence followed, heavy as the darkness in Rivka's bedroom. Then Aaron said, more gently, "I'm sorry. You had to do as you thought best."

"He wouldn't understand," Ada answered. Another silence fell. Rivka sat up, straining to hear more.

"Nat didn't tell me." Ada again. "I found the letter in his pocket when I shook out his trousers. He usually puts away his clothes. If I hadn't checked on him just now—"

"Maybe he was taking time to think before he said anything."

"Think? About what? His home is with us. Just because Ezra wants—" She broke off. "I shouldn't have told Ezra anything. I should have guessed this might happen…he might try to claim Nat…after all he's been through…"

"Hush." Aaron's tone was loving now. "We'll talk to Nat. He must be surprised by this, too. He won't do anything right away. Can you speak to Ezra tomorrow? Make him see sense?"

Ada's reply was muffled. "Pray God I can."

# THIRTY-TWO

*July 30, 1872*

N at had told Ezra he went to the Mantern School. A quick check of the city directory in Mrs. Kelvin's parlor yielded the street and number. Ezra had meant to go there at the end of the school day but, after a night of restless dozing, felt too keyed up to wait. A dashed-off note to John Jones in Tuesday's early post, claiming a stomach complaint, and he was on his way. When Nat arrived, they could go somewhere and talk. It wouldn't hurt the boy to miss schooling this once. He sidestepped all thought of Ada's reaction if she learned about it. They were only talking, he and Nat. The boy was old enough to make up his own mind about his future.

The walk from the boardinghouse was long and hot. His mind on his son, Ezra paid scant heed to the passing city blocks. A cooling puff of breeze, a second's break in the heat, briefly caught his attention. Clouds were building in the southwest, promising a storm later. With the baked-wood smell of the boardwalk and the pungent odor of horse manure filling his lungs, he longed for the clean, clear scent of rain. The night-dark bayou flashed through his mind, and his breathing quickened. No matter what, he had to stay safe. Keep Nat safe, too.

The school came in sight, a low-slung building of pine boards with a tin roof and a small side yard, packed dirt dotted with beaten grass. The yard was full of boys and girls, all Negro or mulatto. Several boys were playing a scratch-up ball game, while girls played tag and jumped rope.

Still more students were coming down the boardwalk, on their own or accompanied by their mothers or elder siblings. As he drew nearer, Ezra scanned the arriving students' faces. Maybe Nat was part of the ball game. Ezra stopped at the far edge of the yard and watched for a few minutes, but none of the ball-throwing players was his boy. *His boy.* Even unspoken, he savored those words.

He eyed the street again and stiffened. There was Nat, striding down the boardwalk, swinging his books and a small sack. Talking easily, comfortably, with a tall man at his side. A white man.

Cold shock washed through Ezra. Abruptly, he felt like a fool. The short walk on Saturday to where Ada lived, instead of a horsecar ride south to the Negro part of town. The white faces of all the people they'd passed on the way. Of course her husband was one of them. "'Papa Aaron…'" Only when a sturdy youngster playing outfield gave him a puzzled look did he realize he'd spoken.

He moved away from the ball game, his pulse thudding in his temples. He wasn't ready to meet this man, say so much as a word to him. That he was white felt like a betrayal of what Ezra and Ada had once been to each other, years gone though it was. He breathed deep, pressing a hand to his forehead. This man had never done him harm, had been good to his son…dear God, Nat. Had the boy seen him yet? Muted thunder muttered from the far-off wall of cloud. He could walk away, come back later and find Nat alone. Or go up to him right now, right in front of the white man, stake his claim—

*Too late.* Nat was staring at him from the middle of the boardwalk. Ada's husband had stopped also. Ezra drew himself up, tall and proud. Let Papa Aaron see who Nat's *father* was.

A grim look came over the white man's face. "Go inside, Nat."

"But—"

"Do as I say. I will come for you later." He talked like he was born someplace foreign. He brushed Nat's shoulder with one hand, then moved forward. Nat followed. *Not obeying orders*, Ezra thought with approval. He sized the man up as the fellow drew nearer. Broad shouldered but lanky, likely not so strong as Ezra was. Some younger, not much. Plain homespun clothes, a small round black cap on his dark hair. No yielding in his face, just that icy look. Arrogant, like *he* was in charge.

The man drew breath to speak, but Ezra beat him to it. "That's my son you're walking to school."

"So I understand." The man clipped his words, as though each one cost him. "You are Ezra Hayes?"

To answer felt like surrender. Ezra gave a brusque nod.

"I am Aaron Kelmansky. Ada's husband."

"I figured." Ezra glanced past him to Nat. The boy caught his eye with a pleading look that twisted Ezra's heart. What was he doing, with his son right there, confronting this man who'd been a father to Nat for nearly half his life?

Fresh anger flared. He, Ezra, should have done that. He should have been able to stay with Ada, help her raise their boy, not been sold away. He clenched his fists. White men like this one had cost him his family. They'd cost him his freedom. They'd cost him everything.

"—know you wrote to Nat," Aaron was saying. "I ask you not to do it again. He is my son now, mine and Ada's, and we—"

"The hell he is." Harsh and loud, the words escaped before Ezra could bite them back. With effort, he reined in his temper and spoke to Nat. "I'd have been a father to you all along if I could…if I'd known about you, if I'd known where you and your mother were. Now I can be. You're old enough to choose. That's all I'm asking."

Aaron stepped forward. "*No.* You will not do this to him, or to Ada. Keep away, or I will make sure you do."

Pent-up fury burst its bounds. A low cry escaped Ezra as he drove his fist hard into the white man's gut.

Aaron doubled over. The *whuff* of his breath and Nat's shocked cry brought Ezra to his senses. He saw confusion on his son's face, pain on Aaron's. Then rage as the white man met his gaze again. Aaron coughed and drew a ragged breath as Nat hurried to him. He draped an arm around Nat's shoulders and pulled the boy close. "Stay away from us. Or you'll wish you had."

"Nat. Son." Nat wouldn't look at him. Passersby were staring, wide eyed. The ball game had halted. Ezra felt hot, hotter than the air alone could make him. Unbearable to leave, useless to stay. He lingered another moment, hoping Nat would catch his eye. Instead, the boy and his stepfather showed him their backs as they moved toward the school.

Sick with anger and regret, Ezra turned and strode away.

# THIRTY-THREE

Hanley overslept Tuesday morning and hurried in to work with a churning in his stomach that owed as much to nerves as to the extra beer he'd drunk the night before. He'd gone to Cleary's as planned after his encounter with the rail cop, but the Norwegian card players he sought never showed. No chance of breaking Mahoney's alibi without them. Which would leave him stuck in place, with two prime suspects who couldn't have committed the crime, and no leads pointing anywhere else. *Just my luck, like everything on this damned case.*

His apprehension proved justified at the sight of Patrick Coughlin filling out a form at the lobby desk. The rail yard boss looked up, glaring as he recognized Hanley. "I warned you," he said, each word clipped. "Unless you want worse trouble, don't show your face at my rail yard again." He signed the form with a flourish, then strode past Hanley and out the double doors into the fitful sunshine.

Hanley watched him go, then turned to the desk sergeant.

"You're for it, I'm thinking," the sergeant said, sympathy on his lean face.

"What'd he fill out?"

"Trespassing complaint." The sergeant picked up the form. "You want to take it to the chief, or should I?"

☙

Seated at his desk, the complaint in hand, Sergeant Moore gave Hanley a stern look. "So. Tell me what you thought you were doing."

His rebuke roused Hanley's temper. "Finding evidence for a search warrant. Something solid, like you said. Only I didn't get that far."

"Don't use me as an excuse." The whiplash of Moore's voice jolted Hanley back to good sense. He was in the wrong, and he knew it. Might as well take his medicine.

The chief of detectives set the complaint down. "Trespassing after hours with intent to break into the rail yard office? That's what Officer Walker said and Coughlin swears to. Right here." He thumped his index finger on the paper. "Tell me you didn't actually break into the building. I assume not, or Walker would've pinched you, and you'd still be in lockup somewhere."

"He's only guessing I meant the office. He caught me a few yards shy of it. I told him I'd come to watch the riverbank where O'Shea went in, at the time he went in, to see who might be about and could've seen or heard something the night O'Shea died."

"You're lucky Walker believed you, at least enough not to arrest you then and there." Moore sighed and shoved the form away. "If you *had* gotten into the yard office *and* been caught there, did you really think you'd be able to talk your way out of that one?"

He'd thought exactly that and flushed when Moore said it. "I need to see those ledgers, to know if Coughlin was bilking his employer. But because of who Coughlin is, and the damned railway, nothing I have on him so far is enough to do it legally—not his gambling debts or his lying about them, not his claiming permission from the company lawyer to show me that one ledger when he had no such thing—"

"You can't prove that without the lawyer's admission. As to the gambling debts, it would be good to have someone more respectable than a known madam, an infamous gambling prince, and a crooked saloon owner from Custom House Place to back you up." Moore snagged the complaint again, yanked open a desk drawer, and dropped the paper into it. "I can just about get away with burying this, *only* because Walker caught you in the open. Don't act so rash again. Am I clear, Detective?"

Hanley could count on one hand the number of times in the past few years Moore had called him by rank instead of by name. "Yes, Sergeant."

Moore's expression softened. "You're good at your job, Frank. Because of that, sometimes I let you bend the rules, likely more than I should. But you can't do that whenever the fancy strikes you. Especially not if you want to move up."

"You're considering me for senior? Chamberlain's job?" He'd hoped for it, even though he knew it was a long shot. He was damned well good enough, better than Chamberlain, and God knew he could use the pay raise. But there were skilled detectives who'd been in the squad far longer and had better connections than he. "I've no angels, apart from you. You really think I've a chance?" If he hadn't wrecked it already…

"Maybe." Moore let out a sigh. "Superintendent Sheridan owes me a favor. I can get him to listen, at any rate. But the precinct captains will weigh in, and the superintendent will listen to them as well. As chief of detectives, my word should carry the most weight. But you and I both know *should* doesn't always matter. You've baggage enough with Captain Hickey, especially after that business involving Miss Kelmansky this past spring. I don't want to join him in talking you down, lose you the only pull you have. So don't make me."

The mention of Hickey sobered him like nothing else. "No, sir. I won't."

"All right, then." Moore nodded toward his office door. "Go down and ask the desk sergeant for the cases that came in this morning. I believe one's a theft, the other's a shooting. You're to spend the next day or so on those. Report to me once you've cleared both. And leave Patrick Coughlin and the rail yard alone."

Not as bad a punishment as he'd expected, but it still left Hanley feeling hollow.

# THIRTY-FOUR

Ezra's fury drove him on an aimless walk away from the school through Chicago's streets. The hot, stinking air choked his lungs, and the noise of people and traffic grated on his ears. Always before, when anger gripped him like a fever, a long walk had simmered him down. Not this time.

He took a swig from the bottle he held, bought from the first ten-cent saloon he'd stumbled across. Cheap whiskey burned his throat. Near a third gone by now. He'd meant to buy himself and Nat a meal while they talked things over someplace quiet and decent. So much for that. He coughed, wiped his lips on his sleeve, and kept moving.

A white man. Holy God, a *white* man. Raising *his* boy. Taking *his* place. *Papa Aaron...* Another gulp of liquor couldn't wash away the thought. It clawed at him, sharp with anger and guilt. He'd ruined everything. Nat had gone inside the school with his stepfather, left Ezra standing like a fool in the street. He hadn't even glanced back when Ezra called his name. What chance, what hope, was there now for building any kind of life with his son—here in Chicago, out West, anywhere?

A choking sob rose in his throat. He jammed a fist against his teeth to keep it back. The pain of bitten knuckles cleared his head long enough for him to notice the averted gazes and hurrying footsteps of passersby. White, all of them. Where in hell had he gotten himself to? Despite the muggy heat, a chill rippled through him. He wasn't safe here. What if some white went to the police, reported the lunatic Negro wandering around? He halted in the middle of the boardwalk, stomach churning with rotgut and nerves. What if Aaron had reported him for assault?

Thunder rumbled, close. He looked around. Gray clouds covered the sky. His gaze took in weathered frame buildings, rundown brick ones, worn cobblestones dotted with horse manure. A swirl of wind brought odors of mud and dead fish. Must be close to the river, though he couldn't see it. Dust devils and a torn handbill scudded down the street. He'd no notion where he was, except he was far from home. The word stuck in his craw. Chicago wasn't *home*. No place was. Or would be, now.

Noise erupted a few yards behind him—a shout, the shriek of hinges, a heavy thud on the wooden boardwalk. "And don't be comin' back!" someone yelled in a thick Irish brogue.

Brief silence followed, broken by a muttered oath. Then two words cut through the air and Ezra's brain like lightning through deadwood. "Hey! Darky!"

Ezra turned around. A white man, burly and bearded, glared at him from several feet away. Above the man's head, a wooden sign sticking out over the walk read *Jacky O'Toole's*, with a crude drawing of a liquor bottle—the saloon the fellow had just been thrown out of. Ezra's heart pounded against his ribs. A drunk, angry white man spoiling for a fight. And here Ezra was, a perfect target.

*Run,* said the sensible portion of his mind as the white man strode toward him. From deep inside came, *Why? Got nothing to live for.* Ezra stood his ground, his grip tightening on the bottle in his hand.

The drunkard reached him. The smell of liquor rolled off the man like a stinking fog. Red faced, he spat his next words inches from Ezra. "The hell you doin' on *my* street, boy? Hereabouts is for *decent* folk. You get your darky ass gone!"

Fool that he was, Ezra shook his head. The drunkard threw a punch, landing a hard blow on Ezra's shoulder. Ezra staggered back, then slammed the whiskey bottle against the man's jaw.

Glass shattered. The drunkard hit the boardwalk. Blood welled from cuts across his cheek. He shook his head as if dazed, then started to rise. Beyond him, the saloon door opened. Two more white toughs came out. They caught sight of Ezra and the drunkard and charged.

Ezra made it a dozen steps before they beat him down.

✧

He woke to rain, gentle on his battered body. Clothes soaked, every inch of him hurting. Taste of blood harsh on his tongue, each breath like knives at his rib cage. Was he dead? Maybe he was, and this was hell.

Thunder. He remembered that. Couldn't hear it now. He lay in the wet street for what felt like forever, too racked with pain to move. Storm must've saved him. Second chance? Maybe. He had to get up. Get home and sober and patched up some, then back to Mantern School. Catch Nat leaving, fix things between them. If he could just get *up*…

Rough hands rolled him over. He bit back a grunt of pain, glimpsed a copper star on blue cloth. Above it, blond hair, white skin. "*Scheisse*," the policeman said. He knelt, slid a brawny arm under Ezra's shoulders, and hauled him upright. "Come on. We go to the station."

✧

Hanley was heading for the squad room to write up preliminary notes on the theft case when Rolf Schmidt came through the stationhouse doors with a Negro in tow. Big and muscular, the fellow moved as if drunk, or in pain, or both. He was mumbling loud enough to be heard across the lobby. "Tired of running…free man…got no *right*…" His voice rasped, as if someone had punched him in the throat.

Rolf tugged on the Negro's arm, herding him toward the hallway that led to the holding cells. "Quiet, you. Come on." To the desk sergeant he called, "Anybody in holding? Fella's drunk, got beat up near Jacky O'Toole's. Needs to sleep it off before we move him to the Negro jail at the Armory."

161

The sergeant gave Rolf a sour look. "Holding's empty right now. Guess you can put him there, if he don't stay long enough to stink up the place too bad."

"Not goin' to jail—" The Negro tried to pull away and flinched. His breath hissed between his teeth.

Rolf took a firmer grip. "Fighting get you nothing but hurt some more. Don't want that, *ja?*"

The fellow stood still, head and shoulders bowed, as if spent beyond endurance. Whatever was weighing on him, Hanley felt it from several feet away. Then the man gathered himself and looked up. Hard determination gleamed in his eyes. "No jail. I've done no wrong."

"*Ja*, jail," Rolf answered as Hanley started toward them. "Then police court, unless you got somebody to bail you out." The patrolman's skeptical tone made clear what he thought of that.

The Negro's reply surprised them both. "John Jones. Cook County Commissioner." He gritted his teeth as if against a fresh surge of pain, and Hanley noticed a bleeding gash on one of his hands. "Get me paper. Write the note myself."

෨

Writing to Jones—the fellow's employer, he said curtly when Hanley asked—seemed to ease him a bit. After handing the note to a runner, and watching the runner leave the station, he finally allowed Rolf to lead him to a holding cell. Curious about his presence, apparently inebriated, in a rough area by the river where a man of his color was a walking target for white toughs, Hanley lingered by the lobby desk until Rolf came back alone. "So what happened? Did he tell you what he was doing, drinking around here in the middle of a workday?"

Rolf nodded to the desk sergeant, who produced a logbook. "He don't tell me anything, not even his name. Just kept saying, *got no right*." He flipped the book open, uncapped the fountain pen tied to it, and began writing the particulars of the arrest. "Jacky O'Toole sent a guy to find me, said get rid of the darky by his place. Bad for business. I get there, O'Toole's by his own door, waiting to see if I show. Little ways past him I see that fella, laid out and soaking wet from rain. Brown glass all around. Somebody broke a bottle. Maybe him, maybe who worked him over. O'Toole just wants him gone, don't know nothing 'bout any fight must've happened on the street. Didn't see, didn't hear." Rolf snorted at that. "Whiskey stink everywhere. Whoever beat him, long gone. Lucky that fella's alive." He closed the book and slid it back to the desk sergeant. "Goin' back out. Put him in the next wagon to the Armory if bail don't come by then, *ja*? Maybe he sobers up a little before he gets on it."

# THIRTY-FIVE

L et me see you home, Fraylin." Moishe hovered in the doorway between the schoolroom and the tailor shop. He hefted something, and she saw it was an umbrella. "The rain is coming down again. You will need this."

And Moishe came with it, of course. Rivka tightened the strap around the stack of readers in front of her, only four now. She'd lost another student last week. Soon she'd have no one left to teach.

She bit her lip to squelch rising anxiety. "I can't take you away from your work, Reb Zalman."

"Reb Nathan says he can spare me for a little while."

She picked up the books and held them close like a shield. "The rain is not so bad. I'll be fine on my own." Her last words were nearly drowned out by a staccato rattle of raindrops on the shop roof.

"Rivka." The tenderness in his face and voice brought a pang of guilt. "Don't shy away from me. I want only what is good for you."

"But you don't know what is good for me."

"I know you and your books should not get soaked on the way home." He held out one arm toward her. "It is only a little walk. Will you come?"

Saying *no* to that earnest face, those bespectacled eyes full of hopeful entreaty, was impossible. So was going with him. *Walking out*, as people put it. The more they were seen together, the more inevitable certain things became. There was no use hiding from it. What was she going to do, anyway? Wait in the schoolroom until the rain stopped, whenever that might be? And what about tomorrow, the next day, or the next? With a little sigh, Rivka let him shepherd her out of the room.

The summer rain smelled fresh and clean, and a brisk wind ruffled Rivka's kerchief as Moishe opened the umbrella over them both. They went around the shop and headed north. Her scalp itched, and she wished she could strip her kerchief off for a good scratch. She didn't dare, here on the street where anyone might see. Here with Moishe beside her.

They traveled most of the block in silence. She was aware of Moishe mainly through his footsteps, a solid rhythm on the boardwalk not quite matching her own, and his outline in her peripheral vision. Soon they would pass the Nathans' house and then be at her own door. Five minutes had never felt so long. What would Moishe say to her? He must mean to say something, or he wouldn't have suggested this. If he pressed her for an answer about their marriage…she swallowed, her mouth gone dry. He wouldn't. Not yet. He'd promised to give her time, and Moishe was a man of his word.

When he finally spoke, he surprised her. "Is it so awful, the thought of being my wife? Because I don't understand why."

So bewildered, he sounded. They reached the corner, and she briefly closed her eyes. "I'm sorry. I don't mean to hurt you." She couldn't tell him how trapped she felt, how weighed down by expectations. His, everyone's. How much she wanted free of them, wanted something else. Some*one* else. *Don't think it. It can't be.* "I don't know. I don't know what I'm saying."

"Then…there is hope yet? Is this what you are telling me?"

She could hear in his voice, see in his thin face with its scraggly reddish beard, how much he wanted it to be true. And why shouldn't it? Because she was stubborn and foolish, with her yearning for the impossible that she scarcely dared name. "I don't know why you want me," she said without thinking. "Especially now."

He looked startled at her bluntness, then nodded. "Because of Aaron's goyische wife, you mean? Aaron is a good man, and his wife seems a good woman. Hashem will judge more clearly than we can, and it will blow over anyway, once they are gone." His expression shifted, still serious but a touch shy now. "You're not like other girls. You never back down from anything. I saw it last spring, when you stood up for

Aaron and his family. And when those men came to the tailor shop and threw stones at us. I don't know anyone so brave, except for my mother, and that was only after my father died. Are you surprised I should love you for it?"

*Love.* She hadn't expected that word, felt flustered that he'd said it. "I doubt Fray Zalman will love me for it. I say things I shouldn't, I get into trouble, I hate keeping house, I can barely make a decent loaf of challah. You'd be miserable."

He drew in a breath, then raised a hand and brushed his fingers across her cheek. She froze. Looking amazed at his own daring, he let his hand fall. "I honor my mother. But I am my own man and will make my own choice." A pause, weighted with hope. "Have you made yours, Rivka?"

She could barely manage, "Not yet." His own choice, where she had none. The unfairness of it hit her in the pit of her stomach. "We should go on," she said when she could trust her voice. "I'll have supper to start soon."

He sighed and fell into step beside her. Gazing down the street as they walked on, she could see where the three branches of the Chicago River came together. She could see Lake Street Station, on its little patch of ground where the river turned toward the lake shore. Hanley would be there, working at his desk. Or out in the city, talking to people and tracing some crime, far from Market Street. Had he truly meant what he'd said that night in May when he walked her home from the dance? That he'd played that heart-aching fiddle tune, "If Ever You Were Mine," because he was thinking of her? She thought so, but…

*What if I'm wrong?*

As they reached her house, Moishe laid a hand on her sleeve. "You must decide before your brother leaves. Whatever I can do to help you make the right choice, I will."

She managed a nod, then fled inside as if for shelter from a storm. But there was none to be had.

☙

166

The cell at the Armory stank like the slave quarters at the sugar plantation—a foul mix of old sweat, piss and shit, and dead hope. Ezra breathed shallowly even though it made him dizzy. His skull pounded like a drum. Or was it fever, that feeling? He knew the signs. Floating head, heat in his skin, taste like swamp water at the back of his tongue. Ague? Fear crawled up his spine. He could die of it here, and who'd care?

Damn, his head hurt. All that liquor he'd drunk...*how long ago? Can't remember....* He swallowed and fought the urge to spit, afraid of heaving his guts into the flea-ridden straw that covered the dusty floor.

"You ain't lookin' too good." Rumbling voice, flat Chicago accent. Ezra blinked, struggled to focus. His cellmate eyed him from a corner. Scrawny, hard faced, blacker than he was. "What they git you for? Drunk? Not havin' no place to go?" He frowned. "Va-gran-cy. Fancy word for walkin' down the street mindin' your own business till somebody don't like it. Then they grab you up, throw you in here."

Ezra licked his dry lips. "I'm not much for talking. Sorry."

The vagrant shrugged. "That's fine. You stay the night, they give you beans in the morning. Ain't too bad, you don't mind a few dead flies in 'em."

Nausea surged. Ezra fought it down. "Thanks for the warning." He glanced around the cell, spied a rough-hewn wooden bench against a wall. He gestured toward it. "You want...?"

"Naw." The vagrant shook his head. "Tried it first time they put me here. Got splinters in my ass. Floor's better."

Too exhausted to care, Ezra stretched out on the bench, his head at the end farthest from the slop bucket. Did white prisoners get to go take a piss or a crap in an outhouse, or did they get buckets too? His cut hand throbbed. He should probably feel grateful he wasn't dead. Hah. Only beaten near to it, and now he was stuck in this pesthole. For how long? Long enough to kill him, maybe, if he really was ill and not just hungover all to hell. Fresh fear jolted him. What if he wasn't released until *after* Ada and Nat left town? He'd likely never see his son again. He took slow breaths until the clawing panic in his gut receded. After a time, his aching head and body, the hard wood beneath him, and the stench in his nostrils drifted away into darkness.

Next thing he knew, someone was shouting over the jangle of keys and the scrape of metal. "Get up, boy! You're leaving. Not *you*, Skinny. The big one." The cell door creaked open as he sat up, wincing, and turned to face whoever had entered. The turnkey, a pock-faced white man with untidy hair and a stained shirt, jerked his head toward the open door. "Go on, git. Hurry up. I ain't got all night."

John Jones must've paid his bail. Gratitude and guilt washed through Ezra. He stood, moving cautiously against ripples of pain. "What about my arrest?"

"Don't know, don't care." The turnkey spat into the sawdust. "You gittin'? Or you so dumb you *like* jail?"

"Gonna miss the beans," the vagrant muttered. "'S all right. More for me."

Shaky legged, Ezra walked out. The cell door clanged shut behind him.

Outside, it was near dark. Must be well past supper time. Traffic was scant, on foot and in the street. Ezra lingered on the boardwalk, getting his bearings. Sleep had done him no good. He still ached all over, and his gut felt like a hollow tree. Too bad he had no money—it was long gone with the thugs who'd jumped him. He could do with some grub. Where was he, exactly? A lamppost beckoned at the corner, maybe fifty yards away. Something to lean on while he worked out what cross streets it stood at, and how far a walk Mrs. Kelvin's boardinghouse might be from here. He was so goddamned tired...

Nat's face floated into his mind—the boy's shocked stare after Ezra gutpunched his stepfather. He thought of Ada, and a sick shudder ran through him. God knew what Aaron had said to her about the morning's confrontation. She'd never let him see Nat again, must regret having told him about the boy. They were going west to homestead. How soon? How long did he have?

He clenched his fists. Fresh pain shot through his injured hand, reminding him he was alive. While he was alive, he had hope. Not much, but better than none. *Get home. Rest up. Then go find my boy.* What should he say when they met again? He'd figure it out when the moment came.

He drew a slow breath, gathering strength, then jumped half out of his skin at a footstep nearby. "Easy now," someone said, with a touch of Irish lilt. "I won't hurt you."

Dry mouthed, every muscle taut as wire, Ezra looked around. A white man stood a few feet from him. A stranger. Ezra's head swam. He closed his eyes and willed himself to stay upright, ready to run. "Who are you? What do you want with me?"

The Irishman smiled, his eyes shrewd and hard. "I've business with you. You have something *I* want. Let's take a little walk, you and I."

# THIRTY-SIX

*August 1, 1872*

By the end of the day on Wednesday, Hanley had settled the two cases to the satisfaction—such as it was—of all parties involved. He stopped by Lake Street early Thursday morning and added to his case notes, then headed upstairs toward Sergeant Moore's office. *Every "i" dotted and every "t" crossed, as a sign I've learned my lesson.* Then more sober thoughts intruded. Moore was right, he couldn't afford to cut corners and trust his luck to make things come out well. Not if he wanted promotion. *Senior detective gets a rise in pay. With more money, I could buy lumber for a house. Build a home for—*

He cut the thought off, afraid to give it shape. Useless anyway, when he couldn't even see Rivka alone for two minutes, thanks to her guard dragon of a brother. He shook his head, like a dog shaking off rain. He'd a report to give and a murder case to take up again. He schooled his face and walked into Moore's office.

The chief of detectives glanced up, his expression easing as he recognized Hanley. "Thank God it's you. I'm in no mood to deal with that ignorant fool Chamberlain again. Thinks he's too good for the case he got. Had the nerve to tell me he didn't see why he should be bothered about a dead Negro." Moore shook his head, dismissing the thought. "So. The theft complaint?"

Hanley drew himself straight, as if for a military report. "Two spinster sisters, Elspeth and Tansy Gordon. Sixty-one and fifty-nine, respectively. Miss Tansy Gordon took their fine china teapot to show it off to a neighbor, set it down while chatting with said neighbor, and managed to leave it behind. Don't ask me how one forgets a teapot. Miss Elspeth Gordon swore out the complaint to teach her a lesson, 'a sad duty that often falls to the eldest in a family.'"

Moore pursed his lips, a glint of humor in his eyes. "And?"

Hanley kept his face straight. "The neighbor brought the teapot back just as Miss Elspeth finished explaining the…unusual…circumstances. Tansy Gordon took the chance to berate her sister, starting with, 'I *told* you!' and not letting up. When I left, they were bickering like two sparrows fighting over a scrap of stale bread."

"And the shooting?"

"That was in the Hairtrigger Block. Alderman Whitman's son suffered a graze wound to his scalp. The young fool wasn't involved in the gunfight, just unlucky to be seated at a gaming table nearby, and too witless to duck. All the witnesses agreed on who the culprit was and were only too happy to tell me where to find him. It was one of my easier arrests."

"This is all in your notes, of course."

"Every bit. Anything else you'd like me to tackle, sir?"

A snort of laughter. "Go on, Frank. Get back to your murder case. Just use your head and tread lightly where Coughlin is concerned."

❧

Hanley's first order of business was to follow up on the possibility that Mahoney was the one who'd killed O'Shea. The alibi provided by the man's fellow rail yard workers and their night out at Cleary's was a stumbling block that needed dealing with.

He arrived at Cleary's just before ten, determined to accomplish *something* on the O'Shea case. At the bar, he greeted Gabe Cleary and ordered coffee and a roll. When the saloon keeper set them in front of him, Hanley asked, "The men Mahoney played cards with a couple of weeks ago, July thirteenth. The Norwegians, the ones I asked about when I was here Monday night. Any chance you'd know where I can find them?"

Cleary nodded. "Here, as it happens. Saw 'em come in a little bit ago. No work today, apparently." He glanced past Hanley, around the crowded room. "There. Front corner."

Hanley followed his gaze. Two bearded giants in checked flannel shirts, one forest green, the other dark blue, dwarfed the table where they sat with a foaming beer glass each. Green Shirt shuffled a deck of cards, while his companion looked on. "They speak any English?"

"Enough to order food and drink." Cleary gave Hanley a wry grin. "Good luck. You'll need it, I'm thinking."

*Luck of the Irish. That'd be useful.* Coffee in one hand and roll in the other, Hanley ambled over to the two Norwegians. "Mind if I join you?"

Blue Shirt looked up, blank incomprehension on his face. Green Shirt frowned, more in puzzlement than annoyance, and stilled the cards between his hands. "Irish, you?"

"American. Irish born."

Green Shirt pursed his lips. "No play with Irish. Last one cheat." He shifted in his chair, angling a shoulder toward Hanley. The gesture said *Go away* more clearly than words.

"It's that fellow I want to ask you about." Hanley sat down at their table, prompting startled looks from both Norwegians. "Mahoney's his name. You played faro with him a bit over two weeks ago. A Saturday night."

Green Shirt was looking lost now, as well as irritated at Hanley's intrusion. Silently, Hanley cursed the limits of language. He knew not a word of Norwegian, and English clearly wasn't Green Shirt's strong suit. He dug out his badge. "Detective," he said, tapping his chest. "Hanley. I want to know about the Irishman who cheated you."

At the sight of the badge, Green Shirt's eyes widened. Then he scowled and shook his head. "No. No cop. Don't want trouble. You go."

"I just—"

Green Shirt jerked his head toward the saloon at large. "We play now. You go."

Hanley weighed his options. A wary Green Shirt watched him for a few seconds, then pointedly started dealing cards as if Hanley wasn't there.

Hanley bit into his roll, washed the mouthful down with coffee, and pulled out his sketchbook. A few minutes' work was all he needed, the scratch of the pencil on paper oddly soothing amid the rising voices and laughter as more customers entered the saloon. When he was finished, he laid the drawing he'd just made of Grace O'Shea in front of Green Shirt and lightly tapped her penciled cheek. "Widow," he said quietly. "Husband dead. Killed." He drew a finger across his throat, a gesture he hoped was universal. "I find who killed him. You can help." He waited, his gaze locked on Green Shirt's face.

Sympathy warred with the guarded look in the big man's eyes. Thank God he'd understood, at least enough for Hanley's purposes. Green Shirt brushed the sketch with his fingers. "Don't know nothing," he said, but he sounded uncertain.

"Saturday." Hanley held up two fingers. "Two weeks ago. You play cards with three Irish. Sully, Rourke, Mahoney…"

At the names, recognition flashed across Green Shirt's face. "Mahoney. He cheat. Not first game. After."

"Tell me about Mahoney."

"No trouble for us?"

"No trouble." Hanley allowed himself a grim smile. "Trouble for Mahoney, maybe."

Green Shirt's answering grin was cold as snowfall. "What you want to know?"

"What time was Mahoney here? Did he ever leave the saloon during your game?"

"We play," Green Shirt said, nodding toward the dog-eared card deck beneath his thick fingers. "Me—Aksel, my brother Gottmar." He pointed to Blue Shirt. "And cheat Mahoney, two more Irish. Bet small to start. Bigger when we drinking more, *ja*?" At Hanley's nod of understanding, he continued. "Mahoney play, not long. Half hour, maybe. Then stop. Cards on table, like this." Aksel slapped down a five-card hand, hard enough that one pasteboard rectangle fell to the floor. "Say, bets too small. He come back when we play for real. Then he leave."

"Leave the table? Or the saloon?"

"Leave. Outside." Aksel gathered the five cards and shoved them into the deck. "Back door, like he go for a piss. Only he don't come back soon. Don't come back for *long* time."

"How long?"

Aksel spoke rapidly to Gottmar in Norwegian. Gottmar replied, his voice soft but definite. Aksel translated, a somber look on his face. "Gottmar get more beer. Clock over there, up high." He waved toward the bar, where Cleary was merrily serving his morning customers. "Say almost nine. Back door open right then, Mahoney walk in. Right past us, go get himself whiskey." Aksel clicked his tongue against his teeth. "That some damn long piss, I think."

It certainly was, as confirmed by Gabe Cleary. "I did see Mahoney get up, now you mention it," he said, frowning slightly in an apparent attempt at fuller recall. "He said something about the betting, but I didn't catch what. And he didn't seem worked up. Offhand, if anything. Why it slipped my mind, must be. Not like the night before last, when he set off a regular donnybrook. Lost all his cash and couldn't take it, mad drunk as he was. I had to call the police, have him hauled off." Cleary shrugged. "The place was damned busy that Saturday you're asking about, I'll tell you. I didn't see if Mahoney went outside or not. I'd have thought nothing of it if he had."

"What time did he leave the card game that night?"

"Bit after eight. No more than a quarter past."

Half to three quarters of an hour he'd been gone, then. Plenty of time to nip back to the rail yard, lure O'Shea out of the office, crack his skull with the scale weight, and dump him in the river. Time even for a quick washup, if he'd gotten hit by any of O'Shea's blood. Then back to Cleary's Saloon, a shot of whiskey instead of another beer. He could have slid back into the card playing like nothing happened. *And for it he gets the week's salary in O'Shea's pocket plus whatever Coughlin promised him. All right…how to prove* that *part of it?*

He'd no answer for that problem yet, but he trusted one would come to him. For now, it seemed good luck enough that Mahoney was probably still in town, since he'd no reason to think Hanley suspected him for O'Shea's murder.

# THIRTY-SEVEN

Breakfast had been a silent affair, no one speaking beyond requests to pass the milk for porridge and coffee. Things had been like this since Monday evening, but no one said a word as to why. *Something happened*, Rivka thought uneasily, not for the first time. Something to do with Nat, from the boy's subdued look and his anxious glances at Ada and Aaron. Nat and Ezra, Rivka guessed, recalling the nighttime conversation she'd overheard. When he caught the boy eyeing him, Aaron smiled as if to reassure, but the strain in his expression had the opposite effect. By the time Nat and Aaron left for school and work the tension in the kitchen was thick as coal smoke.

Ada was taking a rare day off, using the time to prepare for the upcoming trip west. She and Rivka were spending the morning sorting through clothing together, deciding what needed to be mended or altered before being packed and what would be sent to the ragman.

They'd been working for a couple of hours when someone banged sharply on the front door. Startled, Rivka clutched at the shirt she was folding. "Who on earth?"

Across the kitchen table, Ada's worried gaze met hers. The banging came again, louder. Rivka set the shirt down and went to answer.

"Police," said the burly stranger on the front step. Brown hair and unkempt mustache, wrinkled shirt and trousers instead of a uniform. Only the badge pinned to his chest confirmed what he was. He loomed over her, a stern look on his face. "Does"—he eyed a notebook in his hand—"Ada Kelmansky live here?"

"I…" Rivka's voice sounded faint in her ears. *A detective looking for Ada? Why?*

The stranger stepped forward. "I'll just have a look around—" He broke off, gazing past Rivka's shoulder. "Well," he said with quiet satisfaction. "Well, well."

His tone made her skin prickle as Ada stepped up beside her. "I'm Ada Kelmansky. How can we help you?"

"I need a word with you. Down at the station."

"If this is about what happened the other day—"

"It is. It most surely is."

Ada gripped her apron. "My husband doesn't want to press—"

"Don't know what your husband's got to do with it. Yet." He eyed Ada up and down in a way that made Rivka cringe. Beside her, Ada went still as ice.

Three heartbeats of silence. "I need to be here when my son gets home from school, sir," Ada said.

"Not today."

"I'll come with you." Rivka flashed the stranger a challenging look. "Detective Hanley knows us. We'll speak to him when we get there and straighten this out."

The detective snickered, a puff of air through the nose. "You do that. Let's go."

☙

The detective wouldn't answer questions, or even give his name. By the end of the first block Rivka quit asking. At the station, he led Ada to the squad room. Rivka followed. A breath of hope died in her chest when she saw Hanley's empty desk. He must be out on a case. Still, whatever this was, and no matter the strange detective's unpleasant manner, they would surely be home before long.

The detective grabbed Hanley's straight-backed chair and dragged it next to his own desk, then gave Ada a brusque nod. "Sit." She perched on the edge, her spine stiff with anger or fear. Her closed expression

177

made it hard to judge. He ignored Rivka. "Now. Let's talk about what happened the other day."

The twitch of Ada's fingers around her string purse betrayed her nerves. "As I said before, sir, my husband doesn't want to—"

"Do you know an Ezra Hayes? Lately a resident of Chicago, at Mrs. Kelvin's boardinghouse on Twelfth Street?"

Stone faced, Ada said, "Why are you asking?"

"Do you know him?"

Ada stayed silent. Then, as Rivka opened her mouth to speak, "Yes."

"How?"

"From work. At Mr. John Jones's cleaning and tailoring establishment." She paused, as if weighing her next words. "Is Mr. Hayes in some kind of trouble?"

"You could say that." He folded his arms and gazed down at her, clearly savoring the moment. "He's dead."

Color drained from Ada's face. Her spine sagged, and she closed her eyes. Through her own shock, Rivka saw tears rimming Ada's eyelids. She moved forward and wrapped an arm around the other woman's shoulders. Ada leaned into the hug.

"I'm...sorry to hear that," Ada said after a moment in a hoarse whisper.

"Not going to ask how it happened? Or when?" The big detective was almost smiling now. "Or maybe you don't need to. Given your... connection to the deceased."

Ada's face looked frozen. "I would like to go home."

"Not yet. How do you know Hayes? Besides work."

Rivka drew a sharp breath. "Leave her alone. She has nothing to do with—"

"Officer Hawkins!" the detective shouted. The desk sergeant appeared in the squad room doorway. The detective jerked his head at Rivka. "Get this girl out of here."

Resignation flitted across the sergeant's face. "Yes, sir." He walked over to Rivka. "Best you come quietly, miss."

"No. I will wait here for Detective Hanley. When do you expect him—"

"I'm sorry, miss." Hawkins reached for her arm.

She backed away. "I won't go, I can't—" Her gaze met Ada's. "I can't leave you here. I—"

"I'll be all right." Ada's expression belied her words. "It's some misunderstanding. I'll be home before you know it."

"Miss," Hawkins said, more firmly this time. "I don't want to lay hands on you, but I will if I have to."

He meant it. She could see it in his face. With a last worried glance at Ada, Rivka let him escort her out. Behind her, the detective was speaking again. "Now. What's your connection to Hayes…and what were you saying about your husband?"

෩

Rivka couldn't settle to anything as the day dragged on. The idea of teaching her English class—now down to just two girls—left her feeling overwhelmed. She dashed off a note to the Zalmans and one to the Kleins, canceling the afternoon's lesson. Half past one, two o'clock, two thirty. Aaron was out working whatever job he'd found for a day's wage. She didn't know where to start looking for him. At three o'clock she tied her kerchief over her hair and walked out the door, ready to search the streets and hope for good fortune, but the thought of Nat coming home to an empty house drove her back inside. And then she felt useless. What was she to do if Ada didn't come home? What to tell Nat and Aaron?

By three thirty, she was ready to claw the walls down. The soft flap of the mail slot startled her—the post had come an hour ago. She hurried to the front hall. A single folded sheet of paper lay on the floor, bright white against the wood.

She snatched it up. Her heart sank at the sight of her name across it in Ada's hand. Hesitantly, she opened it. *They are taking me to the Armory on suspicion of murder. Find Aaron. Don't tell Nat yet. Pray for me.*

She couldn't have said how long she stood there, staring at the words as they blurred in front of her. Her throat burned as she crumpled the paper into a ball. With a hard swallow and a murmured prayer, she dropped it and ducked into her father's study. One more note of her own, scribbled and stuffed in her pocket. Then she was out the door and heading toward Lake Street Station.

# THIRTY-EIGHT

Hanley's next move, after learning of Mahoney's absence from Cleary's saloon on the night of O'Shea's murder, was to determine the man's current whereabouts. A quick question at his own stationhouse confirmed his suspicion that, after his latest arrest Tuesday night, Mahoney had been released on Wednesday morning once he'd sobered up. The next likely place to find him was at the rail yard. But when Hanley arrived there and asked after him, Sully shook his head. "Damn fool didn't show up for work today, nor yesterday neither," he said, grabbing a cotton bale and heaving it off the scale bed. "Don't ask me why, 'cause I don't know. Still sleeping off a bender, most like."

Hanley thanked him and left. Mahoney's boardinghouse was on Putnam Street, a stone's throw from the river's North Branch. If the man was spending more than one day home ill from too much drink, he'd be easy pickings. Feeling hopeful, Hanley set off to nab his quarry.

❧

"He's not here," the landlady, Mrs. Nolan, said when Hanley arrived. "He's paid up, though, like always. All my lodgers are. Every two weeks in advance, or they're out. They know the rules." She reminded him of a schoolmarm, sharp faced and stern. He could imagine her bringing a wooden ruler down with a slap on some luckless pupil's tender palm. "Mind you, I've little complaint of Mr. Mahoney. He pays on time and doesn't bring fancy women here, even if he does drink too much. That's no worse than many. I'm sorry to lose him, and that's the truth."

Startled, Hanley said, "Lose him? But you just said he paid you in advance."

"He did." She shrugged, her brown stuff dress pulling taut over bony shoulders. "He was called away of a sudden, he said. Family problems. He didn't say what, or when he'd be back. Just packed his bag and left yesterday morning. Told me to keep the extra rent for my trouble at losing a lodger so abruptly."

Now *that* was unusual—a workingman like Mahoney being so free with his funds. Possible evidence that he'd gotten some kind of payout. It seemed the surly Irishman had gone to ground, likely with help. Hanley could guess whose, and why. "Did he say where he was going? Are his people in the city, or elsewhere?" There weren't any 'people,' he felt sure, but the man might have dropped some hint of his present whereabouts.

Mrs. Nolan pursed her lips. "He didn't tell me that, either. And I didn't ask. My business is hiring out rooms and collecting rent. I don't trouble myself with anything else."

Hanley bit back an oath. "If Mr. Mahoney comes by, or you hear from him, let me know. He witnessed a death at the Illinois, St. Louis and Grand Southern rail yard. The police need to talk to him."

&

Hanley returned to Lake Street and stood on the steps of the stationhouse, his shirt sticking to his back as the air grew hotter. He mopped sweat off his face and considered his next move. Why had Mahoney vanished? Had he gotten the wind up over Hanley's investigation after all, and left Chicago? If so, he was likely gone for good. But, if he'd decided to lay low instead, there was a chance Hanley could root him out. If he were Mahoney and needed to hide, where would he go?

The answer hit Hanley like a bolt between the eyes. *This time of year, it'd be easy. He could hide out in an empty freight car at the rail yard and wait for a chance to stow away on a train leaving for some far-off point.* Then came the disquieting thought—*Who says he hasn't done that already? How many freight trains leave that yard in a day, and him flush with whatever money he got from*

182

*Coughlin that he didn't lose at Cleary's or get taken from him in jail Tuesday night.*
*There's his grubstake for a new life wherever he ends up.*

Still, it was worth the chance. If he meant to nab Mahoney at the
rail yard, though, he'd need help. Where would Rolf Schmidt be now
on his beat? He lingered on the corner of Lake and Market, peering in
all directions. No sign of the big German patrolman. When he caught
himself looking for Rivka as much as for Schmidt among the passing
people, he made himself stop, and then eyed the sun. Past three, close
to four at a guess. They'd have to move fast.

As he reached the next corner, someone called his name. A voice he'd
heard in dreams almost every night since the ceilidh dance at the end of
May. He halted and turned. Rivka was hurrying toward him. "Hanley!
Thank goodness." She reached him, hands held out. Automatically, he
took them. She gripped his fingers, and he saw tears in her eyes. "Ada's
in trouble. They've taken her to the Armory jail. They think she killed
someone…a man named Ezra Hayes."

 confused

Hanley set a cup of coffee by Rivka's elbow. She'd composed herself
on the short journey to Lily Stemple's place, and now she glanced up at
him with concern in her face. "You're hurt. What happened?"

"It's nothing. An accident a week ago." He sat across the table from
her. He knew he should be heading to the rail yard but helping Rivka
had to come first. "Go on about Hayes."

"He's Nat's father, I think. I haven't met him. Ada and Aaron spoke
of him." Her cheeks pinked. "I didn't mean to eavesdrop. But their
room is next to mine, and…"

"And a detective thinks Ada murdered him? Why?"

"I don't know. I know they work at the same place. For Mister…"
She paused. "Jones. Yes. John Jones. The detective had me thrown out
before I could hear more."

Jones was a county commissioner. The Negro Schmidt had brought
in on Tuesday—he'd written Jones a bail note, said he worked for him.

"Is Hayes a Negro?"

"I think so. Why?"

"Did the detective give his name?"

"No." She shivered and cradled her cup as if for warmth. "He was a big man. Broad, like a barrel. Brown hair and a drooping mustache. Wrinkled clothes. His eyes were hard as stones."

Anger shot through him. "Chamberlain," he muttered. "He sent her to the Armory jail already, you said?"

She nodded. "She wrote a note. I was going to leave you one at Lake Street. I didn't know if—" She swallowed and pushed her chair back. "I need to find Aaron. But when I saw you, I thought…I wanted—"

"You did right to tell me." He knew she needed to hear it, so he said it, even as he reminded himself that Chamberlain's case was none of his business. Hayes must be the "dead Negro" Sergeant Moore had spoken of, that Chamberlain couldn't be bothered about. *Bastard. Didn't want the case to begin with, so he goes for whoever's convenient, to settle it fast.*

The anxiety in her face eased. "You'll help us, won't you? Whatever this man…Chamberlain…thinks, it can't be true. Ada wouldn't hurt anyone. Come with me, talk to Aaron, he'll tell you—"

The door to the eatery swung open. Rolf Schmidt stepped in and headed for the order counter. Hanley eyed him, then turned his attention back to Rivka. If he had any sense, he'd explain to her how things stood, but he was beyond sense where she was concerned. "Where's your brother now?"

"I don't know exactly. He takes odd jobs. But he can't be far. He would stay within walking distance of home, and there are plenty of building sites that need men to clear rubble…"

*Damn.* He couldn't spare the time for a goose chase. He needed to grab Schmidt and go after Mahoney before the man skipped. But he couldn't leave Rivka in the lurch. Why did it have to be Chamberlain's case? Hanley getting involved would only make things worse. Though they could hardly *be* worse for Ada Kelmansky.

Schmidt, waiting for a sandwich, spotted Hanley and nodded a greeting. Hanley waved back. "I can't come now," he said. "There's a man I have to find for the case I'm working. I'll drop by your house later."

"How much later?"

He thought fast. "I'm not sure. Could be an hour or two." God help him, he was really going to do this. Deep down he felt a warm glow at the thought of spending time in Rivka's company. Seeing her often, maybe every day.

She stood. "I'll tell Aaron. We'll be waiting."

# THIRTY-NINE

At the rail yard, Hanley and Schmidt bypassed the office. Mahoney, not Coughlin, was today's target. Hanley would tackle the rail yard boss later, after Mahoney spilled his guts. "What if he's not here?" Schmidt said in Hanley's ear as they walked along the meandering wooden pathway that skirted the busiest sections of the yard. Around them, the whistle-shrieks of arriving and departing trains mingled with men's shouts and the hollow clang of rail cars being loaded and unloaded.

Hanley pitched his voice above the din. "We'll check the holding area where the empty cars are. I'm thinking that's where he'd be holing up, in a boxcar or some such. We'll pick up a railway cop or two, search the cars until we find him."

The words had hardly left Hanley's lips when trouble approached in the form of Officer Walker. "You're trespassing," Walker said as he strode up to them, with a swift and dismissive glance at Schmidt. "Mr. Coughlin made it clear—"

"Mr. Coughlin doesn't tell me how to do my job. The police department does. Where's Liam Mahoney? Have you seen him today?"

"What do you want with him?"

"Questioning. About a murder."

Walker's eyes widened, but his scowl remained. "I'm sure that's nothing to do with the railw—"

Schmidt nudged Hanley. "That him? Big redhead over there?"

Hanley glanced where Schmidt gestured. Liam Mahoney was just darting out of sight between two freight cars.

Hanley swore. Schmidt's curse, in loud German, flew out a second afterward. The patrolman charged off in pursuit, Hanley right behind him.

"Stay on the walkways," Walker shouted. "You'll get yourselves killed otherwise." Hanley and Schmidt pounded onward, straining to keep Mahoney in sight as he dodged and wove through the chaos of the yard. The shriek of train wheels and brakes, the boom and crash of cars, the shouts and footsteps of hurrying men, blended into a fog of noise and motion. Mahoney was heading toward the empty car storage area. If he reached it, and Fourth Street beyond, they'd lose him.

Ahead of them, the walkway angled rightward. Mahoney hurtled around the turn and vanished. Hanley sped up. He skidded around the corner seconds later. No sign of Mahoney. His head throbbed and his side ached. He slowed, taking in more of the rail yard. Where the hell had Mahoney gone? Off the walkway? *The damn fool.* A switch engine pulling four cars moved slowly past, cutting off his view. He jogged forward, breathing hard, peering through gaps between the freights. There. A moving human shape, ten yards or so distant. The last car trundled past, clearing Hanley's field of vision. A chill spread from the pit of his stomach as he realized Mahoney was running across the tracks toward empty car storage…with another switch engine and its load bearing down on him.

Schmidt came puffing up. "*Hundesohn* going to kill himself!"

"He thinks he can beat it." Hanley watched in horror as Mahoney put on a burst of speed, angling to cross the track in front of the engine. Hanley charged ahead, desperately scanning the gap between himself and Mahoney. No more trains coming for the moment. He vaulted over the walkway railing. His feet struck packed dirt with a spine-rattling jolt. Sunlight glinted off the rails that covered the ground in front of him. He dashed toward Mahoney, knowing he'd be too late.

Mahoney jumped—not in front of the engine, but toward the first freight car. He caught hold, clung like a possum to its mother's back. Then he was climbing, up and over the top of the car. "Sonofabitch," Hanley muttered. The freights had ladders so the brakemen could climb up and down. Even as he watched, Mahoney scuttled over the car's roof and started down the other side. By the time the switch engine and its cars cleared enough space for Hanley to see beyond them, Liam Mahoney was gone.

Nearby, Schmidt stood bent over with his hands on his thighs, blowing like a winded horse. "Now what?" he said once his breathing slowed.

Hanley ran a hand through his hair and pulled in sheer frustration. "Nothing. Damn it."

☙

Hanley stopped at Lake Street a short while later to add to his case notes and down some rotgut coffee from the pot on the squad room stove, hoping the harsh brew would clear his head. It didn't help. He finished his coffee, set the empty mug on his desk, and pushed the O'Shea case—and the fiasco at the rail yard—from his mind as he left the station. Outside, dusk was falling. Rivka would be expecting him. In spite of everything, the thought of her put a spring in his step, and he let himself daydream as he walked southward. What were the odds of their stealing a moment together, maybe a kiss, before he spoke with—

*Aaron.* Who was also expecting him. The notion of dealing with Rivka's brother made Hanley grit his teeth. The man made no secret of wanting Hanley gone from Rivka's life, the sooner the better. That he needed Hanley would only make this evening more difficult. *High-handed son of a—*

With effort, he reined in his annoyance. What Aaron thought of him with regard to Rivka didn't matter. All that mattered was the help she'd asked for. If he could give it. He picked up his pace. Time enough to make that judgment after he spoke with Rivka's brother.

Rivka answered his knock, her eyes red rimmed and puffy. Relief, and something warmer, glimmered in her face at the sight of him. "Aaron should be here soon. I didn't find him earlier, he doesn't know…I had to come home, I didn't want Nat to…he's upstairs now, I haven't said a word about…" She bit her lip. "I'm sorry. Please, come in. I'm sure Aaron won't be long."

Hanley stepped over the threshold. Words tumbled through his brain—*Don't worry,* mavourneen, *it's all right, I'll fix everything.* Useless to say, no matter how much he wanted to. Useless as well to take her in his arms, though it almost hurt to hold back. But how would she respond to such a brazen act? He couldn't stand the thought of distressing her further. "I'm sure you're right," he said instead and followed her down the hall to the kitchen. The scent of chicken soup hung in the air, rich and comforting.

"I made supper. Nat ate a little. I'm keeping it warm for Aaron," Rivka said as she crossed to a steaming pot on the stove. He savored her grace as she moved, even as habit made him soak up other details of his surroundings. Carrot greens and onion tops lay in a bowl next to the sink. The polished wooden table in the center of the room held spoons and knives in a heap, a plate of bread in the middle. "I had to do something, I—" She clenched her fists around handfuls of skirt, then slowly uncurled her fingers. When she turned to face him, her eyes were overbright. "Would you like some soup? Unless you've eaten…"

*Alone together for the first time in months, and we're talking about soup.* The awkwardness of it made him want to laugh, but he recognized how much Rivka needed the semblance of normality just now. He could give her that, at least. "I haven't. Soup would be welcome." He picked up the silverware and began to lay the table. As he finished, he glanced up and saw Rivka watching him, ladle in hand.

He shrugged. "I helped my mother keep house until my sister was old enough. Some habits die hard."

A smile flitted across her face. Then she drew in a sharp, sobbing breath. The ladle clattered to the stovetop as she turned away—from him, or from the table with three places set instead of four.

He didn't think, just went to her. At his touch on her shoulder, she turned and burrowed against him. He cradled her close as she fought for composure. "It'll be all right, *acushla,*" he murmured. "You'll see."

A heavy tread sounded on the stairs outside. Hanley let go of Rivka, who quickly stepped away as the back door opened and Aaron walked in. Shock crossed the man's face at the sight of them standing less than an arm's length apart. Then his expression darkened. "Get out," he told Hanley. "*Now.*"

Hanley stood his ground. "Not until we talk, Mr. Kelmansky."

"Get out of my house or I'll throw you out!"

"*Er geyt nit avek!*" Rivka's tone was sharp as a blade. "*Es iz nit—*"

Aaron cut her off. Rapid-fire Yiddish flew between them. Hanley caught the name *Moishe*, saw Rivka blanch at a cutting phrase and fling a question back at her brother like a fistful of stones. Hanley's own temper flared, and he drew breath to defend her just as Rivka said Ada's name. That brought Aaron up short. A glimmer of uncertainty showed through his anger as he turned toward Hanley. "What about my wife?" He glanced around the kitchen, as if aware for the first time of Ada's absence. "Where is she? Has something happened to her?"

Hanley kept his tone calm. "I'm sorry, Mr. Kelmansky. There's no easy way to say this. Your wife's been arrested."

"*What?* Why? Did you…were *you* the one who—"

"No. But I know the detective who took her away. Miss Kelmansky found me and told me. That's why I'm here." *Miss Kelmansky. Acushla. My heart…*

"Took her away where? What for?"

"She's at the Armory jail. On suspicion of murder."

Aaron turned sheet white. He groped for a chair and held onto the back as if only his grip on it kept him from falling. He stared at Hanley, then at Rivka. His voice cracked as he asked, "Does Nat know?"

"I couldn't tell him." Abruptly, Rivka hurried toward the stove. "Let me get you some soup. You need to eat."

Aaron sank into the chair, hollow eyed as he met Hanley's gaze. "Who is Ada supposed to have killed?"

"A Negro named Ezra Hayes." Hanley took a seat nearby. "Tell me about Hayes and your wife. Miss Kelmansky said he's your stepson's natural father?"

"Yes." One word, clipped from fatigue, or embarrassment at discussing such private matters with Hanley. "Ada told me about him not long after we met, years ago when I was teaching with the Freedmen's

Bureau in Virginia. She and Hayes—" He pressed his lips into a thin line. "She cared for him. They were...together. On the plantation. Not married. It wasn't permitted." A hard swallow, visible against his throat. "Until Hayes was sold. Ada didn't know she carried his child. For thirteen years, she didn't know where he was. They met here in Chicago by chance a couple of weeks ago."

"At John Jones's tailoring establishment, I take it. Your sister told me." He paused, but Aaron said nothing.

Rivka spoke up. "Ada and Aaron are saving money to go west. They'll have enough before much longer." She set a bowl of soup in front of her brother, then another in front of Hanley.

He thanked her and picked up his spoon. "Did your wife tell Hayes about the boy, Mr. Kelmansky?"

Aaron had gone rigid, staring at Hanley's meal. Abruptly, he shifted his glare to Rivka and spoke sharply in Yiddish.

"Would you have our guest go hungry?" she snapped back.

"*Er iz nit*—"

"*Neyn, Aaron. Makh zikh nit narish.*" She turned to Hanley. "Please forgive my brother. He'll regain his common sense in a moment."

Aaron barked out a single Yiddish word. Rivka flushed as she held his gaze. "No. I *won't* hush. If you want to see Ada again, Aaron, then talk to Hanley. Tell him everything you can."

# FORTY

It was nearly eight thirty by the time Hanley, and then Aaron and Nat, left. A little more than an hour had gone by, yet Rivka felt as if she'd lived a year. She stood by the kitchen table, fists clenched against the well-scrubbed wood. She wanted to scream, but why bother? Aaron wouldn't hear.

*You will stay home*, he'd said. This *is your place. Not police stations and jails. We will give Ada your love.* And then he and Nat had departed, once Aaron made sure Hanley was well gone. No chance of Rivka being foolish again. Of forgetting her place. Or Hanley forgetting his.

She pressed her palms against the smooth pine. Anger warred with anxiety and confusion as other moments from the past hour circled through her mind, like the head and tail of a spinning coin. Hanley holding her, his arms warm and strong, murmuring comfort while her tears dampened his shirt. Then talking with Aaron, all his gentleness gone, coolly alert as a cat at a mousehole. *Was there some dispute over the boy? If Chamberlain somehow learned your wife and Hayes shared more than a workplace, that they have a son and a past—*

*There was no dispute. You have my word.*

*That's not good enough.*

No comfort in those last four words. None at all.

The need to move sent her around the table gathering dishes and silverware. The untouched soup went into a hastily fetched crock, the dirty bowls and spoons into the dishpan. She placed the brimming crock in the icebox that sat on one end of the kitchen counter. Wash water next. No...bread. Put the bread away first. Four slices on the plate. Aaron had taken the rest, two pieces wrapped in oiled paper, and given them to Nat who held them reverently like a *siddur* as he followed Aaron out the door. She recalled Hanley again, answering her question about what Ada might need. *They're not much for decent food at the Armory jail. Something to eat might be welcome. Only enough for tonight. And tell her to get rid of crumbs. They draw rats.*

Rivka shivered. Ada didn't belong in such a filthy, horrible place. Hanley had sounded gentle again, even regretful, when he spoke of her situation. Yet with Aaron, an underlying hardness that made her uneasy. *That's not good enough.*

A knock at the front door brought fear, sudden as a thunderclap. What now? The accusing detective, Chamberlain, come back to harass them? But why would he? Or perhaps Hanley had returned, to tell her… what? He hadn't been gone long. There was nothing he *could* tell her this soon. She wanted, and didn't want, to see him. He hadn't believed Aaron, had virtually said as much.

The knock came again, light but insistent. Maybe it *was* Hanley. Maybe she was wrong about him and Aaron, and he'd come to explain himself. She hurried down the hall. Never mind who saw her let him in, or what her brother would say. One look at Hanley's face and she'd know everything was all right.

His name died on her lips as she opened the door. "Moishe."

Hope lit Moishe's eyes, and she could have cursed herself for using his given name. "Rivka," he said with a shy smile. Then he sobered. "I have heard a strange thing…that a policeman came here today and took Aaron's wife away. Is it true?"

On edge all day, and now cruelly disappointed, the question was more than she could bear. Renewed anger swept through her. "You've *heard*? Who is saying this? Why are you listening to gossip?"

"Calm yourself." He said it with unexpected firmness and laid a hand over hers on the doorknob. "I put no faith in *lashon hara*. You must know that. I came to speak with Aaron. To ask if I can help."

"He isn't here." Her throat felt tight. Moishe's hand was too warm, too heavy. She slid hers out from under it. "He's gone to see Ada. I don't know when he'll be back."

"So she *is* gone, then." Moishe let out a breath. "What happened?"

"I…" Words failed her. "I don't want to talk about it."

"A hard thing, whatever it is. I can tell from your face. And you are alone, you and the boy." Moishe moved closer, crowding her, one foot on the threshold. "You should not be alone like this, Rivka. Someone should protect you, care for you—"

"I have Aaron. And Onkl Jacob." She felt a warning sense of something irrevocable looming. "Please, I must finish cleaning the kitchen. I'm sure Fray Zalman is expecting you home—"

"You are more important. Much more." He clasped her hand in both of his. "I know I said I would wait for your decision. But how can I wait when you need me? I cannot do it, Rivka. I love you too much. I will arrange things with Aaron tomorrow. And with Reb Nathan. All will be well soon. I promise."

*No.* She couldn't force the word out. She shut her eyes, unable to look at him. She wanted Hanley here instead, with a longing so fierce it stole her breath. Wanted him holding her close again, safe and beloved.

Moishe pulled her toward him. His lips brushed her kerchief, then moved down to her temple. As they touched her bare skin, she stiffened. He slid his hands up to her shoulders, tightening his grip. *"Mayn libe…"* His beard and the curve of his spectacles felt rough against her cheek. Then he released her. She stumbled backward and caught herself against the door frame. Moishe gazed at her, his eyes full of wonder. And something else, a sureness she hadn't seen in him before, as if he had laid claim to her.

"Goodnight, Rivka," he murmured. "I will come back tomorrow, before *minyan*. We can plan the wedding then." Finally, mercifully, he turned away.

She stayed where she was long after he left, too spent to move as the shadows deepened. The air, still warm from the day, felt like fog in her lungs. She stared down the street, but the boardwalk stayed empty. No one was coming.

# FORTY-ONE

*August 2, 1872*

S o how did Hayes die?" Hanley asked. He stood a few feet from Will Rushton, breathing shallowly through his mouth. Never a pleasant place, the morgue in early August was extra ripe with corpse stink.

The adjoining deadhouse held its typical summertime share—folk who'd succumbed to heat stroke or this year's cholera outbreak, hotheads killed by gunfire in the Hairtrigger Block, drunkards who went lake diving off a dock or the partly built breakwater and discovered too late that whiskey didn't magically enable them to swim. How did Will stand it day after day? The man must have a stomach and nerves of iron.

Will leaned against the table where he'd been working when Hanley walked in. The body of a young woman lay atop it, most of her decently shrouded in a plain white sheet. "Someone knifed him," Will said. "A small blade, about two inches, a single clean slice across the neck. I'd guess a pocketknife, but it could be a shorter fixed-blade. He was struck from behind first, with a rock or a chunk of brick, judging from the lump on his head. Only one blow. Fresh bruising on his face, and defensive wounds on his hands. He fought back before his killer slit his throat."

"A clean slice," Hanley murmured. "Someone used to handling a knife, then."

"Or any kind of blade. Knife, dagger, bayonet. Strong, too."

"Was the killer right- or left-handed?"

"Left-handed, from the angle and depth of the cut. That alone should help narrow your list of suspects." Will pursed his lips. "A bullyboy might carry a small blade, similar to a push knife. It'd be interesting to know if Hayes gambled, and if he won money off the wrong person. Maybe more than once. He had a lot of bruising, several hours older than the fresh marks and the slit throat. Someone gave him a real working over earlier on the day he died." He tilted his head. "He spent part of Tuesday in the Armory jail, you said?"

"Yes." Hanley described Hayes's appearance at Lake Street Station Tuesday afternoon, drunk and apparently the victim of Irish toughs from Jacky O'Toole's tavern. For the moment, he left out the man's connection to Ada, though he knew he'd have to get to it soon. He needed Will's unvarnished assessment of how Hayes died, and of Chamberlain's investigation thus far, but he couldn't conceal the truth for long. Will had a right to know. He'd be devastated, and furious, and desperate to help his sister. *Let him be spared that for a few more minutes.* "Schmidt booked him for disorderly conduct and vagrancy and sent him over. His employer must've paid his bail. He wrote to John Jones while at Lake Street and made sure the message went out before he'd let Schmidt put him in a holding cell."

"John Jones," Will said, with a cynical twist to his lips. "So that's why the detective squad cares about a poor darky getting knifed in an alley...because a county commissioner does. I'm not used to seeing your lot down here on a dead Negro's behalf. Certainly not Chamberlain, of all people."

The phrase *your lot* gave Hanley pause. He'd never heard Will use it before, never heard him separate himself from the rest of the police department that way. "There's something else," he said, choosing his words with care. "Ezra Hayes was...acquainted with your sister. He's Nat's natural father."

Will gaped. "Good God. Does Ada know he's dead? Does she even know he was in Chicago? She never mentioned...I mean, we don't meet much, I've gone to see her a few times since…" He stopped, and Hanley watched the blood drain from his face. "Don't tell me she's involved. Don't tell me Chamberlain thinks so."

Hanley reached out, then checked himself. Time was, he'd have bucked Will up with a clap on the arm and not given it a second thought. Regret for that loss, as well as for what he had to say, colored his tone. "I'm afraid he does. She's been at the Armory since sometime yesterday. Apparently, Chamberlain thinks she can handle a knife, and a fistfight, well enough to make a plausible suspect. When did he come here, and what did he ask you? What did you tell him?"

Will looked like he might sick up his breakfast. He gripped the edge of the work table. "It's not your case. What's your interest?"

"Miss Kelmansky asked for my help. I don't like rushes to judgment." His friend's pallor worried him. Will was taking it worse than Hanley'd expected, which was saying something. "Can I get you some water? Have you whiskey about?"

"I'll be fine. I—" Will gave a sharp headshake. "You've talked to Ada? Seen her? How is she? Has she said anything to anyone?"

"Don't know yet. I'm going to the Armory next. When did Ezra Hayes die? Where was he found?"

"I'll come with you." Will pushed away from the table, then went still with a bewildered look. "She'll need things…food, clean linen… what else?"

"Best wait till after I've talked with her. I can ask what she needs, then tell you. All right?" Something was eating at Will beyond the stark fact of his sister's plight. No time to tease it out now. Hanley waited for Will's reluctant nod. "Now tell me more about Hayes. Who found him, where, and when?"

Will drew in a breath. "Commissioner Jones. He came here with the body about half past ten Wednesday morning. He looked shaken up. Said he'd been to Hayes's boardinghouse to check on him, was looking for him when he saw what he took for a drunkard sleeping near the mouth of an alley. He went over, and…" Will ran a hand through his hair. "I got the sense he cared about Hayes. Beyond employer and employee, I mean. There was a friendship there, I'll wager. I don't know if that helps you."

Hanley nodded. He needed to talk to Jones, the sooner the better. "And Chamberlain?"

"He came here Wednesday afternoon. Asked the usual questions—how the man was killed, time of death, whether he died where he fell." Will let out another breath. "Which was in an alley off Thirteenth Street by State, about half a mile from the Armory. Not far from where he lived, I gather. Jones said he grew concerned when Hayes didn't turn up for work two days in a row. On Tuesday Hayes sent a note, claiming illness—but if Jones paid his bail that night, he'd have known that was a lie. Then, when Hayes didn't turn up on Wednesday..."

"What about time of death? And did anyone find the knife, or whatever he got hit with?"

Will shook his head. "No weapons nearby, from what Jones said. Rigor was leaving by the time I saw Hayes's body. Given the heat, even after dark...I'd guess he was dead for twelve hours at least, maybe as much as fourteen, when Jones ran across him. Jones couldn't give me an exact time, but nine a.m. is a good guess. Which puts Ezra's death sometime between seven and nine on Tuesday night, nine thirty at the outside. No later than that."

"And after he left the Armory, whenever that was." A question for the jailhouse sergeant when Hanley got there. He looked at Will again, and the thanks he'd meant to say died on his lips. Will stood with his hands clenched, anguish so raw in his face that Hanley felt it like a gut punch.

"Ada didn't do this," Will said. "A blow to the head hard enough to stagger a man, then a brawl ending in a slashed throat? The father of her child, killed so brutally...it makes no sense. Why does Chamberlain think she did it? Maybe it's those Irish toughs you should be looking for, the ones that beat Hayes up."

The same question—why Ada?—was bothering Hanley. Some quarrel over the boy, despite Aaron's denial, or something else from her and Hayes's past—but how did Chamberlain know of those things, let alone leap from them to murder? Presumably he'd gone from the morgue to Hayes's lodgings. Hanley would have. Had Chamberlain found something there? As to the rest, he didn't point out how far away Thirteenth Street was from Jacky O'Toole's saloon, or how conspicuous a gang of white men was likely to be in the Negro part of town, especially after nightfall. "I'll find out what happened."

Will swallowed. "Be careful. Please."

"Chamberlain's on his way out. Retirement. I can handle him." Hanley wasn't at all sure of that, but he wanted to sound confident for Will's sake.

"That's not what I meant. If Ada's investigated…other things might come out."

It took a moment before realization dawned. Hanley drew breath to offer reassurance, then shut his mouth. Who knew what Chamberlain would uncover, let alone what the man might do with it? "Bloody hell. I'm sorry, Will."

They looked at each other in silence. "I want my sister safe," Will said finally. "That matters most. But if you can keep me out of it?"

This time, Hanley obeyed the instinct of friendship and gripped Will's shoulder. "I'll do my best. I promise."

☙

The hot breeze outside the hospital brought Hanley the odor of horse manure from the surrounding traffic-choked streets. Not pleasant, but a welcome change from the morgue stinks of chemicals and death. The manure smell brought to mind his too-close encounter with Mike McDonald's omnibus ten days earlier. Who had shoved him in front of it? Maybe no one. Maybe it was an accident after all. He remembered the moments just before— the harsh whisper, *mind your business*, then two flat palms striking the small of his back. *No accident.*

The end of the line for Young's Omnibus Company wasn't far from here. Though McDonald was probably already busy hauling well-heeled travelers from hotels to passenger depots and vice versa. Still, it might be worth a quick trip before heading back north to

Harrison Street and the Armory. Maybe he'd be lucky, and the man hadn't started his shift yet.

McDonald was there, harnessing his horse, when Hanley arrived at the drafty barn on Wabash off Twenty-Second Street. He glanced up at the sound of Hanley's step and scowled. "I told you days ago, I didn't see who shoved you into the street. And I've not magically recalled anything since. So you can take your cop self off and go to blazes."

"Good afternoon to you, too." Hanley fished a fifty-cent piece from his pocket and held it out. "I've come to settle up for that omnibus ride. I owe you forty cents. Here it is, plus the value of my ten-cent piece you left lying in the street."

McDonald eyed the coin as if it stank of something worse than manure.

"Last chance," Hanley said. "You don't want it, that's your lookout. Either way, I've paid my debt. I just wanted to make clear that some of us do."

McDonald shifted his gaze to Hanley's face. "'Us' meaning coppers?"

"That's right."

Silence stretched between them. It crossed Hanley's mind to tell McDonald, *I know who you are.* Nagged by the pinprick of memory and the man's abrupt change from friendliness to hostility after driving Hanley home, he'd asked around at Lake Street. McDonald was a gambling prince, small time but ambitious to rise. Police had raided his establishments more than once in the past several years, even when he paid protection money. At the moment, he was between gambling hells, reduced to working for a living to pile up cash for another go. No wonder he hated cops.

McDonald gave a short laugh and plucked the coin from Hanley's palm. "No more'n what's mine, isn't it? Most folk wouldn't've bothered. You've a nerve on you, boyo, I'll give you that."

"So I'm told. We're square now. Pleasure doing business with you." With a wry salute, Hanley turned to leave.

He was two steps shy of the big double doors when McDonald called out to him. Hanley turned to face the man, eyebrows raised in question.

"You said to tell you if I remembered anything. Happens I do recall a bit. What it's worth to you, I don't know. Something, I'd guess."

Hanley moved closer. A little smile played around McDonald's mouth, and Hanley realized the gambling prince was enjoying this. *He's tossing out a fresh marker, putting me back in his debt. Or so he thinks.* "A description of whoever pushed me would be good. Though it would also mean you lied before about not seeing anything. You sure you want to confess to that?"

McDonald's laugh this time was genuine. "You *have* got a nerve. Must be the Galway in you. Like I said, I didn't see what happened. Mostly, my mind was on the fella my horse'd just kicked—that'd be yourself— and whether you were still breathing. But I did see something after."

"Which was?"

"A fella...ducked out of the crowd around where you fell and went hurrying away soon's you opened your eyes. Damned near running, like all the hounds of hell were after him."

*Coughlin?* "What'd he look like?"

"Big fella, kind of square, like. Not so tall as you. Plain clothes. And red hair."

*Mahoney. Christ.* Had Coughlin told him to...no, that didn't make sense. Hanley'd been investigating O'Shea's murder for what, a week, when Mahoney attacked him? He'd barely gotten past the first steps, hadn't settled yet on any suspects. How in blazes had he posed enough of a threat then for Coughlin—or Mahoney on his own—to resort to attempted murder? He clenched his fists, wishing Mahoney was here for him to pound the truth out of. God knew where the fellow'd gotten to now, little chance of nabbing him any time soon.

*Help Ada Kelmansky. Do something useful.* He thanked McDonald and left for the Armory jail, feeling as stymied as ever.

# FORTY-TWO

Which darky was it again?" The ruddy-faced officer in charge of the Negro jail at the Armory scratched his greasy scalp. A yard or so to his right, Hanley spied something small and many legged crawling across the floor. The officer turned his head, hawked, and spat, hitting the insect dead-on. "Damned deathwatch beetles. They're everywhere. Can't get rid of 'em, no matter what I do. What'd this feller looked like? Hell if I can figure one darky in here from another. All look the same to me, you want God's honest truth."

With gritted teeth and a silent prayer for patience, assuming the Almighty was bothering to listen, Hanley gave Ezra Hayes's name a second time and described him as best he could. "He was released late Tuesday afternoon or in the evening. John Jones paid his bail."

The officer frowned. "Jones? Naw. I know what *he* looks like. Seen his picture on 'lection posters for the county. He wasn't here Tuesday." The frown gave way to a thoughtful look. "Seems to me I recall a darky gettin' out that night, though. Older fellow, big in the shoulders, hurt his hand? I 'member a guy with a big old cut near his thumb, looked pretty fresh. From his face, it was still hurtin' him. Something surely was." He flipped through the logbook on the desk in front of him. "Tuesday, off the wagon from Lake Street…what in tarnation one of *them* was doing in your part of town, I don't know. Lemme see…"

"Drinking and getting beat up," Hanley said. "You're sure Commissioner Jones didn't spring him? Jones was his employer."

"I *tole* ya," the man said. "Jones didn't bail out nobody. But I found yer fella." One fat finger stabbed at a scrawled entry in the book. "Ezra Hayes. Patrol wagon driver signed him in at two, bail logged at twenty past seven. Turnkey told him he was free to go maybe ten minutes after that."

"You know where he went?" A fool's question, but Hanley asked anyway because you never knew. The officer gave him a skeptical look. "Who paid his bail, if Jones didn't?"

The man shrugged. "Some white fella."

"A white man?" A thrill of unease ran up Hanley's spine. "You have a name? What'd he look like?"

"Jimmy O'Rourke, he said. Dark brown hair, blue eyes…mustache, but no beard. Tall as you, almost, big in the shoulders like a railroad navvy. Map of Ireland on his face, as they say. Bit of a brogue, but he wasn't fresh off the train or anything."

*Coughlin?* The description certainly sounded like it could have been him. Relief and confusion flooded through Hanley. *So not Aaron. But why on earth would Coughlin be involved with Ezra?* "Thanks," he said. "I'm here to see a prisoner as well…Ada Kelmansky."

❧

The privy stench hit him first—an indignity the Negro jail shared with the one for whites, along with bad food and vermin-ridden straw on the dirt floor. Being here conjured memories of Hanley's own time in a cell this past winter, though he knew his skin itched because of sweat, not phantom lice. He shook off the feeling and searched the row of cells in the women's section for Ada.

She was in the fourth cell down, along with two other women. One lay on the floor, snoring as if sleeping off a binge. The second, with a weathered face and matted gray hair, huddled in a corner muttering to herself. She took no notice of him, or of Ada when Aaron's wife rose from the wooden bench and hurried toward the bars.

"Detective Hanley." Ada's face looked ashy, her eyes rimmed red. Her wrinkled dress told him she'd lain down at some point, but he doubted she'd slept. "Aaron said you'd come. Can you get me out? I want to go home…I need to go home."

Damn Chamberlain. This woman shouldn't be here. He answered gently to put her at ease. "I'm working on it. Will sends his love, by the way. If there's anything you need, I'll pass the word to him, and to your family."

"Oh, God." She closed her eyes. "I suppose he's part of this, isn't he? They'd have brought…Ezra's body to him, to…" She looked away, brushing straw from her hair. "I need to be with Nat. He…I saw his face last night, I…he only just met Ezra, and…" She pressed a hand to her lips. "I'm sorry. I just…I can't believe this is happening, *did* happen. There's no reason."

"About that." He moved closer to the bars. Ada clasped her hands as if she'd nothing else to hold onto, and he sensed the effort she was making not to break down. A quick glance around told him no one was paying them much mind, but he lowered his voice nonetheless. "I know you didn't do this. But you need to help me. The detective who arrested you—Chamberlain—wants shut of this case, the quicker the better. He's not stupid, but he might well be careless. That's our best hope. Tell me everything that happened from last Saturday to Tuesday, starting when Ezra Hayes met your son."

She answered slowly, as if marshaling her thoughts. "Saturday through Tuesday?"

"Yes. Everything involving Hayes and you…and your husband. What you said and did, where you all were." His fleeting fear that Ezra's bail payer might be Aaron had died the moment he heard the jailhouse officer's description. Still, Aaron hadn't told him the whole truth about Hayes and the boy. Hanley had felt it the other night but shied away from pushing too hard in Rivka's presence.

Ada looked worried. "Aaron? But…he wasn't there Saturday." She eyed the floor. "I didn't want Ezra to know I married a white. He wouldn't have taken it well."

Hanley recalled the bitterness in Hayes's face during their brief conversation in the Lake Street lockup. "He wasn't fond of whites, I gather."

She looked up, a glint of anger in her eyes. "He was a slave, Detective. As I was. White men's property, from when he was nineteen.

White men took everything from him. The free life he was born to. Me. Nat. The war gave him back his freedom, at least. No remedy for the rest."

The way she said "white men" brought an unexpected sting of shame. "I fought for the Union—" Hanley said, then stopped, realizing he'd spoken loudly enough to rouse the dozing woman. She lifted her head and glared, then settled back to sleep. Hanley got hold of himself. "I'm sorry. Tell me about the visit with Nat and what happened after."

Ada drew in a breath. "I left them alone together, mostly. They deserved their own time after thirteen years." A shaky smile flitted across her face. "When I came back to the parlor, Nat was showing Ezra one of his carvings. He whittles little animals. He gave it to Ezra. A rabbit." Above the smile, her eyes were wet. "I walked with Ezra to the horsecar stop, afterward. The whole way, he held that rabbit like it was gold." Tears spilled over, and she swiped them away with her thumb.

"And after that? Did Hayes speak to you or your husband about the boy?"

Her fingers worried at her skirt. "We don't work Sundays. Monday the shop was busy. Not much time for talk. Then...then Tuesday, Ezra was out sick, Mr. Jones said, and—"

"You asked about him?"

"Yes." Wariness tinged her eyes. "We meant a great deal to each other once. When he didn't come to work, I was concerned."

"Did you check on him? Did anyone?"

"I...it was a working day. We don't get much time to go anywhere."

"Did Chamberlain give you any idea why he suspected *you* of killing Hayes?"

"He said someone at our workplace saw us arguing...fighting. I don't know what they think they saw. We talked at work several times, but it was always calmly. I wanted him to know Nat...but I never saw him again after Monday."

Chamberlain apparently felt a purported disagreement was enough reason to come after Ada instead of looking for some thug who jumped Hayes for money. But brute-strength fisticuffs followed by a throat slitting in a dark alley wasn't a woman's kind of murder. What was

Aaron's role in all this? The real story was like an incendiary bomb Hanley had to find and douse before Chamberlain built a case on pieces of it. *Unless Ada or Aaron, or both of them,* are *involved—*

No. He wouldn't think that. "Your husband can't have been happy about Hayes turning up, meeting the child he'd fathered."

"Aaron is an understanding man." The chill in her voice could have cooled the surrounding air by ten degrees. "Which it seems you are not. I'd thought better of you, Detective Hanley. I know Rivka does."

The mention of Rivka threw him off stride, but only for a moment. "So there was no fight over you and Aaron taking Nat out West, far away? Hayes had no objection?"

She met his gaze steadily. "No."

"Hayes was found unconscious Tuesday afternoon near Jacky O'Toole's tavern. That's on Franklin Street by the river, not far from where you're living. There's not many Negroes who're safe in that part of town if the wrong folk take an interest. Would you have any idea why Hayes was there? He didn't go from your workplace…he'd lied about being off sick. Do you know why he did that? Market Street is a stone's toss from where he was picked up. You were at work, and he'd have known that. Maybe he came to see your husband, and Aaron didn't tell you?"

"My husband and I don't keep secrets from each other. Are you going to help us, like you said, or not?"

"A white man paid Hayes's bail Tuesday night. If Detective Chamberlain—"

"Bail?" She looked stunned. "Ezra was locked up?"

"Yes. Here. Chamberlain might think it was Aaron who got him out. You see why I have to know everything you know? Without that, I *can't* help. Where was Aaron Tuesday evening…and where were you?"

"Home," she said, too quickly. "We were home. Where else would we be?"

He didn't believe her, and it dismayed him. "Rivka can vouch for that?"

She raised her chin, a defiant gesture. "Yes. I'm sure she will."

# FORTY-THREE

Thunder muttered as Hanley headed north from the Armory toward Lake Street Station. His feet were sore, and he'd get a soaking if he didn't beat the storm, but long walks helped him think. And he needed a good think just now.

*Bail logged at twenty past seven. Turnkey let him go maybe ten minutes after.* Ezra Hayes had left the Armory by seven thirty Tuesday night and was dead less than a mile away no later than nine or half past. Where had he gone, whose path had he crossed on his way home? Aside from the man who'd paid his bail. Someone who sounded a lot like Coughlin. The jailhouse officer's description matched, though Hanley couldn't figure why Coughlin would bail Hayes out, or how he knew the man was in jail. And why would the rail yard boss harm him? What possible connection could there be between the two cases? Far more likely some footpad jumped Hayes, hoping there was money in his pockets. Which wouldn't help Ada Kelmansky at all.

The next thought carried a chill with it. *There was no dispute. You have my word.* Hanley could hear Aaron saying it, see the man's face as it had looked yesterday evening at the Kelmansky house. Shuttered, the fear and anger Aaron had to be feeling under tight control. The face of a man working hard not to let anything slip. And now Ada had lied about Aaron being home Tuesday night. Hanley was sure he hadn't been, sure there was more to the story than either of them would admit. If Ada had evaded Chamberlain's questions to protect Aaron, no wonder the bastard had clapped her in jail. To a man who cared more about closing the case fast than being sure of the right killer, Ada Kelmansky made a convenient culprit.

The chill deepened, spread through him. Ada and Aaron had better not be involved. It would shatter Rivka. And if Hanley were the one who brought it to light...but he couldn't dwell on what that meant, couldn't put words to it even in his mind.

The wind kicked up, its sudden coolness weaving through the hot summer air. Off to the west, lightning flashed amid looming blue-gray clouds. Hanley could still outrun the threatening weather, but he'd best hurry.

He arrived at Lake Street Station just as the storm broke. A glance into the squad room told him Chamberlain was absent. Scattered papers covered the man's desk, but with three other detectives present, Hanley chose not to walk in and look them over. Someone would talk, and then there'd be trouble. Not even Sergeant Moore would excuse him meddling in a fellow detective's case—at least not without a damned good reason. A check of the dusty storage room where files were kept yielded no notes, a disappointment but also a relief. Chamberlain wasn't finished yet. He'd do a passable job at least, enough to ensure his case held up in court. Hanley loitered next to the crammed cubbyholes, running a hand through his hair. Would confronting Aaron about Tuesday night be worth a damn? No, the man would just evade him some more. *Talk to John Jones about finding Ezra's body, retrace Chamberlain's steps. You know this job as well as he does. Better.*

Paying scant heed to the roar of sheeting rain hitting the stationhouse roof, Hanley hurried out of the storage room.

ɷ

In all his time working with the police, Will had never been to the Armory jail. The stationhouse a few times, the old one and the new—following up with coppers who'd found this or that dead body, digging out the details of when and where. But never the jail cells, too often the last stop on the way to trial and prison. *Or hanging.* He drew a sharp breath and bit his lip, counting on pain to drive that terrifying thought from his head. *Ada's innocent. Hanley will prove it.* He clung to that notion instead, wouldn't let himself think anything else.

"Place getting to you, is it?" the turnkey said over his shoulder, with a grin that didn't reach his eyes. Hard eyes, in a pockmarked face that resembled pitted brick. "That's all right. You ain't gotta stay long. Gent like you." He reached the bottom of the stairs and squinted as Will joined him. "You been here before? I swear I seen you somewheres."

"Not here. I'm a doctor. I don't spend much time in jails." The response came out faster than thought, and Will clamped his jaw shut to cut off the spate of words. Fear would make him say something stupid, betray himself, and his undeserved luck at not running into any copper he knew on the way in here would be tossed to the winds. He shouldn't have come, shouldn't have risked being seen with his sister and identified as like her. *But how could I stay away and still call myself a decent man?*

The turnkey spat sideways onto the floor. "Makes me no never mind." He jerked his head down the narrow corridor in front of them, lined with barred cells. "You got ten minutes." Another ugly grin, wider than the first. "Unless you want to pay for double. Twenty's enough time for a ride on your black mare, give the rest of 'em something to watch."

Revulsion at the crude insult robbed Will of breath. He clenched a fist, felt his arm rising to punch the turnkey's leering face. Restraining himself took all his strength. Too angry to speak, he stalked toward Ada's cell. The turnkey's snicker echoed behind him, mercifully followed by the man's footsteps retreating up the stairs.

Ada sat on the floor, sagged against the damp brick wall with her eyes shut. As he drew breath to call out, her eyes flew open. Fear, surprise, and a hint of relief, even gladness, flashed across her face, then gave way to a guarded look. "You shouldn't be here," she said.

He felt like he'd missed his footing and gripped the cell bars to steady himself. "I had to come. Are you all right? Nobody's hurt you? Have they given you any food, or—"

Her short laugh held no mirth. "You could call it food. Beans with fat pork, they said. Only the pork was moving." Slowly, she stood. "Why *are* you here, Will?"

The off-balance feeling hit him again, and he gripped the bars tighter. "I came to help, see what I could do—"

"For me? Or for yourself?"

"Jesus." The word escaped him on a breath, part curse and part prayer. "I'm here, aren't I? Isn't that answer enough?"

"I don't know." She sounded hollow, as if speaking from farther away than the few feet between them. Abruptly, she looked down at the moldy straw beneath her shoes. "I'm sorry. I don't know much of anything right now. Except Ezra's dead, and I'm here, and I shouldn't be, and I want to *go home*." Her voice shook on the last few words, and she swallowed as if choking back tears.

God, if only he could reach her, hold and comfort her like she'd done for him when they were children and he'd suffered some hurt or loss. "I know you don't belong here. Why *are* you? Why—" He faltered, searching for words. "Why did Chamberlain arrest you? Why in hell's name does he think you did Ezra Hayes any harm? How did he know there was anything between you in the first place?"

She blinked and wiped her eyes. "He must've found the letter I wrote for Ezra when Nat was born. Even though Ezra was long gone by then. Sold away." Her lips twisted, as if she hurt deep inside. "I gave it to him…I meant it as a comfort. I thought…I wanted…and he wrote to Nat, Ezra did, after I let them meet. He wanted Nat to live with him. But that awful man…Chamberlain…he can't know about that. I don't think."

"Ada." Will pressed closer to the bars. "Tell me everything, about Ezra and you and his time here in Chicago. You never know what may help."

Her smile then, shaky and wet eyed, sent his heart plunging. "Nothing can help. Not if the police have made up their minds. The world doesn't work that way for people like me."

He knew what she meant, and the knowledge curdled his stomach. Half a dozen responses galloped through his mind, each one useless. There was no guarantee he could give, no reassurance whatsoever, that wouldn't ring as false as the promise of freedom after Jubilee.

What came next, even he hadn't expected. He eased one hand's grip on the bars and held it out toward her. "People like us," he said.

She stared at him for what felt like forever. Then she moved forward and clasped her cold fingers around his.

❧

Wet and irritable as a soaked cat, Hanley stood in the slackening downpour outside John Jones's cleaning and tailoring shop. "You just missed him," the shop assistant had said. "Mr. Jones left half an hour ago, for a political meeting. I'll give him your name if you like, tell him you want to talk with him." Hanley had agreed, biting back frustration he'd no earthly right to take out on the pleasant young Negro in front of him. He felt as if he'd wasted what was left of the day and done Ada—and Rivka—no good at all.

He headed wearily down Dearborn toward Madison for the long trek home, sore footed and his head throbbing with an overwhelming sense of failure.

# FORTY-FOUR

The scent of challah filled the Nathans' kitchen. Rivka wished she could take comfort from it. Today, for the first time in her life, it brought a sense of dread. They would eat the challah at Shabbos dinner, after the men returned from shul, and then—

"Come and help me, Rivka," Tanta Hannah called from the dining room adjacent to the parlor. Reluctantly, Rivka obeyed. Hannah stood by the sideboard Onkl Jacob had built, shaking out a length of pale blue linen. Her best tablecloth, a survivor of last autumn's Great Fire, and a sign of what was coming. Rivka went still. *No way out.* Aaron had made up his mind, Moishe had broken his promise to her, and as for Onkl Jacob...

"Help me lay the places," Hannah said. "Then go upstairs and change. You may use my room. The girls will finish the cooking, so you needn't worry about protecting your best dress." Though her face showed the strain of the past few days, she managed a warm smile. "It's good to know you'll be settled. Things will work out, *baruch Hashem.* You'll see."

*Baruch Hashem*...but Hashem wasn't listening. Moving like a sleepwalker, Rivka went over and took up one end of the tablecloth. *Things will work out.* And, *it's* bashert*, meant to be.* Two sentences repeated at her like morning prayers too often since that night in May when she let Hanley walk her home from the ceilidh dance. She'd kissed him on the lips and fled. *That* was *bashert*—or perhaps a fool's dream, destined to end in mere hours. Words would be spoken this evening, pledges made, that would set the pattern of her life forever. Unless she kept it from happening. *How?*

The blue linen rippled like water as she and Hannah draped it over the table. Mechanically, Rivka smoothed the fabric. *I don't want this. I don't want to marry Moishe.* She'd considered it, tried more than once to convince herself of what everyone else believed—that she could be a good wife to Moishe Zalman, give him children, make a happy home with him. And Moishe had been so kind, so understanding, that she'd been partway to convincing herself. Until yesterday, when Hanley held her as she cried, and she hadn't wanted him to let her go.

Was there any point in telling Hannah, or anyone? Joyful consent was not required, only acquiescence. Rebellion flared, and she clenched her fists as words tumbled out. "Please, Tanta Hannah. I need more time. I—"

"Time? For what? To change your mind?" Hannah's gentle tone belied her blunt words. She piled silverware on the table, then laid out spoons one by one. "You're stubborn, Rivkaleh. You always have been, so those of us who know what's best must make choices for you. You don't like it, but you'll adjust. Women always have."

"What about Tamar? Will *she* adjust?" Rivka grabbed a handful of forks. "She loves Moishe. She'd marry him in a day if he asked her. You must know that. Don't you want your own daughter to be happy?"

Guilt flashed across Hannah's face. "Tamar will do well enough. She has her choice of suitors—"

"And I don't. Especially since Aaron came home." She left *with his goyische wife* unspoken, though Hannah's expression said she knew full well what Rivka meant. "But Moishe wants me no matter what, so I'm to gratefully accept him. Is that it?"

Hannah's frown deepened. "Since you ask, yes. Now set the table and go change."

Rivka slapped a fork down. "I don't love Moishe. He doesn't love me. He thinks he does, but it isn't true. He loves who he wants me to be."

"You think love has anything to do with it?"

"You love Onkl Jacob. Don't tell me you don't. I've seen it."

"Because I learned to love him. What *you* call love is nothing. A trick of the body, a silly girl's daydream." There was anger in Hannah's voice now…and regret, faded but present, like a flower pressed in a book long since put away.

Carefully, Rivka set down the remaining forks. "Who did you love, Tanta Hannah?" she asked softly. "Before Onkl Jacob?"

Hannah placed the last spoon. "It doesn't matter. We were too young, his family had no prospects…it was a lifetime ago." She shot Rivka a sharp glance. "Though he was Jewish, at least."

Heat rose in Rivka's cheeks. "That was in the old country. Things are different here."

Hannah snatched up the knives and laid them out, her movements brusque and quick. "Forget your Irish policeman. He has no place among us. *You* have no place with his people. You know that!"

"But—"

"You will do as you must, Rivka, and there's an end."

In the sudden quiet, save for the whisper of slackening rain outside, the sounds of chopping and sizzling carried from the kitchen. One of Tamar's sisters, giggling about Moishe, was met with a barked, "Hush! Take the challah out before it burns." Hannah had turned her back to Rivka and was counting out linen napkins. No ceremony would be spared in marking this occasion. The knowledge squeezed Rivka's heart like a fist. *No way out. No way—*

A new thought formed, and the pressure in her chest eased a little. She eyed the window, gauging the time, as she took the napkins from Hannah. When Onkl Jacob came, she would speak to him.

❧

The men returned just before sunset, clothes damp from the last of the rainstorm, talking and joking and stamping dirt off their boots in the entryway. Rivka heard them from upstairs. Her best dress, dark green broadcloth with mother-of-pearl buttons at sleeves and throat, lay draped across Hannah and Jacob's bed. She hadn't been able to put it on, or comb and re-pin her hair, or do anything except splash lukewarm water from the washstand basin on her hot face and listen for the men's arrival. Her breath came fast as she hurried out of the bedroom. From the top of the stairs, she saw Aaron and Moishe head into the dining room, Aaron clapping Moishe on the shoulder like a younger brother. Nat, fetched from home after minyan ended, followed in their wake. Jacob lingered in the hallway, straightening his shirtsleeves.

Rivka started down the steps. "Onkl Jacob!"

He glanced up with a broad grin. "Rivkaleh! An important night for you, this will be. A good night." He paused, as if waiting for an answer. When she didn't respond, his smile gave way to concern. "Did Hannah speak with you? Go to her. There's nothing to look so nervous about. She'll tell you every—"

"We've talked." She reached the foot of the stairs and hurried over to him. "Onkl Jacob, I cannot promise myself to Moishe. Not yet. I am still in *shanah* for Papa. It isn't right to end the mourning time this soon. Tell him and Aaron, they'll listen to you."

He shook his head, still smiling. "We've settled that. Mourning can be shortened when circumstances require, and your circumstances certainly—"

"My circumstances?" What had Aaron told Onkl Jacob? Surely not about the kiss. He'd *promised.* "What circumstances? I don't understand—"

"Is something wrong?" Aaron stepped back into the hall, Moishe behind him. Rivka's mouth went dry. Aaron gave her a cool glance, then eyed Jacob.

"Your sister is concerned about shanah. I was telling her not to worry. I suppose a bride can't help it." Jacob patted Rivka's arm. "Aaron and I discussed things even before this…misunderstanding…with the police. He wishes your future settled before he and his family leave. This present trouble with Ada is all the more reason. We can hope it will be cleared up before long, but you need someone to help and protect you. It's long past time. Your father, baruch Hashem, would understand."

"No. I can't do this. It's wrong." Her reply came out as if of its own accord. Moishe flinched, and guilt washed through her, mixed with anger. If he hadn't broken his promise… "I can't…I'm sorry, I'm not ready—"

"Nonsense," Aaron snapped, as if only the other men's presence held deeper anger in check. "It's decided, Rivka. There is no more to be said."

"I'm only asking—"

"I know what you're asking. The answer is no. The law permits—"

"The law?" Her voice cracked. "Is that the only thing that matters? What about me, what I want, what I feel? You say it's *decided*. When do *I* decide? *You* did, for yourself, but I am not allowed?"

Moishe broke in, with a wounded look. "Is it so terrible, the idea of being my wife? Have I not shown how much I care for you?"

Tears stung her eyes as she faced him. "Yes. Yes, you have. I know it. I'm sorry. But I can't do this. Not now." What could she say? Not the truth. Not an outright lie. Moishe deserved better. "If you really care for me...then let me finish mourning for Papa. A few more months, and then..."

Moishe bit his lip. "This is for your father? There is...no other reason?"

She meant to say yes, but the half-truth died unspoken. Hanley came to mind—his arms around her, his voice gentle in her ear. A lump rose in her throat. *No more dreams. It can't happen.* "And for myself. To...accept what must be." She swallowed hard. "I need more time. Just a little. Please."

She watched his expression, could almost hear him thinking. He had waited so long already, been patience itself with her, and she still couldn't consent? Then his troubled frown cleared. He shifted his gaze to include Aaron and Jacob. "I have an answer...if you approve?"

"Go on," Jacob said.

Moishe blinked like a nervous owl. "We will hold the wedding as soon as may be but, after the first night, refrain from living as husband and wife until the shanah time ends. That should satisfy everyone, yes?"

A chill spread through Rivka. "But there *can't* be a wedding. To celebrate during mourning is not allowed—"

"Mourning can be cut short," Aaron said curtly, his gaze on Jacob instead of her. "Which is what we agreed. We should keep to it."

Rivka turned to Jacob, but his thoughtful look was on Moishe and Aaron. Were they actually going to do this? Marry her off in, what…a week, a few days, wedding night included? And then leave her for the next five months as wife in name to a husband she didn't want? For a wild moment she considered defying them, refusing Moishe outright. And then what? Would they force her? Would she run away? Where would she go? *To Hanley*…but what place was there for her in Hanley's world? How could she be sure he even wanted her with him?

Madness, such thoughts. "Onkl Jacob," she whispered.

He glanced at her, compassion in his face. "I cannot decide this. We need a rabbi's advice."

"My father would want —" Aaron began.

"We can't know what he would want. There are other rabbis we can go to."

"Yes? Which one?"

Jacob touched Aaron's shoulder. "We'll talk it over. Things will still be settled quickly enough."

Rivka's heart pounded in her chest. She had bought herself a few days. A few days to persuade Moishe to keep waiting, or better yet, turn his heart elsewhere. A breathy laugh, almost a sob, escaped her. Little chance of that. Still, surely she could do *something*.

Moishe cupped her chin and tilted her face upward. His touch was dry as paper. Nothing like Hanley's, so warm and alive that she'd felt his embrace through her dress as if he'd touched her skin. "It's in Hashem's hands, *mayn libe*. All will be well soon."

# FORTY-FIVE

*August 3, 1872*

I t's a bad business." Jones's deep voice rumbled through the small back office at his Dearborn cleaning and tailoring establishment. Neatly stacked papers, receipts, an inkwell, and an open ledger shared the top of his desk, whose red-brown surface gleamed with polish. A tall bookcase against the rear wall held more ledgers arranged by year, plus a few other books on an upper shelf. One was a bound collection of the *Cook County Statutes*. Next to it was a copy of *Chicago and the Great Conflagration*. That had come out last December, just seven months ago. Clearly, Jones kept up with current events. "A bad business. Ezra Hayes didn't deserve what happened to him. And Ada Kelmansky doesn't deserve what's happening to her now."

"You're sure she's not guilty?"

Jones's expression turned thunderous, and Hanley realized he'd chosen his words badly. Before he could undo the damage, Jones said, "I know my workers, Detective, and I'm a fair judge of character. If Mrs. Kelmansky is a murderess, I'll eat this ledger." He thumped the open book. "I already told the other detective—that big untidy fellow—as much when he came here asking questions. Don't you people talk to each other? You're rowing down the wrong river in any case."

Hanley chose not to correct the impression that he was here officially. He leaned forward in his straight-backed chair. "As it happens, Commissioner, I disagree with Detective Chamberlain. I don't think

Mrs. Kelmansky killed Hayes. Why didn't you bail Hayes out? He wrote you from my station. I gave him paper and pen myself."

Jones looked bewildered. "I never got word. The only note from Ezra on Tuesday came in the morning post, saying he was ill, but he'd be back at work the next day. I got worried when he didn't show on Wednesday morning, and…" He shrugged. "You know the rest."

"You found him. Tell me about it." As Jones drew breath to protest, Hanley held up a hand. "I know, you already told Chamberlain. I'd like to hear for myself."

Jones looked skeptical but did as Hanley asked. "I'd gone to see Mrs. Kelvin…she runs a boardinghouse on Twelfth Street, where Ezra was living. I wanted to check on him, make sure he was all right. She told me he came home briefly Tuesday night, just after eight o'clock, then went out again. She didn't know where, and he didn't turn up at breakfast. I started walking around the neighborhood, hoping I'd find him in some tavern or other. I passed the alley off Thirteenth Street, saw what I thought was a drunkard sprawled there. I went over to see if I could help…" He swallowed, his cheeks tinged with gray. "I saw Ezra's face. The red mess of his throat. Bit of white sticking up in the middle. His windpipe, the morgue doctor said."

"I'm told he was clubbed down and then cut. Did you look around for weapons—the knife, or anything the killer could've hit him with?"

"Not more than a glance. As soon as the first shock wore off, I ran for the nearest signal box to report the crime."

"Do you recall anything else about that alley—rubble, garbage, bloody marks on the pavement, footprints?"

"I saw a trash heap a ways down. I couldn't tell you what was in it. Cobblestones stained all around where he bled out." Jones's brow furrowed. "There *was* another mark, now I think of it. A smudge, separate, but not far from Ezra's head. About the size of my fist, I'd say. It could've been blood, it looked dark enough. Deeper into the alley, not near the street."

Hanley let out a breath. A shoe or boot print, maybe…but partial at best. And a trash pile that might not contain a damned thing useful.

Still, the alley was worth a look. "Would it surprise you to know a white man paid Ezra's bail?"

Shock, twinned with anxiety, crossed Jones's face. "A white man? Was he a Southerner, by any chance?"

"An Irishman, I'm told. One who's been here awhile." Hanley cocked his head. "You had someone else in mind?"

"An Irishman makes more sense," Jones said slowly. "O'Shea, that'd be the name. Though why O'Shea wouldn't have..." He sighed and shook his head. "I told Ezra to go see the man. O'Shea's son was lynched outside New Orleans. Ezra saw it. He promised the boy he'd get to Chicago and tell his family how he met his end."

This information startled Hanley. So Ezra Hayes was the "darky" who'd brought Michael O'Shea's mother the news of her son's death? That could explain Coughlin bailing him out of jail. The two cases were intertwined...though exactly how, he didn't yet comprehend.

"It wasn't Lawrence O'Shea," he said grimly. "He's dead. Murdered at the Illinois, St. Louis and Grand Southern Railway yard three weeks ago."

Jones's eyes widened. "Then I don't understand this at all."

Something Jones had said belatedly registered. "What did you mean, 'why O'Shea wouldn't have'? Wouldn't have what? And who were you thinking of when you asked about a Southerner? Someone to do with the lynching? Did Ezra give you a name?"

"I wish he had." Jones studied Hanley as if taking his measure. "Did you fight in the war, Detective?"

"As a proud Union man. Chicago Irish Brigade."

"Then you saw a bare fraction of what Ezra—and Ada, and others of my workers—lived through. I'm fortunate. I was born free, and I've achieved a great deal in my life. Which is why it matters to me that my people are done right by. Will you do right in this case? No matter who might want otherwise?"

"As in?"

A thin smile crossed Jones's face. "As I said, I don't have names. But I know how the world works. And I'd like it not to work that way this time."

"Then tell me what you know, sir." Hanley leaned forward, elbows on his knees. "I want to find Ezra Hayes's murderer as much as you do."

"May I ask why?"

"Because I'd like the world not to work as usual this time, too."

Jones gave him another measuring look, then pulled open a desk drawer and took an envelope out of it. Wrinkled and mud smutched, the envelope bulged with whatever it held. "Look at these first. Ezra left these with me for safekeeping. I hope you've nowhere to rush to. I've a story to tell, and it may take a while."

# FORTY-SIX

Rivka had spent a restless Shabbos under Tanta Hannah's watchful eye. At home, at shul, at the Nathans' for supper, her thoughts running in the same closed circle. She couldn't marry Moishe, yet she must. Unless he changed his mind. Either that, or—

Standing in the Nathans' front hallway, the evening's *havdalah* blessings said and Shabbos mercifully over, she clenched her fists hard enough to hurt. Thinking beyond *or* was chasing the impossible. *Why impossible? Because people say?*

*Forget your Irish policeman,* Tanta Hannah had said yesterday. *He has no place among us. You have no place with his people.* She wished she were with Hanley now—the two of them holding each other, his lips brushing her hair, her cheek, her mouth—

"—stay here tonight." Aaron's voice broke into her thoughts. She knew that too-level tone. He used it when he wanted no questions about something. A few feet away, near the parlor door, Nat leaned with his head down as if trying not to overhear. "It's kind of Hannah to offer, and it will be convenient for all the work before the wedding."

"What?" Belatedly, Rivka recalled Hannah taking Aaron aside after supper and the two of them murmuring together. "Stay here…you mean me?" Her scattered wits collected around *all the work before the wedding.* Her bride's chest, he meant. Linens for her new home with Moishe. She and Hannah and the Nathan girls would spend the next several days until the wedding, and weeks after that, making them. Tablecloths, napkins, pillowcases, bed sheets—

A shiver passed through her. "There isn't room. Or need. We're only next door, I can just come over—"

"You should stay here. You'll be busy, and it's one less thing to worry about."

"Worry? What worries you about my living in my own home?" Anger sparked as an answer suggested itself, though she lowered her voice for Nat's sake. "Do you think I need a keeper to stay out of trouble? Why not for the months of mourning after the wedding night as well? Oh, but Fray Zalman will watch me then. And Moishe, when he isn't at work. So *that's* all right."

He flinched at her bitter tone. "Rivkaleh, I didn't mean—"

"Don't 'Rivkaleh' me. And yes, you did." She turned sharply away from him as Hannah stepped into the hall. Without giving herself time to reconsider, Rivka marched up to her. "Aaron tells me you invited me to stay. It's very kind, but I can't possibly inconvenience Tamar and her sisters. Thank them for me, won't you?" She threw Aaron a look of challenge. "Shall we go home? Nat needs his rest and so do I."

෬

But rest eluded her, as she woke yet again from a fitful doze in her own bed. The same thoughts she'd had all day skittered through her head like chickens in a hen yard. What was she to do? Either accept Moishe as her husband—pain lanced her heart at the thought—or turn his attentions elsewhere. Toward Tamar Nathan, who would take him in a second. But how? Intimate conversations as if the two of them were bosom friends, while they sewed Rivka's bridal linens for the husband Tamar wanted? Tamar's resentment must run deeper than Lake Michigan. Why would she trust Rivka, or believe a word she said? And, if the scheme succeeded, then what? A mirthless chuckle escaped her. *Scheme.* She couldn't even call it that, had no sense of how to make Moishe's change of heart happen. Or of what might come after.

She pressed her fingers against her scalp. Here it was—the question she'd been avoiding since the engagement celebration Friday night. What did she truly want with Hanley? Did she love him…and did he love her? Enough for her to give up what she *should* want—a marriage and a home among her own people, a future she knew the shape of—for a life she could scarcely imagine? Or had he held her, kissed her, because she needed help and he felt sorry for her? And she'd responded so eagerly because…?

She thought back, past the day of Ada's arrest, to last spring and the Champion murder case she'd helped Hanley solve. Those terrifying moments in the deserted ground by the riverbank, when he confronted her kidnapper and she feared the man had shot him. Hanley had held her afterward as if he never meant to let her go. She'd felt his heart against her chest, beating in rhythm with her own. And at the dance days afterward, the song he'd played thinking of her: "If Ever You Were Mine."

She closed her eyes. If it *was* bashert that she should be with Hanley, then—

Downstairs, something hit the floor and shattered. Rivka stiffened, then relaxed as Aaron's voice rose in a muttered oath. What was he doing out of bed? She heard a dull *thwack* like a fist against a wall, then the scrape of a chair. Then silence.

For a moment, she debated leaving her brother to stew. Then her better nature took over. She was still angry with him, but the past three days had been hard on him, too, and it might do her good to worry over someone besides herself. She eased out of bed, shoved her feet into slippers, threw a shawl around her shoulders, and left the bedroom.

Lantern light glowed from the kitchen. Aaron sat slumped at the table with his head on his folded arms. On the floor near the banked stove lay shards of white china and the cracked-off handle of a coffee mug. The grinding mill stood on the counter, and steam rattled the lid of the coffeepot on the boil.

She wrapped a trailing end of shawl around her hand and shifted the pot from the hot stove lid to a cold one. Aaron didn't stir. Looking at him, huddled there as if pinned by the weight of Ada's absence and his fear, Rivka felt a wave of sympathy. She snagged a fresh mug from a cabinet, poured it full of coffee, and set it in front of her brother. "Here," she murmured as she sat across from him. "Have a little. Then we'll see to cleaning up."

He raised his head, looking past rather than at her. "I didn't mean it to happen," he said, his voice hoarse. "It just did." His breath stank of liquor—sharp and sour, like Onkl Jacob's homemade *slivovitz.* Which Aaron disliked and they didn't have in the house.

"It's only a coffee cup. Not even one of Mameh's best. Easily replaced—"

"Never mind. Go back to bed, Rivka." He pulled the mug closer, gulped coffee, grimaced, then blinked at her. "I'm surprised you came down. Surprised you even want to speak to me."

"I don't. But you're my brother." *Who went out and got drunk instead of going to bed, and now you're trying to sober up before anyone sees you.* Impulse pressed her to ask what he hadn't meant to happen, but she took a leaf from Hanley's book and waited.

Aaron stared at the tabletop. After a moment, a corner of his mouth lifted. "Remember when I taught you how to sneak out at night? Down the tree outside your window and onto the lean-to roof?"

"After I caught you sneaking back in." She felt herself smiling too, wistful at the memory. Where had *that* Aaron been these past few weeks—the one from before the war, who told her secrets, shared his thoughts, listened to hers as if they mattered?

"Fair payment for you not telling Papa and Mameh." He drank more coffee, then fixed her with a serious look. "Promise me something, Rivkaleh."

"What?"

"Don't talk to Hanley. At all. If he comes here again, avoid him."

She felt as if he'd punched her in the stomach. "How can you ask that? He's trying to help Ada. Trying to help *you.* Or do you still think I—" She shoved her chair back and stood. "You're right. I *don't* want to speak to you. Good night."

"You don't understand."

The ragged need in those three words halted her. "Understand what?"

Seconds ticked by. "Tuesday," Aaron said finally. "When Ezra Hayes was killed."

"What about it?" Her mind raced over the events of that day. Aaron walked Nat to school, Ada went to work, everything was as usual...no, Aaron went out after supper, now she recalled. To see Onkl Jacob. Rivka had gone upstairs to read, not feeling much like company, and fallen asleep over her book. She'd woken much later to the sound of Ada and Aaron coming up the stairs, retiring for the night...

"I didn't only go to Jacob's," Aaron said. "I also went to the boardinghouse where Hayes lives. To talk to him. He came to Nat's school that morning and...we had words." He swallowed hard. "I didn't find Hayes that night. But I saw Ada there."

# FORTY-SEVEN

*August 4–5, 1872*

Sunday Mass passed in a blur for Hanley. Sweating in his best clothes, the morning's heat wrapping him like a blanket, he didn't absorb a word of Father Gerald's homily. He said his profession of faith and Our Father by rote. His mind was stuck on the story John Jones had told him yesterday, on the contents of the envelope and a sworn statement Jones had pulled from his desk drawer.

"I asked Ezra to set this down, with a lawyer acquaintance of mine as witness," Jones had said, his dark eyes shadowed as he set the statement and the dirt-stained envelope within Hanley's reach. "I meant it for the white boy's father, Lawrence O'Shea, but now you tell me he's dead. There are drawings in the envelope, and a written testament. Michael O'Shea made them before he was killed. Look at the drawings, read Ezra's statement. I'll fill in the rest as best I can."

Ezra Hayes's statement was brief and harrowing. Scattered phrases floated through Hanley's mind, snagged in his thoughts like debris caught by rocks in a fast current. *Arrested for vagrancy…couldn't pay the fine…sold me by contract to a sugar plantation.* For two years, officially, but the sentence kept lengthening. New fines—and time—were added for working too slowly, for eating too much, for oversleeping once. For attempting escape. That transgression earned Hayes a beating. Which hadn't discouraged him, only made him more careful. It was after another escape attempt that his path crossed Michael O'Shea's.

Hanley set the statement aside, then emptied the envelope of its contents—a sheaf of papers covered in cramped handwriting, and three sketches in charcoal pencil. From memory, he guessed, given the detail and care evident in each stroke. The scenes depicted would be damned hard to forget. They'd stay imprinted on your eyelids at night, haunt your dreams…

He forced himself to examine each drawing. The first showed a tall pole in a dirt yard, edged by ramshackle huts. A Negro was tied to the pole by his wrists, his bare back and his face clearly visible. The former bore stripes from the whip wielded by the man standing behind him—a white man, hard-muscled and grinning. A silent scream contorted the Negro's face. In the second sketch, another black figure lay hogtied around the base of a similar pole, half naked, his eyes shut. *Already whipped, or waiting his turn?* A white man stood a pace or two away, a length of rope stretched between his hands.

Hanley's jaw clenched against phantom pain. With a sense of foreboding, he eyed the third drawing. The huts had given place to towering trees with cone-shaped trunks, the dirt yard to marshy ground. A line of Negroes, chained together at their wrists and ankles, gazed up at one particular tree. A body dangled from it, the head at an unnatural angle. White men were sketched in like ghosts, guarding the Negroes… except for one white man who stood near the hanging tree, hauling hard on the rope. *The executioner.*

"The boy worked for the Freedmen's Bureau in New Orleans," Jones said, in response to the first question Hanley could stammer out. "There'd been rumors about plantations up and down the Mississippi, between the river and the bayou, and a scheme to supply slave labor for them by trumping up criminal charges against Negroes. Toss a black man in jail, levy a fine he can't afford, then lease him out to 'work off the debt.' Only, somehow, the debts never shrank and the 'terms of contract' never ended. Unless someone escaped…or died." Jones drew in a breath and nodded toward the drawing in Hanley's hand. "More often the latter. Laborers were whipped, beaten, chained to posts, and left in the day's heat without a bit of shade or a drop of water. Michael O'Shea came to investigate the rumors. Ezra said he was an artist. The boy drew things he saw and wrote notes as well. He meant to send everything to his father—some fool's hope of getting the word out, I guess—but the bastards caught him first."

Hanley's grip tightened on the sketch he held. He unclenched his fingers and carefully laid the drawing on Jones's desk. "Why didn't the Freedmen's Bureau help?"

Jones raised an eyebrow. "Do you follow politics, Detective?"

"I try not to."

"You and too many others." The man sounded more saddened than angry. "Which is partly why the world works as it does. The bureau's been shut down. Our esteemed Congress never did give it sufficient monies to do its work, and things have gone from bad to worse over the past few years. Federal troops are leaving the South, and outrages perpetrated against the freedmen increase every day. Negro farmers murdered for daring to own land. Negro holders of office run out of town by jeering mobs, and that's if they're lucky. Negro businesses set afire, freedmen caught and jailed and lynched on whatever pretext can be devised, in every rebel state. And all I've just told you merely scratches the surface. The Union won the war, but we're losing the peace. That poor young man, Michael O'Shea, was a casualty."

☙

A red-faced churchgoer coughing into his shirt sleeve pulled Hanley back to Saint Pat's. Father Gerald was bidding them go in peace to love and serve the Lord, but Hanley's mind remained on what he'd seen and heard in Jones's office. The name of the plantation Ezra Hayes had escaped from was Sweetbay. *Sweetbay Sugar Company. Coughlin's client.* Now it made sense why the rail yard boss had been spending so much time around Grace O'Shea lately. *He knew those sketches, and Michael's testament, were coming. Lawrence must've told him. He'd lose everything when Lawrence went to the papers with them, like Michael wanted. He had to silence the man and get hold of the evidence. But he didn't know when it would get here. Until Ezra Hayes showed up, and Coughlin was there at Mrs. O'Shea's home to hear everything he said...*

He felt punch drunk and half sick as he stood with the rest of the congregation and the opening chords of "Faith of Our Fathers" rolled through the stifling air. He didn't have all the details, but John Jones and Ezra Hayes between them had given him a motive for Ezra's murder, and possibly his killer's identity…and confirmed the reason behind Lawrence O'Shea's death, though Hanley still couldn't prove it. *Yet.*

❧

Monday morning found Hanley at Lake Street Station early enough that Chamberlain wasn't in yet. A swift glance into the squad room showed the night shift detectives packing up and heading out, joking with each other. One of them gave Hanley a friendly nod as they passed in the doorway.

Chamberlain's desk was clear of paperwork, though not of traces of the man—a dirty coffee mug, a broken pencil stub, a grease-stained handbill advertising an upcoming gathering of the Nineteenth Illinois Regiment. The sight of the handbill gave Hanley an odd turn. Of course Chamberlain had served in the war, likely with honor. Stationhouse jaw had never suggested otherwise. It felt strange to think of Chamberlain as a fellow veteran, to acknowledge any similarity between them. Hanley's mouth twitched in a grim smile. *Probably the only thing that bastard and I can agree on.*

He glanced over his shoulder, saw no one, and quickly searched the desk drawers. The paperwork on the Hayes murder was in the first drawer on the left. Hanley grabbed the thin sheaf and riffled through it. Initial case notes, the arrest record with Ada Kelmansky's name across the top of the page. Seeing it made Hanley uneasy. Chamberlain wasn't finished yet, but how close was he? How much more time did Ada have before trial, followed by conviction and prison or hanging?

Beneath the arrest record were two pages that looked like personal letters. No time to read them, only to note a few details. The first page was worn and creased, the second newer looking but with several crossed-out phrases, and the letters appeared to be in different hands. Hanley's unease deepened as he caught familiar names amid the scripts: *Ada, Ezra, Nat.*

230

The fifth sheet of paper brought a fresh jolt of worry. A complaint form for a search warrant...*Market Street, home of Asher Kelmansky (the late), and immediate vicinity thereof.* Hanley frowned. Why bother with a warrant? The Kelmanskys had no pull, except what little Rivka might claim through him, which would matter less than a damn to Chamberlain. *Of course—John Jones.* The county commissioner's involvement explained it, had made a poor Negro's death worthy of investigation in the first place. Hanley chewed his lip. So what was Chamberlain looking for? He skimmed further down the page. *Small-bladed knife...correspondence from victim to—*

"Get the hell away from my desk!" Chamberlain's voice boomed through the squad room. Before Hanley could move, the big Englishman strode over and snatched the papers out of his hand. "Give me those, you goddamned Mick. What d'you think you're doing in my business?" He broke off as he eyed the papers. "You sneaking bastard. You're checking up on me? Well, you listen, Paddy boy. Hayes is *my* dead darky, and it's *my* damned case. You keep your drunken Irish nose out, or I'll break it for you."

"Go ahead and try it." Hanley kept his voice level, his gaze locked with Chamberlain's. "I expect we'll both of us end up with something broken."

"You'd like that, eh?" Chamberlain dropped the papers on his desk. "Let's get to it, then. Out the back, here and now. Before the brass comes in."

"So you can claim I threw the first punch? I won't risk my badge for that!"

"You already have." Chamberlain was grinning now. "If I tell the sergeant you searched *my* bloody desk for notes on *my* case, he'll want to know why. And what the hell else you've been doing." The grin became a sneer. "Moore may like you, Irishmen together and all that, but he won't save you if you cause trouble in the squad."

Hanley's gut tightened. He'd not a leg to stand on, and he knew it. His badge wasn't at risk yet—Chamberlain was surely bluffing—but his prospects for advancement might be. As far as Sergeant Moore knew,

Hanley had no reason for poaching on the Hayes murder. Doing it made him a problem, and problems didn't get promoted.

"You've got the wrong suspect," he said, even though he knew it was futile. "You really think a woman attacked Hayes, fought bare knuckle with him, and then slit his throat? Have you even looked for anyone el—"

"How do *you* know how he died?"

"I'm a fast reader." Better the man believe that than guess he'd spoken to Will Rushton, retracing Chamberlain's steps. "I'm telling you—"

Chamberlain's eyes narrowed. "What have you been up to with my case…and why do you care about some black-and-tan who killed her lover, anyhow?" Abruptly, the sneering grin came back. "It's that girl, isn't it? That little Jew girl who followed me here with *Missus* Kelmansky. She's turned up here before, looking for you. That girl your bit of skirt? Or you think she'll be, if you help out her darky kin?" He gave a theatrical shudder. "Mongrels, the lot of them. Makes me sick to think of it—"

Fury took over. Hanley drove his fist into Chamberlain's face. The big man staggered backward, regained his balance, and glared at Hanley, blood welling from a split lip. "You—"

Someone grabbed Hanley's shoulder. A familiar voice spoke roughly in his ear. "Detective! With me—*now!*"

Chamberlain spat, then squared his shoulders. "He struck me, sir. Unprovoked."

"I saw what happened. Appropriate steps will be taken." Then, to Hanley, "My office. Get moving."

Hot with rage and embarrassment, gut roiling with fear, Hanley marched out of the squad room. Three other detectives lingered near the door, wide eyed, and Hanley knew he'd be the subject of gossip for the rest of the day. Likely the whole week. He strode up the stairs, head high, gaze fixed forward, until he reached Moore's office.

Sergeant Moore closed the door behind them. He walked to his desk and leaned on it, crossing his arms over his chest. "All right, Francis. What's this about?"

# FORTY-EIGHT

*August 5, 1872*

I t wasn't unprovoked." Hanley stood in the middle of Moore's office, stiff as a soldier on parade. "He brought it on himself. That's all I'll say."

"The hell it is," Moore snapped. "You've every right to be angry at Chamberlain. But not to haul off and hit him! What brought Miss Kelmansky into it, anyway?"

Fighting down his temper, Hanley drew a deep breath. He needed a clear head or there'd be no hope of getting Moore on his side, even unofficially. "Miss Kelmansky came to me after Chamberlain arrested her sister-in-law...on flimsy evidence at best." He shoved the thought of the letters and *Ada, Ezra, Nat*, out of his mind. "The sonofabitch doesn't *want* this case. You saw that yourself. He's trying to get shut of it as fast as he can."

"And your feelings for Miss Kelmansky didn't enter into it, of course."

The question brought heat to Hanley's face. "All right. Yes, they did. But he's got the wrong person in jail."

"How do you know? Good Christ, how far have you gone with this? Tell me it's not beyond your snooping around five minutes ago—"

"Hayes was jailed at the Armory until half past seven Tuesday evening. Ada Kelmansky didn't know that." Recalling her shock when he'd mentioned it, Hanley felt certain of his judgment. "Yet she just happened to intercept him near that alley off State and Thirteenth, half a mile from the Armory and well east of Hayes's boardinghouse, within the next couple of hours? No—less than that. Commissioner Jones says—"

"You spoke with the county commissioner? God *damn* it, Francis!"

Hanley's voice rose, defying his efforts at self-control. "Sir, Chamberlain hasn't even *looked* for other suspects! He latched onto Ada Kelmansky because she's convenient. A Negress, married to a poor Jew, the pair of them not even living in Chicago until this past April. He's railroading—"

"You bloody fool!" Red spots flared in Moore's cheeks, a warning sign Hanley recognized. "Meddling in Chamberlain's case because you've a personal stake in the outcome? If he complains to the police board, you could lose your badge, let alone any chance at promotion. And what if Mike Hickey gets wind of this? Hell, if I stick my neck out for you—again—*I* could lose my job. You've just risked the squad for your self-righteous crusade—"

"Goddamn it, Hayes's murder connects with my case!"

"*Your* case?" Moore stared, then shook his head. "Lawrence O'Shea? Don't even try that on."

"Swear to God, sir." Swiftly, watching for any change in Moore's stony expression, Hanley summed up what he'd learned from John Jones. "What Michael O'Shea discovered outside New Orleans was bad enough to string the boy up over. Patrick Coughlin knew there was proof, knew it was coming. Lawrence O'Shea told him so. And—"

"You don't know O'Shea told his boss anything. And Coughlin's got nothing to do with ugly goings-on at a sugar plantation in Louisiana, in any case. Even if the story got out, it'd be an embarrassment to Sweetbay Sugar until the next eye-catcher knocked it aside. It wouldn't affect Coughlin—or the Illinois, St. Louis and Grand Southern, for that matter—at all."

"Yes, it would. Coughlin owes his job, his position, everything, to a major shareholder at the railway…Hugh Denham, his patron saint. Denham was an abolitionist, and Coughlin himself told me the man wouldn't abide a client tainted by slavery. Coughlin brought Sweetbay

Sugar's business to the St. Louis and Grand Southern—he must have heard rumors of enslaved workers even then and should have looked into them. Denham would blame him, pull his support, probably fire him if he learned the truth. You know as well as I do that among the blue blood money-grubbers who own railroads, an Irishman without a wealthy backer is just another lazy, drunken, thieving Mick."

"Speaking of thieving, what happened to your theory about Coughlin skimming the till and O'Shea finding out?"

"Who says Coughlin wasn't doing that, too? Yet another reason he couldn't afford scrutiny from higher-ups at the railway. Stealing profits would cost him his job *and* land him in jail. If I could get a damned warrant for the accounts—"

"Which you won't, even if I put in a word. Not without hard proof of wrongdoing, from a respectable source. And what's any such scheme got to do with Ezra Hayes?"

Hanley gritted his teeth. The bitter realities of pull in Chicago made him want to punch something more than just Chamberlain's sneering face. "Hayes went to the O'Sheas' house a week ago Sunday, to tell them their son was dead. July twenty-eighth, just two days before Hayes himself was murdered. Coughlin was there. I saw him and spoke with him. Whatever Hayes said to Mrs. O'Shea, he heard it. He must have known Hayes had Michael O'Shea's drawings and testament about the slave labor. That's why he paid Hayes's bail."

"Can you prove that was his reason? Or put Coughlin anywhere near the alley off State and Thirteenth last Tuesday night? For that matter, why bother killing Hayes? Why not buy the evidence from him? Gambling debts or not, Coughlin has money, and it'd be a lot less risky. Without proof of his story, Hayes was just a workingman and a Negro. Who'd believe his claims?"

"Maybe Coughlin tried a payoff, then changed his mind. Or Hayes refused. Coughlin offered him money before, at Mrs. O'Shea's, and he turned it down."

Moore sighed. "Do you hear yourself? It's all *maybe, must have, if.* And it's not your case. You want to save Ada Kelmansky? Keep working on

Lawrence O'Shea. Find the bullyboy Coughlin paid to murder *him*, get a confession. Find one of Coughlin's wealthier acquaintances who'll attest to his gambling debts. Plenty of respectable men drop in at Carrie Watson's place. If one of them talks, that might be enough to convince a judge. You'd get your warrant, at least."

"Sir, that'll take too—"

Moore raised a hand, the gesture sharp as a blade. "Stick to your own case, Detective. I'll not warn you again."

A vivid memory came then, of Rivka four nights ago, huddled in his arms and choking back tears. *It'll be all right,* he'd told her. *You'll see.* A promise he could no more break than he could stay alive without breathing.

He gave Moore a stiff nod and strode out of the office.

☙

A trip to the rail yard, and a quick question to the junior clerk, netted him Coughlin's whereabouts, and Hanley ran his quarry to earth at the Carroll Street Tavern. At the sight of him, Coughlin's face darkened. "This is harassment," he snapped as Hanley approached his table. "I'll file another complaint if I must, until you damned well leave me alone. I respect the law and the police, but there are limits."

Hanley ignored the implied threat. "I've questions. Again. Answer them honestly this time. Shall we do this here, or at your office?"

"If this is about the railway accounts—"

"It isn't." Not to start with, anyway. He'd get to those.

Motion off to one side heralded a waiter's approach. Coughlin glanced toward the advancing young man, then pursed his lips and nodded at the chair opposite his own. "Be quick about it. I'd like to finish my dinner in peace."

Hanley sat, ordered a coffee when the waiter arrived, and kept his attention on Coughlin as the waiter retreated out of earshot. The rail yard boss looked puffy under the eyes, as if he hadn't slept well for the past few days. "Ezra Hayes," Hanley said. "You paid his bail Tuesday evening. Why?"

Coughlin sawed at the pork chop on his plate. "That's my business, not yours."

*So, it* was *him.* "Really? You didn't know Hayes from Adam, apart from running into him by chance at Mrs. O'Shea's. Yet you kept track of him and went to some expense on his behalf."

"I was protecting Grace." Coughlin's stocky frame relaxed a bit as he set his knife down and stabbed his fork into a chunk of meat. "I told you I meant to send a telegram to the Freedmen's Bureau in New Orleans, to make sure the darky was who he said. I did that, first thing on the Monday. It seemed best to keep an eye on him in the meantime, until I got a reply. He told us who he worked for here. That much turned out to be true. Then on Tuesday he didn't go to work. My man followed him to a Negro school, where the darky—"

"Hayes. Ezra."

Annoyance flashed across Coughlin's face. "Where *Hayes* met a white man and a mulatto boy. He and the man exchanged words. Then Hayes hit the fellow and ran off. It wasn't hard to guess he'd be locked up after that. I'm familiar with the Armory jail. I've had occasion to bail out good workers of both races who drank too much and got in trouble. Provided they don't repeat the offense, I don't mind giving them a second chance."

Hanley's gut felt hollow. *A white man and a mulatto boy.* With effort, he kept to his line of questioning. "Hayes doesn't work for you. Why help him? What did you want from him?"

"I've no idea what you mean. I acted out of simple decency. As a copper, you might find that hard to believe, but it's true."

"The Sunday he showed up, you told me you'd no notion how to find him again. Yet you knew where he worked. And you gave the bail bondsman a false name. Jimmy O'Rourke. Two lies you didn't have to tell, for 'simple decency'?"

"His place of employment slipped my mind at the time. As to the name, I like to keep my acts of charity private, as the Bible says. Tuesday evening, I paid the bondsman and left before they brought the darky up from the cells."

"You didn't see Hayes at all? Didn't speak to him that night?"

"I told you, no."

"Hayes turned up dead within an hour or two after you sprung him."

Coughlin's face went white. "That's nothing to do with me. I paid his bail, I left."

"Where did you go?"

"You want to know that, haul me off to your damned police station. And then I'll charge you with false arrest." He jerked a thumb toward the tavern's front door. "Get out, before I have them throw you out."

Hanley didn't budge. "I'll stay, thanks. I've a coffee coming." He pulled out his sketchbook and pencil. "Tell me where you went after you left the Armory and when. And about the white man Hayes struck, if you know anything more."

# FORTY-NINE

*A white man and a mulatto boy.* The thought pounded in Hanley's brain as he turned onto Market Street, still unsettled from the encounter with Coughlin. He hadn't been prepared to arrest the man, with so much of his case still conjecture. He hadn't even had the chance to mention Michael O'Shea's papers. And when Coughlin described Hayes's run-in with Aaron…Hanley tried to tell himself it could have been someone else—Coughlin hadn't seen the incident, merely had it reported to him—but he didn't believe it.

Did Detective Chamberlain know Ezra Hayes had struck Aaron in the street? Was that why he'd latched onto the Kelmanskys? But why would he think Ada, rather than Aaron, was the one who'd killed Hayes?

*There was no dispute. You have my word.* Hanley swore as he hurried along. He'd known Aaron was lying but hadn't pressed him hard enough. Because Rivka was there, and he'd heard her indrawn breath, seen the worry in her face.

Rivka's house lay just ahead. He strode to the front door and knocked. Waited. No one came. The boy must not be home from school yet. Aaron would be working some odd job, God knew where. Rivka would be out on whatever daily errands women did. Frustrated, he tugged at his hair. Where in heaven's name should he look for her—the butcher's, the greengrocer's, the…

*Tailor shop.* She taught English to girls there, he recalled. He eyed the slant of the sun and guessed the time at somewhere around two o'clock. Not too late to catch her, maybe. *If I get that damned promotion, I'm buying myself a pocket-watch.* He turned and loped down the boardwalk toward Madison Street.

Nathan and Zalman's shop was busy when Hanley walked in. At the jangle of the bell over the front door, Jacob Nathan glanced up from the coat sleeve he was pinning. The customer wearing it turned his head just enough to see who'd entered. He and everyone else in the shop regarded Hanley with startled looks.

Nathan recovered first. "Detective. What brings you here? You have news for Aaron? Good news, I hope."

"No news. Is Miss Kelmansky here?"

Nathan glanced at Moishe Zalman, who stood behind a slanted table draped in dark gray wool, a pair of shears in his hand. Something unspoken passed between the two men, and Nathan gave Zalman a nod. Then Zalman set down the shears and stepped out, his spine straight and shoulders squared as if answering a challenge. "You talk to me."

Hanley frowned. "Is Miss Kelmansky here or not? I need to speak with—"

"Rivka cannot see you. You ask *me*. *Vos iz?*"

Hanley knew enough Yiddish by now to recognize *what is it*. Short, blunt, and combative, nothing like the young man's usual diffidence. And he'd used Rivka's given name. What *that* meant... Turmoil gripped Hanley, and his temper took hold of his tongue. "This is police business," he snapped. "I can arrest you for obstructing—"

At the rear of the shop, a curtain slid back. Rivka stood framed in the doorway, wide eyed. The sight of her hit him like a gut punch.

Zalman turned and hurried toward her. *"Alts iz gut, mayn libe. Er geyt avek."*

Rivka stepped forward. *"Moishe, Ikh—"*

Zalman blocked her path. *"Neyn, mayn libe."* His fingers brushed her cheek.

Hanley's gut punch feeling deepened. Ada had warned him. He should have seen this coming, should have known.

Moishe turned to face him again, taking firm hold of Rivka's hand and keeping her beside him. "We are promised, Rivka and I. You understand, *ja?*"

Jumbled words stuck in Hanley's throat. *Get out of my way, you bastard. She's coming with me.* Beneath the churning mix of jealousy, embarrassment, and anger, heartache loomed like a thunderhead. What if he bulled his way over and grabbed her? What would Zalman—or Nathan and the rest—do? He couldn't risk it, for Rivka's sake.

He locked eyes with her instead. "Miss Kelmansky, I need to speak with you about your brother and sister-in-law. Can we talk privately, outside?" *Where they can see us, but not hear...*

Her only answer was the pleading in her face. For him? To do what—stay, go? A wild vision overcame him of tearing her from Moishe's side and cracking the man across the jaw, and to hell with what anyone thought. Appalled, he realized his fists were clenched, his arms aching with the effort not to throw a punch. Best leave now, before he lost all mastery of himself.

He held Rivka's gaze a few seconds longer. "I won't give up," he said. Please God she'd understand everything he meant.

Rivka shut her eyes and turned away.

❧

Hanley walked for a long while, paying little heed to his surroundings beyond keeping clear of street traffic. The smell of the river, close enough to gag him at first, gradually receded. At some point his feet hurt enough that he wanted to sit down, and his heart hurt enough that he needed a damned drink. He barged into the next saloon he saw, laid what coin he had on the bar, snagged the glass he received in return and carried it to a table in the dimmest corner he could find.

He tried to focus on the case, on Coughlin's claim to have gone straight home after leaving Ezra Hayes definitely alive and well at the Armory jail Tuesday night, but he couldn't bring his thoughts under control. Couldn't do anything except sit in this damned saloon whose name he didn't know, staring into the single whiskey his scant funds afforded him. It tasted like it last saw the inside of a horse, and a sick one at that. He gulped it anyway, in hopes it would help him forget the past hour or so. His head throbbed, and he closed his eyes. Images swirled in the darkness. Rivka gazing at him in the tailor shop. Turning from him, hiding her face against Zalman's shoulder. Her *promised*. Soon to be her—

He choked down the remaining rotgut. Of course she would marry one of her own. She was well over twenty…it was long past time. Why did the idea hurt him so? She wasn't an Irish girl, anyone he'd a right to think of. Her brother had made that clear since the ceilidh dance. Thoughts of that brought fresh memories to swamp him. Rivka laughing as he pulled her through the fast steps of reels and jigs. The heart-stirring music and her bright eyes making his blood race. Her kerchief sliding off her shining dark hair as they danced. Walking her home after…that kiss, her lips soft and sweet against his own…

He shoved himself upright and stumbled around the fat barrel that served as a table. *Not drunk. Nowhere near, damn it.* Behind him, someone snickered. He couldn't see who, didn't care enough to find out and teach them a lesson. Work. Work would help. What was Rivka Kelmansky to him, anyway? Just a girl he'd met on a case. A girl he'd no business wanting, dirt-stupid fool that he was.

He hurried outside, wincing in the bright late-afternoon sun.

♋

He was near drunk enough to spend a while hunting for Aaron at random building sites within a reasonable walk of Market Street, before common sense took hold. *Aaron could be anywhere around here. I'm wasting time.*

Ada, now. He knew exactly where she was. Back to the Armory, then, with the story Coughlin, damn him, had told—*a white man and a mulatto boy*—ringing in Hanley's brain. *She'll have to say where Aaron was on Tuesday night. She won't have a choice.*

Unfortunately, he was wrong. "I told you before. We were home." Ada stood rigid in the middle of the cell, her expression grim. "I've nothing else to say."

"How about the truth?" It came out harshly, and he made an effort to gentle his tone as well as lower his voice. "I know what happened in front of your son's school Tuesday morning. I know Aaron had words with Ezra, and Ezra struck him."

She flinched, then rallied. "Then you must also know Aaron didn't press charges." Suspicion flickered across her face. "He didn't even report it. How do you know about it?"

"I'm a cop. We have our sources. It doesn't matter." The setbacks of the day, and a looming sense of time running out, made him grip the cell bars as if sheer pressure could snap them. "What matters is, if I found out, Detective Chamberlain will, too. Once he does, I'd not give a plugged nickel for my chances of clearing you—or your husband. Chamberlain will happily see you both on trial if it makes a lick of sense and gets him shut of the case."

A sickly pallor washed over her, and she shut her eyes briefly. "It's hopeless, then."

"Not if you tell me the truth. Where was Aaron, and where were you, Tuesday night?"

She turned away, her spine and shoulders so taut it hurt him to look at her.

"Mrs. Kelmansky." He pressed against the bars. "Please. I can help you if you trust me."

He counted five heartbeats before she faced him again. "We were home," she said, each word brittle as glass. Her eyes gleamed wet in the dim light of the cell block. "That's all I can tell you. I'm sorry."

# FIFTY

*August 6, 1872*

The patch of sky outside Rivka's window was pearl-gray edged with pink when she got out of bed. Her head felt stuffed with cotton wool, the effect of a sleepless night. She'd kept reliving Hanley's appearance at the tailor shop, when Moishe had barred her from talking to him. She'd seen in Hanley's face the wild impulse to take her away, seen him wrestle it into words instead of action. *I should have gone with him. Never mind what they think, what Aaron thinks. It's my life, not his!*

Outrage drove her to the washstand, where she splashed lukewarm water on her hot face and scrubbed it dry. Aaron and Nat would be astir soon and needing breakfast. The thought of Nat blunted her anger, reminded her of their precarious situation. Ada was still in jail, facing conviction for murder, unless Hanley could save her. *I can help him. I have to help him. I owe Ada that.*

A spark of hope flared. *He said he won't give up.* The spark brightened, spread its warmth through her. She knew what Hanley meant, had spent all night thinking of it between bouts of heartache and rage. It wasn't just Ada he wouldn't give up on.

She took a day dress from her wardrobe and laid it across the bed. She knew what she had to do now and felt her spirits rise to the challenge.

☙

Rivka drew shallow breaths through her mouth as she followed the turnkey downstairs and through a short, dank underground corridor lit by flickering gaslights. At the far end was a lighter patch of dimness—the entrance to the Negro jail, she guessed. Bile rose in her throat. She choked it back. Ada shouldn't be here. No one should be locked up in a place like this.

She put from her mind the trouble that surely awaited her when she got home. Tanta Hannah had arrived too conveniently this morning, for breakfast and "to start work on your bride's chest. There's a lot to do and not much time." Another thing Rivka didn't want to think about. She knew why Hannah was really there—to get in the way if Hanley turned up. After yesterday, Aaron, Jacob, and Moishe were taking no chances.

Hannah would soon know Rivka was gone, if she didn't already. The excuse of a headache and needing to lie down in her room would only last so long. But Hanley had meant to ask her about Ada and Aaron. He must know something connecting them to Ezra Hayes's death. Before Rivka could say anything to him, she had to know what had happened the night Ezra died.

They emerged from the tunnel into a wide-open chamber lined with barred cells on both sides, a walkway down the middle. The turnkey nodded toward one. "Fifteen minutes, then I'll come get you." He held out a cupped hand. "I'll take them safety pins now, miss."

Rivka dug the pins out of her small satchel and handed them to him. The turnkey had inspected the satchel before bringing her here, his ears turning bright pink when he realized what it contained. Tense and uncomfortable as Rivka felt, this unexpected touch of humanity had made her want to laugh…or cry. The turnkey pocketed the pins and nodded toward Ada's cell. "Quarter hour, mind. That's it."

Ada was standing at the bars, gripping them tight, when Rivka hurried over. She looked exhausted beyond endurance. "What are you doing here? Is there news? Is Aaron all right…and Nat? Nothing's happened since yesterday?"

"They're fine. They're well." Rivka fished in the satchel again and brought out a fistful of soft cotton rags. "I brought you these. I know it's near that time…"

"Thank you." Biting her lip, Ada took the rags and tucked them in her skirt pocket. The cell's other occupant, a gray-haired woman in a ragged sack dress, huddled in the corner a few feet away, snoring. "What's happening? Aaron doesn't tell me much when he comes." She hesitated. "Does Detective Hanley tell you anything? When did you last see him?"

"I saw him yesterday. Not to speak to." Rivka's throat tightened and she drew a deep breath. "He is still trying to help you. And I want to help *him*, for your sake and Aaron's."

The worry in Ada's face deepened. "Aaron's done nothing. I'll swear it on the Bible if I have to—"

Rivka paused as she considered her next words. "When Detective Chamberlain first came…when he brought you to the police station from our house…you asked if he came because of 'what happened the other day.' Something to do with Aaron, yes? What was it?"

Ada let go of the bars. "Nothing that led to murder."

"Chamberlain seems to think it did."

Ada stiffened and glared at her. "Do *you*?"

"Of course not. I know you didn't kill Ezra Hayes. I know Aaron didn't kill him. But what we *know* doesn't matter. Only what we can prove." She grasped the bars where Ada had done so moments before. "What happened the day Ezra died? Is that why you and Aaron both went to his boardinghouse last Tuesday night?"

"I wasn't…we didn't—" Ada's shoulders sagged. "How did you know? Does that detective know, too?"

"Aaron told me. After Shabbos. It was late. He was very tired." She chose not to mention that he'd been drinking, or that he'd also said, *Don't talk to Hanley. If he comes here, avoid him.* "I've said nothing to anyone. But I think Hanley knows. Part of it, all of it." She shrugged. "I'm not sure. I do know he believes you're innocent, and he doesn't trust Chamberlain. But he cannot help you, or Aaron, without the whole truth."

Ada stood motionless for several seconds. Then she sighed and covered Rivka's hands with her own. "Detective Hanley knows there was a fight between Aaron and Ezra…somehow, I don't know how.

But he doesn't know what the fight was about." She took a deep breath, squeezed Rivka's hands, and continued. "Ezra sent Nat a letter. He wants...wanted Nat to live with him, not go west with us. I told Aaron. He walked Nat to school Tuesday morning. Ezra was there, and...he and Aaron had words. Then Ezra struck Aaron and ran off." She swallowed. "When Aaron came home that night, he told me what happened. I was concerned about Ezra because he hadn't shown up for work that day. I decided to find him, try to talk him out of taking Nat away from us... so I slipped out after Aaron went to the Nathans'. I thought he'd be there for most of the evening. I didn't think he'd follow after me." A sad smile flitted across her face. "I should have known. It's like him, to think he had to rescue me from my own foolishness."

"And did you find Ezra there?"

"No, and his landlady didn't know where he was. I didn't know where else to look for him."

Footsteps sounded from the tunnel. The quarter hour must be up. "Did anyone besides Aaron see you at the boardinghouse? Can the landlady prove you were there, and when?"

Ada nodded, with a worried glance past Rivka toward the approaching turnkey. "Her name is Mrs. Kelvin. It's at 148 Twelfth Street."

∾

Hanley had choked down what breakfast he could, and it lay in his stomach like bricks as he hurried toward Lake Street Station. After a mostly uneasy night, he'd finally managed to sleep upon realizing that, without a formal assault complaint, Chamberlain would have to stumble on the story of Ezra's confrontation with Aaron near young Nat's school, just as Hanley himself had. That gave him some breathing space, at least.

He was sweating by the time he reached Canal Street, the temperature already climbing past bearable levels. He turned north and headed toward Lake, bypassing his usual route over the river and down Market Street in front of Rivka's house. He couldn't face her just now. As always, the steady rhythm of his stride helped marshal his thoughts. Ada Kelmansky's best hope was for him to prove who'd really killed Ezra Hayes. Had Coughlin done it, or hired it done, so he could get his hands on the evidence of slave labor at Sweetbay Sugar that he surely knew Hayes had? Sergeant Moore's words came to mind, from their tense conversation in his office. *Why bother killing Hayes? Why not buy the evidence from him? Gambling debts or not, Coughlin has money, and it'd be a lot less risky.* Except Ezra had died in an alley off State and Thirteenth Streets, a considerable distance from Coughlin's house on Elizabeth Street.

*If Coughlin's not lying again.* The man had no live-in domestics, hadn't helpfully chatted with a neighbor out for an evening walk upon his arrival home. On the other hand, Hanley couldn't prove he *hadn't* gone straight to his own house from the Armory jail. *Stalemate.*

He tugged his hair in sheer frustration. *Drop it for now. Come at it fresh in a few hours. There's work to do still on the O'Shea case.* Like running Mahoney to earth again, making the surly bastard say why he'd shoved Hanley in front of an omnibus almost two weeks ago. Had that muttered, "Mind your business!" been a message from Coughlin after all? Were the two of them in cahoots even then?

He crossed the Lake Street Bridge and turned toward the stationhouse. Too much to hope that he'd find Mahoney in Lake Street's lockup, but the fellow was a habitual brawler who frequented Jacky O'Toole's, so it wasn't impossible he'd fetched up at some station in the area. At this point, the "luck of the Irish" felt like the only thing Hanley could count on.

⁊

No Mahoney at Lake Street, but something nearly as good—an incident report charging him with assault the previous evening, against a night shift patrolman Hanley knew as a friend of Rolf Schmidt's. Hanley's next stop was the West Chicago Avenue station, where the stout desk sergeant eagerly shared the juicy story. "That damn fool can't stay out of trouble. Drunker'n hell out on the street, singing some goddamn thing at the top of his lungs, slugged the beat cop who told him to pipe down, there's working people sleeping hereabouts. Happened near some rail yard, I heard. He didn't hurt your man bad, but you *don't* take a swing at them big Germans if you got any sense. German fella put him down with one gut punch, called him out for assaultin' an officer. Your house was full, so they parked him here overnight. We sent him off to police court earlier this morning. Mahoney's looking at prison time, 'less the cop he hit was feeling charitable."

Hanley thanked the sergeant and headed west toward the Second Precinct Station police court at Madison and Union Streets, determined to squeeze the truth out of Mahoney. The proceedings might be over by the time he got there, but Mahoney would surely be held. *Finally, something's breaking my way.*

The prisoners' wagon stood out front, the grim-faced driver just climbing onto the box, when Hanley arrived. A few patrolmen huddled by the steps leading to the stationhouse entrance, talking excitedly. Swift inquiry established that Mahoney wasn't aboard the wagon, or still in Union Street's lockup. The opposite, in fact.

"Sonofabitch punched me," the duty officer said, when Hanley tracked him down in the station lobby. He sat on the visitors' bench, a handkerchief pressed to his bleeding nose. The skin beneath his right eye was turning purple. "Socked me a good one and ran off. We gave chase, but the bastard's fast. Lost him in the crowd." The man sniffed hard and pinched the bridge of his nose. His hair was white, though he didn't look more than ten years Hanley's senior. "That's two cops he's assaulted now. You want help hunting him down, count me in. Son of a damned bitch."

So much for squeezing anything out of Mahoney. "He's a suspect in a murder investigation," Hanley said.

The officer swore. "Didn't know that when we were loading him up. Just that he punched a cop. Why'nt your patrolman *say*? Never mind." He waved his free hand. "Hadn't charged him with more'n assault yet, had you? Still, a word in the ear 'bout murder would've been nice." He sniffed again. "Name's Hamish. Hamish McGowan. You?"

"Hanley. Frank." He shook the hand McGowan offered him. "Which way did Mahoney go? How far did he get?"

"Fella ran east. I didn't get more'n a block after him, with this pouring like Niagara," McGowan said, gesturing toward his nose. "But some of my men kept on him. Saw 'em turn the corner at Clinton, where the horsecars run. Big Swede on the boardwalk tried to grab him there, but your man hit him and yanked loose. Swede said he kept going down Clinton and ducked inside someplace. By the time my men caught up, he was out of sight. We're checking saloons hereabouts, 'specially the Irish ones."

*Damn.* Mahoney could be anywhere in Chicago by now. He'd likely avoid the rail yard, where Hanley'd tracked him down before. He'd still need money to leave town, must've stashed it somewhere. With his drinking mates, Sully and Rourke? Maybe.

"Mahoney's a regular at Cleary's, up north on Kingsbury Street," he said. "At Jacky O'Toole's on Franklin as well. We can branch out from those to other saloons in the area. He's got friends at the Illinois, St. Louis and Grand Southern rail yard, too. I've names back at Lake Street. He's likely got money stashed someplace. I figure he'll skip once he gets hold of it."

McGowan gave him a thumbs-up. "Right you are. I'll get up a posse."

❧

Hanley was sweating, tired, and cranky when he got back to Lake Street. He found Rolf Schmidt and dropped a quiet word in his ear about rounding up patrolmen to check Cleary's and Jacky O'Toole's, then headed into the squad room, where he copied the names and addresses of Mahoney's friends from his case notes and tucked the paper in his pocket. No time to hunt for Chamberlain's case notes again, even if he dared try it.

He ran a hand through his hair. How long had Ada Kelmansky been in the Armory? Six days. Chamberlain must be damned near done building his case against her. Hanley remembered the search warrant complaint, tried to recall what Chamberlain had written in it. *A letter, almost surely from Hayes to Nat, and a small-bladed knife.* Probably young Nat's whittling knife, but anyone in the Kelmansky house could have gotten hold of it. God help Ada if it was a two-inch blade.

He wanted a good long think in the quiet of his room, not another mad chase after Liam Mahoney. But Ada, and Aaron, were running out of time. And Rivka…but he couldn't think of her without his heart feeling squeezed like a wrung-out cloth.

He stalked out of the squad room and was nearly at the stationhouse doors when one of them opened. He stopped dead at the sight of Rivka in the gap. She looked as startled as he felt but recovered swiftly. "I need to talk to you," she said. "I found out where Ada and Aaron were last Tuesday night, when Ezra Hayes was killed."

# FIFTY-ONE

Y ou went to the Armory jail?" Hanley stared at Rivka across the little table at Lily Stemple's eatery, unsure whether he felt more admiring or dismayed. "Good God, that's no place for a woman—"

"Tell that to Ada," Rivka replied. Around them, the murmur of conversations rose and fell. No other coppers in the place just now, no one to overhear them and drop a word in Chamberlain's ear. *Half an hour*, Hanley'd promised himself. He could spare Rivka that much before going after Mahoney. Hamish McGowan and his men were already fanning out from where Mahoney was last seen, and they'd be able to cover a fair amount of ground before Hanley rejoined them.

Rivka toyed with the coffee he'd bought her, which she hadn't touched. Pale and drawn though she was, Hanley savored the sight of her. "How long does Ada have before…whatever happens next?" she asked.

"Arraignment, that'd be." He didn't name the charge. Neither of them needed the reminder. "I can't say exactly how long. It depends on how close Chamberlain thinks he is to being finished. But soon. Within a few days, probably."

"Hashem." The Hebrew word slipped out in a whisper.

*Is that her people's name for God?* Hanley wondered. His landlady, Ida, had told him once that Jews considered God's true name too sacred to say, so they used other words instead. *Fine time to be thinking about that.* He moved his hand to cover Rivka's and felt heartened that she didn't pull away. "Try not to think about it," he said. "Just tell me what you found out."

Rivka relayed to Hanley what she'd learned from Ada about the fight between Aaron and Ezra over Nat, and Ada's subsequent visit to Ezra's boardinghouse to try and talk him out of taking the boy.

"That's all very helpful to know." He chose not to bring up his own second visit to Ada, or the danger Aaron was in now. He would spare Rivka that for as long as he could. Chamberlain still might not know about the incident, if Ada hadn't let anything slip and Hayes's landlady had kept quiet. If he did know, or had pieced things together, Aaron could be in more trouble than his wife.

"And Aaron?" He waited, but she stayed silent. "Where was he that night?"

Beneath his palm, her hand curled into a fist. "Rivka," he said gently. "Trust me."

She let out a breath, and her shoulders sagged. "He followed her to the boardinghouse."

"And then what?"

"When she told him Ezra wasn't there, they decided to return home. There wasn't anything else they could think to do." Rivka unclenched her fist and turned her hand to clasp his, hope warring with anxiety in her eyes. "This helps, doesn't it? To know they were at Ezra's boardinghouse and he wasn't there? So they couldn't have been...out wherever that poor man was killed?"

Hanley eyed his coffee mug, a brief respite from looking her in the face. Ezra Hayes had died between eight and nine o'clock, no later than nine thirty from what Will Rushton had told him. Within that time, Ada and Aaron were only blocks away from the alley off Thirteenth Street where Hayes's body was found. Maybe *at* Thirteenth, if they'd ridden a horsecar back north. The State Street line ran right past that alley. Chamberlain would latch onto this like a mouser on its prey, if he hadn't already. And if he also knew Aaron and Hayes had come to blows...

Maybe he could narrow the time frame. "When did they get home? Do you remember?"

She frowned in thought. "I fell asleep reading. I woke up when I heard them come upstairs. It was close to nine, I think."

"How close?"

She went still as ice, and Hanley cursed inwardly. Something in his tone, or maybe the question itself, had given him away. "We need to know the time as exactly as possible. Just do your best to—"

"When did Hayes die?" she asked.

"I can't say exactly. There's a range—"

"When?"

He couldn't answer. Couldn't bring himself to tell her that her effort to exonerate her sister-in-law and brother had done no such thing and whatever she'd risked to do it was for naught.

She caught his hesitation. "Don't protect me. Just tell me the truth."

He closed his eyes and sighed. "Hayes was bailed out from the Armory at seven thirty that night. His landlady saw him just after eight. Whoever killed him did it between then and nine o'clock, half past at the latest."

She let go of his hand and pressed both palms to her cheeks. He watched her, sick at heart. "Let's just hope Mrs. Kelvin didn't tell Detective Chamberlain she saw Aaron as well as Ada that night," he said, hoping to reassure her. If they weren't in the middle of an eatery, he'd take her in his arms, and to hell with propriety. "Chamberlain's an arrogant bastard...pardon my language. He puts people's backs up. I'd bet Mrs. Kelvin told him as little as she could get away with." Enough to turn his sights toward Ada, obviously. But, if he suspected Aaron as well, surely he'd have gone after Rivka's brother by now. A faint ray of hope, but Hanley clung to it for Rivka's sake.

"It would take time for them to get home," Rivka said. "They would walk, to save the horsecar fare. Someone might have seen them. If they were back at nine o'clock—"

"Hayes could've been dead before then," he reminded her, hating himself for it. "And you're Aaron's sister, and Ada is his wife, so—"

"You think I would lie for them?"

"It doesn't matter what I think. It matters what Chamberlain thinks." He paused, a weight in the pit of his stomach. "Would you lie? Even to me, to save them?"

She stared at him, then pushed back her chair and stood. "I've told you what I know. Do what you will with it." She turned away and stalked toward the door.

"Rivka—" He started after her but hadn't taken three steps before she was gone.

# FIFTY-TWO

**N**ow what? The question wouldn't leave Hanley as he headed toward the rail yard. At this time of day, Sully and Rourke should still be working. If they weren't, or if they clammed up about Mahoney to save the fellow bad trouble, he'd go on to Conley's Patch and see what he could learn from the landlady at the boardinghouse where both men lived. Or should he save that step for later, head back to the station on Union Street, and join McGowan? How far could Mahoney have gotten since his escape, on foot and with empty pockets? Overnight in lockup meant no money for horsecar fare or a day's food and shelter. The man would have to lie low somewhere, or keep moving, until he could get at his grubstake, wherever it was.

He crossed the Lake Street Bridge and turned north onto Canal. Up ahead near Fulton, a horse drawing a hackney cab shied as a brewer's dray crossed its path. Watching the near collision, Hanley thought of Rivka and what had happened at Lily Stemple's. A disaster all its own, that was. Christ, how had he handled it so badly?

Slowly, punctuated by swearing and rude gestures, the traffic snag cleared. *Mind on your job*, Hanley told himself sternly, and strode onward.

❧

As he'd feared, Mahoney's drinking mates no longer wanted to talk, and neither man knew where the fellow kept his money. Last Thursday's chase through the rail yard, and Mahoney's absence from work since, had made clear he was in deeper trouble than Sully and Rourke wanted to deal with. "Got cargo to move, no time," Sully said, regret on his face as he hurried off toward a newly arrived train. Conn Rourke had simply shrugged, then scuttled away. A question to Jamieson, the clerk, confirmed Mahoney had missed payday on August 3rd. "What happens if you don't show to collect?" Hanley asked.

"Goes in there." Jamieson jerked a thumb toward a tall wooden safe with a combination lock, in the back corner of the office. "He'll get it next payday. The men sign for their wages, so the railway has a record. Mahoney all right?"

"Far as I know." He thanked the clerk and left, sharply aware of time passing. One more stop before linking up with McGowan. But Mahoney's former landlady hadn't seen hide nor hair of him either. Nor had she agreed to keep his money safe. "All I've got is what he left me of his room and board," she sniffed, as if offended Hanley would ask. "I'm not a bank for my lodgers. I've quite enough to do, between cooking and washing and keeping track of room rents. Now I'll thank you to clear off, before someone gets the notion there are criminals on the premises."

The station on Union Street, finally, and a quick catch-up with Hamish McGowan in the stationhouse lobby. "No sign of him so far in any saloon hereabouts, but there's plenty of lowlife hangouts left to check," McGowan told him. His left eye was purple-black and so puffy Hanley wondered how he could see out of it. "I'm happy to haul that bastard back here soon's we nail him. Better yet, straight to the goddamn Armory."

They left the station together while Hanley filled McGowan in about Mahoney's likely shortage of cash and his own efforts organizing searches near Lake Street. "Though we can't be sure he went anywhere near his home ground. Unless he's a fool, he has to know we'll be looking in all his usual haunts."

"Right." They headed west on Madison, and McGowan waved toward the upcoming intersection. "Plenty of Irish watering holes along Halsted and Peoria. See what we find, eh?"

Five saloons later, with no luck at all, Hanley's fledgling hope had turned to baffled fury. "Where the hell is he?" he muttered as they left the site of their latest failure. He didn't recall its name; they'd all begun to blur. "Vanished into thin air?"

As McGowan drew breath to reply, a patrolman in blue came puffing up to them. "They sent me to find you, sir," he said, eyes on McGowan. "Officer Turley spotted a fellow, looks like the one we're after, breaking into a house. A fine one, near Lake and Elizabeth."

*Elizabeth.* The street name nagged at Hanley. Then it hit him. "Good God. What's the house number?"

The patrolman told him. Hanley turned to McGowan. "I know the place. Let's go."

The patrolman peeled off at McGowan's order, to gather more men for the arrest. The stocky Scotsman kept pace with Hanley's ground-eating stride, and they reached Elizabeth Street faster than expected. "I'll take the front door. You take the back," McGowan said. Hanley nodded and hurried around the house. He reached the backyard and halted. The kitchen window was open, curtains fluttering in the breeze.

He drew breath to shout, then checked the impulse. Quietly, he approached the back steps. As he drew near, he appraised the gap between the sash and the windowsill. Large enough to admit an average-sized man...maybe large enough for the burly Mahoney, if he didn't mind a scrape or two. A jagged scratch in the window frame drew Hanley's gaze, and he leaned forward to peer at it. The window must have stuck, and Mahoney had forced it. The golden brown of bare wood shone through the green paint.

Something creaked. The back door flew open and Mahoney hurtled out of it. Fast and low, he swung something at Hanley's midsection. The impact doubled Hanley over. Burning pain shot through him as he and Mahoney went sprawling.

Breathing was agony. *Broken rib. More than one?* The pain held him immobile for precious seconds as Mahoney scrambled to his feet and dashed toward the low fence that separated the yard from its neighbor. The railman flung something large and dark away from him and leapt the fence, turned toward the alleyway, then vanished behind a shed at the edge of the neighboring lot.

*McGowan. Call out.* Hanley sucked in air, ignoring the feeling of knives in his lungs, just as McGowan charged around the side of the house. "That way," Hanley gasped, jerking his head in the direction Mahoney had gone. He struggled to prop himself on an elbow and fought down panic as he waited for the fresh surge of pain to clear. *I'm not dying. Not passing out. It just hurts.*

McGowan ran toward the alley, then stopped and looked back at Hanley. "Sonofabitch," he muttered and hurried over. "What'd he do? Don't see any blood—"

"Hit me." Hanley ground the words out. "Something hard. Broke some ribs." He sucked in another breath through clenched teeth. "Tossed it…by the fence."

"Let's get you off the ground." McGowan helped Hanley sit up against the side of the house. "By the fence, aye." He went over and peered at the grass, then bent and grabbed something. "The missus here won't be happy, I'm thinking," he said, holding the object out so Hanley could see.

Hanley's disbelieving *whuff* of a laugh sent fresh agony through him. "An iron skillet. Goddamn."

# FIFTY-THREE

Rivka's steps dragged as she neared home. What had she been thinking? In trying to help Ada she'd only made things worse. And Hanley…but she couldn't think of him without knots in her stomach. That he could ask whether she would lie to him! Did he think she had? The thought that he no longer trusted her left a hollow place inside. She would have to face Hannah and Jacob soon, Moishe as well, after sneaking out from under Hannah's nose this morning. At least Aaron probably wasn't home yet. She should have one night's peace before the storm broke.

She realized how wrong that notion was when she walked in the back door and found Tanta Hannah in the kitchen, peeling potatoes. Hannah gave her a single, piercing glance, then turned back to her work. Her silence offered no relief. *Do I speak first and bring fury down on my head? Or wait until Hannah is ready?*

She moved further into the room and began untying her kerchief. "Leave it," Hannah snapped. "You're coming home with me. To stay until the wedding, as your brother wants. The boy can come, too, until Aaron returns. Find a pot, we'll take the potatoes with us."

Rivka's hands briefly stilled. Then she finished undoing the knot and slid the kerchief off her head. "I'm staying. Aaron needs me, Nat needs me—"

Hannah thumped the potato and paring knife on the counter. "Aaron and the boy will do well enough on their own. You won't. You proved that today. Where were you, Rivka? What were you doing? We checked the shul, we checked with your friend Sisel Klein, we checked everywhere. Including the police station at Lake Street. You were nowhere to be found, nor was Detective Hanley. Were you with him while that other man was here, searching this house?"

"What?" Fresh anxiety shot through her as she guessed who Hannah meant. "What did this man look like? Did he tell you his name?"

"He was big. Square. A policeman's badge on his wrinkled shirt." Hannah pursed her lips in disapproval. "He wouldn't say who he was. That German patrolman—Schmidt?—was with him. They had a paper. Schmidt showed me. They were looking for a knife and a letter. They went all through the house. They weren't here for long, baruch Hashem, no more than half an hour. And you…you were gone, who knows where, I didn't know what to tell Jacob when—"

"I was with Ada. I've been doing what I could to help her, bring her home. I told Detective Hanley what I found out." The letter would be Nat's, from Ezra Hayes, the knife maybe Nat's as well. Rivka felt her breathing quicken. "Did you see what they took…or if they took anything at all?"

Hannah folded her arms. "It doesn't matter. This situation has gone far enough. Jacob and I have indulged you too much since your father died. We never should have let you stay here on your own. You haven't the sense of a baby rabbit about how other people see things, and with your brother's foolishness, and now this—"

"That he married Ada, you mean, and calls her son his own? Is it *foolishness* because they're *goyim* or mulattoes? Or both?"

A flush stained Hannah's cheeks. "You can't be that naïve, Rivka. I've served as *rebbetzin* for ten years, ever since your mother passed on…I hear things no one would say to your face, or Aaron's. It was hard enough when Ada and her boy first came. Now she's in jail, some think she must belong there." The flush deepened. "I do not say this. Jacob, either. Even after today, there may be some other explanation. But others *do* say it. Our neighbors, our friends. Part of us, just as much as you and Aaron are."

"Fray Zalman, you mean." Moishe's mother, more than likely, and others who'd objected to giving Aaron's family refuge here less than five months ago. "So, because of her, and a few other *foolish* people, we should abandon Aaron's wife to be punished for a crime she didn't commit? Because she isn't 'one of us'?"

"Rivka—"

"'You shall love the stranger who dwells among you, for you were strangers in the land of Egypt.' What about that, Hannah? We offered them sanctuary! You spoke for Ada then. How can you say now—"

"Jacob and I have to think of your future! Your position is precarious enough. People avoid you on the street. Jacob says you're losing students. And now the police have searched your house for evidence of murder! Do you really think you can go traipsing around the city, with your Irish policeman or on your own, in the midst of all this and no one will notice or care?"

"Does Moishe care? What does he say?" Not that it would stop her if he objected. The thought crossed her mind that, if he disapproved and she defied him, he might look elsewhere for a more biddable bride. *Or his mother will force him to.*

Hannah pursed her lips. "He doesn't know. When I went to Jacob and told him—about the police search and that you'd gone—we agreed to say nothing. But Moishe is not stupid, nor is his good nature boundless. You have taken enough advantage of it, don't you think?"

Rivka's answer was quiet but firm. "I won't abandon Ada. She's innocent. The detective who came today is wrong. I'm going to help Hanley prove it. And I won't be packed off to your house until my wedding day as if I'm an errant child. So, unless you're prepared to drag me with you, this discussion is over."

"You cannot be so reckless, so unwise—"

"It won't be the first time, will it?"

Hannah stared at her. In her face, Rivka saw worry and regret, a look both painful and familiar. "Whatever you may think, Rivkaleh, we have only your good at heart."

"I know." The words came out through a tight throat. "You are doing what you believe you must. So am I."

ભ

After Hannah left, Rivka went upstairs. Nat was sitting up in bed, eyeing a well-creased sheet of paper in his hand. "How are you feeling?" she asked softly. And then thought how absurd that question was, with things as bleak as they were.

Nat glanced up. He looked exhausted from more than a summer cold. As he drew breath to answer her, a booming cough engulfed him. "They took my knife," he croaked, when it subsided. "Not my pa's letter, though. I keep it under the mattress. That dumb cop missed it."

Despite his bravado, she heard the tremor in his voice. Her heart hurt, as if someone had twisted it. "Nat—"

Loud banging echoed from downstairs. Someone was pounding at the front door. "Police! Open up!"

Chamberlain. A jolt of panic held her still. *He knows about Aaron. The landlady told him.* But Aaron wasn't here. He was out working, and Rivka could truthfully say she didn't know where. That thought gave her courage. She met Nat's frightened gaze as the pounding came again. "Stay here and keep quiet," she said, and went to answer the door.

Chamberlain and Officer Schmidt stood on the front stoop. Schmidt looked as if he didn't want to be here. "Aaron Kelmansky," Chamberlain said. "Is he here?"

Fresh fear shot through her. "No. He's working."

"Where?"

"I don't know."

"'Course you don't." He shouldered past her into the house. "Kelmansky! Come on out. We're going to the station."

"He isn't here." Despite her best efforts, Rivka's voice shook. "What is this about? Why do you want my brother—"

"Murder." Chamberlain tossed the word over his shoulder as he peered into the empty parlor. "Or accessory to it. You warn him or help him, you're an accessory, too." He glanced at Schmidt and nodded down the hall toward the kitchen. "Check that way. I'll take upst—" At the creak of floorboards above, a wolfish grin crossed his face. "By God, we've got him! Keep her quiet." He turned and strode toward the staircase.

"Nat! Stay where you are!" Rivka hurried after him.

She was halfway up the stairs when she heard Chamberlain growl, "Your stepdad hiding in here, boy? He come home from wherever he was this morning? Out of my way!" She ran faster and reached the top as the detective shoved Nat backward through his bedroom doorway and sent him sprawling.

Angry as well as afraid, she hurried to Nat's side. She helped him sit, then glared at Chamberlain while the man prowled the small space. "I told you, my brother isn't here. Leave us alone!"

"I could haul the pair of you in. Maybe that'd loosen your tongues." He eyed them coldly, as if considering. Rivka stared back at him. After a few seconds, he looked away. "Schmidt!"

Another brief silence. Then she heard the patrolman climbing the stairs.

"Keep an eye on them," Chamberlain said as Schmidt appeared in the doorway. "If Kelmansky's odd-jobbing, he can't be far. I'll go roust a few men."

♋

She couldn't talk Nat back into bed. The boy was too agitated to rest. "He can't take Papa Aaron. We have to find him, warn—"

"Hush." Rivka glanced over her shoulder. Schmidt was pacing the hall outside Nat's bedroom. Had he heard? She waited until the patrolman was out of sight, then turned to the boy. "I'll take care of things. I promise." *Idiot, you don't even know if you can leave the house.* But of course she would. If Schmidt refused to disobey Chamberlain, she'd walk off anyway. What was he going to do, chase her down the boardwalk? Her mind raced as she eyed the doorway again. Go to Lake Street, find Hanley, tell him… but she couldn't go to Lake Street. Chamberlain was there, rounding up men to search for Aaron. If he saw her…no, she had to handle this on her own. Nat, though. She couldn't leave him here.

She went to the clothespress in the corner and took out a shirt and pants. "Get dressed and go next door to the Nathans'," she whispered. "Tell Tanta Hannah to find Detective Hanley. I'll warn Aaron."

Nat nodded as he took the clothing from her.

Schmidt was loitering at the top of the stairs. He followed Rivka down to the kitchen, where she turned to face him. "Detective Chamberlain is wrong. Ada didn't kill anyone. Nor did my brother. Hanley can prove it if he gets the chance."

Schmidt looked uneasy. "Best stay here, Fraulein. You cross Chamberlain? Trouble."

"And we don't have trouble now?" She folded her arms, listening for Nat's quiet footfall on the stairs. "I need to tell Hanley. He'll want to know what's happened." A white lie at worst. She *would* tell Hanley, as soon as she dared go where she hoped he was. *But first, find Aaron.*

"Hanley is out on a case." Schmidt cocked his head. "You won't go to Lake Street. You think you find your brother before Chamberlain does. Thought you don't know where he is?"

"I don't. I know where he worked yesterday. He might still be there." A soft creak and a flicker of motion at the far end of the hallway told her Nat had reached the front door. As the boy slipped through it, she looked Schmidt in the eye. "If you're afraid of being blamed, we can think of some excuse…"

He looked doubtful a moment more, then shrugged. "You go to outhouse, don't come back."

☙

Aaron wasn't at the building site by Washington and LaSalle, where he'd been clearing rubble the day before. "We're done with that," the foreman said when Rivka explained her purpose. "It's skilled workmen I need now, not just willing hands and a strong back. But they're clearing another lot down the street." He pointed. "I told him to check there for work. Steady man, that brother of yours. If he knew how to lay brick, I'd hire him in a heartbeat."

"Thank you." She hurried off down LaSalle, praying she'd be in time. Praying Aaron would be there. Praying Chamberlain wouldn't. So far, she hadn't seen the detective or his search party. Maybe her luck would hold.

She could see the building site ahead, swarming with workmen shoveling rubble into wheelbarrows and dumping it in a pile on the east side of the lot. Aaron was there, pushing a barrow, his *kippah* marking him out among the fifteen or so other bare-headed men.

A flash of blue caught her attention. She halted in the middle of the boardwalk, heart pounding. Four patrolmen walked onto the site, Chamberlain leading them. They strode up to Aaron and surrounded him. He let go of the barrow, his startled look giving way to shock and anger as the big detective laid hold of him. The patrolmen closed in, cutting off her view.

Instinct propelled her forward, as if to grab Aaron and drag him from his captors, but fear and cold logic checked her. If Chamberlain saw her, he'd arrest her as well. He'd threatened as much. The stinking, vermin-ridden Armory jail came sharply to mind, and clammy sweat rose on her skin. *Get help. Where?* Hanley was on a case. Find him? Impossible. Onkl Jacob, Moishe? What could they do, against the police and the law?

The coppers with their prize were turning toward her. She slipped out of sight, through the small crowd that had gathered to watch, and ran.

# FIFTY-FOUR

Y ou'll be fine," the ward doctor told Hanley after a thorough examination that hurt like hell. McGowan had called a patrol wagon from the Union Street station to ferry Hanley to Cook County Hospital. "One broken rib, two cracked. Take it easy for the next few weeks, and don't stint on the willow bark tea." He tucked in the end of the bandage he'd wrapped around Hanley's midsection. "Strong drink helps, too. Doesn't kill the pain, but swallow enough of it and you won't care."

Damn Mahoney. Hanley had no time to play invalid. "How long is a few weeks?"

"Four to six. You'll want to sleep sitting up the first couple of nights. Have you got family or someone to keep an eye on you? There's warning signs of a bruised lung, or God forbid, pneumonia—high fever, pain in your shoulder or gut, increasing chest pain or shortness of breath. If you start coughing up mucus or blood—"

"How soon am I fit for duty?"

The doctor sighed. "Rest up through Sunday, and you can go back to work on Monday. *If* the pain goes down and *if* you take things easy. No chasing suspects or breaking up saloon brawls, understand? Or you'll be right back here with a bruised lung or worse, and I won't guarantee I can save you."

⁕

The doctor had cleared him for the trip home—"Better off walking than riding the cars, as long as you rest when needed. Walking around helps with breathing, in fact." Hanley had no intention of going home yet. He'd a fugitive to find, who might well have fled toward familiar ground while Hanley was being poked and prodded. And Chamberlain—the bastard must be nearly finished with his case against Ada, to be swiftly followed by arraignment and trial, unless Hanley figured out a way to stop it.

He shortened the journey to Lake Street Station by riding the horsecar partway, though several blocks' walk awaited him at the north end of the State Street line. The trip offered ample time to think despite the dull throbbing that spiked whenever the car went over a bump or pulled in at the curb. The pain disjointed his thoughts, made it hard to focus. Mahoney, Coughlin. Two murder victims, Lawrence O'Shea and Ezra Hayes. Rivka. God in heaven, what a mess he'd made of things there. He'd as good as called her a liar. That was how she took it, though he hadn't meant it so. His head ached, and he pinched the bridge of his nose. He was in no shape to think about how to explain himself. Yet he had to make things right between them. Rivka needed his help. He needed her to trust him. Had he sacrificed that, and more, with his careless words? Painful thought. He didn't want to think it.

The horsecar lurched, throwing him back against the wooden bench. He sucked in a harsh breath, then forced himself to concentrate on the questions at hand. Why had Mahoney broken into Patrick Coughlin's house? How did he know where it was? Bosses like Coughlin didn't normally share their home addresses with mere laborers like Mahoney. Unless there was more between these two men than a workplace and a shared taste for gambling at dog tracks and ten-cent dive saloons. Maybe Lawrence O'Shea's murder wasn't the first time Coughlin had paid Mahoney for violence, just the most lethal.

A memory nagged at him, something Rolf Schmidt had said about arresting Mahoney in May for brawling. *He jumps a fella in the street. Fella owed him money, I guess, the way Mahoney's yelling, 'Pay up.' Other guy didn't want to talk, ran away like a rabbit soon as he could.* Was it Coughlin the beating victim owed, and had the yard boss paid Mahoney to collect? God knew Coughlin needed as much cash as he could lay hands on, if a gambling prince like Johnny Dowling had the fellow in his sights.

Carts and hackneys rattled past, and the smell of horse carried on the hot breeze. Sweat made the bandage around Hanley's ribs itch, but trying to scratch only hurt more. He gritted his teeth and did his best to ignore the pain. Skimming from the railway was another obvious source of extra funds. How did Coughlin manage it—and how did he keep track of the money he stole? He'd need his own private record of what sums he'd diverted, if only to keep things straight. Was Mahoney looking for that at Coughlin's place? Though how he'd have known it existed, or anything about Coughlin's scheming…surely to God the yard boss wouldn't have told him. Could be Mahoney was smarter than he seemed and had guessed.

Hanley shifted on the bench, vainly seeking relief as a fresh jolt sent agony through his ribs. *If I were stealing money from a railroad, how would I do it?* Seamus Reilly had said there was big money in sugar and molasses. That had to be part of it, the slave labor another. No wages paid at the Sweetbay Sugar plantation, and no bother about working people to death in the cane fields or boiling houses, producing more hogsheads than their competitors who didn't use slaves could. What had Coughlin said about Sweetbay, when he'd let Hanley see that June ledger? Something about "a good deal" for the railway, Sweetbay Sugar paying a lower rate but making up for it by shipping a higher amount of goods. If sugar producers were awash in money, why didn't Coughlin charge more? With hugely lowered costs from enslaving its workers, Sweetbay could afford it. Wouldn't that be an even better deal for the Illinois, St. Louis and Grand Southern?

He buried his head in his hands. None of this got him any closer to proving who'd killed Ezra Hayes. Unless…had Mahoney done it at Coughlin's behest? He straightened, wincing. That couldn't be, he realized with a sinking heart. Mahoney was in lockup at the West Chicago Avenue station the night Hayes died, far away from where the killing happened. Maybe Ezra's death was a random street crime, the perpetrator unlikely to be found. Or had it been Aaron Kelmansky after all? He only had Ada's word—through Rivka—that she'd been with her husband that night.

The horsecar pulled in at Randolph, the end of the line. Hanley got off and headed west toward the stationhouse. Seven blocks and he'd be there. Could rest for a few minutes, maybe, while Schmidt or somebody caught him up on whether Mahoney'd been spotted anywhere around. As for what to do next to save Ada...*I'll think of something. I'll have to.*

⌘

"Message for you, Detective," the desk sergeant said as Hanley walked into the stationhouse lobby. He held out a small white envelope. "Miss Kelmansky dropped it by, said it was urgent."

Hanley grabbed the envelope, tore it open, and pulled the letter out. A shiver went through him as he read. *Aaron was arrested. Chamberlain took him. The house was searched this morning, and Chamberlain found Nat's whittling knife. Please come as soon as you can.*

Hanley crumpled the note in his fist. "Where's Detective Chamberlain? Is he here?"

The desk sergeant shook his head. "Out. Escorting a murder suspect to the Armory, I heard. Don't know when he'll be—"

The stationhouse doors swung open. Rolf Schmidt strode through them, his round face flushed with exertion. Relief gleamed in his eyes as he spotted Hanley. "That *hundesohn*, Mahoney," he said, breathless. "Jacky O'Toole's. He was just there. I saw him. Tried to arrest him, but he ran out the back. Don't know which way he went, 'cause goddamn O'Toole gets in front of me. Time I shove past him, Mahoney's gone." He swept off his hat and shook out sweat-damp hair. "I got men like you asked, five plus me. We find him, swear to *Gott*."

Nerves taut as fiddle strings, Hanley nodded. "I'll join you as soon as I can."

⌘

He strode down Market Street as fast as he could make his sore body move. The afternoon shadows were lengthening as he neared Rivka's house. She must be beside herself. What had Chamberlain discovered to make him arrest Aaron? Had Hayes's landlady told him about seeing Aaron by the boardinghouse? Or had he simply drawn the most damning conclusion from the incident near Nat's school? Ada had said Aaron pressed no charges, but there were witnesses, and Chamberlain clearly knew they'd been arguing over the boy. Hanley picked up his pace, ignoring his ribs. Rivka could tell him more. Then he'd catch up with Schmidt. But Rivka first. He wanted—*needed*—to see her, comfort her. Let her know he'd make everything all right somehow.

He was steps away from her front stoop when her voice, frightened and furious, carried to him from the house on the warm evening air. "—no money here! Get out!"

The answering voice was male, Irish. Familiar. *What the hell?* "Don't give me that, girl. You Jews've always got something. I want it. Egg money, jewelry, whatever you have. Get it. *Now.*"

*Round the back.* Moving as fast as he could, Hanley ducked around the corner of the house. The back door stood partway open in the dusky light. No one was visible in the gap. *Other side of the door, both of them. Mahoney's closest. Has to be.* He took a moment to gather himself, then charged.

He hit the door shoulder first and hurtled through, saw Mahoney turn toward him, shock on his red-eyed face. Rivka stood a few feet beyond, both hands gripping a wooden rolling pin. The door's edge had missed the sonofabitch...Mahoney was still standing. With a roar like a bull, Mahoney threw himself forward. His tackle slammed Hanley against the wall. Dazed with fresh pain, Hanley registered Rivka's scream and the sound of hurrying footsteps from upstairs. *The boy. Christ.*

A hard shove and an uppercut. Mahoney staggered backward. "Give it up," Hanley wheezed, pushing himself off the wall. The fire in his ribs made him want to pass out. "I've men coming. You're outnumbered. Give up, you bastard."

271

Mahoney lurched at him, swinging both fists. Hanley sidestepped, too slowly. One fist caught him and sent him reeling. Mahoney grabbed him in a bearhug. "I won't swing for a goddamned darky," he growled. His hot breath reeked of whiskey. Hanley fought for purchase to break Mahoney's grip. Darkness hovered at the edges of his vision. He was dimly aware of rapid steps and a dull *thwack*. Mahoney's hold abruptly loosened. The railman swayed, arms dropping to his sides, face going blank. Then he crumpled to the floor.

Hanley thrust out a hand. Barked his knuckles. Grabbed the table and hung on. Blinked to clear his head.

Rivka stood next to Mahoney, rolling pin raised. "I hit him," she said. "Is he dead? Hashem, don't let him be dead. I had to. He was hurting you. I thought he would kill you."

"'M all right." He wasn't. Damned if he'd let her see it. The rolling pin slipped from her fingers as Hanley moved toward her. He meant to take her in his arms, but his body betrayed him. He and the rolling pin hit the floor, the sound of the pin's impact lost in the thump of his knees striking wood. *Damn.* He couldn't give way. *Things to do, people to tell...*

Rivka beside him, arm around his shoulders, hand bracing his chest. Beyond her, Nat in the hall, lamp in hand and fear on his face. Rivka's voice, sharp with worry. "Nat, get water and a cloth." Then, to Hanley, "What now? Who do we send for at Lake Street? Tell me. Nat and I will do it."

The lamplight gleamed off her hair. Beautiful. He wanted to stroke it. "Not wearing your kerchief." *Hell. Am I delirious? Must be.*

"Hanley...Frank. Who do we send for at Lake Street?"

"Moore. Sergeant Moore." The darkness rose around him, or maybe it was the twilight deepening. "You have rope? Tie Mahoney. His hands. Tight. Then Moore. He'll bring men. Tell him..." God, he was dizzy. His chest felt like an elephant was sitting on it, after some bastard ran him through with a bayonet. "Tell him...Mahoney. Not Ada. Not Aaron. Mahoney killed Ezra Hayes."

# FIFTY-FIVE

**D**ark. *Floating.* No pain, God have mercy. Not quite true. Someplace far off, something hurt. A lot. Hanley drifted above it. *Stay like this. Forever. And ever…Amen…*

But something was tugging him back. A nagging itch, a splinter in his skin. It weighed him down, forced him toward the thing that hurt. He drew a breath. A steel band tightened around his chest.

Someone spoke…Rivka. "…went for the doctor. They'll be here soon." Her voice wobbled. Frightened. She shouldn't be frightened. He'd come in time, he'd saved her from harm, from…

*Mahoney.* Memory flooded back. Hayes's murder. Aaron. Ada. Moore. *Got to find Moore, tell him—*

"Shh." A damp cloth at his forehead, cool fingers stroking his cheek. From somewhere the scent of lavender and a freshness like new leaves. "Onkl Jacob is bringing the sergeant. All will be well. Try to breathe. Slow and easy."

He did his best. The steel band loosened and awareness of the rest of his body returned. He lay against something soft that moved in a heartbeat rhythm…in-out, in-out. He focused his scattered wits, felt the line of a torso, a shoulder, an arm curved around him to stop him from slipping. Rivka was keeping him upright. This was wrong, he shouldn't be here with his head pillowed on her chest, and the rise and fall of her breath buoying him up, but he didn't care. He wanted to stay like this until the darkness came back and swept the pain away. *Forever and ever…*

His lips formed words he shouldn't say. He didn't care about that, either. Her voice went on, soothing as rain. "*HaKadosh Baruch Hu yimalei rachamim alav…*" Had she heard him? It mattered, it mattered immensely, but he couldn't stick in the here and now. He tried to listen to the Hebrew, felt his breath come easier. Moore was on his way. Rivka said so. *All will be well.*

The darkness beckoned, and he sank into it.

෴

Soft sounds woke him. A shuffle of feet, the clink of a spoon against china. He was lying down, on something sturdy this time, propped partway up with pillows, chest and head screaming agony at him. He heard a grunt that ended in a whimper and realized it had come from him. Was he home in bed? Where was Rivka? Where was Moore? She'd said Moore was coming, she'd *promised*—

"Ah, awake." A stranger's voice, though the accent reminded him of Jacob Nathan. "You are a lucky fellow, Herr Hanley, *nu*? I have willow bark, very strong. You will drink, please. Then you can talk with Herr Moore. *Ein bitte*, a little, only. You understand?"

Hanley opened his eyes. Rivka's front parlor swam into focus. Rivka herself wasn't there. Moore was, sitting in a straight-backed chair near the sofa where Hanley lay. He must be badly off if they hadn't moved him any farther than this. The black square of the window beyond told him it was night. He hadn't been out for too long, unless he'd slept the clock 'round?

Not-Jacob stood by the sofa, brimming mug in hand. He was thin and stoop shouldered, with kindly dark eyes and a black skullcap perched atop salt-and-pepper hair that matched his beard. "I am Dr. Gershon," he said, handing Hanley the mug. "And you have a bruised lung. Nothing worse, baruch Hashem. I would like to hear the story, how you ended up on Fraylin Kelmansky's kitchen floor with cracked ribs and an unconscious man beside you." He nodded toward Moore. "After you talk to him and then rest again."

Hanley thanked him and grimaced as he sipped the willow bark. "Mahoney," he said, eyes on his sergeant's.

"In lockup, pending transfer to the Armory." Moore leaned forward, elbows on his knees. "Miss Kelmansky tells me you said *he* killed Hayes. What's your evidence?"

"Aaron and Ada…where are they? What's happening?"

"Nothing, for the moment. It took some doing to halt the proceedings against them, but I managed. Chamberlain hadn't sent his final report to Captain Hickey at the Armory—a problem with the supposed murder weapon, plus he can't place Aaron Kelmansky near the scene at the right time. All he has is the fight with Hayes from earlier in the day. I called in a favor, so everything's suspended until we hear your story." He tilted his head. "Tell it, Frank. And make it good."

❧

Exhausted as he was, Hanley couldn't relax after Moore left. Worry plus pain made sleep impossible. Had he told Moore everything? Mahoney's knife, confiscated at the station on Union Street—get it to Will Rushton. If it matched the wound on Hayes's throat, *and* if anyone had seen Mahoney near the alley by Thirteenth Street where John Jones found Hayes's body, would that be enough? Moore had promised to canvass the area. Please God, they'd get lucky and find a witness. And then find out exactly *how* late on Tuesday night Mahoney had landed in the West Chicago Avenue lockup for starting that brawl at Cleary's Saloon, since it appeared he might have been out on the streets at the relevant time after all.

As to why Mahoney killed Hayes…Hanley let out a sigh. All he had was the plain fact that the man had clearly said, *I won't swing for a goddamned darky.* Had Coughlin promised to pay Mahoney, as with Lawrence O'Shea? Get Michael O'Shea's papers, kill Hayes because he was living proof of slavery at Sweetbay Sugar, bury the story so deep that no partner or shareholder in the Illinois, St. Louis and Grand Southern—especially the abolitionist-minded Hugh Denham—would ever know of it? The profit skimming was secondary. But Hanley had no proof. No proof Mahoney broke into Coughlin's home to steal the man's private ledger of his theft from the railway, no proof such a record existed…though Moore had agreed it probably did, said he'd write up a complaint and get a warrant first thing in the morning.

So…a declaration in the heat of the moment, not enough to save Aaron and Ada without other evidence, and maybe not even then. Motive, and salvation, had to come from Mahoney's own mouth.

The sofa arm was giving him a crick in his neck. Dr. Gershon had left a lamp turned low, in case Hanley needed aid during the night. Gershon himself snored softly from a pallet nearby. Hanley envied him. Rivka must be sleeping, too, upstairs. He wished she were here instead of the doctor, awake so he could talk with her. Selfish thought. He should be wishing her sweet dreams. He shut his eyes. If he stopped thinking, maybe sleep would come.

Sometime later, the creak of a floorboard woke him. He turned his head and saw Rivka standing in the parlor doorway. The lamp she held illuminated her face, her dark hair spilling over her nightdress. She made a startled sound as their gazes met. Then, with a brief downward glance at the slumbering doctor, she spoke. "I thought you were sleeping. I didn't mean to wake you."

"Can't sleep." He kept his voice low, matching hers. *Don't rouse the chaperone.* "Are you…have you slept much?" What an idiot he sounded. But just looking at her made him feel better. So did the smile that brightened her face as she came into the room.

"I have hardly slept at all. Little catnaps…and then I think of Aaron and Ada and that man Mahoney, and—" She lifted her chin, a defiant gesture. "I'm glad I hit him so hard. He killed Nat's father. He would have killed you if he could."

Her fierceness surprised him, though by now nothing about her should. "I'm still breathing, thanks to you." He shifted his feet to make room for her, ignoring sharp twinges from his rib cage. "Stay and talk with me. It hurts too much for me to drop off."

"Do you need more willow bark? I can—"

"No, please. I'm sick of it. Stay. Just for a little while."

She moved closer and sat, setting the lamp on the floor. The light cast odd shadows on her face and body. Loose as it was, her nightdress couldn't hide the curves beneath. Hanley felt hot and kept his eyes on hers. Had he embarrassed her? Was she blushing? Hard to tell. She was still smiling. That must be good.

"Your mother and Fray Kirschner will come tomorrow," she said. "Dr. Gershon thinks you might safely be moved by then. I sent them a note."

"That was kind. Thank you. Mam would be frantic otherwise." What would his mother think of him now, here with Rivka at this ungodly hour? He shifted position and winced. There had to be more to say than this…parlor conversation, as if they were chatting over coffee and cake. There *was* more to say. He'd said it. Caught up in pain, fighting to stay conscious, some part of him was afraid he might be dying and not get another chance. Fresh heat made his face flame, and he drew in as deep a breath as his battered ribs allowed. "Rivka…before, when…in the kitchen, when I was…hurt, and you held me up."

"Yes."

Her stillness made Hanley's anxiety spike, but he plunged on. "What I said…I meant it. It wasn't delirium talking." He didn't quite dare repeat the words he'd spoken—*I love you, marry me*—but he saw in her face that she recalled them precisely. He hadn't been sure, in the moment. He wasn't sure of her now. But he had to take the gamble, before Mam came to bring him home. Once he left here, he'd likely be barred from seeing Rivka again.

"I know what you said." There was warmth in her voice…and more, unless he was deluding himself. "And…I love you also."

Her words should have delighted him, except he heard the one she didn't say. Dry mouthed, he said it for her. "But?"

"What I want…" She shook her head. "I *shouldn't*. Everything I know, everything I've been taught, tells me that. So I don't know how to answer you."

"'Yes' would do." Good sense asserted itself a heartbeat too late, and he clenched a fist against the soft nap of the sofa. He was wrecking his chances, *their* chances, with his damn fool tongue.

Distress roughened her voice. "You don't know what you're asking. You are goyische. Your world is not mine. My family, my people…I will be dead to them."

"But if…" He floundered. "I mean…surely they'll come around? They can't throw you aside forever."

"They can. They will." Her eyes glistened in the lamplight. "And your family—your mother, your sister—will they accept *me*? What if they don't? What then?"

"Rivka…" Her anguish hurt more than his injuries. God, if only he could *move*. Wrap her in his arms, kiss her breathless. Frustration, desire, a piercing sense of loss…he hovered so near that last, it closed his throat as if he'd swallowed stones. "I love you," he finally managed to say. "You love me. Doesn't love matter most?"

She leaned forward and cupped his cheek. The warmth of her palm sent fire through him, a hearth glow on a cold night. She shifted her hand, let her fingers drift across his lips. He caught his breath as the fire blazed. She snatched her hand away, scooped up the lamp, and stood. "I need to think. Try to sleep."

He lay awake long after she left, head and body aching, mind and heart churning between despair and hope.

# FIFTY-SIX

*August 7, 1872*

Our Lord is watching out for you, Frankie. That's all I can say." Mam knelt by the sofa in Rivka's parlor and helped Hanley on with his boots. He felt five years old again, caught between gratitude and embarrassment. God damn Mahoney, inflicting this on him. The thought of the big Irishman made him restless. Only Mahoney could say why he'd killed Ezra Hayes and how they'd crossed paths… and, stone sober from a cell at the Union Street station, there was no guarantee he would. If he didn't, then what? Chamberlain's circumstantial "evidence" against Aaron and Ada won the day? Hanley clenched a fist. *I won't let that happen.*

And then there was Patrick Coughlin. Moore should get a warrant today to search the fellow's house and his office at the rail yard for that private ledger. Hanley was betting on the house, unless the fellow carried the ledger with him everywhere he went. *Hopefully not, or we'll have to see the account books at the rail yard office. Which means dealing with the Illinois, St. Louis and Grand Southern Railway, and God knows if they'll fight us about it.*

"I was that worried when you didn't come home for supper." Mam stood, twitched his collar straight, and drew a comb from her pocket. For a horrified moment he thought she meant to comb his hair, but she handed it over and watched with her arms folded while he did his best to tame the sleep-tousled mess. "Honestly, Frankie, I don't know whether to bless that girl or damn her. That doctor says she saved your life, but if you hadn't come here in the first place…" She gave a sharp sigh. "That's neither here nor there, I suppose. We'll get you home where we can take proper care of you. Ida's borrowed a buggy so you can ride in style."

It took him a moment to sort out who *that girl* was. Rivka. His skin flushed hot at the thought of her. He'd said too much last night, yet he wouldn't un-say a word of it. Would her people really consider her dead because of him? Surely not, or just for a time. He glanced at his mother and bit his lip. Mam would get over it, that he hadn't chosen an Irish girl. Rivka's folk would as well. Somehow, they'd work things out.

*She loves me. She said so.* He clung to that thought like a drowning man to driftwood. *I don't know how to answer* wasn't *No*, exactly…. "Where's Rivka…Miss Kelmansky? I'd like to thank her. I wasn't in any shape before—"

Mam pursed her lips. "She was talking with Ida. I don't know where she's got to now. Let's get you outside."

He didn't see Rivka as he left the house, Mam and Dr. Gershon helping him into the buggy while Ida held the horses. He watched over his shoulder as long as he could while Market Street receded into the distance, but Rivka's door stayed shut and the boardwalk empty.

ॐ

Some time later, a knock roused him from uneasy sleep. Sergeant Moore poked his head through Hanley's bedroom doorway. "I came as soon as I could. I have news."

Hanley blinked sleep grit from his eyes. "Coughlin's place? Mahoney? What's going on?"

Moore came further in and sat on the end of the bed. "Will Rushton found traces of what looks like blood around the hilt of Mahoney's knife. The blade is the right size and length, and Mahoney's left-handed. His workmates confirmed it."

"The canvass by Thirteenth Street…did anyone see—"

"They did." Moore grinned. "I took John Jones with me, figured that might loosen some tongues. He was glad to help. We ran across two workmen heading home after supper at a place four doors down State Street from where Hayes was found. They saw what they thought was a drunkard passed out in the alley around half past eight. When they went to check on him, they saw a man spring up and run away. I can't say we've a good description, but there was decent moonlight, and they both recalled pale skin and red hair. That and size. The runner was tall and burly."

Mahoney, interrupted while rifling Hayes's pockets, hoping to find the papers from Michael O'Shea. The ones Coughlin so desperately needed no one else to know about. "Did they see his face?"

"No. I did ask what time he landed in West Chicago Avenue's lockup on Tuesday night, and they said close to midnight…well after Hayes was killed. So Mahoney was definitely at large when the murder occurred. Still, we'll need a confession to confirm it was Mahoney—and that he was paid to murder Hayes and Lawrence O'Shea. Then we can go after Coughlin. I told Schmidt and a few more men to meet us at Coughlin's home in an hour."

"You didn't already—"

"Search the place? And leave you out of it? You know better than that, Frank. You've earned the right to be in at the kill."

♈

At the Union Street lockup, Mahoney sat slumped in his cell. "Head hurts like blazes," he muttered as Hanley and Moore approached. "If you won't get me any goddamn whiskey, can I at least get on the fucking paddy wagon and go be miserable someplace else?"

"Transfer's at noon," Hanley said.

Mahoney raised his head and winced. "God. You're like the bad penny, always turning up."

"No thanks to you." Hanley parked himself a foot from the cell, while Moore drifted over to lean on the bars an arm's length away. "Why did you kill Ezra Hayes?"

"Who?"

The bewilderment in Mahoney's face gave Hanley a nasty turn. He gripped the bars to steady himself. "The darky. The one you swore you wouldn't swing for."

Mahoney's expression turned furtive. "Don't know what you're talking about."

"At the house you broke into on Market Street last night. 'I won't swing for a goddamned darky,' you said. I heard you. So did the young woman you tried to steal from and frightened half to death. Why in hell else d'you think you're in here?"

Sergeant Moore picked up his cue. "You slit that man's throat. Cut him near to the bone. We have your knife. You missed some blood. And you were seen. You might as well tell us what happened."

"Who're you?" Mahoney hauled himself upright and peered at Moore. "Some Proddy? You are. I can hear it, that fancy way of speakin'. Like Patrick fucking Coughlin."

"We'll get to him," Hanley said. "Hayes first. Why'd you kill him?"

"What do I get if I say?"

Hanley clenched his jaw. "Answer the damned question."

Mahoney threw him a challenging glare. "It was self-defense. You tell the judge that, you want another word out of me."

"Self-defense?" Moore said, disbelieving. "Hayes attacked you first?"

"He fought back. He shouldn'a done that. Not *supposed* to, cowards like them people are. A man's got a right to protect himself."

*Christ*, Hanley thought. "You jumped him by that alley. What for?" He knew the answer already, but they needed Mahoney to admit it. *Hayes first, then Lawrence O'Shea.*

"Some papers the boss wanted." The word *boss* came out with bite. "Planned it all, Coughlin did. I only did what he told me."

"Which was?"

Mahoney locked eyes with Hanley. Hanley didn't waver. After a long moment, Mahoney shrugged and looked away. "I met the darky when he got out of jail, told him I wanted the papers he had. Told him I'd pay good money for them. He said to meet him near his boardinghouse around eight and he'd hand them over. He gave me some papers, all right, but when I looked at them after I walked away, I saw they were all blank." He scowled, as if at the memory of being tricked. "He'd ducked out of sight, so he thought, but I spied him again. I followed him to a good spot, plenty dark and no one about. Found a loose brick by a tumbledown building, threatened him with it. Told him he better get the real papers or I'd bash him." Mahoney prowled the cell, his words coming faster. "I only wanted the damned papers. But he slugged me, that black bastard. I'd my knife in my pocket, and he was bigger'n me. What the hell else was I s'posed to do, eh? Let a goddamned darky beat me bloody? Kill me, even?"

The stupidity of it made Hanley sick at heart. "You dumb sonofabitch. Hayes was no threat to you, until you made him one. All he wanted was to live free somewhere, far away from what he'd been through. If you and your *boss* had just left him alone..."

Mahoney snorted. "You care more about some darky than about me, for all we're both plain Irishmen. D'you care about the lying rich Proddy bastard whose fault all this is? D'you want to see *him* in a jail cell? 'Cause he should damned well be right here, alongside me." He shook his head, as if at his own foolishness. "I shoulda known better. I'm a workingman, I'm nobody. That's what Coughlin thought. Make me do his dirty business while he walks away clean. He's done it before. But I know more than he thinks. I'll tell you all of it, if you take care of me."

Hanley moved closer to Mahoney. "Talk's cheap, Liam. We need evidence. More than just your word for what Coughlin said and did, about Hayes *and* Lawrence O'Shea."

Mahoney wet his lips. "What if I told you he's stealing from the railway? Fixing the books? I figured it out. That's why he wanted O'Shea dead. O'Shea did the accounts, kept track of the money coming in along with cargo going in and out. Poor boyo musta found something bad." A sly look crossed his face. "Like I did, at Coughlin's place. What's that 'evidence' worth to you?"

"You mean the private ledger you burgled Coughlin's house for?" As Mahoney gaped, Hanley shook his head. "You're a liar, Liam. If you had it, they'd have taken it when you got here and handed it over to us."

Mahoney clenched his fists. "What d'you damned well *want* from me?"

Hanley glanced at Moore. At the sergeant's nod, he turned back to Mahoney. "The payment for killing Lawrence O'Shea. How much Coughlin gave you, when, and where. If you tell the truth, we'll put in a word with the judge at your trial. Let him know how…helpful you were."

"I don't want a bleedin' trial. I want the hell out of here!"

"You killed two people, Liam. You really think you can just walk free?"

A taut silence fell. In the distance, a church bell tolled the three-quarter hour. As the last chime faded, Mahoney sagged against the cell bars. "All right," he said, quietly. "Here's how it was…"

# FIFTY-SEVEN

A warrant for Patrick Coughlin's personal account at City Savings Bank, sworn out by Sergeant Moore and swiftly granted by a sympathetic police court judge, gave Hanley and Moore all the authority they needed to confirm a withdrawal that matched the amount and date of the payment to Liam Mahoney. "Friday, July twelfth," Hanley said, eyeing the entry in the ledger brought by a worried-looking bank clerk. "The day before Lawrence died. Mahoney said Coughlin paid him half up front at the rail yard, the other half at Saint Pat's right after Sunday Mass. There's cheek for you…passing blood money to a murderer at church."

Moore ran a finger down the page, stopped at the bottom. "And here's a sizable cash withdrawal on the day Hayes died. For his bail, and whatever funds Coughlin gave Mahoney to buy those papers, I'd guess." He closed the ledger and gave it back to the clerk, who hurried away with it as if from the plague. "You'll ask Father Gerald to confirm he saw Mahoney and Coughlin together on Sunday, July fourteenth? It can't be every day the good pastor inadvertently interrupts two men of his flock having a spat over money in the church vestibule."

Hanley gave a grim chuckle. "I'm sure Father Gerald will remember that. He has a good eye for faces as well. Comes with his calling, I'd guess."

Outside the bank, Moore eyed the warrant. "Coughlin lives on Elizabeth Street near Lake. You all right for the trip?"

"I'm fine." As if he'd have said anything else. Gritting his teeth against twinges of pain, he kept pace with his sergeant as they headed west on Randolph to the nearest horsecar stop. "Lying bastard. 'I never stole a penny. Poor Lawrence was set upon by footpads. He was a valued employee who'll be missed.' And he's responsible for Ezra Hayes's death, too. It'll be my pleasure to give Coughlin his comeuppance."

Moore touched his breast pocket where the warrant was. "If we find what we're looking for, that should clinch it."

Fifteen minutes later, they reached the house, a solid two-story brick affair with a neatly trimmed hedge that suggested a well-paid gardener's touch. Rolf Schmidt and another patrolman waited on the front porch. "Awful quiet inside," Schmidt said as Hanley and Moore joined them. "Nobody here, I think. Maybe our man gone to work."

"Or someplace else." Hanley turned to Moore. "May Street isn't far from here. Coughlin may have gone to court the Widow O'Shea again."

Moore nodded. "We'll get started. Go."

༡

Grace O'Shea answered Hanley's knock. She looked surprised to see him but stepped back readily enough to let him inside. "Detective! Is there news?"

"Have you seen Patrick Coughlin today? Do you know where he is?"

"Funny you should mention him." She raised a hand, and he saw she held an open envelope. "I've a letter...it came in the late morning post. I was just settling in to read it."

"May I see it?"

She handed it over. He took the letter out of the envelope and read swiftly, absorbing phrases that tightened his gut. ...*going to New Orleans...regret I can't come and tell you goodbye...may stay there, as Chicago feels played out...my love to you, and good wishes always.*

When he looked up, the widow was staring at him. "I'm sorry, Mrs. O'Shea. Patrick Coughlin engineered your husband's death. He's leaving town. I need your help to stop him."

Money borrowed from Mrs. O'Shea paid for a cab to the Chicago and Alton depot at Madison and Canal. She'd volunteered to go to Coughlin's home to tell Moore where Hanley was headed and why. The sickening thought that it might all be for nothing nagged at him as the cab bowled along. Had Coughlin personally mailed his farewell today, or asked someone else to—a housekeeper, a neighbor—while he skipped town the night before? The cab slowed, and Hanley swore. A glance out the window told him they were stuck in traffic at Desplaines. He dumped coins from his pocket and banged on the roof. When the cab stopped, he opened the door and slid out. "Fare's on the seat," he called up to the driver, then headed toward the depot, cursing the slowness forced by his injuries.

The depot was all noise and crowds, a roar of voices and hurrying footsteps pierced by the shrieking whistles of arriving and departing trains. A porter gave him the platform for New Orleans. "No. 5, sir. She leaves in twenty minutes." Hanley thanked the man and picked up his pace, jaw clenched against jolts of pain.

The conductor, walking the platform to check for stragglers, nodded when Hanley showed him a sketch of Coughlin. "He boarded a little bit ago. First-class ticket straight through. Two trunks and a carrying bag. I guess he's fixing to stay down South awhile."

Hanley thanked him, climbed aboard, and headed for the first-class cars. He found Coughlin in the second one, reading the front section of the *Chicago Tribune*, the rest of the paper on the velvet-cushioned seat beside him. A carpet bag sat between his feet. Through its open mouth, Hanley glimpsed a few shirts and the dark corner of what looked like a leather shaving case. "Mr. Coughlin?"

Coughlin glanced up. Only a second's stillness betrayed his tension. "Detective. How can I help you? Best be quick. The train leaves in"—he fished out a pocket-watch—"fifteen minutes."

Hanley nodded toward the bag. "Grab that. You're coming to the station."

"I don't think so. Good day." Coughlin went back to his newspaper.

Hanley snatched it from his grasp. "Do I need to arrest you? I'd thought to keep this discreet. But if you want a scene—"

Coughlin glared. "Try it and I'll have your badge. You've harassed me for nearly a month over Lawrence O'Shea, even though you well know I didn't kill him. Nor am I guilty of any other wrongdoing, despite your efforts to prove otherwise. Now give me my paper and leave me be."

Hanley dropped the section on the rest of the pile. "Of course you didn't kill him. You paid Liam Mahoney to do it. City Savings Bank was most helpful there. Though I'd like to know if you meant for Ezra Hayes to die as well, or whether Mahoney overdid things. I don't suppose you'd care to tell me?"

"You've got it wrong." Smooth as good whiskey, the man's voice was. "Whatever Liam Mahoney did, it's nothing to do with me. I'd no reason to want Lawrence dead, let alone that darky, Hayes. If you've snagged Mahoney for murder, I daresay he'd tell any lie to get himself out of it. Wouldn't you, to escape a hangman's noose?"

"Try again. A witness saw you pay Mahoney at Saint Pat's the day after Lawrence ended up in the Chicago River with a staved-in skull. Are you coming, or do I have to make you?"

Fear flashed in Coughlin's eyes. Then his gaze hardened. "There's a Pinkerton on this train. I can find him and have you removed."

"You can try. I'll tell him why I'm here. We'll see who he believes." Hanley said it with a confidence he didn't feel. Was Sergeant Moore on the way? On his own, with no corroborating evidence in hand, all Hanley had was words. And he was running out of them.

"I have the papers you were after, too," he said. A bald-faced lie— John Jones had kept them—but Coughlin couldn't know that. "Michael O'Shea's drawings and personal testimony from the Sweetbay Sugar plantation outside New Orleans. They're damning. And you were with Mrs. O'Shea the day Ezra Hayes came and told her what happened to her son. A white boy strung up, Hayes himself with hard evidence of the ugly secret Michael died for. Evidence you swore to me didn't exist. You couldn't risk that coming out, could you? Especially with a well-off county commissioner to vouch for Hayes as well. That would've gotten people's attention, if the drawings themselves weren't enough. Once your patron, Hugh Denham, found out about the slave labor at Sweetbay—a client you brought in, a contract you negotiated— you'd have lost your job, and the money and prestige that went with it. No chance to pay off gambling debts without an income, honest or otherwise. And if any higher-ups took a closer look at the books and discovered you were thieving as well—charging Sweetbay a lot more for shipping than you told your employer and pocketing the difference—there goes your freedom, too. From respected senior shipping agent to common thief in a jail cell, overnight."

"Quite a tale you'll have to tell the Pinkerton." Coughlin reached for his bag. Haste or nerves made him topple it, spilling items onto the floor—a shirt, a tobacco tin, a book. Small, black leather, blank cover. *Not a shaving case after all.*

Coughlin dove for it. Hurt or no, Hanley moved faster. He grabbed the book and held it high, out of Coughlin's reach. "Thief!" Coughlin yelled. Around them, heads turned. "This man's a thief, don't let him leave—"

Motion at the end of the car cut him off. Hanley glanced over, spotted a familiar profile and a flash of blue. Coughlin lunged forward, jarring Hanley's ribs. Hanley sucked in air and dropped the book. It hit the floor as Sergeant Moore reached them.

Moore snatched it up. He flipped through a few pages, his expression turning grim. "Quite a record you've got here of all the money you stole. We looked for this at your house. But of course you wouldn't leave it behind." He handed the book to Officer Schmidt, eyeing Coughlin with contempt. "You're under arrest for conspiracy to murder Lawrence O'Shea."

# FIFTY-EIGHT

Sergeant Moore was out on a case, the desk officer said when Rivka arrived at Lake Street Station seeking word of Aaron and Ada's release. "Can't say when he'll be back, miss. You can leave a message. I'll see the sergeant gets it."

She scrawled a brief note and left, with a faint sense of relief that her brother and his wife would be home before long. Tomorrow, maybe even today. Outside on the stationhouse steps, fresh worry engulfed her. Once they were home, what then? Panic spiked, and she drew a sharp breath. *I can't face Aaron. Not now, not when…*

She hurried down the stairs and away from the station, striking out wherever her feet might take her, head bent to keep from seeing the houses and shops along the streets she knew so well. She focused on her stride instead, the tap of her shoes on the scuffed wooden boardwalk. Her head ached from lack of sleep and the thoughts still chasing through her mind. Hanley loved her. Wanted her as his wife. She loved him. Wanted him. How could she deny that? But the price. She was promised to Moishe. To break her word, leave everyone and everything she knew…for what kind of life among strangers?

Two memories refused to go away. Hanley in the darkened parlor, his whole heart raw in his face and voice. *I love you. You love me. Doesn't love matter most?* And this morning, talking in her own kitchen with Ida Kirschner. *Are all your family elsewhere? How do you live among the goyim without your people close by?* Ida had smiled at that. *But I have my people,* she'd said. *Among my friends, at my shul. Not like yours,* meydele, *but not so different as you might think.*

A glimmer of possibility, of hope almost. Yet so much to lose, either way.

෪

As Hanley and Moore hustled Coughlin down the steps to the Armory's dank basement, Coughlin's stone-faced exterior cracked for the first time since his arrest. "I had to do it. Lawrence was going to tell, the minute he got hold of what Michael had. The newspapers, the shareholders. Hugh Denham. He meant to tell all of them. He said so. Even asked me to come with him, back him up. They'd listen better to me, he thought. I couldn't talk him out of it." His anxious gaze met Hanley's. "I worked all my life to get where I am, to be more than just a 'Paddy.' I'm no Catholic, but here it never mattered a damn. Irish is Irish, that's what rich Yankee blue bloods think. Why should what happened to a bunch of darkies down South cost me what I've earned? You're Irish. *You* know…"

Hanley tightened his grip on Coughlin's arm. "Your thieving got two good men killed, murders you paid for. And you're still lying about it. And Michael O'Shea, what about him? The son of your 'valued employee' and friend, tortured and strung up by the slavers you gladly did business with, all to line your pockets. His death doesn't bother you? Good God, you're a disgrace."

Jeers and epithets greeted them as they reached the cell block. "Fresh meat!" "Nice suit, Moneybags!" "Look what the dog chucked up!" As the turnkey unlocked an empty cell and Moore wrestled Coughlin into it, one voice rose above the rest.

"Well, well." In the cell across the way, Liam Mahoney sauntered up to the bars. "Fancy seeing you here, Proddy boy. For all your money and airs, you're just a dirty Mick like me." He gave a snort of laughter. "Isn't it grand, you've finally ended up where you belong?"

෪

Rivka made early supper for herself and Nat, and she did her best to share his joy at the news Sergeant Moore had brought a little while ago. Matters were in hand for Aaron and Ada's release, he'd said. *Once the papers are signed, they'll be free to go. No charges attached, as neither of them was arraigned. They should be home before nightfall. Please tell them I'm sorry for what my detective put them through.*

"Home by dark." Nat grinned at her over his tin cup of milk. A cough racked him but couldn't dim the relief in his face. "Everything'll be all right now." The grin faded. "And my pa can rest easy. He won't be a haunt, stuck 'round here till somebody fixes things."

She reached across the table and squeezed his hand. Unsettled as she still felt, the gesture eased her. "I'm sorry all this happened. I'm sorry things are so—"

"Messed up."

"Those are good words for it."

He sipped his milk, then speared a potato chunk, chewed, and swallowed. "It'll be better out West. Free land if you can hold it. That's what they say. And nobody to bother us for miles around. A whole new life. Startin' over, like."

The hope in his face touched her. A child still, not a man, yet he was unafraid. Words her father had said years ago, quoting Rav Nachman of Breslov, came to mind. *The world is a narrow bridge, and the essential thing is not to fear.*

Nat set his fork down and gave her a wistful look. "I wish you were coming with us. I'll miss you."

Unexpectedly, her eyes stung. "I'll miss you, too. All of you."

# FIFTY-NINE

*August 8, 1872*

Ada and Aaron had gone to work early, both of them eager to resume normal life and earn another day's pay so they could leave Chicago that much sooner. Nat, his cold greatly improved, had gone off to school. Alone in the house at last, Rivka spent a difficult hour composing an even more difficult letter. Then she packed a carpet bag and went downstairs to the parlor, bag in one hand and letter in the other.

A light rain misted the front window. She hoped Nat had reached school in time to stay dry. A pang of sorrow shot through her, and she steeled herself against it. They'd been so happy last night, the three of them—Nat, Ada, and Aaron. Rivka had joined in their glad reunion as best she could. Only Ada had noticed how quiet she was, and only briefly, her attention easily diverted back to her husband and son by Rivka's false, bright smile.

*Don't think of that now.* Rivka looked around the parlor. Where to put the letter, that was the question. Someplace Aaron would see it right away.

She chose her spot and laid the letter down. Her brother's name across the top brought up a tangle of feelings—love, sadness, a fierce desire that things could be different. She swallowed past an ache in her throat, shook it off, and headed for the front hall. As she reached it, a knock at the door startled her. She froze until Moishe spoke from outside. "Rivka? Let me in. I need to talk with you."

She drew in a breath, set down her bag, and reached for the knob.

As soon as she opened the door, Moishe stepped inside. "You are all right? Jacob told me about the housebreaker. You were not harmed?"

"No. I am well, baruch Hashem."

Relief shone in his eyes. He reached for her, then checked himself with a downward glance. Puzzlement, then suspicion, crossed his face. "What is that bag for?"

She kept her gaze on his. "You wanted to talk, you said. About…?"

He blinked, as if surprised by her blunt change of subject, then wet his lips. "Jacob also told me…Detective Hanley was here the day before yesterday. Overnight."

So delicately spoken, that last word. Anger sparked, but she kept her voice even. "Yes. He slept in the parlor, with Dr. Gershon nearby. Hanley was injured defending me. I'm sure Onkl Jacob told you that, too."

Moishe shook his head. "I am saying this wrong. I…it is only that I care so much for you, Rivka. I would not have any ill befall you. I came to tell you we can still marry. I don't care what my mother says."

"And what does she say? Headstrong? Willful? An unsuitable wife for her only remaining son? I imagine those are the milder things."

He scowled. "Can you blame her, after what you have done these past few days? Going about the city on your own, or with Hanley. An unmarried girl keeping company with a man, and a goy at that? Playing at solving a crime? You did it for Aaron's sake, I know, and his wife's. So I forgive it, provided it stops now. There can be no more of this, Rivka. You must behave respectably. And you will not see Hanley again. I'm sure the talk will die down once we're married, and—"

"We won't be married."

Owl eyed, he blinked at her. "What?"

"I don't love you, and you love who you want me to be. So there's no point." She picked up her bag, conscious of his gaze on her.

"You are going to him." Moishe's sudden anger made her flinch, though she should have expected it. His voice rose to a shout. "A *shande*, Rivka! How dare you disgrace yourself this way? You shame your father and mother, may they rest in peace! You shame me, who loved and honored you always! This is how you repay me? And Jacob and Hannah, for their love and care of you? And your brother, who only wants what is best for—"

"My brother married a goy. You didn't shun him for it! At least my children will be Jewish, if Hashem sends—"

"Don't speak that name!" He lowered his voice to a near whisper, though the fury in it remained. "If you do this, you are dead to Hashem. Dead to me. Dead to us all."

Her whole body felt clenched like a fist against the grief that threatened to engulf her. "Then I am dead to you," she managed to say. Bag gripped tight, she pushed past him onto the front stoop. "Tell Onkl Jacob and Tanta Hannah I love them. Goodbye."

She kept a steady pace along Market Street, heading toward Madison and the nearest river bridge. Tears mingled with the drizzle on her face, but every step forward felt steadier than the last, and up ahead the clouds were thinning. She reached the bridge and turned west, felt her kerchief sliding back as she crossed over the water. She eased it off, folded it with care, and tucked it in her pocket.

❧

Will hurried up the street toward John Jones's cleaning and tailoring establishment, every muscle in his body taut with excitement. The contrast in his feelings from the last time he'd come here seeking his sister struck him forcefully as he strode through the front door. He'd been so afraid that day. Afraid of being seen, recognized, known for what he was. No more, ever again.

He made his way to the counter where customers brought garments or placed orders for fine shirts and other clothing items. He gave his name, asked after Ada, and waited while the clerk went to fetch her. The moment she came into view, Will moved toward her and clasped her hands. Weariness lined her face and shadows lingered in her eyes, but she looked a little better than when he'd escorted her and Aaron home from the Armory jail last evening. "Can you walk with me for a bit?" he said. "I have news."

She managed a smile. "Since last night?" The smile gave way to curiosity as she studied his face. "Good news, I'm guessing. Mr. Jones said to take all the time I like."

He ushered her outside, with a half-formed notion of taking them somewhere for a cup of coffee and a sandwich even though it was well before noon, but so eager was he to tell her his news that the words spilled out of him before they'd gone ten steps down Dearborn Street. "I made a decision," he said as they passed the stone pile of the new Tribune Building. "I'm going west with you. Well, not with you, exactly—it'll take me some time to settle things here—but when you and Aaron and Nat find a home place, write me and I'll join you. In the fall, if I can, or next spring. Folks can always use a doctor out West, so I shouldn't have much trouble earning my keep. And you'll probably need an extra pair of hands around once you file a claim…I've lived in this city most of my life, and I'm no farmer or rancher, but—"

She held up a hand, laughing a little. The lightness in her warmed him, convinced him all the more of the rightness of his choice. "Will. You don't have to persuade me. You're a grown man. You can do what you want." Then she sobered. "Are you sure about this? It won't be easy, you know. No telling if we'll even make a go of it. You have a life here, your work, friends, your…" She hesitated. "The Rushtons. Have you told them?"

"I wanted you to know first." He shoved his hands in his pockets. "My life here…I can't keep it. I don't want to keep it. I thought I did for a long time…but the more I think on it now, the more impossible it seems. After…everything these past five months."

"You're afraid they'll find out Will Rushton isn't white? Take your job and who knows what else from you?"

"It's more than that." His steps slowed as he searched for words. "I can't be that Will anymore. The lie of it…it's a weight on me. More than I realized." He stopped and looked her in the eye. "I need to be free of it. Be who I really am. Go back and find that fifteen-year-old boy who made a hard choice years ago, see if I can unmake it. See what happens when I do."

She gazed at him for a long moment, as if absorbing what he'd said. Then, gently, she gripped his shoulder. He squeezed her fingers, then let go. They started walking again, turning east at Monroe and heading toward the lakefront.

"I've news as well," Ada said after a few moments of silence. "About why Ezra was killed and what I plan to do."

The sudden steel in her voice made him raise his eyebrows in wordless question. "Mr. Jones gave me papers," she went on. "Drawings and writings, including a sworn statement from Ezra about the Sweetbay Sugar Company." The name Sweetbay Sugar came out with added bite. "Evidence of slave labor on the company's plantation. They didn't call it slavery, but that's what it was. Ezra was held there for two years before he escaped. The man who killed him—had him killed—wanted all proof of it dead and buried. But it won't be." She drew in a breath. "I'm taking everything to the newspapers. The *Tribune*, the *Daily Journal*, the *Inter Ocean*, any others I can think of. Mr. Jones knows some reporters who'll likely be interested. There was another man murdered over this—a white man, Lawrence O'Shea—so I may ask his widow to join us. Haven't decided yet. Her son, Michael, made the drawings. He died for them, too. He worked for the Freedmen's Bureau, Mr. Jones told me."

Will shook his head, feeling bleak. "I wish I could say I'm shocked at this." He stared down Monroe, at the railroad tracks and the glimmer of Lake Michigan a few blocks away. Too many stories in the papers these days, about the Freedmen's Bureau closing down and federal troops withdrawing from the defeated Confederate states even as outrages committed against the freedpeople rose in number and brutality. "You think it'll make a difference? Getting this one story out?"

"No. But it doesn't matter. What matters is the truth, told out loud. Told where folks can see and hear, whether they want to or not. If nothing else, maybe it'll make some people finally admit what's happening under their noses."

"White people."

"Yes." Her steady gaze toward the distant shoreline never wavered. "They won't like it. They'll turn away from it. But they'll know, just the same."

❧

"You're not going anywhere, Frankie." Mam stood outside Hanley's bedroom, arms folded and lips pursed. "You'll stay home and rest today if I have to camp outside your door till dark."

"I just need to talk to my sergeant. I'll hardly be there any time at—"

"The devil. Work's not where you'd be going. You never could lie to me, there's no sense trying now." Mam's expression softened as she shooed him back into his room. "Rest. I'll bring tea in a bit."

"No more willow bark," he muttered, but she'd already shut his door. Scowling, he shuffled across the room and propped himself against the windowsill. Still no word from Rivka. Nothing when he got home yesterday, nothing in the evening post, nothing yet this morning. He pushed away from the window, ignoring a fresh stab from his rib cage. *The devil with Mam. I can't stay here. I need to see Rivka, talk to her. Hold her...*

Downstairs, the doorbell rang. Other sounds carried—his landlady's footsteps crossing the hall, then Ida's voice, and another. Rapid Yiddish floated up, and then he heard his name.

He dashed for his door, threw it open, and stumbled toward the staircase. "I'm here. I'm coming..." He could see Rivka now, standing in the foyer, gazing up at him. Bareheaded, no kerchief. Carpet bag by her feet. Here to stay?

She met him at the bottom step. He wrapped her in his arms, heedless of his injured ribs and Ida's presence. Nothing mattered but Rivka's soft curves against him, the scent of her hair, the taste of her lips beneath his.

After a time, she pulled away enough to look him in the face. "I cannot be a goyische wife," she said softly. "You should know that, before—"

He laid a finger on her mouth. "We'll work it out." Ida had gone, it was just the two of them there. Lightness of soul filled him, sweet as a fiddle tune. "Rain's stopped. Let's go someplace. A walk on a fine day, and we can talk about...everything."

God, the shine of her as she smiled up at him.

"A good way to begin."

## THE END

# ACKNOWLEDGMENTS

No book is a solo effort, and (as usual) I owe enormous debts to a great many people who offered aid, comfort, advice, expertise, and the occasional glass of wine (or home-baked scone) during the creation of this book. The scones— —pecan, scrumptious—came from my publisher and editor, the exceptional Emily Victorson, who bucked me up with them during an intensive revision session that made this book a hundred times better while preserving the story I wanted to tell. I can't thank you enough, Emily, for your commitment, your friendship, and your story structure superpowers. (And I want that scone recipe!)

Similar thanks go to my writers' group, the Red Herrings. Michael Allan Dymmoch, Irene Reed, Eric Arnall, and Jerry Silbert—collectively blessed with an ear for language, a nose for plot problems, and a gift for asking exactly the right questions—helped make this a far stronger book than it otherwise would be. Special thanks to Irene, whose comments about Ada Kelmansky and Ezra Hayes offered insights into the African-American experience that otherwise would have eluded this white girl. I'm lucky beyond words to have such talented fellow scribes to share Wednesday nights with.

I'm likewise indebted to the volunteer staff at the Illinois Railway Museum's Strahorn Library in Marengo, Illinois, who gave generously of their time and resources on railroads in the 1860s and early 1870s. Railroad guides, books and news articles, photos and artifacts...this place has everything, and the lovely people I met were invaluable guides through it. Any errors of fact about railroads, railmen, and their place in American life during Hanley's time are mine alone.

For assistance with the Yiddish dialogue used in this novel, I'd like to thank Dr. Khane-Faygl Turtletaub (doctorkft.com).

Thanks also to my mother, Alice O'Mara Piron, for stories of the Hanleys, O'Maras, Moroneys, and McGraths who emigrated to America between 1820 and the 1840s, when the Great Hunger drove masses of Irish from their native soil. Through her, I carry memories of people I've never met from a time that's not my own. Though the Irish characters in this novel are fictional, they owe a lot to the real people from "the olden days" who came here fleeing hardship and chasing hope and, against all odds, found it.

My husband, Steve, deserves a medal for unflagging service to a stressed-out author wrangling with plot problems, research overload, and too many tough days when the words refused to come. For listening to me spin story lines, stepping up to take care of family issues so I could have time to write, giving me backrubs and wine when I needed them, and all around being my rock and mainstay, thank you, thank you, and thank you again. (Also, I love you to pieces.)

Finally, I want to thank readers of the Hanley & Rivka Mysteries series. For those who've read *Shall We Not Revenge* and *For You Were Strangers*, and asked if Hanley and Rivka are getting together, I hope you'll like the answer I came up with in this book. I'm not done with these two and their world yet—and it's my hope that neither are you.

# HISTORICAL NOTE

In 1872, the United States stood at the threshold of the Gilded Age, an era defined by runaway capitalism and the greed, corruption, and racism that drove it. From the robber barons of the railroads to the southern planter elites, the drive to pile up ever-greater fortunes dovetailed with the crusade to restore white supremacy in the South, and with increasing indifference in the North toward the fate of African Americans below the Mason-Dixon line. The era between the end of the Civil War and the dawn of a new century was one of betrayal—of the freed slaves and black people in general, and of laborers whose hard work mainly enriched their wealthy bosses. The tragedy of Reconstruction lies in the triumph of white domestic terrorism over common decency, fueled by lust for money and power.

Sweetbay Sugar and the Illinois, St. Louis, and Grand Southern Railroad are both fictional companies, but they are patterned after very real companies of the time. The railroads were the "big tech" of their day, their upper echelons a bastion of wealth and privilege, their daily operations the engine of economic survival for thousands of Chicagoans. Sugar was an immense source of wealth in the South, especially in Louisiana, and fueled much of New Orleans's economic revival in the years after 1865.

Two characters in this book, both historical figures, deserve particular mention. John and Mary Jones were among Chicago's leading African American citizens, educated and prosperous and well placed to aid others. John Jones built his wealth on a cleaning and tailoring business at 119 North Dearborn Street, and the Joneses' home at that address became a center of anti-slavery and civil rights activity as well as a stop on the Underground Railroad. That building burned down in the Great Fire. However, by the late spring of 1872, Jones had rebuilt a four-story brick building for his business. Jones also served as Cook County Commissioner from late 1871 through 1875. Historical sources are unclear as to when the Joneses moved to 43 Ray Street, south of downtown. For simplicity, I've chosen to locate them there rather than invent a home that never existed. Their ongoing actions in helping people like Ezra, a forerunner of Southern blacks who later fled Jim Crow, are based on what I learned of their wartime activities and their staunch commitment to advancing black people's freedom.

The Freedmen's Bureau, constituted by Congress in 1866, made valiant efforts to aid newly freed blacks, and often poor whites as well, across the defeated Confederate states. The bureau helped former slaves find their families again; distributed relief supplies immediately after the war; enforced labor contracts made with white landowners, who frequently did not wish to pay their former "property"; built and staffed schools for black people, including Howard University, a respected institution to this day; and dealt as best they could with "outrages" against the freedpeople, from assault to robbery to arson, rape, and murder. Unfortunately, Congress's financial commitment to the bureau never matched the need. Funding was cut and the bureau's focus narrowed to building and maintaining schools by 1869, and the bureau was shut down by the end of June 1872.

As always, I am indebted to numerous authors and sources for the historical underpinnings of my writing. Douglas A. Blackmon's excellent and disturbing *Slavery by Another Name* provided the theme that prompted me to write this story in the first place. It describes in chilling detail the system of "convict leasing" that arose in the Southern states as early as 1868, and over time re-imposed de facto slavery in the former Confederacy. In 1872 this system was just getting started. It spread and worsened over the next seventy years, and its effects are felt to this day.

Douglas Edgerton's *The Wars of Reconstruction* effectively lays to rest the myth of that period as one of Northern scalawags and carpetbaggers picking over the carcass of the prostrate South. Impressively thorough, it paints a dismaying picture of a sundered nation unable to knit itself back together without betraying its founding ideal—that "all men are created equal"—on the backs of its black citizens. Christopher Robert Reed's *Black Chicago's First Century* provided valuable information on how black citizens in Chicago responded to these challenges, and the many ways they survived and thrived. I was surprised to find that Chicago in the 1870s was more integrated than it later became. The repeal of Illinois's harsh Black Laws in 1865 removed many legal barriers to African Americans' full participation in public life, and Chicago schools were legally desegregated in 1874. Whether national or local, the history of race in America is too often oversimplified or ignored because it makes us uncomfortable. With this novel, I hope to shed light on one small piece of that history and prompt interested readers to dig further.

No book in the *Hanley & Rivka Mysteries* series could exist without the copious materials available through the Chicago History Museum, in its reading room and through the *Encyclopedia of Chicago* online. Additional online sources provided treasure troves of information: The National Museum of African American History and Culture website, The Freedmen's Bureau Online, the *Chicagology* blog, and the *Chicago Crime Scenes* blog. Specifics on the Freedmen's Bureau in Louisiana came from Tulane University in New Orleans, via their archive on the subject (https://libguides.tulane.edu). The websites BlackPast and Black Then offered biographical data on John and Mary Jones, as did the DuSable Museum of African American History website. The historical archive service Fold3 gave me access to Chicago city directories and provided details such as prices for food and lodging in 1872.

Background on the Chicago Police Department is largely taken from John J. Flinn's *History of the Chicago Police*. Mike McDonald, a historical figure just getting started as a gambling prince, really was driving an omnibus in 1872, his former gaming hells having been raided out of existence despite his dutifully paying the police their protection money. I relied on Richard C. Lindberg's excellent biography of McDonald, *The Gambler King of Clark Street*, and was delighted to find the Young's Omnibus Company tidbit in a footnote to chapter 2. McDonald's hatred of cops is illustrated by an anecdote from later in his career, when he was approached by a man collecting funds to bury a policeman killed in the line of duty.

When requested to give two dollars, McDonald allegedly handed over a ten-dollar bill, saying, "Here. Bury five of 'em."

Readers interested in exploring further the theme and background of this novel can find excellent works in the following bibliography, which includes some, but not all, of the sources I consulted in writing this book.

❧

Blackmon, Douglas A. *Slavery by Another Name: The Re-Enslavement of Black Americans from the Civil War to World War II.* Anchor Books, 2009.

Cutler, Irving. *The Jews of Chicago.* University of Illinois Press, 1996.

Edgerton, Douglas. *The Wars of Reconstruction: The Brief, Violent History of America's Most Progressive Era.* Bloomsbury Press, 2014.

Flinn, John J., and John E. Wilkie. *History of the Chicago Police: From the Settlement of the Community to the Present Time.* Kessinger Publishing Legacy Reprints; originally published by the Chicago Police Book Fund, 1887.

Lindberg, Richard C. *The Gambler King of Clark Street: Michael C. McDonald and the Rise of Chicago's Democratic Machine.* Southern Illinois University Press, 2009.

Reed, Christopher Robert. *Black Chicago's First Century, Vol. 1, 1833-1900.* University of Missouri Press, 2005.

Web Resources

BlackPast (https://blackpast.org)

Black Then (http://www.blackthen.com)

*Chicago Crime Scenes* blog (http://chicagocrimescenes.blogspot.com/)

*Chicagology* blog (http://chicagology.com)

DuSable Museum of African American History
(https://www.dusablemuseum.org/)

*Encyclopedia of Chicago* (http://www.encyclopedia.chicagohistory.org/)

The Freedmen's Bureau Online (http://freedmensbureau.com)

National Museum of African American History and Culture
(https://nmaahc.si.edu)

# ALSO PUBLISHED BY ALLIUM PRESS OF CHICAGO

*Fiction with a Chicago Connection*

Visit our website for more information:
www.alliumpress.com

# THE HANLEY & RIVKA MYSTERIES
## D. M. Pirrone

### *Shall We Not Revenge*

In the harsh early winter months of 1872, while Chicago is still smoldering from the Great Fire, Irish Catholic detective Frank Hanley is assigned the case of a murdered Orthodox Jewish rabbi. His investigation proves difficult when the neighborhood's Yiddish-speaking residents, wary of outsiders, are reluctant to talk. But when the rabbi's headstrong daughter, Rivka, unexpectedly offers to help Hanley find her father's killer, the detective receives much more than the break he was looking for. Their pursuit of the truth draws Rivka and Hanley closer together and leads them to a relief organization run by the city's wealthy movers and shakers. Along the way, they uncover a web of political corruption, crooked cops, and well-buried ties to two notorious Irish thugs from Hanley's checkered past. Even after he is kicked off the case, stripped of his badge, and thrown in jail, Hanley refuses to quit. With a personal vendetta to settle for an innocent life lost, he is determined to expose a complicated criminal scheme, not only for his own sake, but for Rivka's as well.

◆

### *For You Were Strangers*

On a spring morning in 1872, former Civil War officer Ben Champion is discovered dead in his Chicago bedroom—a bayonet protruding from his back. What starts as a routine case for Detective Frank Hanley soon becomes anything but, as his investigation into Champion's life turns up hidden truths best left buried. Meanwhile, Rivka Kelmansky's long-lost brother, Aaron, arrives on her doorstep, along with his mulatto wife and son. Fugitives from an attack by night riders, Aaron and his family know too much about past actions that still threaten powerful men—defective guns provided to Union soldiers, and an 1864 conspiracy to establish Chicago as the capital of a Northwest Confederacy. Champion had his own connection to that conspiracy, along with ties to a former slave now passing as white and an escaped Confederate guerrilla bent on vengeance, any of which might have led to his death. Hanley and Rivka must untangle this web of circumstances, amid simmering hostilities still present seven years after the end of the Civil War, as they race against time to solve the murder, before the secrets of bygone days claim more victims.

# THE EMILY CABOT MYSTERIES
## Frances McNamara

## *Death at the Fair*

The 1893 World's Columbian Exposition provides a vibrant backdrop for the first book in the series. Emily Cabot, one of the first women graduate students at the University of Chicago, is eager to prove herself in the emerging field of sociology. While she is busy exploring the Exposition with her family and friends, her colleague, Dr. Stephen Chapman, is accused of murder. Emily sets out to search for the truth behind the crime, but is thwarted by the gamblers, thieves, and corrupt politicians who are ever-present in Chicago. A lynching that occurred in the dead man's past leads Emily to seek the assistance of the black activist Ida B. Wells.

◆

## *Death at Hull House*

After Emily Cabot is expelled from the University of Chicago, she finds work at Hull House, the famous settlement established by Jane Addams. There she quickly becomes involved in the political and social problems of the immigrant community. But, when a man who works for a sweatshop owner is murdered in the Hull House parlor, Emily must determine whether one of her colleagues is responsible, or whether the real reason for the murder is revenge for a past tragedy in her own family. As a smallpox epidemic spreads through the impoverished west side of Chicago, the very existence of the settlement is threatened and Emily finds herself in jeopardy from both the deadly disease and a killer.

◆

## *Death at Pullman*

A model town at war with itself . . . George Pullman created an ideal community for his railroad car workers, complete with every amenity they could want or need. But when hard economic times hit in 1894, lay-offs follow and the workers can no longer pay their rent or buy food at the company store. Starving and desperate, they turn against their once benevolent employer. Emily Cabot and her friend Dr. Stephen Chapman bring much needed food and medical supplies to the town, hoping they can meet the immediate needs of the workers and keep them from resorting to violence. But when one young worker—suspected of being a spy—is murdered, and a bomb plot comes to light, Emily must race to discover the truth behind a tangled web of family and company alliances.

# THE EMILY CABOT MYSTERIES
## Frances McNamara

### *Death at Woods Hole*

Exhausted after the tumult of the Pullman Strike of 1894, Emily Cabot is looking forward to a restful summer visit to Cape Cod. She has plans to collect "beasties" for the Marine Biological Laboratory, alongside other visiting scientists from the University of Chicago. She also hopes to enjoy romantic clambakes with Dr. Stephen Chapman, although they must keep an important secret from their friends. But her summer takes a dramatic turn when she finds a dead man floating in a fish tank. In order to solve his murder she must first deal with dueling scientists, a testy local sheriff, the theft of a fortune, and uncooperative weather.

### *Death at Chinatown*

In the summer of 1896, amateur sleuth Emily Cabot meets two young Chinese women who have recently received medical degrees. She is inspired to make an important decision about her own life when she learns about the difficult choices they have made in order to pursue their careers. When one of the women is accused of poisoning a Chinese herbalist, Emily once again finds herself in the midst of a murder investigation. But, before the case can be solved, she must first settle a serious quarrel with her husband, help quell a political uprising, and overcome threats against her family. Timeless issues, such as restrictions on immigration, the conflict between Western and Eastern medicine, and women's struggle to balance family and work, are woven seamlessly throughout this mystery set in Chicago's original Chinatown.

### *Death at the Paris Exposition*

In the sixth Emily Cabot Mystery, the intrepid amateur sleuth's journey once again takes her to a world's fair—the Paris Exposition of 1900. Chicago socialite Bertha Palmer has been named the only female U. S. commissioner to the Exposition and she enlists Emily's services as her social secretary. Their visit to the House of Worth for the fitting of a couture gown is interrupted by the theft of Mrs. Palmer's famous pearl necklace. Before that crime can be solved, several young women meet untimely deaths and a member of the

Palmers' inner circle is accused of the crimes. As Emily races to clear the family name she encounters jealous society ladies, American heiresses seeking titled European husbands, and more luscious gowns and priceless jewels. Along the way, she takes refuge from the tumult at the country estate of Impressionist painter Mary Cassatt. In between her work and sleuthing, she is able to share the Art Nouveau delights of the Exposition, and the enduring pleasures of the City of Light, with her husband and their young children.

◆

## Death at the Selig Studios

The early summer of 1909 finds Emily Cabot eagerly anticipating a relaxing vacation with her family. Before they can depart, however, she receives news that her brother, Alden, has been involved in a shooting death at the Selig Polyscope silent movie studios on Chicago's northwest side. She races to investigate, along with her friend Detective Henry Whitbread. There they discover a sprawling backlot, complete with ferocious jungle animals and the celluloid cowboys Tom Mix and Broncho Billy. As they dig deeper into the situation, they uncover furtive romantic liaisons between budding movie stars and an attempt by Thomas Edison to maintain his stranglehold over the emerging film industry. Before the intrepid amateur sleuth can clear her brother's name she faces a serious break with the detective; a struggle with her adolescent daughter, who is obsessed with the filming of the original Wizard of Oz movie; and threats upon her own life.

◆

## Death on the Homefront

### (coming in Dcember 2020)

With the United States on the verge of entering World War I, tensions run high in Chicago in the Spring of 1917, and the city simmers with anti-German sentiment mixed with virulent patriotism. Shockingly, amateur sleuth Emily Cabot is present when a young Chicago woman, who is about to make a brilliant society marriage, is murdered. Was her death retaliation for her pacifist activities, or was it linked to her romantic entanglements? Emily has a personal connection to the woman, but she's torn between her determination to solve the murder and her deep need to protect her newly adult children from the realities of a new world. As the country's entry into the war unfolds, Emily watches with trepidation as her sons and daughter make questionable choices about their own futures. Violent worker unrest and the tumultuous arena of automobile racing provide an emotionally charged backdrop for this compelling mystery.

## Set the Night on Fire
### Libby Fischer Hellmann

Someone is trying to kill Lila Hilliard. During the Christmas holidays she returns from running errands to find her family home in flames, her father and brother trapped inside. Later, she is attacked by a mysterious man on a motorcycle. . . and the threats don't end there. As Lila desperately tries to piece together who is after her and why, she uncovers information about her father's past in Chicago during the volatile days of the late 1960s . . . information he never shared with her, but now threatens to destroy her. Part thriller, part historical novel, and part love story, *Set the Night on Fire* paints an unforgettable portrait of Chicago during a turbulent time: the riots at the Democratic Convention . . . the struggle for power between the Black Panthers and SDS . . . and a group of young idealists who tried to change the world.

## A Bitter Veil
### Libby Fischer Hellmann

It all began with a line of Persian poetry . . . Anna and Nouri, both studying in Chicago, fall in love despite their very different backgrounds. Anna, who has never been close to her parents, is more than happy to return with Nouri to his native Iran, to be embraced by his wealthy family. Beginning their married life together in 1978, their world is abruptly turned upside down by the overthrow of the Shah and the rise of the Islamic Republic. Under the Ayatollah Khomeini and the Republican Guard, life becomes increasingly restricted and Anna must learn to exist in a transformed world, where none of the familiar Western rules apply. Random arrests and torture become the norm, women are required to wear hijab, and Anna discovers that she is no longer free to leave the country. As events reach a fevered pitch, Anna realizes that nothing is as she thought, and no one can be trusted…not even her husband.

*Honor Above All*
## J. Bard-Collins

Pinkerton agent Garrett Lyons arrives in Chicago in 1882, close on the trail of the person who murdered his partner. He encounters a vibrant city that is striving ever upwards, full of plans to construct new buildings that will "scrape the sky." In his quest for the truth Garrett stumbles across a complex plot involving counterfeit government bonds, fierce architectural competition, and painful reminders of his military past. Along the way he seeks the support and companionship of his friends—elegant Charlotte, who runs an upscale poker game for the city's elite, and up-and-coming architect Louis Sullivan. Rich with historical details that bring early 1880s Chicago to life, this novel will appeal equally to mystery fans, history buffs, and architecture enthusiasts.

◆

*The Reason for Time*
## Mary Burns

On a hot, humid Monday afternoon in July 1919, Maeve Curragh watches as a blimp plunges from the sky and smashes into a downtown Chicago bank building. It is the first of ten extraordinary days in Chicago history that will forever change the course of her life. Racial tensions mount as soldiers return from the battlefields of Europe and the Great Migration brings new faces to the city, culminating in violent race riots. Each day the young Irish immigrant, a catalogue order clerk for the Chicago Magic Company, devours the news of a metropolis where cultural pressures are every bit as febrile as the weather. But her interest in the headlines wanes when she catches the eye of a charming streetcar conductor. Maeve's singular voice captures the spirit of a young woman living through one of Chicago's most turbulent periods. Seamlessly blending fact with fiction, Mary Burns weaves an evocative tale of how an ordinary life can become inextricably linked with history.

*Where My Body Ends and the World Begins*
Tony Romano

On December 1, 1958, a devastating blaze at Our Lady of the Angels School in Chicago took the lives of ninety-two children, shattering a close-knit Italian neighborhood. In this eloquent novel, set nearly a decade later, twenty-year-old Anthony Lazzeri struggles with survivor's guilt, which is manifested through conflicted feelings about his own body. Complicating his life is a retired detective's dogged belief that Anthony was involved in the setting of the fire. Tony Romano's delicate handling of Anthony's journey is deeply moving, exploring the complex psychological toll such an event has on those involved, including families…and an entire community. This multi-faceted tale follows Anthony's struggles to come to terms with how the events of that day continue to affect him and those around him. Aided by a sometime girlfriend, a former teacher, and later his parents—after long buried family secrets are brought into the open—he attempts to piece together a life for himself as an adult.

◆

*Sync*

K. P. Kyle

Every day we each make thousands of decisions. Sometimes it's the big ones that change our lives, sometimes it's the tiny ones. What if all the choices not made led to billions of alternate realities where different versions of our lives unwind? On a cold and rainy night in New England, the paths of two strangers collide—a young man fleeing from his past, and a forty-something woman dreading what her future holds. When his past catches up to him, the two of them embark on a journey of danger, adventure, and self-discovery. Ultimately, they each need to face the question, How far would you go to help someone in need? K. P. Kyle's debut novel is a riveting technothriller/road trip/parallel universes combo with a healthy dollop of romance. It will keep you hooked until the very end and make you ponder the choices you've made in your own life.

# FOR YOUNGER READERS

## *Her Mother's Secret*
## Barbara Garland Polikoff

Fifteen-year-old Sarah, the daughter of Jewish immigrants, wants nothing more than to become an artist. But as she spreads her wings she must come to terms with the secrets that her family is only beginning to share with her. Replete with historical details that vividly evoke the Chicago of the 1890s, this moving coming-of-age story is set against the backdrop of a vibrant, turbulent city. Sarah moves between two very different worlds—the colorful immigrant neighborhood surrounding Hull House and the sophisticated, elegant World's Columbian Exposition. This novel eloquently captures the struggles of a young girl as she experiences the timeless emotions of friendship, family turmoil, loss...and first love.

A companion guide to *Her Mother's Secret*
is available at www.alliumpress.com. In the guide you will find resources
for further exploration of Sarah's time and place.

◆

## *City of Grit and Gold*
## Maud Macrory Powell

The streets of Chicago in 1886 are full of turmoil. Striking workers clash with police...illness and injury lurk around every corner...and twelve-year-old Addie must find her way through it all. Torn between her gruff Papa—who owns a hat shop and thinks the workers should be content with their American lives—and her beloved Uncle Chaim—who is active in the protests for the eight-hour day—Addie struggles to understand her topsy-turvy world, while keeping her family intact. Set in a Jewish neighborhood of Chicago during the days surrounding the Haymarket Affair, this novel vividly portrays one immigrant family's experience, while also eloquently depicting the timeless conflict between the haves and the have-nots.

A companion guide to *City of Grit and Gold*
is available at www.alliumpress.com. In the guide you will find resources
for further exploration of Addie's time and place.

# OUTLIER BOOKS

Novels without a Chicago connection that will appeal to
those who've enjoyed other Allium Press books

◆

*Never Walk Back*
Adam J. Shafer

(Coming in October 2020)

All Ruth Casper wants is to make her mark on the world, but in the post-Civil
War South she's considered a person of no consequence. After witnessing a
speeding locomotive massacre a herd of wild elk, she conjures up the design
for an improved railroad brake. It's based on an invention that her husband,
Henry, a tinkerer and a dreamer, has been unable to bring to reality. Ruth
encourages him to construct the brake, and the two of them undergo a
perilous trip north to Washington to have it patented. There they encounter
Augustus Windom, the man-child heir to his father's railroad empire, who's
obsessed with establishing his own legacy. When he decides that he'd rather
steal Henry's creation than pay for it honestly, the three of them set upon
a collision course with each other that has far-reaching consequences. Rich
in historical details, this novel will appeal equally to railroad enthusiasts
and readers who enjoy stories about women who chase their dreams with
boldness and grit.

Made in the USA
Columbia, SC
13 October 2020